Acclaim for Elf Child

"*Elf Child* is a warm-hearted, weird, and wonderful first novel. Pierce's lush and magical story is reminiscent of Francesca Lia Block and her supernatural take on Southern California."

—Marshall Moore, Author
The Concrete Sky

"What if you could look like any man you desire? Or, better yet, look like every man anyone else could desire? That's the imaginative conceit at the heart of *Elf Child,* a finely tuned blend of several genres of fiction, among them the supernatural thriller, the queer cruising-for-sex read, and, most winningly, the romantic love story. David M. Pierce brings strong plotting, plausible characters, and a true element of suspense to his fantasy, along with something rare in contemporary gay fiction—originality. I can't think of another gay novel which uses the rich concept of body transformation at will to deal so ably with matters of male beauty, attraction, and commitment. *Elf Child* is an entertaining light read with some unusually serious things to say about gay life."

—Richard Labonte, Reviewer
Book Marks and *Q Syndicate*

"David M. Pierce's tantalizing first novel is a literary changeling that metamorphoses from gay romance to fantasy thrill to modern-day morality play. Figuratively and at times literally, the identity of all characters in *Elf Child* shifts as they come to terms—or not—with the darker secrets of their lives.

In the tradition of Dr. Jekyll, Dorian Gray, and Tom Ripley, the talented Russ Lincoln leads a treacherous double life. His identity always in flux, Russ has inherited his changeling mother's uncanny gift to temporarily assume myriad human and animal forms. More his mother's than his father's son, the elf child may die but never age. Until he meets Eric, Russ's life is a narcissistic merry-go-round in which each night a 'new' Russ cruises San Diego's bars and clubs. Falling in love, however, profoundly upsets Russ's sense of self as the elf 'child' unravels into a man who, to salvage his romance, entrusts his lover with his family 'secret.' But revealing secrets carries costs, as Russ quickly discovers when Eric falls victim to a murderous hate crime that prompts Russ to turn sleuth and 'become' his lover in order to uncover whodunit."

—Clare Colquitt, Editor
A Forward Glance: New Essays on Edith Wharton;
Associate Professor of English,
San Diego State University

NOTES FOR PROFESSIONAL LIBRARIANS AND LIBRARY USERS

This is an original book title published by Southern Tier Editions, Harrington Park Press®, an imprint of The Haworth Press, Inc. Unless otherwise noted in specific chapters with attribution, materials in this book have not been previously published elsewhere in any format or language.

CONSERVATION AND PRESERVATION NOTES

All books published by The Haworth Press, Inc. and its imprints are printed on certified pH neutral, acid free book grade paper. This paper meets the minimum requirements of American National Standard for Information Sciences-Permanence of Paper for Printed Material, ANSI Z39.48-1984.

Elf Child

HARRINGTON PARK PRESS
Southern Tier Editions
Gay Men's Fiction
Jay Quinn, Executive Editor

Love, the Magician by Brian Bouldrey

Distortion by Stephen Beachy

The City Kid by Paul Reidinger

Rebel Yell: Stories by Contemporary Southern Gay Authors edited by Jay Quinn

Rebel Yell 2: More Stories of Contemporary Southern Gay Men edited by Jay Quinn

Metes and Bounds by Jay Quinn

The Limits of Pleasure by Daniel M. Jaffe

The Big Book of Misunderstanding by Jim Gladstone

This Thing Called Courage: South Boston Stories by J. G. Hayes

Trio Sonata by Juliet Sarkessian

Bear Like Me by Jonathan Cohen

Ambidextrous: The Secret Lives of Children by Felice Picano

Men Who Loved Me by Felice Picano

A House on the Ocean, A House on the Bay by Felice Picano

Goneaway Road by Dale Edgerton

The Concrete Sky by Marshall Moore

Edge by Jeff Mann

Death Trick: A Murder Mystery by Richard Stevenson

Through It Came Bright Colors by Trebor Healey

Elf Child by David M. Pierce

Huddle by Dan Boyle

The Man Pilot by James W. Ridout IV

Elf Child

David M. Pierce

Southern Tier Editions
Harrington Park Press®
An Imprint of The Haworth Press, Inc.
New York • London • Oxford

Published by

Southern Tier Editions, Harrington Park Press®, an imprint of The Haworth Press, Inc., 10 Alice Street, Binghamton, NY 13904-1580.

PUBLISHER'S NOTE
This is a work of fiction. Names, characters, places, and incidents either are the products of the author's imagination or are used fictitiously, and any resemblance to actual persons, living or dead, business establishments, events, or locales is entirely coincidental.

Cover design by Jennifer M. Gaska.

Cover photograph by Steven Zeeland.

Library of Congress Cataloging-in-Publication Data

Pierce, David M., 1958-
Elf child / David M. Pierce.
p. cm.
ISBN 1-56023-428-8 (alk. paper)
1. Gay men—Fiction. 2. Immortalism—Fiction. 3. San Diego (Calif.)—Fiction. I. Title.
PS3616.I35 E43 2003

2002014124

Acknowledgments

I would like to thank the talented and supportive team at Haworth Press, including Bill Palmer, Jay Quinn, Rebecca Browne, Patricia Brown, Peg Marr, Karen Fisher, and Josh Ribakove, for helping to bring *Elf Child* to life.

Closer to home, I wish to express appreciation to Clare Colquitt and Bonnie Anderson. Jerry Bumpus, wherever you are, thank you. Laurie Okuma, who died too soon, I miss your insight, sensitivity, and friendship.

I would also like to express appreciation to my great-great grandmother, Adelaide Mariette Pierce, who is the inspiration for a character in this story, and whose letter, quoted within, serves as a turning point in the novel.

And close to my heart, I wish to thank my mom, sister, godparents, and cousin, Karen. Dad, your memory is more precious than rubies. To my partner, David, thank you for your love and support.

1

Russ tipped the magazine slightly to reduce the glare from the lamp. The dishwater blond in the picture smiled at him, Russ thought, in just the right way. His piercing blue eyes were an invitation. The eyes, Russ knew, were important; they could be everything. It was as if the model had been waiting for him.

Russ tore out the page and took it to the bathroom, where the light was better. The model had beautiful hands, large and masculine with the veins showing. The guy's face wasn't bad either; he had an angular face with high cheekbones, a mouth just a tad on the large side, and full, sexy lips. "You're it," Russ told the model in the magazine. "Hope you don't give me trouble."

Russ closed his eyes and tried to imagine the blond looking back at him, but he couldn't get the image right. Were the eyebrows a darker blond? He waited a moment and then tried again. Was the skin tone olive or fair? Growing impatient, he went to his bedroom and found some tape so that he could hang the picture on the wall next to the mirror. Once the picture was in place, he stood very still; he gazed alternately at the model and at his own image. Russ's green eyes stared back at him hauntingly. He wondered why the process wasn't working. The model's facial structure was similar to his own, although his eyes were a little more sunken and set closer together. Even so, it should've been easy.

He thought again about going out that night. Although he yearned for adventure, a small part of him kept saying "no." Over the last few months, there had been an endless stream of one-night stands, all with terrific guys and sex. But even variety, which always excited him, had become predictable. Lately, the rate at which he was compelled to find sexual partners alarmed him. Maybe what his mother had said about sexual addiction was true.

Russ studied the face of the model more closely. "This should be so simple," he whispered. When he thought he had the picture memorized, he closed his eyes and allowed himself to relax. The image floated in front of him, very similar to the model in the catalogue. He smiled. It was the same angular face, the same bright blue eyes, even the same expression.

Finally, a success, at least with the first step. He let the image float in his head for awhile. The trick was to keep the image and nothing else, to let all other thoughts breeze through. Usually the change came easily, second nature to him. This time, once he was past the initial difficulty, the transformation was automatic.

At a certain point, when the image became even more defined, he felt a familiar tingling at the base of his spine. The feeling quickly spread up his back and to the top of his head. All the while, he kept the image of the blond before him. For an instant, he felt as though he were floating, somewhere above his own head. The tingling brought him back—a thousand pinpricks along his spine. The feeling electrified him. He smiled again. There was no turning back now.

The tingling continued, unabated, in waves. His body felt fluid. Russ expanded the mental image of the man to fill his entire body. At the last minute, Russ opened his eyes, wanting to see the change for himself.

All at once, his hair lightened to a dark blond, and his facial structure changed just slightly, becoming more angular. Then the transformation spread, and he grew taller and more lanky. All the while, he had the feeling of being weightless, of being lifted up into something and someone else. He could feel his bones lengthen, his skin growing more taut one moment and more fluid the next as it found its new form. No matter how many times he transformed, he was amazed at its speed and grace.

His eyes, as always, were the last things to change, this time from a bright green to piercing blue. He was momentarily blinded. Suddenly, Russ felt as if someone or something were pitching him forward into the mirror, but just as he thought he might topple over, he regained his sight and was able to grab the edge of the sink to find his balance. Keeping his eyes open had made the transformation more difficult. Slowly, he lifted his head to look at his reflection again. He felt as though the transformation were complete.

When he was able to focus, the image looking back at him was that of the model in the magazine. He studied the picture again, then checked his new reflection. It was almost perfect. He grinned at himself with the pleasure of success. His teeth hadn't changed. When he looked back at the picture, he realized the model didn't have his mouth open.

"No one ever recognizes teeth anyway," he muttered to himself and smiled again. "What a good-looking guy," he said to the reflection in the mirror. "I'd pick you up."

After he parked the car, Russ peered into the rearview mirror one last time. In the darkness, his eyes looked almost like slate. He opened the door a crack to make the light come on and the eyes were blue again. He noticed with dismay that he already had a five o'clock shadow. Sometimes, immediately after a change, his body produced hormones so rapidly that hair, especially facial hair, grew abnormally fast. He closed his eyes and concentrated to get rid of the shadow. When he opened them, it was gone. He smiled. Of course, there were certain benefits to the hormones racing a little faster.

He stepped out of the car onto a deserted street. Club Nova was just a few blocks away, in a commercial district filled with warehouses and old buildings. Given the shadows and lack of people, Russ usually felt a little uneasy, at least until he got close enough to hear the beat of the music, which couldn't be entirely contained by thick walls. The dance bar was housed in a nondescript building that hinted nothing of the host of handsome men within. As he walked to the building, his body felt as if it were springing off the pavement in anticipation. He hoped he'd find some young guy, preferably big and muscular, who would match his own energy and libido.

Club Nova was packed, especially for a Thursday night. Russ usually tried to arrive at about midnight on weeknights. This was the magical hour when most of the guys would still be there and, more important, thinking about finding some company for the night.

Just inside the door, he checked himself again in the mirror. He'd worn tight Levi's and an even tighter T-shirt, one of his own designs. He kept various sizes of shirts at home, though a large size generally did the trick. Sometimes he had to wear extra large. In his current form, the shirt showed everything off to good effect. This body had nice definition, especially the arms. He had to admire his taste. He knew how to pick them.

Something about the eyes, though, was troubling. Did the model have blue eyes? The longer he questioned himself, the more perplexed he became. Thinking about it made him dizzy, so he quickly stepped away from the mirror. To dwell on the feeling might be dangerous; besides, he was ready for some fun.

Club Nova, a fairly large bar, was housed in a two-story building. A large, sunken dance floor took up most of the main level. Along its perimeter were places to stand and sit, to drink or not drink, to watch and be watched. A bar ran along one side of the large, square room. Multicolored lights helped to create a carnival atmosphere, which provided an extra measure of safety for Russ, concealing any unwanted changes in his form.

Once he got his bearings, Russ headed for the second bar upstairs to buy a drink. There were a lot of attractive guys to choose from; one in particular caught Russ's attention in the stairwell. The man was headed downstairs—a big, hunky guy well over six feet tall with jet-black hair and a goatee. He was dressed in a black muscle shirt and blue jeans. He gave Russ a glance too.

After he arrived on the second level, Russ bought a screwdriver and headed for the balcony overlooking the dance floor. He loved to watch the action from above. On a good night, a sea of writhing bodies would be dancing below him, turning and twisting to the heavy beat of the music. Russ found his usual spot and let his eyes sweep the dance floor, searching for the dark-haired hunk he'd seen in the stairwell. He couldn't find him. As he continued to search, Russ spotted a few other candidates: a shirtless black guy, dancing and spinning in the middle of the pit, and another energetic dancer, this one a blond who resembled the form that Russ had taken on for the evening. Neither of them sparkled quite like the man in black. As Russ finished his drink, he finally caught the guy standing along the perimeter of the dance floor, gazing up at him. The man immediately averted his eyes, but Russ was sure he had been watching him.

Russ made his way back down to the main level and bought another drink. In the mirror behind the bar, Russ spotted his target. He fancied that the man was being careful not to return his look. Russ sensed that the man wanted him. Russ found a spot along the railing within a few feet of the man in black, with only one other guy between them. A shot of adrenaline rushed through him. The man's body was almost perfect, about the same size as his own, with beautifully defined chest and arms. His face sported a strong profile with a Roman nose and square jaw. His black hair was slicked back, fairly long on the top, but short on the sides.

Finally, the guy standing between them moved off and Russ edged closer. The dark-haired man was moving in time to the music, a strong invitation to dance. "How about a dance?" Russ asked.

The man glanced at him sharply. "Sure," he said, without smiling.

As they danced, the man continued to stare at him with an intensity that Russ hadn't seen in awhile. He seemed much younger than Russ had first guessed. He had a wonderful, natural leanness that usually came only with youth. His upper body was spectacular, with huge arms and chest. Even better, Russ sensed he would be a wildcat in bed, just the kind of guy he was always hoping to find. Russ could tell by the way the man moved that he wanted him. Every other beat or so, the man inched a little closer. The stalking was Russ's favorite part of the game. He didn't have to show too much interest or encouragement: Russ let the other guy do most of the work. His philosophy was to always keep them wondering and unsteady.

Even though the man was wearing a black T-shirt, Russ could clearly see that it was beginning to get soaked. Soon it would be the right time to ask the man to join him for a drink on the rooftop. Russ most definitely wanted him; he figured they'd make a perfect pair physically.

After the song ended, they ordered drinks at the rooftop bar. This was Russ's favorite spot, where he could get away from the loud music and find out a little more about his potential partner. A dozen or so tables with lawn chairs were scattered around. Some of the tables had umbrellas. The rooftop was contained by a high wall. It would be difficult, Russ thought, for anyone to jump off even if he wanted to. In spite of the glare from the city's lights, Russ could faintly see stars in the clear dark sky.

They sat at a table graced with an umbrella in the colors of the rainbow. Russ wondered why the man hadn't smiled yet.

"It feels great up here, doesn't it?" the man asked in a dark, deep voice. "That dance floor is like an oven."

"Yeah," Russ agreed. "I'm Russ, by the way."

"Troy," the man replied.

Russ doubted that was the guy's real name: it sounded phony. Suddenly, dizziness came over him. Russ regretted taking on this body; it appeared to be unstable, but it was too late to change his form now.

"Haven't seen you around before." Troy fed him a standard line, obviously unaware of anything amiss. He took another gulp of his drink. "You go out much?"

"I get out enough," Russ replied, the dizziness almost gone. Something about the guy's voice bothered him. It was so rough that it almost sounded garbled—like a voice on the radio, marred by static. His body, however, made up for the lack of music. Just the thought of getting close to him was sending Russ off. "You're a pretty good dancer," Russ added encouragingly.

"You're not bad yourself." Troy took a slug of his drink. "Can I buy you another one?" he asked.

"Sure," Russ replied, although his was barely touched. Troy's glass was already empty. He wondered why Troy was drinking so fast. A bad sign.

"Another screwdriver?" Troy added in his gritty voice.

"Sure." A line of about ten people had developed at the bar, so Russ had to be content to wait. It was obvious to him that his new friend was after the same thing he was, which would make things easier. The problem was that he wasn't sure he really liked the guy. On a purely physical level, though, he'd seldom seen anything better.

As he waited, two other guys caught his attention; in fact, they caught everyone's attention. A huge parrot perched on the shoulder of one of them—a parrot that let out an incredibly loud shriek.

"Squaaaaawk!"

The three of them, men and bird, sat down at the table next to his. The man with the bird on his shoulder was overweight, almost to the point that he had trouble sitting down. Russ hadn't seen anybody so big in a long while. Even more imposing was his height, a good six feet or so. Underneath all of the fat, though, Russ could tell the guy wasn't that bad-looking; he had good bone structure and his brown hair, though on the short side, was thick and wavy.

The other guy was a different story. He looked like he'd just walked in from playing touch football with his buddies at the park—athletic and ruggedly handsome, with long dark hair, prominent nose, and an easygoing air about him. He was wearing a baggy white sweatshirt that seemed totally out of place in this bar and hid whatever he had. Even so, for a moment, Russ almost wished he'd seen this new man, this touch football player, first.

When he came back with the drinks, Troy looked a little jealous. Russ wondered if Troy had noticed that he'd been watching the other guy. This didn't concern him. A bit of jealousy intensified the pursuit and the fun.

"Squaaaaawk!" Several other men at the bar came over to greet the bird. Russ had to admire the parrot's array of colors. It constantly moved its head up and down, which Russ thought would be enough to drive anyone crazy.

Troy handed him the drink instead of placing it on the table. "Here you go."

As Troy took his seat, the touch football player stood up and went to the bar. Russ heard him say over his shoulder, "No line at the bar, Kevin," before he left. Russ couldn't help but follow him with his eyes.

Troy also looked. "He's cute like a big puppy dog," he said, turning back to face Russ. He slowly ran his fingers through his dark hair with both hands, showing off his arms in the process.

"Yeah," Russ said, smiling, although he fought an urge to come to the young man's defense. Out of the corner of his eye, Russ caught the bird glaring at them. He turned his chair slightly and tried to concentrate on Troy.

"So what are you into?" Troy asked, leaning forward, gazing at him.

"I'm flexible," he replied coolly. Usually he liked a strong come-on, especially from such a gorgeous guy. But this time it seemed rushed. Still, he pushed on, eager to connect. "How about you?"

"I'd say anything with you," he replied, narrowing his dark, unsmiling eyes.

As Troy leaned forward to talk more intimately, Russ felt something hit the bottom of his chair, and a large something crashed into him, spilling what smelled like beer. The cute football player was piled in a heap on the floor in front of him, still clutching the plastic pitcher. "Oh, no," the man groaned.

The man's friend let out a sigh, which told Russ that this wasn't the first time he'd tripped and spilled a pitcher of beer.

"Squawk!"

"Off the tap?" Russ asked jokingly and smelled his shirt.

"I'm sorry." The guy remained sprawled on the floor in front of Russ. "This is so embarrassing." He reached for one of the empty plastic glasses, which had landed between Russ's legs. "I'm a total klutz."

"You can say that again," Troy added, obviously angry, even though it didn't appear that any beer had splashed on him.

"That's okay," Russ said, apologetically, not understanding Troy's reaction. Could he really be that jealous? The beer had soaked through Russ's pants, both on his lap and through one of the pant legs. The wetness felt strangely comforting, almost sexy. "I'm Russ, by the way," Russ said to smooth things over. "And this is Troy."

"Hi," the football player said sheepishly. "I'm Eric, and this is Kevin," he pointed to his friend, "and the bird is called Bird."

"Squawk!" Bird said, as if in response.

"I'm really sorry about this," Eric repeated and smiled.

Russ thought he looked so cute, sitting there in front of him, beer spilled everywhere.

"Look, can I buy you guys a drink or something?"

"Not for me," Troy stood up. "We were just leaving."

Russ looked first at Troy, then at Eric, hesitating before replying. Something about this football player urged him to stay. The problem was that he wanted Troy, at least for the night. There was an awkward pause that probably seemed longer than it really was—it puzzled him. He looked back at Troy, who was grimly waiting and watching. "Yeah, I guess we were," Russ finally agreed and stood. "Don't worry about the beer. I've had a lot worse spilled on me." On impulse, Russ extended his hand to help Eric to his feet.

Eric gladly took his hand and staggered up. "Thanks," he said and smiled. Eric's grip felt strong and firm. All at once Russ felt dizzy, maintaining the handshake long enough to get his balance back. He closed his eyes for an instant.

"Are you okay?" Eric asked.

"Yeah, thanks." When he opened his eyes, he almost became lost in Eric's gaze —it had been years since he'd seen eyes so brown, as brown as the earth.

"Nice to run into you," Eric said.

"Likewise."

Once Russ and Troy had made their way out of Club Nova into the warm, humid air, Russ felt dizzy again and sick to his stomach. The only thing that helped him to find his center was remembering Eric's steady handshake, along with something more intangible that Russ didn't understand. Some kind of promise had been made, though Russ couldn't imagine what it could be, since he doubted he'd ever see Eric again. The feeling mystified him.

"What a jerk, huh?" Troy said with a laugh as they walked down the street.

Russ didn't reply. He wanted Troy to forget about the accident; in fact, he wished *he* could forget about it. He couldn't shake the image of Eric sprawled on the floor at his feet, embarrassed and vulnerable. He considered ditching Troy. It would be so easy to go back and find the football player again. But as he looked over at his companion, the original attraction reasserted itself. Troy's body was perfect—strong and completely sure of itself. "Where do you want to go?"

"Your place, my place." Troy stopped and faced him. "I'd take you anywhere." Russ smiled. This was what he wanted to hear. It helped him forget. Troy was attractive, especially his dark, intense eyes. Russ's body ached for contact. "You're hot," he finally said, although he felt dizzy again and imagined his eyes might be slipping into another color. Once again, he wondered if he'd gotten them the right color in the first place. There was a tingling behind both eyes that bothered him.

"How about we do something right now?" Troy asked and edged closer to him. Russ instinctively backed away, turned, and led him off the sidewalk and close to one of the deserted commercial buildings. Finally, his body touched a bare wall. Troy pulled him into a recess of a doorway.

Troy's arms quickly encircled his waist as their bodies slipped together. Troy's strong hands felt good; his hard body felt even better up against Russ's own. Russ slowly pulled up Troy's shirt and slipped his hands underneath it, exploring the contours of Troy's muscular arms and upper back. As they continued to grope each other, Russ felt a momentary release from his own emptiness. There was only a feeling of closeness, of skin touching skin. It was one of the only things he could still look forward to, this abandonment to the senses. He didn't understand why it never lasted.

When Troy began to kiss him, though, the feeling went away and the tingling in his eyes started again. The memory of Eric came back. There he was, sprawled on the floor. There were his brown eyes. Suddenly someone else's consciousness crowded into his own. Russ could see a bedroom and he knew, somehow, that a boyfriend was in the next room. With a sick feeling, Russ realized it was the thoughts of the model whose form he had taken. The model was lying naked on a bed, waiting for his boyfriend to come back from the bathroom. The model kept thinking about some problem he had at a photo shoot that day.

Russ would have to do something quickly. "Wait a second," Russ stammered and tried to pull away.

"Why stop?" Troy said and continued to grope him.

"Something's wrong."

Troy backed away. "Are you sick?" he asked, almost as an accusation.

"Just a second," Russ pleaded and kept his eyes closed. Why did this have to happen again? Especially now. He had to change at least a part of his body, to make it different enough from the model's to break the connection. He tried to keep the transformation to a minimum; he hoped the eye color would be enough. The tingling, though, came all over his body. He felt himself lose at least a couple of inches from his height and he felt hair growing on his chest, which at least would be out of sight. He let his hair color change slightly too. Finally, he felt that his eyes had reverted to green. As soon as the change was complete, Russ felt better; the dizziness and unwanted images and impressions were gone. He opened his eyes.

"Are you okay?" Troy asked him again.

"Yeah, I feel better now," he replied, worried that the changes might be too obvious.

"Good," Troy said and reached for him again. "You must've had too much to drink."

Troy was all over him again, oblivious to any change. Instead of feeling relieved, though, Russ felt angry. Why hadn't he noticed any changes? Was he really that self-centered? Now the groping, the tangle of arms, the kisses, felt like violations.

"Look, this isn't going to work out."

"What do you mean?" Troy asked as he continued to kiss him.

"You and me," Russ replied. He firmly put his hands on Troy's shoulders and pushed him back.

"Hey," Troy said and tried to muscle in on him again.

"Cut it out!" Russ commanded in a deep voice, putting even more pressure on Troy's shoulders.

"Damn!" Troy backed away. "That hurt."

"I said enough," Russ repeated more softly.

"For a second I thought you broke something," Troy said, rubbing his shoulder. "I don't believe this."

"Like I said, it's not going to work out."

"Screw you," Troy muttered and turned away from him.

Russ waited in the entryway for a moment. His body felt fine now, but the anger wouldn't leave. Troy hadn't noticed even one of the changes. Russ thought twice about going back in. He could change form again, perhaps find his touch football player, but he wasn't sure he'd be up for another transformation and he couldn't go back into the bar in his present, altered form. Somehow, he suspected that of all people, Eric would notice the changes, especially the difference in height. He finally decided he had to give up and go home.

As he waited another minute to calm down, he heard a loud squawk and figured that his other friends were leaving the bar. Soon enough, he saw them walk by on the opposite side of the street, talking about some cute guy they had seen. Russ wondered if they were referring to him. After a few moments, he heard one last squawk from the parrot before two doors slammed and a car drove off. They were gone.

There was nothing but quiet. He couldn't even hear the music from the dance bar. In his mind's eye, he followed them home, wondering where they lived, if they were roommates, and how often the bird man had to feed his parrot.

When he thought no one would see him, he came out of the shadows and found his car. For the first time in a long while, he drove home alone.

2

Eric opened his eyes to find Bird gazing at him. The parrot was perched on the arm of the couch within easy reach of Eric's face. They stared at each other. Finally, Bird fluffed out all of her feathers and tried to take a bite out of Eric's nose, which Eric easily avoided by moving his head back into the pillow.

"I thought you liked me," Eric whispered to the parrot. "Squawk!" Bird didn't sound quite as loud as usual. Eric marveled at the colors—the green and blue especially. Such a vibrant bird on a Friday morning could easily cause a headache.

"Squawk!" Bird was getting louder. Eric sat up and tried to stretch the kinks out of his body, put there by Kevin's couch. His watch told him it was nine o'clock, but it felt much earlier. He was still in the same clothes he had worn the night before at Club Nova. He hadn't bothered to take off his shoes. He knew that Kevin wouldn't care if he got the couch dirty. It was already dirty enough.

When he got up to visit the bathroom, the parrot followed, hopping from couch to coffee table to armchair. Eric couldn't see how Kevin could possibly get more furniture into his small one-bedroom apartment. According to Kevin, most of his things were second- or third-generation hand-me-downs. Kevin, a freelance computer programmer, had other priorities—like computer equipment, tons of which were set up in the bedroom.

Eric quietly slipped into the tiny bathroom, where Kevin had hidden a dozen or so dirty magazines. Eric considered looking at one of them, but decided it was too early in the morning for something like that. On the way back out, he paused at the bedroom door and pushed it open a crack, releasing a musty kind of smell that was hard to place. Inside, Kevin was lying flat on his back on the bed, a mountain of a guy. Strangely, although he was snoring loudly, Kevin's chest didn't seem to be moving. The longer Eric watched his friend, the more still the room became. "Kevin?" Eric asked, a little worried. "Kevin?" he said louder.

Finally, there was movement—a leg lifted slightly, a half turn of the head. "Huh?" he replied.

"Do you want to get up?" Eric asked.

A moan. "Not really."

"You don't have to." Eric backed away from the door. "Go back to sleep." Eric returned to the living room, certain that Kevin would soon follow. Now that he was awake, Kevin would feel hunger pains. Sure enough, he came lumbering out a few moments later, dressed in a white terrycloth robe. Eric figured that Kevin was nearly twice as big as he was. Kevin headed directly for the kitchenette, just off the living room.

"Hungry?" Kevin asked and yawned.

"Sure." Eric followed him in, along with the parrot.

"Hash browns?" Kevin pulled out a huge bag of hash browns from the freezer.

"Sure," Eric agreed.

"Franks?" Kevin found a package of hot dogs and dangled them in front of Eric.

"Okay," he said, not as certain.

"Squawk!" The parrot hopped onto a chair near the kitchen doorway. "Squawk!" "Shut up, Bird," Kevin told her and pulled a large bag of pastries from one of the kitchen drawers. "Danish?" he asked Eric. Eric gave him an incredulous look. "Well," Kevin said with a mock sigh, "I'm a growing boy."

"I could say something mean right now," Eric teased him.

"Shut up, Eric," Kevin replied in the same tone of voice he had used with his pet. "Why did you insist on staying here last night, anyway?"

"Oh, I don't know," Eric paused, wondering why Kevin invited ribbing about his weight yet always acted so hurt when he received it. "I guess I'm tired of living at home."

"I don't blame you," Kevin added more softly, intent on getting an entire package of hash browns into the microwave.

"Squawk!" Bird began to pace back and forth on the arm of the chair. "Why don't you move in with me and split the rent?" Kevin suggested. "It would be cheap."

"Not as cheap as it is at home," Eric said. "Besides, I don't want to use up too much of the money my grandparents left me for college."

"A professional student in the works!" Kevin said as he put water on to boil for the hot dogs. "What you need, my friend, is to become more independent."

"Don't tell me," Eric said, sticking out his finger just out of reach of the parrot. "How about rent? And food?"

"Get a part-time job until you start grad school."

"Doing what?" Eric asked, inching his finger closer and closer to the parrot, who periodically tried to take a bite.

"Become a male escort or a professional masseur." Kevin tossed an entire package of hot dogs into the boiling water. "You've got the looks for it."

Eric hated it when Kevin gave him compliments. He was certain that Kevin was attracted to him, but Eric had absolutely no interest in Kevin in that way. "I couldn't handle male escorting," he finally replied. Kevin asked him why. "With my sense of direction, I doubt I'd be able to escort anyone anywhere."

"My dear," Kevin said and opened the large bag filled with Danish, "you take the term 'escort' a bit too literally." Kevin handed him a Danish with grape jelly filling.

"You know what I mean." Eric popped the Danish in his mouth. "This is good."

"Thank you." Kevin checked the hot dogs. "I wonder if you got your looks from your mother or father?"

"Don't even bring it up," Eric replied, licking the sugar coating from his fingers, wondering why Kevin had to start talking about his birth parents. "You know I don't like being reminded that I'm adopted." Eric paused. "Especially so early in the morning," he added, not wanting to spoil the mood.

"Sorry," Kevin said with a shrug. "I forgot."

"You know," Eric added to change the subject, "these Danish are nothing but sugar and fat, but they're good."

"Don't get started on me again about healthy eating, okay?"

"Fine," Eric said, satisfied that Kevin wouldn't bring up his looks again for at least another ten minutes.

Kevin took out two light blue ceramic plates from the cupboard. "Here," he said. "Dish up what you want."

Eric took another Danish, several heaping spoonfuls of the hash browns, and one hot dog. "Thanks."

Kevin piled the rest of the hash browns and hot dogs on his plate. "Bliss," he said, and took the bag of Danish along with him as they walked back to the living room. After they set everything on the coffee table, Kevin lumbered back for something else.

"Orange juice?" he asked. Eric tried not to look at the food piled high on Kevin's plate. He couldn't imagine eating so much at one meal. When he came back, Kevin had a half gallon of orange juice along with a bottle of catsup. "Dig in." Kevin immediately began to wolf down his food. Eric tried to ignore the way his friend shoveled it all in and picked at his own food. "Sweet dreams?" Kevin asked him between bites.

"What do you mean?" Eric asked.

"I mean the hunky blond model you met last night." Without a sound, Bird waddled over and perched on Kevin's shoulder.

"Oh, yeah." Eric smiled and fed a piece of hot dog to the parrot. "He was kind of cute."

"Excuse me!" Kevin said. "Kind of cute?"

"All right," Eric agreed. "He was very cute."

"He might have been cute, but he had a weird guy with him." Kevin shoved an entire Danish into his mouth.

"You mean the dark-haired guy?"

"Yeah, he said that you were cute like a puppy dog, or something like that," Kevin said angrily and reached up to give Bird a piece of Danish.

"He was just jealous," Eric laughed. "He didn't like it because his friend was paying more attention to me."

"Why wouldn't he, after you dumped a whole pitcher of beer?"

"He still liked me," Eric insisted. "That's why his friend wanted to leave."

"That's not the only reason." Kevin picked up the bottle of catsup and poured a bunch on his remaining hash browns, now almost gone.

"What was the other reason?"

"Me," Kevin said and stopped pawing his food for a moment.

"Oh, really?" Eric asked, bracing himself for another over-the-top Kevin story.

"His name is Troy," Kevin explained. "We met in an online chat room. I think it was San DiegoM4M. We got to talking and I finally told him how big I am. He said he wanted to get it on with a very big guy and I fit the bill."

"What happened?"

"It was strange," Kevin continued. "I knew that he'd be a chubby chaser, but he asked me to do some strange things."

"Like what?"

"Well," Kevin said more reluctantly and began to eat the few remaining hash browns and the last Danish. "We met at a street corner and he barely looked at me. He wanted to come up to my apartment and when we got here, he told me to get him in a bear hug. He said he wanted to feel crushed, so I got face to face with him and squeezed him as tight as I could, but he kept telling me to do it harder."

"Into pain, huh?" Eric asked, laughing.

"Yeah, but that wasn't the weird part," Kevin continued, finishing up the Danish. "Then he wanted me to sit on his face."

"Sit on his face?" Eric repeated.

Kevin paused for effect and Bird cocked his head to look at him. "He passed out."

"Oh, God," Eric said in shock, but then began to giggle.

"It wasn't funny at the time," Kevin complained, stone-faced at first, but then laughing too. "When I revived him, he wanted to do it again." More laughter from Eric. "Just think of what this means about your dream boy," Kevin suggested.

"Sounds kinky," Eric joked, but he wondered. "Why didn't you tell me about Troy last night?"

"You were too busy talking about your blond boy."

Eric supposed that he was right—he had been preoccupied. If only Russ hadn't been with someone else already. He would have loved to dance with him. Russ and Troy had seemed all wrong for each other. Eric got up and turned on Kevin's stereo. It was tuned to a progressive radio station, and a loud, driving beat filled the room. Eric began dancing in front of Kevin. "God, this is great," Eric shouted.

"Squawk!" Bird screamed and started flapping her wings.

"The music's too loud!" Kevin complained. "Why are you doing this?"

"Because I'm happy," came the reply.

"It's too early to be happy!" Kevin shouted.

"Everybody's at work, come on!" Eric encouraged his friend. "Dance with me."

Kevin shook his head no but stood up anyway. "I may throw up or something," he said, and began to shake his body, standing in place in front of the couch. Bird flapped her wings, still perched on his shoulder. Eric swung his hips and gyrated to the music. "Go on, girl!" he shouted at Kevin. He was always amazed at how well Kevin could dance, despite the extra weight. Every move, no matter how slight, Kevin timed perfectly. Eric danced in a circle around Kevin and didn't stop until he fell to the couch, exhausted.

3

Russ didn't think that his doorbell was working, but it woke him up anyway. He chose to ignore the irritation, assuming that it was an errant neighbor or someone who had the wrong apartment. A few minutes later, though, the bell rang again. Russ begrudgingly rolled out of bed and trudged down a short hallway, out into the living room, making sure to check himself in the mirror before opening the door.

Although he had reverted to his usual self the night before, he had to be sure he got the transformation just right—it could be his landlord or the attractive delivery man who had knocked on his door by mistake one day. He studied his reflection. Everything was fine. Whoever it was, he planned to be rid of them so that he could get back to sleep.

He opened the door. His mother, a tall, raven-haired woman with flashing eyes and a shy smile, stood in front of him.

"What are you doing here this early in the morning?" Russ asked.

"Is that any way to greet your mother?"

"I suppose not," he replied, walking to the couch to sit down. He could tell by her appearance that nothing was amiss, so he let himself be annoyed. "You're never up this time of the day, are you?"

"Perhaps I didn't go to bed last night," she said slyly. "Since you let me in, I'll assume that you don't have a boyfriend lurking in the bedroom."

Russ wasn't sure he was ready for bantering. "No, I don't," he replied. "You know I don't bring tricks here."

"I'm glad you've been exhibiting some control over your passions." Her eyes sparkled. "How do I look?" She twirled around.

"Of course, you look great," he replied. To any casual observer, Russ knew that his mother would appear to be in her twenties or thirties. Lush black hair fell down her back and around her shoulders in cascades of loose curls, framing a face with high cheekbones, a fine aquiline nose, and bright blue eyes. For as long as Russ could remember, his mother had favored a dancer's body—lithe and flexible, with long, beautifully shaped limbs and quick, sure movements.

"Mom," Russ said in a hopeless tone. "What do you want?"

"I have a surprise for you," she said wistfully. She opened the front door again, stepped out, and returned with a little pot in her hands. "I've brought you a patient."

The poor thing, which resembled a Swedish ivy, had dropped most of its leaves, and what leaves remained were a sickly, light green. There didn't appear to be much hope for it. "You know I'm not interested in growing plants anymore," he protested.

"I thought you might take pity on it," she said.

His mother had never been good with plants. It was one of the few things for which he had a talent and she didn't. "Well, perhaps I can do something for it," he reluctantly agreed. He took the pot from her and tested the soil. It was sopping wet and he could smell mold.

"What's wrong?"

"Too much water and not enough light." He gently blew some air over the plant to get some dust off its leaves and placed it on the floor in a patch of sunshine. "Say a little prayer."

She studied his face. "You seem moody."

He sighed. She always seemed to know when he was having a difficult time. There was nearly always understanding in his mother's eyes, an empathy that seldom wavered no matter what her mood. Here was the only person he could confide in.

She waited for his response. He debated whether to tell her of his previous night's escapades. Although he knew that she would be sympathetic, he was less sure of his own reaction to delving into feelings he usually kept hidden. "I guess there is something wrong," he finally admitted.

"I thought so," she said gently. "Let's get some breakfast. My treat. We can have a good talk."

After he changed into something more presentable, they decided to eat at the Avalon Cafe, not far from Russ's apartment. Hillcrest was one of the most livable neighborhoods he had ever found. It had the feeling of a small town, even though it was part of a larger city. There was a substantial commercial area filled with restaurants, bookstores, a few boutiques, and an old movie house, in addition to a gay bar or two. A nice residential area bordered three sides of the commercial district—a mix of single-family houses and small-to-medium sized apartment houses and condo complexes.

This was San Diego's gay ghetto; there were plenty of men to look at. His mother checked them out right along with him, something to which Russ had long ago grown accustomed.

The Avalon was one of the few places that still served a good breakfast. They chose a table next to a window, and Russ ordered a cheese omelet from a man he'd dated a year or so ago. He hardly recalled the man—they had only been together a few times. He was attractive, but in a bland sort of way with his perfectly sculpted hair and flirtatious eyes.

"You were alone last night?" his mother asked.

"Yeah," Russ admitted. "I met a guy at a bar; he was incredibly good-looking. I was going to take him home, but my transformation unraveled." He paused to gauge her reaction, but she didn't say anything. "The consciousness of the man whose form I took came over me, and I had to change again to break the connection."

"The unraveling took place in the presence of this other man, the man you picked up?" she asked.

"Yeah," he said, "the guy didn't even notice."

"The changes weren't pronounced?"

"Eye color, hair color, at least a couple of inches shorter."

"Oh, no," she said, relieved. "I'm glad you got rid of him. It's amazing how completely self-absorbed some people can be."

"I agree," he said, wondering how often others thought him to be self-absorbed.

"That's not what's bothering you, is it?"

She was always so perceptive, sometimes too perceptive.

"I met someone else there," he said, "but I wasn't able to get his phone number or address."

"A lost opportunity?" she asked, and pulled her hair back. She had changed her eye color as they talked—her eyes were now deep violet.

"I felt a connection with him that was more than a sexual attraction." He reached out his hand, which she took. "When I helped him up, it felt like this." He attempted to recapture the electricity of the touch of the night before, the feeling of connection and promise.

She smiled. "Things are finally coming along for you."

Had she felt it? Her eyes told him that she had. "But I lost him," he added.

"You'll find him again if it's meant to be." She released his hand. "The important thing is that you were receptive to the opportunity."

He knew she was right; he could feel it along his spine, the energy coming up. He attempted to change his eye color to match hers and was blinded only momentarily. He thought of a dark, violet sky just before sundown.

When his sight cleared, she nodded, letting him know that his transformation had worked.

"I'm not sure that I'm ready for a relationship," he told her. "It would be difficult to keep so many secrets."

"Yes," she agreed, her eyes clouding over a little, "it was difficult for me as well." She paused. "Perhaps even more difficult was having to leave my friends." She looked away, focusing on something out the window. "Even today, I miss some of them."

"You could never go back," he ventured, encouraging her, looking for any hints on how he would be able to cope.

"Never," she replied, turning back to him. "If I made friends with the same people all over again, I could never let on that I knew them before. It would've been difficult to watch them grow older while I remained young. I attempted it once, and it created such a void that I've never tried it again."

Russ cringed. He knew that he'd be going through the same things, eventually. In some ways, Russ thought, it was a blessing for his father to die when he did. His mother didn't have to watch him grow old, or leave him.

"Having to keep so many secrets from your father hurt me most of all."

Again, he thought, she had read his mind. "That's why I'm not sure I could ever have a long-term relationship," he confided.

"You should give it a chance." She paused, considering him. "I may not always be here for you, Russ. You're going to need some other companionship. Even if that companionship only lasts for as long as you can remain with him before he knows that you are too old to look so young." She studied his face. No matter what, her eyes always comforted him. "Perhaps you will find him."

He knew she was referring to Eric, his football player. "Did I tell you that he spilled a pitcher of beer all over me?"

"That's promising," she teased.

"There was something about him that I felt kinship with," he repeated, trying to make sense of his encounter for himself as much as for his mother. "The physical attraction was only a part of it. There was something else about him that drew me in. Something about his spirit. It's hard to describe."

"You will see him again," she said.

Though her statement pleased him, he wondered how she could be so sure. "I don't know. Remember, I didn't get his phone number or even his last name."

His mother glanced out the window with a look that was both sad and bemused. "If it was meant to be, you'll find him again."

"You don't think that it's silly for me to have such a feeling about someone I hardly know at all?"

"No. I don't think it is silly." Her eyes sparkled again. "You might be able to find him by using your abilities," she added quietly. "You could take his form and allow yourself to see the world through his eyes. Find where he lives or where he works."

Russ shook his head. He'd never been able to control that aspect of his abilities. It had seldom worked—at least not as well as his mother could do it. "It would be such a violation. Besides, you know that I don't have the same ability that you do."

"Yes, I suppose you're right," she said, disappointed. "There will have to be another way."

As soon as he returned to his apartment, Russ checked on his new friend. Since he'd been gone, the splash of sunshine that had been bathing the sick plant had moved away. He knelt down to nudge the pot back into the sun.

It already looked a little better, he thought. He placed one of his hands close to its leaves, feeling the energy. Life was flowing there—getting stronger. He smiled. The leaves, ever so slightly, turned toward his hands, eager to grow.

4

Eric bounded into his room and threw off his sweatshirt and Levi's so he could shower before his mother returned. The run back from Kevin's had been invigorating; he'd managed to work up a good sweat.

He often thought how lucky he was that his parents lived in Mission Hills—just a stone's throw away from Hillcrest. The family home was small by Mission Hill standards, but still comfortable—four bedrooms, two baths, a large living room and dining area with French doors to a backyard garden filled with his father's collection of cacti and succulents. Since his father's death, the garden had lost some of its glory, but most of the plants were still green and healthy. One of the bedrooms had been converted into a genealogy library for his mother, and another bedroom had been his father's study.

Since his father died, Eric's mother had become obsessed with her genealogical research and spent hours at the local Mormon family history center. Eric had joked that she spent so much time there that it would make her an honorary Mormon. At first, she took him seriously. It didn't stop her.

After his shower, Eric put on some khaki walking shorts and a tank top in honor of the beautiful, sunny day. While he waited for his mother to show up, he reclined on the bed and studied his room. It was not much changed from the way it was in high school, which depressed him. Several track awards sat on the dresser—mostly for sprinting, but some for longer races, too. One entire wall was filled with shelves of books; he had never thrown out a book from his school years. There was barely room for the wedding photo of his grandparents.

He gazed at the photo—his maternal grandparents, whom he'd never known. His mother often told stories about them—especially her mother, who was something of a bookworm and inclined to be stern. Though the family had started out poor, Grandma Jessie had always found ways to acquire books and had even worked in a small bookshop at Berkeley when the city was young. Eric had always loved this photograph—his grandmother had a yearning in her eyes that he'd never been able to fathom or convince his mother to explain. He wasn't certain that she'd been all that happy. He searched their faces, still looking for some kind of family resemblance between himself and them, though he knew this was impossible. In her wedding dress, his grandmother appeared to be sitting in a white cloud.

Being adopted had meant a life of uncertainty where family resemblance was concerned, since he had no idea who his birth parents were. He often searched faces in public places, wondering if he were passing one of his cousins. The only clues he'd ever had were based on a vague story his mother had told him about a chance encounter at an adoption agency, the location of which she had never divulged. His father, of course, had seldom talked about the adoption.

On the floor near his bed sat an open box filled with maps—some purchased, others specially drawn by friends and family. There were maps from all of the places he had visited since he could remember—twenty-eight state maps, twenty city maps, and countless hand-drawn maps. As his mother often told him, he was never meant to have any sense of direction, so he might as well learn to live with it. He had. The maps didn't do him much good—but he was fascinated with them anyway. Eric was never sure exactly where to go.

He closed his eyes and thought of the guy he'd met the night before. He'd never felt so immediately attracted to someone. Eric wasn't sure exactly why—it wasn't how the guy looked or what he said; there was only an awareness of something else binding them together. It was strange, because now Eric had a hard time remembering what he looked like. He recalled that he was blond, but that was it. The yearning stayed with him, though—the feeling of connection he had felt. Their handshake had been electric—strange and familiar at the same time.

Finally, Eric heard the front door being unlocked, opened, and then closed again. "Eric, honey?" his mother called.

"Yeah, Mom," he replied and ran downstairs to greet her.

Just as he suspected, she was carrying a couple of book bags she usually took on her genealogy fishing trips. Since he'd been home from college, he'd especially noticed how gray her hair had become since his father died. He liked it better gray. It made her look more sophisticated. She was still as slender as she always had been and rather slight. His father had often joked that she looked so fragile that she could break in two. But he'd been the first one to break.

"Hi, Mom." He gave her a hug.

"Did you have fun?" she asked. She carefully placed the bulging book bags on a chair.

He had told her that he wouldn't be home, yet he was still surprised that she seemed so blasé about his being out all night. "Yeah, I did," he replied. "I met someone special."

"Another someone special?" she asked lightly and began walking to the kitchen.

"This one really is," he insisted and followed.

"I don't mean to offend you, honey," she continued. "But you always say that you've met someone special."

Eric figured it was probably true, but didn't want to agree with her too quickly. She was spoiling the moment. "Find any good stuff at the library?" he asked to change the subject.

"I worked on the Skinner family today," she replied and paused, looking around the kitchen with blank eyes.

"Mom?" he asked.

"What was I saying?" She looked directly at him. "Oh, I was working on the Skinners today, mostly with the census records. Would you like a sandwich for lunch?"

He wasn't all that hungry but said yes anyway. Eric seldom turned down an offer of food. It was a simple lunch of peanut butter sandwiches, sliced apples, and milk. His mother had never been interested in cooking. From the time he was young, she had told him that cooking was a waste of time. He had never wanted more than this—he had always resented his father quietly berating his mother for her lack of skill in the kitchen. Eric didn't mind eating the same thing as long as it was nourishing.

"Tell me more about last night," she said.

"Well, I met this guy named Russ." Eric paused and laughed. "Actually, I spilled a pitcher of beer on him."

His mother nodded without surprise or a smile. "You were bound to get his attention that way."

"I felt drawn to him," Eric continued, searching for the right words. Although he'd been out to his mother prior to his father's death, talking about some aspects of his life still felt awkward. "It wasn't only his looks, it was much more than that."

"Love at first sight," his mother said in a light voice and took a sip of milk. "That's what happened to your grandparents."

Sometimes Eric thought his mother's acceptance came too easily, as if she were playacting to keep him happy. "Yeah, I guess it must have been like that," he agreed.

"When are you going to see him again?" she asked.

"I don't know if I ever will," Eric said. "He was with someone else and I didn't get a chance to get his phone number."

"Oh, Eric." His mother stood and took her plate to the sink.

"I'll probably see him around again," he said, apologetically.

"You are such a dreamer," she added, exasperated. Then she softened it by turning to give him a hug. "You've always been this way, honey. It's your nature."

He wasn't entirely sure if this was supposed to make him feel better or worse. "Things will work out," she said, still embracing him. "It takes time and persistence."

He cringed. This was a constant refrain.

"I've been thinking about getting a part-time job before grad school," he said.

She released him and picked up his plate and glass. "That sounds fine. What would you do?"

"I'm not sure," he admitted, smiling.

She looked at him softly, with a hint of amusement.

"I'm going to sit on the patio for a few minutes." His mother took the newspaper and went out the French doors. "Then I have a few more errands."

By errands, she meant going back to the genealogy library. He shook his head. He wondered what held such a fascination for her—a whole line of dead people she'd never be able to really know. Some of the family lines went so far back as to lose all meaning.

As his mother settled down outside, Eric heard the mailman drop the day's mail through the slot. He went to the front door and took the mail out—several bills and something from the Grant County, Minnesota, Historical Society. As usual, there was nothing for him. Eric took the letters into his mother's genealogy room, sat down at the desk, and flipped on the computer. Piles of papers were stacked everywhere—on the desk, on the chair next to the desk, even on the floor. This was by far the most cluttered room of the house. He imagined what his father would have said—his father, the neat freak. Actually, the lack of order made Eric feel comfortable. He liked the fact that his mother could finally let things go—even if it was only in one room of the house.

On the wall in front of him hung a framed photo of his parents, taken just a few months before his father's death. This was one of the few photos in which his father had put his arm around his mother. Oddly, neither of them was smiling. Even so, Eric thought it was an attractive shot. His father looked very formal, with his ash-blond hair that had turned white at the temples, his thoughtful eyes, and that look of confidence that Eric had seldom seen shaken. His mother's eyes were dancing and she looked as though she was ready to take the camera away from him. Eric had taken the photo; his father had insisted on having the cactus garden as the backdrop.

As he waited for the computer to boot up, he sifted through the piles of genealogy charts his mother had left there—pedigree charts, family group records, descendancy charts, dozens of them with names vaguely familiar to him. Eric took more of an interest in his mother's quest than he would ever let on—he just didn't want to encourage her.

In one of the piles, he came across a letter dated several months ago from New York State. He didn't recall his mother mentioning any family ties there. He took a closer look. It was from a woman named Marie Thompson.

Dear Frank and Helen Taylor,

I apologize for writing. The adoption agency gave me your names and address, indicating that you would be receptive to a letter from me, based on correspondence they have on file.

On February 25, 1974, I gave birth to a baby boy at St. James Hospital in Albany, New York. I gave the baby up for adoption that same day. I've been told that you are his adoptive parents. I would like to contact my son—who is now twenty-two years old.

I would very much appreciate your help. I am completely at your mercy and hope that you can find the strength to contact me.

Sincerely,
Marie Thompson

Eric read the letter twice before it began to sink in. February 25, 1974, was his birthday. This was a letter from his birth mother. His hand began to tremble. All these years of waiting were over. He glanced at the signature again. The handwriting was so neat that the letter could almost have been typed.

His birth mother had held this same letter in her own hands. Eric raised his eyes, blinking back tears. There was the photo of his parents, the couple who had raised him. What would his father think now, if he were alive? His father had rarely mentioned anything about the adoption. Eric had always resented that. His mother was the only one to ever talk of it, though this too was rare. His mother had told him that she would let him know if she ever heard anything. How could she have kept the letter from him for so long?

He glanced back down at the letter, his whole body numb. There was a name: Thompson. It might have been his name. He found a piece of blank computer paper and, with a shaky hand, wrote down the woman's name, address, and telephone number. His birth mother. He quickly folded the letter and put it back, covering it with the genealogy charts. He turned off the computer. He wasn't sure that he could face his mother now, knowing what she knew.

Fearing that she might have seen him, he sneaked into the living room. From there, he could see her, sitting in her favorite spot on the patio. He had found her there nursing a cup of tea, hundreds, maybe even a thousand times, with her perfect posture, her elegant line. Now Eric gazed at her as if it were the first time. After a moment, she seemed to sense his attention. She turned to him and smiled—as if nothing had happened.

5

Kevin and Bird had already finished eating breakfast by the time Eric arrived. "Squawk!" Bird greeted him.

"You look awful," Kevin told him.

"I didn't get enough sleep last night," Eric explained as he sat on the couch. Various computer components littered the coffee table, along with a tangle of cable and two computer manuals. "What's all this stuff?"

"My latest project," Kevin replied, flopping down on the couch next to Eric. "You went out last night without me?"

"No, it wasn't that kind of late night."

"Oh, I see." Kevin began to fiddle with a computer cable. "Too bad."

Why did everything have to revolve around his sex life? Eric wondered. Now that he was here, he wasn't sure he wanted to go through with it, sharing his news with Kevin, at least not yet. "Are you building a computer?" he asked.

"You could say that," Kevin replied.

As Kevin began one of his technical discourses, Eric's mind wandered back to what he'd been thinking about all night. He couldn't believe how close he was to finally being able to talk with his birth mother. He had been playing the scenario over and over, imagining variation upon variation. His mother would have a soft voice; she would start crying; she would insist on flying out to meet him the next day; she would claim that she never sent the letter and hang up on him.

All the questions started coming back again, too. How could she have left him at the adoption agency? Where was his father? Why did she want to find him after all these years? And why hadn't his own mother shown the letter to him sooner?

Eric's eyes hurt from lack of sleep; he'd tried to dismiss the questions and images from his mind, but they only came back stronger all night long.

Kevin poked him in the arm. "You're not listening to me, are you?" Kevin asked, smiling.

"What?" Eric asked, startled and a little embarrassed.

"I've been talking nonsense for the last minute, and you haven't noticed." Kevin paused. "What's going on?"

Eric laughed. "What kind of nonsense?" he asked, stalling for time.

Kevin stared at him. "Tell me."

"Well," Eric began, "I found something."

"Something?"

"A letter at my mom's."

"And?"

"It was from my birth mother."

Kevin stared again, incredulous. "From your birth mother? No kidding?"

"No kidding."

"And it was addressed . . ."

". . . to my mom," Eric added. "My birth mother got the information from the adoption agency."

"Your mom had the letter, and she didn't show it to you?"

"That's right." Eric handed him the slip of paper with his birth mother's address and phone number. "Here it is."

Kevin shook his head. "After all these years of wondering." He paused. "You want to call her from here?" Kevin asked.

"Yeah, that's what I was thinking."

Kevin brought the phone to Eric, pulling the cord after him. "This is incredible."

"Yeah," Eric agreed, taking the phone. "I still can't believe it." He stared at his friend, not quite sure he was ready for this moment.

"Remember when we were in school together?" Kevin asked, offering the slip of paper back to him. "All the times we fantasized about who your birth parents might be?"

"Yeah." Eric took the paper, clutching it in his hand. He remembered. All the times Kevin would stay for a sleepover. He and Kevin would sit up late into the night in his room, spinning all kinds of unlikely stories and giggling about them until his father would yell at them to shut up.

"Now you don't have to imagine any longer."

Eric picked up the receiver. This was it. His heart began to race as he dialed the number. It rang. Three times.

A woman answered. "Hello?"

What a young voice, he thought. Was this his sister? "Hello," he said, his own voice cracking. "I would like to speak with Marie Thompson."

A pause. "Who?"

"Marie Thompson?" He felt his stomach sinking.

"I'm afraid you have the wrong number."

The wrong number? He began to panic, fearful that it really was his birth mother and that somehow she didn't want to talk with him. "I'm sorry," he said quickly, "could I repeat the number to you?" He repeated it.

"That's my number," she replied. "I don't know a Marie Thompson."

"But," he stammered, "how long have you had this number?"

"Just about four months," she replied. "I'm sorry that I can't help you."

"No, that's okay," he said, crushed. "Thank you." He hung up the phone. Four months? It was a long time. Where was she now? Eric just sat there, stunned. All of the worry, for nothing.

Without a word, Kevin stood up, taking his hand.

"What are you doing?" Eric asked, perplexed.

"Let's try to find her."

Eric allowed himself to be led, too shocked and stunned to protest, or even to wonder how foolish he might appear. When he realized that he was being led into Kevin's bedroom, he only resisted a little. "We're going to find her in your bedroom?"

"Stop joking."

After the sleepless night, the whole thing seemed unreal. He began to wonder if he'd written down the correct number. He sat on Kevin's bed as Kevin took a seat at his computer.

"What's her name?" Kevin asked.

Eric ignored the question. "What are you doing?"

"We can go online and access telephone directories for the entire country," Kevin said, poised in front of his computer terminal. "What was the name again?"

"Marie Thompson," Eric replied.

"The state again?"

"New York."

Kevin rapidly clicked his mouse and began typing. Suddenly, a whole page of Mary Thompsons appeared, with dozens of addresses and telephone numbers. "Oops," Kevin said. "I typed Mary instead of Marie." He typed the correct name and the screen instantly changed.

Eric could see that there were two Marie Thompsons, one with the address and phone number that he had written down. Eric handed the slip to Kevin.

"You had the right one," Kevin concluded. "She must have moved recently." He picked up the phone by his computer table. "Let's call directory assistance to see if she's still living in that area." Kevin dialed the number while Eric anxiously waited. "Yes, Albany?" he asked. "Marie Thompson." There was a pause. "No Marie Thompsons? How about M. Thompson?" Another pause. "Okay, thank you." Kevin hung up the receiver. "Nothing."

Crestfallen, Eric flung himself back onto Kevin's bed. How could he come so close to find nothing? Then the anger began to seep in, anger at his mother for not telling him. How could she have kept the information from him?

Kevin sat next to him on the bed and rested a heavy hand on his back. Eric nearly sank into him—Kevin's weight created such a huge dent in the mattress. "I'm sorry," Kevin quietly said.

"That's okay," Eric muttered.

"If she filed a change of address form, it should be good for six months," Kevin reasoned. "Did Marie mention the adoption agency by name? You could contact them to see if she left a forwarding address."

"I don't remember," Eric replied, unsure.

"Maybe you could get another look at the letter," Kevin suggested.

"Yeah, I suppose."

"We could also look for other Marie Thompsons," Kevin added. "It's called trial and error."

Kevin shifted his weight, and Eric felt as though he was being pulled deeper into the bed. "You always seem to avoid the subject. It's not like it used to be. When we were younger, you didn't mind talking about it."

"After not knowing for so long, I guess I just wanted to block it all out," Eric replied. It was too painful to dwell on the subject.

"I can't remember when you found out."

"I found out before we started hanging out together," Eric said. Did he really have to go into this? Kevin was waiting for him to continue. "I found out when I was about six." All of the memories of the playground came flooding back to him—the dusty gravel, the shouts of laughter from all sides.

"What happened?"

Eric sighed. "I was in school." He paused, surprised that the memory was still so painful. "The class was out for recess and I got into a fight with Ian, a son of one of my parents' friends. I never did like him." The face of an incorrigible redhead with freckles came back to him—he'd always wanted to smack it. "He was mad at me for keeping a toy, or something stupid like that, so he started chanting 'Eric is adopted' over and over again. I didn't even know what it meant, but I figured it had to be pretty bad."

Kevin rested his big hand on Eric's back again. It felt amazingly comforting.

"When I got home that night I told my father what had happened at school that day. He made a big deal about it—he looked so serious when he got my mom and we all sat in the living room. He told me that I was 'special' because I'd been 'chosen'."

"Did you understand what he meant?" Kevin asked.

"No," he replied. "I had to ask him." Eric shifted his weight on the bed to try to escape from the crater made by Kevin's presence. He wasn't sure he wanted to go on telling what happened, but there didn't seem to be a graceful means of escape. "Then Mom started crying.

Dad told me that I hadn't come from my mother's 'tummy' but some other woman's."

Kevin began rubbing his back gently.

"I think he enjoyed telling me the truth."

"What makes you say that?"

"I always got the feeling he didn't accept me completely." He could still remember the look on his father's face—the hint of a smile under the solemn mask, the same look he had worn when Eric had confessed to his father that he was gay. "I was some other man's son. I think my mother was the one who pushed to adopt."

"Maybe that's why your mother didn't tell you about being contacted by the birth mother," Kevin suggested. "She knew that bringing the issue up would hurt you too much."

"Or maybe she's afraid."

"Of you connecting with your birth mother?"

"Yeah." His mother had rarely discussed his adoption unless he brought up the subject first. It was difficult for him to separate his feelings about being adopted from the emptiness he felt from his father's rejection. After his father's funeral, his mother had told him that she felt that his father really had wanted him, but Eric didn't believe it.

"Don't worry," Kevin told him. "We'll find your birth mother." Kevin gently kissed the top of Eric's head.

Eric tried not to flinch. Kevin's reassurance had the opposite effect on him. He wished that someone else, his new blond friend, had been the one to comfort him. Then he felt guilty. "Thanks, Kevin," he mumbled. "I'll be okay."

6

The routine was so familiar, yet it seemed bittersweet tonight. Russ stood in front of the mirror. He felt like transforming into a massive, muscular form—what he thought of as his lumberjack look. He hoped that tonight, like would attract like. He wanted to find some big guy to manhandle, someone strong enough to take him on without being crushed in the process.

Russ had tried to find his football player for several weeks, going to Club Nova, yet there had been no sign of him. Nor was there any sign of his friend, the one with the beautiful pet bird. Russ had never been so frustrated.

He closed his eyes. It didn't take long for an image to form, an image of his own creation, sprung entirely from his imagination. The image was of a huge man with large, thick hands, heavy-boned and muscled, with a ruggedly handsome face. He let the image float in his head awhile, and the man assumed a very serious expression—not mean necessarily, but very determined. Sometimes it happened this way—sometimes the form took on personality traits of its own. Once he took on the form, the traits tended to color his own. For this reason, he had to be careful.

The change came on more quickly and easily than he expected—the tingling was stronger than usual and he felt his body tremble as it expanded and grew even stronger. As he breathed more deeply, he felt his lung capacity expand. His senses became more acute.

When he opened his eyes, he had to back away from the mirror a bit to see his whole face again. A large man with a hooked nose and square jaw faced him. His huge barrel chest had much more body hair. His bones felt heavier than before; in fact his whole body felt denser. As always, he could count on physical strength.

It took him awhile to find clothing that fit him, but he finally found an extra large T-shirt and Levi's big enough to accommodate his larger frame. At the back of the closet, he found a pair of size twelve athletic shoes left by one of his old tricks. He figured that he had grown to be at least six feet four, and when he weighed himself he wasn't surprised to see the scale climb to nearly 250. "Muscle weighs more," he said to himself to check out his voice, which had turned into a deep bass.

Just as he was ready to head out the door, he realized that he was incredibly hungry, but after a quick look in the kitchen, all that he could find was an unopened bag of Oreo cookies. He sat down on the couch and, one by one, devoured the bag of them, probably fifty or so in all. By the time he finished, he had scattered cookie crumbs all over himself and the couch.

"Better brush my teeth," he muttered to himself in a mean tone that startled him—it was so unlike his own.

As he brushed his teeth, he saw that his beard had already grown enough to create a five o'clock shadow, but he decided to leave it. Energy surged through him more intensely than it had for a long time. He would have to find somebody quickly.

Russ decided to go to The Pit—one of the seedier bars. It was dark and crowded, a hole in the wall with only a couple of pool tables and little else. He had waited until his ideal time to find someone he wanted. The place was a disappointment in that regard, though—there were a few handsome men, but they were all too slight for what he had in mind.

He bought a beer off the tap and felt many eyes on him. As he walked to the back of the bar, one of the bigger men tried to block his way and stare him down, but Russ easily pushed him aside. He was about as tall as Russ, but not as big and probably not strong enough. Russ left the man standing in the middle of the room. He could sense how perplexed and hurt the man was, but didn't let on that he either noticed or cared.

Disappointed in the prospects, Russ finished his beer and began to consider what other bars he would visit. Just as he stood to leave, though, another guy walked in. This man looked familiar. Russ was happy to see that he was tall enough and big enough to be a good prospect. As the man turned his face toward Russ, he realized that it was Troy—the man he had dropped a few weeks ago at Club Nova. Again, Troy was dressed all in black—a tight-fitting black T-shirt, black Levi's, and boots. He seemed larger than Russ remembered from before, but just as attractive. Troy's sharp features seemed to Russ more appropriate for The Pit than Club Nova. Troy's rugged appearance was just what Russ hoped to find, and Russ already knew that Troy liked to play on the rough side.

Troy immediately swaggered over to the bar to buy a drink. Russ smiled broadly and stared until Troy turned and noticed. By his reaction, a long stare back, Russ knew that he was interested.

As Russ moved toward the bar to buy another drink, Troy partially blocked his way. Russ came to a dead stop just a few inches from him. They continued to stare at each other, eye to eye. Of course, Troy did not recognize him. Now that he was so much closer, Russ could once again sense Troy's strength—Russ could almost feel Troy's energy leaping out to touch his own.

"You looking for trouble?" Troy asked with a little smirk.

Russ reached out and twisted Troy's nipples between the thumb and middle fingers of each hand.

"Hey!" Troy flinched, nearly spilling his drink. He handed his glass to the nearest person and stepped forward, digging his thumbs behind each of Russ's deltoids.

Russ continued pinching his nipples until he got an idea of what Troy could take, which was considerable. Troy, as Russ had expected, was good at giving it back too—Russ nearly reached his threshold before Troy let go. Russ immediately released him.

"How much do you weigh, anyway?" Troy asked, impressed.

"As much as you, I think."

"I weigh about two hundred and thirty pounds."

"I've got about twenty pounds on you then."

They started to feel each other out, running their hands along the other's chest and arms. Russ liked what he felt—just as he had remembered, Troy was very strong and built like a young bear. They ended up with their arms locked, each with one arm behind the other's neck, pulling on each other in a test of strength.

"How about I take you home and get you down on a mat?" Troy suggested with a smile.

"You're into wrestling?"

"Yeah," he replied. "Are you?"

Russ considered the question. He had never given wrestling much thought, but the idea intrigued him. He wanted to play rough; perhaps a wrestling enthusiast would give him what he needed. "I haven't been, but I could be," he finally responded. "I'm looking for a rough time."

Troy smiled at him mischievously, which irritated Russ.

"I think I can handle you," Troy coolly replied. "I like it on the rough side myself."

"That's what I thought."

Troy said he lived nearby, so they walked to his apartment. Troy didn't say much, which didn't surprise Russ. From what he remembered, Troy was very self-centered. This suited Russ just fine. After all, he wasn't looking for a new relationship—especially just now. He just wanted some rough, uncontrollable sex. Something about Troy irked him, just as it had the other night. His manner of strutting, rather than walking, implied more than healthy self-confidence. Usually Russ felt nothing for his quick tricks—but he disliked Troy. A part of him wanted to tackle the guy and throw him on the sidewalk right then and there—to wipe the smile off his face.

Russ tried to push the meanness away—it was so unlike him. He blamed it on his failure to find Eric.

When they finally reached the ground-floor apartment, Troy showed him inside and locked the door behind them. Although the apartment was dark, enough light leaked in from outside to reveal a shabby bachelor apartment with a living room and what looked like an entry to the kitchen. Russ's immediate impression was that the place was not lived in; the usual smells of food and inhabitation were missing. All that Russ could smell was a dry, dusty scent, almost like a storage room or attic that hadn't been opened lately.

Russ turned to Troy. "What are you waiting for?" he asked.

"Who's waiting?" Troy slipped his arms around Russ in a bear hug. "This is what I like, man, face to face."

Russ was relieved—the guy was just as strong as he expected. It felt so good to be crushed against another hard body, chest to chest. Troy was strong enough to lift Russ slightly off the ground. Russ didn't struggle yet—he wanted the contact to last as long as possible.

"Give up yet?" he muttered.

"Hardly," Russ replied to encourage him.

Troy intensified his effort, but with no effect—at least physically. The longer Troy tried to smother him, the more disdain and revulsion flooded over Russ. This was the guy who wouldn't take no for an answer. This was the guy who had referred to Eric as a puppy dog. Russ grabbed Troy's head with both hands. Hate such as he had never felt before flooded through him. Russ threw his head back and then slammed it forward into Troy's forehead.

"Shit!" Troy cried, but didn't let go.

Russ grabbed Troy's ears and gave him another head butt. With a groan, Troy let go and staggered back. "Man, that hurt!" Troy complained in a trembling voice. "Why didn't you just give?"

"I don't give in," Russ replied menacingly. "I thought you said you like to play rough."

"Yeah," he replied. "But there's rough and then there's too rough. I bet you gave me a bruise."

Russ could see a bruise already forming on his forehead. Part of him couldn't believe that he'd actually given Troy a head butt. The feeling of hate had left as quickly as it had come over him. He needed to maintain control of this form, he reasoned. The form felt fine now, but it could be dangerous. Perhaps, he thought, it would be safer to leave, but he still wanted Troy. "Do you want me to take off?" Russ asked in a taunting voice that he hadn't intended. He needed to get a grip. "You said you liked it rough," Russ reminded him.

Troy sized him up again. "Shit, no. I think I want another chance."

Russ smiled, relieved. The decision had been made for him. "Where's your mat?"

"In the bedroom," he replied. "Come on." Troy led him into a darkened bedroom—a mat took up almost the entire floor. "This is my playroom," Troy said and turned on a dim light.

"You don't really live here, do you?" Russ asked impulsively.

"Hell no," Troy replied. "This is my other life."

"Your other life?"

"Yeah," Troy replied and began to unzip his pants. "I just use this place to get it on with guys."

It seemed to Russ that it was more than that. He glanced around the room, taking in the mat and the wrestling gear. "What is it about wrestling that turns you on?"

"It's making contact with another guy," Troy explained, pulling off his pants. "It's like a dance. Sweaty contact. It's the competition to see who's the strongest. I love the struggle and the grappling."

This was more like it. "How about the sex?" Russ asked hopefully, glancing down to see if Troy had a hard-on yet.

"The sex is okay," Troy said with a hint of disdain. "There's something about being with a guy. You don't have to worry about hurting him like you do with a woman." Troy sighed and pulled off his T-shirt, revealing a beautiful torso—with much more definition than Russ had expected. "Come on," Troy challenged him.

Russ pulled off his own T-shirt, knowing that Troy would use it to his advantage. Sure enough, Troy grabbed him around the chest, this time from behind. Russ fell forward, so he could feel the guy's entire weight on him.

"Okay, hot shot," Troy said angrily.

Troy hooked Russ's legs with his own and pulled back as hard as he could. Then he rolled Russ over a couple of times. Russ could hear his pants rip. It had been a long time since Russ had found someone so strong, and he relished the feeling of being crushed. Russ wondered how long he could keep things going, without overcoming his weaker opponent. He'd never met a guy yet who could measure up to him in strength, but Troy came close. He considered what kind of hold would make Troy give up and started to anticipate pulling Troy's undershorts off and getting even more physical. In spite of the ongoing struggle, or maybe because of it, Russ started to feel turned on.

After another few minutes of Troy's struggling, Russ had had enough. First he rolled them over again and again to get his opponent dizzy. To Russ's surprise, though, the rolling seemed to give Troy more strength, and he was able to squeeze even tighter. Each time they rolled together, Russ lost a part of himself to his new form, which was turning mean. The tighter Troy squeezed, the more energy rushed through Russ's body. Soon Russ couldn't think of anything but crushing him. After a final roll, Russ grabbed Troy's hand and began to squeeze.

"Stop!" Troy screamed. It only took a couple of seconds for Russ to pry off Troy's other hand.

Russ was all over him immediately, bearing down on him as hard as he could, his arms linked just under Troy's shoulder blades, crushing him.

"All right, man," Troy pleaded. "I give up."

Russ couldn't stop. Something wouldn't let him. All he could think about was crushing him.

"I said I give up!" he yelled. Russ could hear bones cracking. "Fuck! You're crushing me! Stop!"

Suddenly there was knocking at the front door and a voice shouting, "Are you okay in there?" Russ immediately let go and Troy lay prone on the mat, gasping for breath. He stared at Russ with a kind of horror in his eyes. "Are you a freak?"

Russ backed away, not knowing what to do, completely confused, trying to get a grip on this form, which now almost had a life of its own. He could feel a tingling at the base of his spine.

"You've got a beard, man," Troy said, still gasping. "You grew a fucking beard since we came back from the bar."

Russ felt his face—he'd grown a full beard in a matter of minutes.

"Are you okay?" the voice at the front door repeated.

Troy flexed his legs and rolled farther away from Russ. "Call the cops," he yelled.

Russ searched for some way out. He couldn't see another door.

"What are you?" Troy asked.

Russ felt completely numb, which scared him. He finally reasoned that it wouldn't matter if anyone else saw him; he'd never take this form again. Russ turned and ran out the front door, and luckily no one was there to stop him.

Later that night, Russ found himself in Pacific Beach, crouching on the sand, completely exhausted. He didn't remember how he got there. He quickly searched his pants pockets, finding wallet and keys. He felt his face and then glanced down at his body. The transformation had totally unraveled. He stood, and slipped out of his lumberjack clothes, throwing them in a heap on the sand. He'd have to find his car later, he decided.

A strong wind had come up. Seagulls screeched above him. He hated the noise they made. Perhaps a large eagle would take care of them, he thought angrily. He resisted the urge to turn into something capable of silencing them.

He couldn't believe that he'd gone so far with Troy. It was if his new form had completely taken over. How could he have lost control? The guilt was nearly too much to bear. If only he had found Eric instead.

He kicked at the sand and approached the water until it lapped over his feet. The water felt terribly cold. He waded farther into the waves until they encircled his legs, knees, and thighs. Still he went deeper, up to his waist. He could feel the water tugging at his heels. He edged out farther. The waves slipped around his neck.

He plunged in, hoping that the current would take him deep enough to compel his body to mutate into a creature without lungs.

7

Eric sped along the boardwalk at Pacific Beach, exhilarated by the glide of the Rollerblades along the hot pavement beneath him. The rush of air helped to clear his mind. He hadn't been sleeping well. Especially last night.

Everything had come to a standstill. It had been weeks since he'd sent a letter to the adoption agency to ask if his birth mother had left a forwarding address, and Eric had heard nothing. Nor could he bring himself to ask his mother why she had kept the secret from him. Kevin was complaining about Eric ignoring him. Eric hadn't even gone out to look for his lost friend—the beautiful blond whose number he didn't have.

Sweat dripped from his forehead. He didn't realize how fast or how far he had gone until he was well into Mission Beach. On the way back, slowed down.

Just as he rolled into Pacific Beach again, Eric spotted a gorgeous guy at one of the T-shirt booths along the walkway. Even from a distance, Eric saw what a great body he had—broad shoulders, nice arms, trim waist. As he got closer, he had to admire the man's face, too, with its high cheekbones, strong nose, and angular features. Sleek like a cat, he thought. He caught the T-shirt vendor's eyes as he rolled by—beautiful green eyes. The guy looked after him with a sense of expectation, Eric thought, so he turned back.

The man was waiting on a couple of middle-aged women tourists. Eric could tell that he was buttering them up. "This shirt would look great on you," he told one of them. He seemed pleased that Eric had stopped and shot him a couple of quick looks that suggested familiarity. There was something strange about the way the guy looked at him, a smiling recognition.

Eric debated whether to stay. He felt tired, distracted, and worried, yet something compelled him to look at the T-shirts. There were dozens of them, many sporting a stylized dolphin. Shorts and tank tops were thrown in for good measure. As the man glanced at him, Eric felt a little awkward, knowing that he didn't look his best. Yet he still seemed interested, and Eric felt drawn to him.

The tourists finally bought two of the tank tops—they said as gifts for their children at home. Once they were gone, the T-shirt vendor turned his bright eyes on Eric and smiled.

"Hi," he said.

"Hi," Eric repeated. "You've got some nice shirts here."

"Thank you."

Eric was struck by his voice—it was beautifully smooth. "Did you design them yourself?"

"I designed all of the ones with the dolphins," he said with a hint of pride, "and also all of the ones that say 'San Diego'."

"Hm." Eric reached down to look through more shirts. "I don't see any of the San Diego shirts."

"They're here somewhere." He reached into the pile, rummaging through the shirts.

Eric hoped their hands would touch.

"Here's one," the guy said as he pulled out a purple T-shirt with a simple 'San Diego' scrawled across the front.

"Very straightforward," Eric observed, trying without much success to keep focused on the shirt. The guy's looks were too distracting.

"That's the kind of design that sells to the tourists. I guess they want to prove that they've been to San Diego."

It was the green eyes that really pulled Eric in. At first, he wondered if the guy was wearing contacts, but he could see subtle variations in the color, a light green along the outside and darker green near the pupil, with specks of brown. Hardly something that could be done with contacts, he decided. Stunning, no matter what.

"What are you looking at?" the man asked with a smile.

"I'm sorry, was I staring?" Eric said, embarrassed.

"That's okay," he replied. "Very few people really look you in the eye when they talk with you. I don't mind. I like it."

"Are you new around here?" Eric asked, relieved.

"Not new to San Diego, but new to this spot."

"Yes, I think I would've remembered you."

"I'm Russ," the guy said and extended his hand.

"Eric." He took Russ's hand in a wonderfully strong handshake that lingered—it reminded him of his handshake with the other Russ. "It's funny, but I just met a guy named Russ a few weeks ago," he added.

"A popular name, I guess."

Eric's hand tingled just as it had on that other night. He looked at this new Russ, wondering—but this wasn't the same man and Eric decided that he was mistaken. They talked about the T-shirts, but Eric sensed that something else was going on. Russ was obviously interested in him, though Eric thought he seemed too good-looking to be true. Then there was the handshake. It was strange.

"See anything you'd like?" Russ asked, leaning toward him with a flirtatious glint in his eye.

"There are some nice things here," he agreed, flattered that such a great-looking guy was coming on to him.

"I've been here all morning," Russ continued, "and I haven't had anything to eat. Would you like to grab lunch somewhere?"

Eric paused, considering. He'd hoped that he'd eventually run into the first Russ, and accepting an invitation from this guy might take him off track. He had an urge, though, to say yes. "Yeah," he agreed. "I could probably eat something."

"Great," Russ said, smiling. "Just let me lock things up and maybe we can find someplace to eat up on Mission."

They decided to walk to a little taco shop near the corner of Mission and Diamond streets—one of those places by the beach where it's okay to show up in nothing but a swimsuit or a pair of shorts. Today at least a dozen surfer boys were hanging around without their shirts on—plenty of eye candy. A canopy of surfboards hung from the ceiling. Someone had painted a mural on one of the walls reminiscent of Hawaii, with coconut palms and wide sandy beaches.

A big, husky guy sporting a scar on one cheek took their order at the counter—a chicken enchilada combination plate for Russ and a beef taco for Eric. They got their drinks and took them to the only table still available, near the back of the taco shop, along the wall with the mural.

Eric caught his own reflection in a mirror at the far end of the room. Even at this distance, he was alarmed to see circles under his eyes; his hair was still damp from skating. Why was this stud so interested in him?

"How long have you lived here in San Diego?" Russ asked and started on his Pepsi.

"Nearly all of my life," Eric replied. He still couldn't get over Russ's eyes—he'd never seen eyes so green. "I'm one of the few native San Diegans around. How long did you say you've lived here?"

"In San Diego?" Russ asked. "Just five years."

"How do you like it?"

"It's fine," Russ said and gave him a look that indicated that this wasn't all he thought was fine.

"Yeah, it's a great place to live. Especially if you like the beach."

The guy with the scar called out their number and Russ offered to get the food. Eric was thankful for the breather. He wasn't sure he felt up to flirting. Once Russ came back, Eric decided to ask him about his business, a fairly safe topic.

"How long have you been designing T-shirts?"

"About as long as I've lived here," Russ said, digging into his enchiladas. "It's a great way to make a living—you choose your own hours, make as much money as you want, and then quit. You don't have some boss breathing down your neck."

"Is it secure?" Eric said.

"Not really," Russ said, tapping the table with one of his fingers. "I'm always taking a chance, never sure of the outcome."

"In what way?" Eric asked, sipping from his drink.

"You never know what young people will go for," Russ said. "There are thousands of designs out there, but only the good ones will sell."

Eric gave him a quizzical look, wondering what Russ meant by "young people," since he was so obviously a young person himself, but before he could ask, Russ pressed on.

"Lately T-shirts with brand names have been popular—like 'Snickers,' 'Campbell's Soup,' and even 'Mr. Bubble.' Now people would rather wear Mr. Bubble than play in it."

Eric had to laugh; he'd heard his father talking about Mr. Bubble. "Don't the companies that own the brands have something to say about your using their names?"

"You have to pay for the right to use the brands. Most of the companies will go with a royalty rate of seven to eleven percent."

Eric couldn't believe that Russ was that far along with his business. "You have enough money to buy the right to use brand names?"

"No, a bigger T-shirt company usually buys the right to the name," Russ further explained, continuing to dig into his food. "When I work with the brand names, I'm employed as a subcontractor." He paused. "The problem is that I don't make enough money selling them. I'd rather sell more of my own T-shirts." Another pause while he took a bite. "It's so cool when I see a kid wearing one of my own designs."

Eric could understand that—it would be cool—but he wondered what Russ meant by "kid." "You mentioned that young people buy most of the T-shirts?"

"Yeah," Russ replied. "Most of the market is made up of sixteen- to twenty-five-year-olds." Russ paused, almost startled. "You know, Generation X and all of that," he added sheepishly.

Eric thought about what he said—Russ considered sixteen- to twenty-five-year-olds to be young people, or "kids." Russ didn't look any older than he did. Eric had assumed that Russ was about his age—in his early twenties. Eric didn't think of himself as a kid.

In turn, Russ searched Eric's face. "I don't mean any offense by calling them kids," Russ added, as if reading his mind. "I'd rather be a kid than an old person any day."

"Whatever," Eric replied with a bemused smile. He was probably reading too much into what Russ had said. He glanced at the mirror to get another look at himself. He wished he was at his best—he looked so weary.

"How's your food?" Russ asked.

Eric glanced down at his taco, which was practically untouched. "Guess I better start eating."

"No hurry," Russ replied with a smile. "How about you? Where do you work?"

"I don't. Not yet, anyway," Eric explained, and took a bite of the taco. It really wasn't too bad. "I'm going to graduate school in the fall. I'll be working on a degree in geography."

"Do you want to teach?"

"Maybe." The truth was that he wasn't sure what he was going to do with his life. Especially now. There were too many unanswered questions.

"Are you living with your folks?" Russ asked.

The question stung a little, but Eric supposed that Russ had reached a logical conclusion. He wished, though, that he could say he was out on his own. "Yeah, I live with my mom."

"How about your dad?"

Eric paused, surprised at how quickly the conversation had turned. "He passed away."

"Oh, I'm sorry," Russ said and stopped eating. "I didn't mean to pry."

"That's okay," Eric said. He didn't mind talking to Russ about his father. In fact, he was glad Russ would be concerned. Most guys would gloss over it. "It was a few years ago."

"He must have been young."

"No, actually he was sixty-two," Eric replied. "He died of a heart attack while he was working in the backyard."

Russ shook his head, looking genuinely concerned.

"My mother found him after she got back from the grocery store. He had collapsed in his cactus garden."

"It must have been awful for her."

"Yeah." Eric remembered the telephone call as if it had happened yesterday. "I was at college when she called. I knew something was wrong as soon as my roommate said she was on the phone. She never called in the middle of the day. She came right out and told me 'your father has passed away,' just like that. It was weird, because she seemed so calm."

"Maybe she was in shock."

"Yeah," Eric said. "After the funeral, she was wandering around the house with this vacant look on her face. She'd always been quiet, but this was strange. Late that night, I found her at the cactus garden, crying. We just cried together for awhile. In less than a week, I was back at school. She wanted it that way."

Eric couldn't tell what was in Russ's eyes—they had clouded over with some emotion Eric couldn't place. It wasn't sadness, concern, or pity; Eric only knew it was something else.

"Did your mom have friends that she relied on?" Russ asked.

"No, not really," Eric said.

"What has she been doing to get over it then? It must be hard for her to do it alone."

There was something in the way Russ said "alone" that gave Eric the impression that Russ felt it himself, perhaps every day. "Well," he continued, "she took up a hobby—actually it's more like an obsession."

"Nothing dangerous, I hope," Russ teased.

"Sometimes I'm not so sure," Eric responded and started to eat the rest of his taco. "She's hooked on genealogy."

"Really?" Russ asked in a way that made Eric wonder if he was unfamiliar with the term.

"She's searching for her roots—like Alex Haley," Eric explained. "She's been obsessed with it ever since Dad's funeral. She was searching through some of his things and came across a family history that my dad's aunt had put together. Mom decided she wanted to do the same thing for her side of the family."

"Why do you say that she's obsessed with it?"

"She spends all her time in the Mormon family history center going over microfilms of old records," Eric said and paused, looking around him. In the space of minutes, the taco shop had lost many of its customers and the room had quieted. He continued, more softly, "Then she comes home and spends all evening entering this stuff into a database she has on her computer. It's crazy."

"It's comforting," Russ suggested.

"She comes home for lunch every day just so she can check the mail when it arrives to see if there are any letters from historical societies that she's written to."

"I can see why you think it's obsessive," Russ agreed. "But she could do worse. Does she still talk about other things?"

"Oh, yeah," Eric replied. "That hasn't changed."

"That's hopeful," Russ said and smiled again. His eyes were so green. "What about you? It's hard to lose a father."

"Yeah, it is," Eric said. "I'm handling it okay. It was tough at first—especially because it was all so quick. I'm not sure what would be harder—losing your parent just like that or losing him to a long illness."

"I'm not sure either," Russ replied.

Eric felt a little odd. Talking to Russ somehow reminded him of talking with an older friend. He had a way of bringing things out—like a counselor. "How about your family? Has anyone done the family tree?"

"I don't think so," Russ said with a smile, but didn't offer any more information.

"You know, I'm not even sure if you've told me your last name," Eric said.

"Lincoln," Russ said. "Russell Hezekiah Lincoln."

"Wow, what a name," Eric exclaimed. "Sounds English to me."

"It probably is," he replied.

"Have you traced your family?" Eric asked.

With a quizzical expression, Russ said, "Are you sure you're not the one with the genealogy obsession?"

Eric laughed, trying to decide whether Russ was being evasive.

"I don't think I have your full name yet, either."

"Eric Taylor."

Russ extended his hand, and again Eric felt the same energy. "We need to do this again sometime."

They exchanged numbers before they left the taco shop, borrowing some paper and a pencil from the man with the scar. As they walked out together, Eric felt a sense of loss, the same thing he'd been feeling since he'd seen the other Russ.

Eric was determined to call that evening. This Russ, Eric decided, wasn't going to get away.

8

The night was electric. Russ looked up at the sky and saw that all the stars were out, a good omen. As he stood at the entrance to Club Nova, he could feel the vibrations all around him, the driving beat of the music. The scent of sweat and cologne floated out the open doorway.

Where was Eric? He was sure to be here soon, Russ thought. After all, it was Eric who had set the time and place. He ignored the other guys as they filed into the dance club, avoiding searching eyes. Russ felt Eric's presence behind him before he heard his voice.

"Sorry I'm late."

Russ turned, and there was his adorable football player again. He resisted the urge to brush Eric's wavy hair away from his face, so he could better see those big brown eyes. The smile, he couldn't miss. "Hey, Eric." Russ lightly tapped him on the shoulder. "Want to go in?"

"Sure," Eric replied.

Russ insisted he would buy the first round of beer, and they headed up to the the rooftop patio, where it was quieter. Eric led the way through the crowd, past the sweaty bodies. Eric was wearing another one of his bulky sweatshirts, and Russ wished he could see more of what Eric had to offer. After Russ bought the beer, they grabbed one of the tables. Russ sat and smiled, with a playful gleam in his eyes.

"What are you staring at?" Eric asked.

"What do you think?" Russ countered and leaned forward across the table. "I really enjoyed our lunch," he continued more seriously.

"Same here." Eric smiled. "I was worried that you might have changed your mind."

"About getting together tonight?" Russ asked, incredulous.

"Well, yeah," Eric admitted.

"There was never any doubt in my mind," Russ said.

"I'm glad."

Why had it taken this long for them to find each other? Russ wondered. It was just like that first night, only this time Russ wasn't going to let anything come between them. "You look great," Russ said.

"You do, too." Eric swayed to the music. "I've always enjoyed coming here," he added.

"You come here often?"

"Not so much lately," Eric replied. "Kevin's been on my case about it. He thinks I've been ignoring him."

"Is Kevin your boyfriend?" Russ asked playfully.

"No," Eric said, shaking his head. "My best friend from middle school."

From middle school, Russ thought. Perhaps a ten, maybe a twelve-year friendship? Russ had no such blessing in his own life. At least not yet. "That's great," Russ said. "I wish that I could say the same thing about someone," he added, surprising himself with this admission.

Eric looked at him questioningly.

"I hope to meet Kevin sometime," Russ added.

Eric's hand knocked into his beer glass, almost tipping it over. "I'm such a klutz."

Russ had to laugh. This was nearly an exact reprise. "Oh, I don't know. I wouldn't mind having a beer bath." With a flick of his wrist, Russ tipped his own glass over so that the beer rushed over the table and onto his lap.

Eric shook his head in disbelief. "Why did you do that?"

Russ stood and held out his hand to Eric. For a moment, Russ wasn't sure what Eric would do. Finally, Eric stood slowly. Russ pulled him into an embrace. After a moment, Eric began to hug him back. "I can feel the wetness coming off onto my pants," Eric whispered. "It's kind of sexy." Russ held him closer, and Eric began to sway. "You're kind of strange," Eric whispered.

"You're right about that," Russ whispered back. "Come on downstairs, let's dance."

Everything seemed magical—the flashing lights, the heavy beat, and a gorgeous guy twirling around with him. As they careened, spinning and gyrating, Eric started to strip off his clothes, first his sweatshirt and then his tank top, and threw them over one of the railings. He was more beautiful than Russ had suspected; there was incredible definition everywhere. Eric's skin seemed to glisten under the strobe lights.

Russ grabbed Eric's arm a couple of times to feel what Eric had there. Eric pulled at Russ's shirt, an invitation for Russ to take it off, but Russ didn't oblige, at least not yet. As they danced, they grew closer together, until their bodies almost touched. Eric's eyes hardly left Russ's the entire time they were dancing. Being with Eric seemed so natural. The only thing that Russ felt acutely was the need to be closer to Eric—he wanted to be in his arms again.

Eric moved forward and caught him in a long embrace, which Russ immediately returned. Now that he was in his arms, Russ felt an incredible heat—Eric's body was warm and giving. Russ felt as though they'd melted into each other.

"Want to take a break?" Eric asked, shouting in Russ's ear.

"I have a better idea," Russ loudly replied. "Let's go."

"Where?" Eric asked.

"Any place you want."

"It will have to be your place, since I don't have one yet," Eric said. Eric grabbed his discarded clothing, and then he and Russ made for the door.

On their way to his apartment, Russ let his hand rest on the edge of the car seat, hoping Eric would take it in his own. After a few minutes, he did. Russ couldn't quite believe it when Eric had suggested leaving his car at the dance club so they could go to Russ's together. Russ would never have left his car in such a place, but he was glad to have Eric with him.

Elated, Russ savored the moment—Eric's hand felt so warm and giving, yet surprisingly dry even after their sweaty dancing. Although Eric kept up a lively, perhaps nervous, monologue about this or that restaurant or card shop they passed, Russ didn't even pretend to listen, content to feel the vibrant energy of his new friend beside him and somehow knowing that Eric wouldn't expect him to follow or recall whatever was being said. It was as though they were entering their own incredible world.

It wasn't until Russ unlocked the door to his apartment that he realized his place was entirely too messy for guests. He hadn't anticipated bringing Eric home with him after their first night out dancing, being sure that Eric would prefer to take things more slowly. Once they stepped inside, he lost this anxiety, as Eric pulled him into a soft, giving embrace.

"I've been waiting to do this ever since we left the dance club," Eric admitted, slowly rocking Russ in his arms.

"Me too."

Russ let his hands glide over Eric's arms, shoulders, and back, as Eric did with him. Was this a dream? Russ wondered. Eric's warmth surrounded him; he wanted to prolong the moment as much as possible.

It was Eric who pulled back first, and before Russ realized it, Eric was kissing him. Even though the first kiss was brief, the softness of their lips together lingered. Russ took in a breath as Eric exhaled. It was sweet. Russ longed for more, but Eric backed away again.

"I'd like to see your place," he murmured.

The loss of touch was jarring. Russ groped for words. "I'm afraid it's messy." He walked over to a small lamp by the couch. "You may not like it." He flicked on the light.

Eric glanced around the room as Russ waited, embarrassed that it looked so shabby. He watched Eric's face for any sign of disappointment, but couldn't see any. Eric went to the plant that remained on the living room floor where Russ had placed it for a sun bath. "Wow," he said. "What a great-looking plant. Why is it sitting here?"

"For the sun," Russ explained, relieved that of all things Eric had decided to focus on this. "It wasn't doing well a couple weeks ago."

"That's hard to believe."

Russ understood why Eric would think that. Since he'd started to care for it, the plant had erupted into a dazzling spot of life. About twenty or so vines were now growing from the pot, covered with deep green, crinkly leaves. The vines spread over the floor, away from the pot in a spiraling shape. The plant's health glowed especially vivid in the semidarkened room. Russ didn't dare approach the plant, for fear that its leaves would turn toward him in recognition.

"You must have a green thumb," Eric observed, gently touching the leaves.

Russ sensed that the plant accepted Eric's attention, which gave him immense hope and anticipation. Perhaps Eric was really the one.

Eric sat on the couch, beckoning him to sit near. Russ went to him and they were immediately in each other's arms again. There was a tenderness between them that Russ had never felt with any of his partners before, and although the feeling had a sexual element, it wasn't overpowering. One kiss melted into the next. They helped each other out of their shirts and tank tops. Russ wasn't sure exactly when they began a delicate touching; Russ explored Eric's skin, his upper arms, his chest, surprisingly hairy, his belly, and his back. Russ's fingertips lingered. Eric's skin felt so smooth—so moist. Russ became lost in the sweet scent of Eric's hair. Another kiss. How could lips be so giving? Russ gazed into his lover's eyes—there was something unexplainable there.

Though they could have gone on, they didn't. Russ felt the shift first—each of them knew his limit. If their relationship was to be special, fully intimate, physical intimacy had to wait.

They relaxed and curled together on the couch. "It's amazing," Eric whispered. "I feel like I'm floating in your arms."

In response, Russ drew him closer. He was afraid to let go—afraid that what he now had wasn't real.

"I could go to sleep right now," Eric said.

"So, I'm putting you to sleep?" Russ asked, confused.

"No, not like that," Eric replied. "I haven't been sleeping well lately, and for the first time I feel relaxed, just very comfortable and safe."

Russ felt better, although he was concerned about Eric's lack of sleep. He somehow knew there was a good reason for it. "Why are you having trouble sleeping?"

"I'm not sure I want to burden you with my problems."

Russ couldn't help but smile. Eric was already feeling guilty about burdening him. "If you're ready to talk about it, I'm ready to listen."

"I recently got some news that was hard to take," Eric began slowly. "See, I'm adopted," he continued. "And I just found out the name of my birth mother."

Russ paused, trying to take it in. It seemed to him that this would be a good thing—to find your birth mother. But he could hear the pain in Eric's voice and wanted to help. "Have you always known that you were adopted?" he asked softly.

"Since I was about six," Eric said. "But I never knew who my birth mother was until a few weeks ago."

"Did you want to know?"

"Yes," Eric answered. "Part of me has always wanted to know." Eric started caressing Russ's arm. "Another part hasn't. It's always been this battle. For some reason, I've always wanted to see their faces—my birth parents—to see which one of them I look like."

Russ could understand. Sometimes he had dreams of not being able to recognize the faces of his parents. "Have you contacted your birth mother yet?"

"I tried to, but the telephone number she gave wasn't good anymore," Eric said. "I wrote a letter to the adoption agency."

"What about your adopted mother?" Russ asked, sensing that there was much more to the story.

"She didn't tell me," Eric said sadly. "I found a letter from my birth mother in Mom's papers." He paused, snuggling closer. "She received it months ago and didn't tell me."

Russ wasn't surprised that she hadn't told him. "She probably felt threatened," he said.

"She promised she would let me know," Eric replied. "I never thought she'd keep anything from me."

It was as though Eric had never grasped the idea that his mother might be vulnerable and capable of making mistakes. Russ tried to remember the last time he had felt such betrayal himself. "Have you talked with her about it?" Russ asked.

"No," Eric replied and smiled ruefully. "I'm not sure if I will."

Russ decided not to advise him to talk with his mother—after all, he wasn't asking for any advice. But it was difficult for Russ to hold back—he could feel Eric's pain. "Well," he finally said, "I'm sorry that you have to go through this. It's rough."

Impulsively, Russ squeezed Eric. He felt so protective of his new lover. "I hope you can find your birth mother," Russ said. "I know it must be very difficult."

"Thanks. I hope so too," he replied.

They fell asleep together, though some part of Russ wondered at the experience, certain that it would be uncomfortable to remain in the same position for so long; but Russ felt no discomfort, only an intense and later more languid awareness of being content and even safe.

He knew that he had dreamed; however, nothing remained when dawn light touched first his hands, still nestled in Eric's, and then his forearm. The warmth of the light reminded him that he had slept without a cover over his bare shoulders, yet he didn't feel at all cool. A cloud of tenderness still hung around them, though sleep had blown some of it away. He kissed Eric softly on the neck, but he didn't stir. As always, with the first light, Russ felt compelled to get up—even though it meant leaving his lover on the couch alone.

He found it strange, but he thought of Eric as his lover—even though they hadn't consummated their union. It was difficult to leave the warmth of their embrace, and Russ was surprised that Eric didn't wake up.

He walked over to the window and greeted the coming day. Memories of other times flooded back—this was after the point at which he would have taken his leave, or insisted that the other leave him. He wondered how many times that had happened—was it hundreds or even thousands? Always, the fear of being discovered had drowned the need for connection. At least, until now it had.

When Russ looked over at his lover, Eric was silently watching him, with a look of concern mixed with something else that was quite wonderful.

Russ smiled in recognition, as if he'd found himself staring back at him.

9

Helen woke up early, as usual, and quietly made her way to Eric's room. She hoped that he might have changed his plans and come home the night before. The door was still open, showing an empty bed. She noticed that his box of maps had been left in a different spot than usual, so she knew he had been into them and going to new places.

It had been difficult for her to have him at home—at least at first. Now she warned herself that she might not be able to do without him unless she took steps to change things.

She decided to take her morning coffee on the patio—it looked so warm and pleasant outside. She wondered if Eric was upset about something—perhaps upset with her, since he'd made himself so scarce of late. She had been told "once a mother, always a mother" by her own mother so many times that she'd accepted it as truth. But she reasoned that there were different ways of being a mother, and she hoped that leaving Eric alone was the best thing for him at this point in his life. She felt that he needed to find his own way. She only hoped that he would find work and his own apartment soon, before she became too dependent on him and would suffer the loss too acutely when he eventually would leave her.

Through her life, she had found that most things worked out if one only waited long enough. She prided herself on her patience.

The cactus garden looked especially grand this morning, with full sunlight bringing out all the contrasting textures and colors so beautifully. After her husband died, she had let everything grow together, giving the garden a touch of wildness. She had always thought that her husband was too diligent in trimming everything back. He didn't want any of the plants to touch.

She especially liked the way in which a cluster of low-growing aeonium had spread around the loquat tree, creating a sea of fleshy green petal-like leaves. Her husband had planted such a splendid variety of plants—yellow crassulas, brittle, spiny euphorbias, and oddly shaped opuntias. She especially enjoyed the combination of the purple schwartzkopf and the green and yellow agave. A cluster of cactus was crowned with dozens of canary yellow blossoms just closing up after blooming the night before.

He frequently had explained to her that although all cacti were succulents, not all succulents were cacti, so that his patch of thorns and thick, fleshy leaves was more properly called a succulent garden. She, who frequently weeded the garden since he disliked that part of the job, always smiled and agreed with him in spite of the fact that each of them, even Eric, always referred to it as the cactus garden.

After her husband's death, Eric had encouraged her to tear out the cactus garden, since it held a terrible memory for her. She had refused to consider doing such a thing. The memory of finding him there would always be with her, regardless of what happened to the garden. Besides, she had learned to live with what she had seen that day after returning from the grocery store. He had fallen over a cluster of cacti, scraping his arms and face. His eyes were glassy and vacant, his body already growing stiff. The way the body fell made it appear as though he had been gathering them together in his arms. She had recalled what her mother said after Helen's father's death: "an empty vessel, everything gone." Although they had died at least twenty years apart, sometimes it seemed to Helen that the passing of her father and husband had been contemporaneous.

Helen had always thought that she had a pronounced difficulty marking the passage of time. It seemed only yesterday that she was picking up Eric at the adoption agency, yet he was now a college graduate. She had been truly sorry that her letter to Eric's birth mother had come back marked "addressee moved, no forwarding address." She hadn't thought much about it since—she chose not to think about it. She only remembered that there was a girl who could not and absolutely did not want to keep her beautiful baby boy. Helen had been waiting for a son for years.

After she finished her cup of coffee, she went into her study to print out a few worksheets to take to the library that morning. When she sat down at her computer, though, she noticed something amiss. As she sorted through a stack of genealogy papers, she came across the letter from Eric's birth mother. "I thought I'd put this away," she said. It appeared the letter had been tampered with. The paper had been refolded. She was quite sure she hadn't refolded the letter at all, yet there were clearly new fold marks, and crooked as well.

He knew. She had to close her eyes and concentrate to quiet her heart. She had forgotten that the letter was still there—it simply had not entered her mind that he might look through her genealogical papers. But apparently he had.

Why hadn't she told him? she wondered. He had found out in the worst possible way. She didn't dare wonder what he now thought of her. How could I have been so foolish? she asked herself.

After she felt more in control, she considered the best way to handle the situation. They had to discuss the matter; the only question was when. She had no idea when he was coming home. The waiting, she knew, would be dreadful, and he might not return home until evening. However, waiting was all she could do.

At noontime, the mail arrived, with, she hoped, some distraction. There were a fistful of bills and one small packet from a historical society, postmarked Valparaiso, Indiana.

The material from Indiana was one of the things for which she had been waiting. The packet was thick, she noted with excitement. It seemed serendipitous that she should receive it today too—so soon after her research into the census information for the same family and town. She wondered if this was a sign that things would work out in her talk with Eric. She knew it was foolish to be so superstitious, but she couldn't help herself.

She walked out to the patio, sat down, and quickly opened the package. She skimmed the short cover letter, which alerted her to the good news that they had found the obituary for William Hays Pierce. The bottom of the letter also carried the name and address of another person who had requested information on the family—perhaps a distant cousin. She threw the letter on the table and began reading the obituary, hoping to find clues to where he was born. It was a lengthy obituary, a very good sign.

Helen was thankful that the obituary mentioned his exact age—thirty years and seven days. From this she would be able to compute his date of birth. She tried to calm herself—she couldn't believe how fast her heart was racing. This was her great-grandfather, a man she had never known, but someone with whom she felt a close connection. He had died so young.

The obituary indicated that he'd died in a railroad accident. He had been running to catch a train and had fallen into a ditch. An exposed beam caught him in the chest, immediately above the heart.

Helen put the obituary down. It was such a horrible, painful death. She could imagine him lying there, knowing he was dying, but helpless. It was amazing how long he had hung on. Suddenly, she thought she heard something. Was it the front door? But it was nothing. Her head felt vaguely numb—she thought from the stress of worrying about Eric. When she picked up the obituary again, she realized that her hand was shaking.

The obituary noted that her ancestor had been more kind to the world than to himself; her grandmother Kezzie had been like that, she remembered, a life of silent suffering. At the end of the obituary, there was a strange note: "Surely Life is but a vapor which appeareth but a little while and then vanishes away, H.W."

Helen put the obituary down and looked out over the cactus garden. How many mornings had she noticed a slight haze over the garden—very much like a vapor, which disappeared as the sun grew stronger? How many mornings had she watched her husband begin work in the garden, his pants wet with dew? Even now, some mornings, if she closed her eyes halfway, she could still see him there, unsmiling, intent on his work.

She thought of her great-grandmother Mariette. What a horrible thing, to be waiting for her husband's body. How must she have felt to have her husband's body brought back? Her whole life was turned upside down in one moment. Didn't her own dilemma pale in comparison? But she couldn't rationalize her fear away—the thought of losing Eric remained.

She caught a slight movement in the corner of her eye, which snapped her out of her thoughts. She turned and saw Eric standing before her.

"I have the best news," he told her, his eyes gleaming.

"How long have you been standing there?" she asked in a daze.

"A few minutes," he replied and sat down next to her. "You must have got some great genealogy stuff in the mail today—you didn't even hear me come in."

"Yes, I did receive something in the mail," she admitted, still flustered from seeing him and wondering what kind of news he had. It surprised her that he appeared to be in such a good mood—it made her feel nervous. "It's my great-grandfather Pierce's obituary." She paused, trying to connect her thoughts. "What's your good news?"

"I think I'm in love," he replied with a grin.

Helen felt odd—he was talking to her as if he knew nothing about the letter. And now here her son was talking of love. "How exciting," she managed to say.

"I met him at the beach a few days ago and we had lunch," he continued quickly. "This might be the one."

She managed not to smile. Each one of his new boyfriends was always "the one." This new boyfriend, she thought, might explain why he'd been absent so much over the last several days. "Have you been spending a great deal of time with him?" she couldn't help but ask.

"Not yet," he replied, smiling. "We may get together again tonight. Right now, all I want to do is get cleaned up."

She knew immediately that he had really come by for a fresh set of clothes. So he was with this man last night, she mused. She would not, of course, attempt to learn any of the details. "I'm very happy for you." She smiled. "What's his name?"

"Russ," he told her, his eyes glowing. "Russell Hezekiah Lincoln."

"You don't see the name Hezekiah all that often anymore," she replied, trying to remember where she'd seen that name in her own family research—she was sure that she had come across it. "Tell me more about him," she suggested.

Eric began to talk about his latest love in the enthusiastic way that was so like him. She listened patiently, all the time wondering if Eric had read the letter. She kept searching for signs in his manner, reading his face for traces of anger directed at her. She could tell nothing, only that he was incredibly happy. Helen decided that the only way to deal with this was to talk it out, whether he had seen the letter or not.

After he finished, Helen leaned over and gave him a long hug. "I can see that you're happy—that's the important thing."

"I *am* happy," he said, hugging her back, perhaps not as completely as he usually did.

Helen tried to imagine how his father would have reacted to this news. He was not the most flexible person she had known. He'd only asked her once whether she thought their son was "different." She had told him "no," though she suspected that Eric *was* different in the way her husband implied. She had said no because she disagreed with the spirit in which he had posed the question. "Did you get to know much about him?" she added.

"Not as much as I would like," Eric admitted. "It was easy for us to talk, though," he added.

Helen smiled. Communication was so important for any relationship. Her years with Eric's father had been spent with far too many silences, especially in the bad times.

"Well, I better get cleaned up," he said and turned.

"Eric," she said anxiously. "When are you going out again?"

"I'm not sure yet," he replied. "I need to call him first."

"I was hoping we could have dinner together tonight." Helen tried not to sound too demanding, but she desperately wanted to see him. "There's something I need to discuss with you, honey."

He paused, his face clouding over. "Sure, Mom," he said, brightening. "I'll be here." He smiled as he headed toward the stairs. "I promise."

As she heard him run upstairs, Helen felt some sense of relief, reasoning that he probably hadn't read the letter. Even so, she was determined to discuss it with him. It will be best to get things out in the open, she told herself on the way into the kitchen, but she still wasn't sure how she would broach the subject.

This would be a difficult night; she was determined, however, to make things work.

10

At first, Eric was reluctant to step into the shower for fear that the water might wash away the feeling of Russ's arms around him. He hadn't felt so content or safe in weeks. He couldn't imagine how he could fall asleep so easily, especially in an unfamiliar place, yet he had.

Eric knew that his mother wanted to talk about the letter from his birth mother. Part of him resented the distraction because it was difficult for him to think of anything but Russ, but at the same time Eric wanted to talk with his mother and find out why she had concealed her discovery. He steeled himself for their talk, which would be difficult for both of them.

He stepped into the cascading water and closed his eyes. He was relieved that the warmth of the water actually seemed to enhance the feeling of Russ's presence. He stayed in the shower just until the water began to turn cooler. It was wonderful to be oblivious to the world again.

After he dressed and went downstairs, Eric found a note from his mother letting him know that she had gone to the grocery store and would be back soon. Her neat script looked more fragile and tentative than usual.

He went to his mother's office and noticed the computer was still on, although the screen had gone black. He felt certain she had left the genealogy program on. He hit the space bar, and, sure enough, the screen lit up in blue with a five-generation genealogy chart. At the far left, Eric saw his mother's name. Branching out from it to the right were the names of her parents, grandparents, great-grandparents, and great- great-grandparents. As Eric followed the names across the screen, he noticed that something had changed since the last time he had seen the chart. There were now names where before there had been none. He read them back, starting with his mother: Helen Keith,

Jessie Elvira Tate, Keziah Rebecca Pierce, William Hays Pierce, Andrew Pierce. The last name was new, Eric was sure, as well as the name of Andrew's wife, Rebecca. She had pushed the Pierce line back one more generation.

He stared at the screen for awhile. It was actually quite beautiful, glowing blue names swimming in a sea of black. Arrows pointed to the far right of the screen wherever the line went even farther back. Instead of following any of them, though, Eric pressed the "x" key and the screen immediately changed to a three-generation chart showing his mother, father, his mother's parents, and himself. For all of his mother's interest in bloodlines, she had included him. She had explained that it wasn't only about bloodlines, insisting that he, as their son, rightfully belonged. Eric smiled. Across the top of the chart read the word "pedigree." Whenever he saw that word, he thought of horses and dogs, not people. He felt certain that the word referred only to bloodlines. He and his parents didn't share any blood. They had, he reasoned, shared their lives, which was enough for him. He wasn't so sure whether it was enough for his mother.

He reclined in the chair, continuing to stare at the blue and black sea. How was it, he wondered, that anyone could instantly realize that a particular someone was the right someone? How could so much be decided in an instant? As he let his body relax, it was almost as if he could feel the warmth of Russ's body again, pressing against his own. When he was in Russ's arms, it was as though all the cells of his body had found just the right position. It was much more than a feeling of warmth or closeness. He felt like he'd been sitting in the sun.

Eric sat forward in the chair and pulled out his wallet. He would have to call Russ to let him know about the change of plans. He dialed the number, and Russ answered on the fourth ring. "I just got out of the shower," Eric said. "How are you?"

"Happy," Russ replied. "Can you see me smiling?"

"I can hear it," Eric told him with a laugh. "Last night was great."

"Yeah, it was. Would you like to get together tonight?" Russ asked hopefully.

Eric paused, uncertain of how to put this without being too discouraging. "It would be great to see you tonight," he began, imagining that he already could hear a sigh on the other end of the line, "but my mom asked me to stay for dinner. She said she has something important to discuss with me."

"Oh," Russ replied, obviously disappointed. "You think it may have to do with your birth mother?"

"That's my guess," Eric said. "I really need to talk with her about this."

"You're right," Russ agreed. "We can get together another time."

"How about tomorrow?" Eric asked.

"Definitely," Russ said. "How about dinner at my place? We can order some pizza. Maybe go dancing later?"

"Sounds great," Eric said. "What time?"

"How about six?"

"I may need directions."

Eric hung up the phone, feeling like he was glowing again. He looked at the computer screen. The blue names were gone, erased by the screen saver. He tapped the space bar again and the names floated back. He wondered what it would look like to add Russ's name as his spouse. He typed the command for child, to bring him up as the principal person on the screen. His name, along with those of his parents, appeared. He typed the command for adding a spouse. Another screen came up with empty data fields for a name and date of birth. He typed in "Russell Hezekiah Lincoln." He couldn't fill out any more of the fields, since he didn't know Russ's birth date yet. He pressed the key for saving the data and another screen popped up, this time asking for marriage data. He left these fields blank too and pressed the key for saving the data. The original screen showing him came up, and by his name was the name of Russell Hezekiah Lincoln as his spouse. He thought that it looked complete that way, two blue names swimming together in a sea of black.

"I see you've made an addition to our family."

Eric jumped, taken completely by surprise by his mother. "I wanted to see what it would look like and typed it in," he said without turning around. "I haven't had a chance to delete it yet."

"Why would you want to delete it?" she asked innocently, he thought.

"You don't mind it being there?"

"I don't mind." He could feel her presence behind him. Had she moved a little closer?

"You may find this hard to believe, but about a month ago on my online service there was a discussion on the genealogy forum about whether to acknowledge nontraditional relationships in our databases. Most of the people discussing this, including me, thought that we should." She rested her hands on his shoulders. "So I don't mind you keyboarding Russ's name in. My only question is whether you're being premature."

He still wasn't sure if there was a trace of anger in her voice. Nontraditional relationships? She had been thinking about this more than he realized.

"This is a first," she said. "You've never added anything to the database until now."

"I really think that he's going to be the one."

"Honey," she said and released him, "you nearly always say that."

"This time it's different, Mom," he persisted, turning around to face her. "I can feel it in my bones."

She stood there silently for a moment. "I'd like to meet him," she finally said.

"Sure," he agreed, relieved she believed him.

Suddenly she looked very vulnerable and he felt protective. Here was one of the few people who had ever cared for him, mistakes and all. What did she see in him at that moment that would bring such sadness to her eyes? She sat down opposite him in a seldom-used armchair. "There's something we need to talk about."

Here it was, he thought. Ever since he'd been young, she'd always taught him to tackle the unpleasant things first before doing the enjoyable things.

"I don't exactly know how to tell you this," she began. Her face looked so worn. "But I think it's best just to get it out in the open."

"Yes," he began, deciding to admit reading the letter, but she cut him off.

"I've heard from your birth mother."

Now that she said it, Eric had a sinking feeling in the pit of his stomach. "I know," he admitted. "I already read the letter."

She flinched, as if he had struck her. Her hand trembled as she reached over to retrieve the letter. He had never seen her hand shake in that way before.

"I've already seen it, Mom," he said more gently. "You don't need to show it to me."

"This is another letter, one that I sent to your birth mother," she explained, giving him the letter, her hand still shaking. "It was returned to me unopened."

Eric had to blink back a few tears to read it. He had never seen his mother so upset, and it frightened him. What bothered him even more was the fact that his mother didn't seem surprised, concerned, or angry that he had read the letter without her knowledge. This new letter, of which he only managed to read a part, indicated that she would be happy to arrange a meeting if Eric agreed. The letter had been sent months ago. Knowing that she had tried to reach his birth mother helped mollify him, though not completely. The fact was that she had not told him of either letter. At the same time that he felt rather protective of his mother, he also felt anger. He tried to balance the conflicting feelings before he responded. "Why didn't you tell me?" he asked.

She scanned the floor. He could see tears welling up in her eyes, but she didn't cry. "I think that I was afraid," she finally said. "I felt unsure what to do. Part of me reasoned that I shouldn't tell you until I'd heard from her again. I suppose another part of me didn't want her to succeed in contacting you." She glanced up at him. "I'm sorry if I hurt you."

How could he possibly feel any anger toward her now? "I'm sorry that I pawed through your stuff," he said.

"You don't need to be sorry about it," she replied. "I feel terrible, though, that you discovered this news this way."

Any chance that he could become angry with her again melted away; instead, he began to feel a strong sense of loss. He knew that nothing between them would ever be exactly the same again.

"I was worried that I might lose you," she told him.

Nothing could be less true than that, he thought. "You'll never lose me, Mom. I'll always be your son."

"Thank you."

She was still. He wanted to reach out and hug her, but the way she held herself, with crossed arms, stopped him.

"I've written to the adoption agency," he had to tell her, "to see if they have more information about her."

"I should have done that, I suppose," she replied, almost as an afterthought, without a hint of sarcasm.

"No," he said. "This is something that I need to do for myself. It won't change anything between us," he added to console her, even though he knew it probably wasn't true.

"Eric," she said, "it's difficult to anticipate how things will turn out. If you find her, it's bound to change you, and that would be a good thing. There's an ebb and flow in the relations between people, even parents and children."

Eric thought a moment before he responded. "I guess what I meant to say was that it wouldn't change the way I love you."

Tears welled up in her eyes again. "I love you too, honey."

Eric stood up as she did and intercepted her before she could get out of the room, giving her a hug. She seemed so small in his arms. "Don't worry," he said.

"Are you going to see your new boyfriend, your Russ tonight?" she asked.

"No, I planned to spend the evening with you," he said, a little surprised.

"Honey, don't feel that you have to stay here with me. I'll be fine. I just need some time to adjust."

He couldn't believe it, but he was sure that she wanted to be alone. He almost felt as though he were being dismissed—didn't she need him? He wanted to make everything right, but he didn't know how.

"Are you sure?" he asked, still not believing it.

"I'm going to work a little more on the family history," she said firmly. "Don't worry about me. I will be fine."

Something about her eyes told him she wasn't just fine, but he didn't want to be contrary with her, especially now. From experience, he knew that when she was feeling hurt, his mother would withdraw. He'd seen it happen so many times with his father. Now that *he* was the cause, Eric felt helpless and incredibly guilty. "Okay, Mom. I love you," he repeated, more for himself than for her, to be reassured.

"I love you too, honey," she repeated and quietly walked out of the room.

He wanted to see her expression, to gauge her reaction, but she wouldn't turn his way again.

11

Toward the end of the day, clouds billowed along the coast in an upsweep of moisture that would never become rain. The change brought a chill to the air as Russ closed down his T-shirt stand. He debated whether to take a quick swim. He'd do almost anything rather than go back to his empty apartment. Even though he knew it was important for Eric to have a talk with his mother, he wished he and Eric could go out again tonight.

As if on autopilot, Russ decided to swing by Orion, a video bar, instead. He didn't really care how he looked. All he knew was that he didn't want to go home.

On his way to the bar, he looked into the window at the Blue Door Bookstore, an alternative, independent bookseller always on the verge of going under. It surprised him to see more or less mainstream best-sellers featured—though the notices posted closer to the front door told a different story—Bisexuals United was holding a meeting and some guest author he'd never heard of was giving a lecture on the special financial planning needs of gay couples.

As he considered whether to venture into the store, a young man came up beside him. Russ froze. The young man was gorgeous—tall, brunette, well-built, and wearing a green muscle shirt that showed off his arms. The man had a particularly handsome face, though not in a conventional way. His features were sharp and angular, like a jackal's, with a prominent nose and ears. Everything taken together, however, worked perfectly in his favor.

The man nodded at Russ. He couldn't help but nod back.

"Are you waiting for anyone?" he asked.

It was tempting. Russ found him immensely attractive, especially his eyes, a brown so light they were almost deep yellow. To top it off, the guy was available and willing. Russ's body felt drawn to him. "No," he answered.

"Would you like to grab a drink somewhere?" The man asked with a smile.

Russ nearly said yes, but then he thought of Eric. Of course, he rationalized, he had made no promises to Eric; in a sense, though, he had made a promise to himself to give up one-night stands. He quickly looked over the guy again—it was so tempting and his body yearned for contact. Was it worth having a fling with the guy? Russ asked himself. The answer came back in the negative.

"Actually, I think I'll pass," he finally mumbled, not quite believing that he'd managed to utter the words.

If the young man was disappointed, he hid it expertly, for Russ couldn't detect a trace of any emotion on the man's face. "That's cool," the man said and ambled off.

Russ felt proud of himself. He had passed his first test.

Orion usually had a friendly bunch of guys. Tonight it seemed a little crowded, especially so early in the evening. A group stood around the pool table and lots of guys talked and watched the big-screen TVs hanging from each corner of the room, which blared a rock video Russ didn't recognize.

He stood in line at the bar for a soft drink and scanned the room. Several hot guys were there and he was already getting a few looks. But Russ didn't return any of the searching glances. After he got his drink and found a place to sit near the back, he just watched the videos and avoided looking at anyone. This was difficult, though; he had a habit of examining everything around him.

He enjoyed watching the games the guys played with each other. A small, intimate bar like Orion actually was a challenging spot for a pickup. There were lots of guys to choose from, of course, but everyone was too much on display. A guy had to be very careful in approaching someone else; if he wasn't, everyone would know if the attempt at a pickup resulted in failure. This lent Orion an underlying feeling of anxiety. Since no one wanted to be perceived as a failure, pickups were trickier and more subtle—a look of the eye, standing nearer the intended target, and waiting for a sign of acceptance was a typical scenario. Russ could detect plenty of this going on in the room and he was careful not to reciprocate anything.

The young man who'd approached him at the bookstore window walked in just as Russ was finishing his drink. The man barely looked at him and then ignored him. Russ had to smile.

Russ took the arrival of the young man as a sign that it was time to go. Before he could make his way out, however, another newcomer arrived that surprised him. It was Eric. Alone. Russ backed into the doorway that led to the restrooms, being careful that Eric not see him.

It was still relatively early in the evening, and Eric should still have been at his mother's—unless Eric had deceived him. Russ felt completely at a loss. He replayed the conversation they'd had earlier. There was no mistake: Eric had clearly said he wouldn't be available. What was going on? he wondered.

Russ slipped into the bathroom, where he was glad to find an empty stall. He locked the door behind him and considered what to do. He could easily transform and slip by Eric unnoticed. He was not sure, though, of what form to change into. Nothing seemed to come to mind—no images, and there was no mirror to help him in the stall. Then it hit him: why not change into his natural, though flawed, form—the body his genes gave him at birth? The more he thought about it, the more compelling the idea became. In fact, he could strike up a conversation with Eric just to see what would happen. What better way to see for certain what Eric would think of him if he saw what he really looked like?

The process took only a few moments and hardly any concentration at all. It was just a matter of relaxing and letting his body unravel. When he stepped out of the stall, he was confronted with his old self—someone he rarely saw anymore.

He decided that he wasn't bad-looking after all. All of the flaws were there—the too-round face, the crooked nose, the freckles, the drab hair. But he had a look about him, he concluded.

He waited a moment before approaching Eric, just to get his bearings. Eric was standing near the spot where Russ had ended up after first entering the bar. Russ thought he looked lonely.

Russ walked over to him and stood nearby, hoping Eric would glance at him. He did. "Hi," Russ said, surprised at first by his voice, which sounded so different than it usually did—deeper and less smooth. He still forgot how much altering the facial features changed the voice. "Busy night, isn't it?"

"Yes," Eric agreed, but didn't look at him long.

"Are you waiting for anyone?" Russ asked and, with a start, realized it was the same line the young man at the bookstore had used with him.

"No, I'm not." Eric glanced back at him and finally let his eyes linger. For an instant, Russ feared Eric might somehow recognize him. "I've just finished a visit with my mom." Eric smiled weakly. "I needed to decompress, if you know what I mean."

"Yeah, I do," Russ said, relieved. At least Eric hadn't lied to him. Russ also sensed that Eric was upset about something and regretted not being able to come out and simply ask him how his talk went. He wondered if he could bring it up somehow but finally decided not to. "The same thing happens when I visit my folks." Russ began to tell a story, only slightly flinching at the lies. "I can only stand so much of it until I need to be around my other family."

"Exactly." Eric looked away from him again, but at least he was smiling.

To keep Eric's attention, Russ continued his story about his "parents," and what it was like spending holidays with them. He was surprised at how easy it was to spin a yarn for Eric. It was something he'd done all his life, but it bothered him when Eric laughed at the silly jokes he made up about his mother's special regimen for baking a turkey. It was as though he were contaminating their relationship, even though it was harmless. At least so far. Russ ended his little monologue by asking Eric if he wanted another beer.

"I don't think so," Eric replied.

Russ couldn't decide if he was happy about this or not. On the one hand, he didn't want Eric to respond to his come-on, yet he yearned to feel again the closeness they'd had the night before. Russ tried to hide his disappointment but didn't think he was too successful.

"Look," Eric added, "I'm sorry. Actually you're an attractive guy, but I just met somebody special, and I usually try not to get interested in anyone else during this stage. I want to give it a chance and see what happens."

Now Russ tried to hide his relief. "That's great," he said.

Eric gave him an incredulous look.

"No, really, I think it's great. It's no problem, really."

"Okay," Eric agreed with a bemused smile. "Maybe you should let me treat *you* to a beer?"

"No, that's all right," Russ answered. "I think I'll get going. But thanks for being honest with me."

"No problem."

When Russ returned home that evening, alone, he found a message on his answering machine from Eric, who hoped that they could get together after all. Delighted, Russ picked up the phone to return Eric's call, only to realize that this might not be the right time. Even if Eric was home by now, he might be talking things over again with his mother. No, he'd have to wait until morning.

Wait until morning. How long had he waited for someone to trust, a partner with whom to share his life? Were all the years of loneliness soon to come to an end? Russ walked over to his patient, the beautiful Swedish ivy that wouldn't stop growing. As he reached out to the plant, a cluster of dark green leaves turned toward him in silent recognition. Now everything seemed right with the world, except for the guilt Russ felt over his ruse.

12

Russ stole a couple of kisses while they were in the car and let his hand rest on Eric's thigh. The Independence Day fireworks at Mission Bay Park had been magnificent, creating an evening sky filled with color.

Russ had lost track of time, though some part of him realized with great joy that instead of counting days, he was able to count two weeks of their being together. They'd fallen into a wonderful rhythm of dinner, dancing, and making love. Never had Russ felt such bliss and never had he been more terrified of revealing too many secrets.

As they hurried up the steps, Russ grabbed him around the waist.

"Someone may see us!" Eric complained, but he was laughing.

Russ closed the door behind them. If only he could be free to transform! He'd grow his hair so long that it would drop to the floor, making a blanket for them both. "I love you," Russ said and drew Eric closer.

Russ caught his lover's eyes. Brown depths gazed back at him. Russ ran his hand up and down Eric's back, feeling the length of his spine under the cotton shirt. He stroked his hair. It felt so good to be this close. Russ kissed his forehead again.

Eric took Russ's hands. They had to be careful to step over "Sylvia," the Swedish ivy gone wild. Sylvia was now taking over a corner of the living room—its vibrant green vines were poking up everywhere. Eric had wanted to trim it, but Russ refused. Eric thought he was crazy.

As they stepped into the bedroom, Russ could feel his spine begin to tingle, all of his energy welling up. He'd need to channel it into the lovemaking. He hoped, someday, for something else, but not tonight.

"Did you lock the front door?" Eric whispered.

"It'll be fine," Russ answered.

There, even in the dimness of the room, Eric's large brown eyes sparkled like they had the night of their first meeting. Russ pulled off his lover's T-shirt, and kissed his shoulder, close to the neck, tracing his lips on Eric's soft skin. When their gaze met again, Eric kissed him on the mouth, gently taking Russ's arms in his own.

Eric slowly reclined on the bed, bringing Russ down on top of him, and they caressed each other with a tenderness Russ had never experienced with anyone else. Eric burshed at the hair above Russ's ears with his fingertips and lightly moved his hands along Russ's shoulders and back, slowly reaching down, underneath Russ's jeans.

For a moment, they struggled together to remove each other's clothing. With their bodies free, Russ fell back onto him. The rest was so easy, so simple. It all seemed to flow, arms and legs, grasping, holding. Their embrace meant everything to him. When Russ momentarily paused, Eric didn't hesitate, moving back, lifting his legs onto Russ's shoulders. Russ gently press forward as he gazed into those brown eyes.

Russ remained stretched on top of him for several minutes, feeling his body relax and melt into his lover's. Eric stroked the hair at the back of his head, and Russ could feel his breath on his ear. Russ rolled to the side and pulled Eric up against him, tracing his fingers along Eric's chest and draping a leg over one of Eric's. Eric snuggled closer.

"It just gets better," Eric said quietly.

"That's what I wanted to hear," he replied. Nothing had ever quite matched it before, not only the intensity of the release, but something else—a sense of spirit between them. It made Russ wonder if he hadn't changed somehow—he felt that some part of his body must have changed without him knowing about it. The idea frightened him.

"Look at my face," he asked Eric. "Have I changed?"

Eric moved away from him slightly to get a better vantage point. "Your face looks softer," he finally said with a smile. "The expression is softer."

As Eric nestled back into him, Russ relaxed, knowing his secret would be safe—at least for now.

Light from the window, as always, woke up Russ early. No matter how closely Eric shut the blinds, no matter how late they had stayed up the night before, Russ always woke up at dawn.

Eric still lay close to him—their limbs were such a tangle that they might as well have had one body. Russ kissed him on the cheek and Eric stirred, allowing a hint of a smile to cross his face. Nearly every morning it had been like this— waking up and waiting until Russ kissed him lightly, as if not to awaken him. Eric wondered if the warmth of them nestled together would be enough to coax Russ back to sleep.

Sometimes Eric wished they could remain in each other's arms forever. Less often, he wondered if he'd ever feel trapped by it. After waiting as long as he thought he should, Eric stretched his legs.

"Good morning," Russ quietly said.

"You're always waking up before I do," Eric replied, with eyes half-closed.

"I've always awakened at dawn," he agreed.

"We need to get some of those black-out shades."

"I don't want to block out the light," Russ said. "It's natural to wake up with the sunrise."

"It's not natural as far as I'm concerned," Eric groused and began to kiss each of Russ's fingers—something that had turned into a morning ritual.

"Did you have fun last night?" Russ asked.

"Yeah," Eric said between kisses. "I think . . . that it's only getting better . . . and . . . better . . . almost . . . perfect."

"What would make it perfect?"

Eric just looked at him and smiled.

"You're thinking what I'm thinking?"

"Probably."

"Tell me, then," Russ said, starting to kiss each of Eric's fingers.

"Do you know what this is leading to?"

"I have . . . the feeling . . . that you might . . . be thinking . . . of . . . moving in . . . with me?"

"Is that something you'd like?" Eric asked, almost coyly.

Now it was Russ's turn to simply smile and say nothing.

What did Russ really think of it? Eric had been getting mixed signals.

Eric watched his lover get out of bed and pick up his clothes, which had been discarded on the floor the night before, noting with amusement that Russ, by mistake, or perhaps on purpose, had slipped on the wrong pair of undershorts. It was as though it had all been preordained—their meeting and courtship. Now it seemed as though they were on the verge of making a commitment. Never had he dreamed that this would happen to him.

Russ reached down, offering his hand. Eric took it, allowing himself to be pulled up, out of bed and into his lover's arms.

"Let's get something to eat," Russ suggested.

As Russ fiddled around in the kitchen, Eric called Kevin to make amends. They hadn't seen each other for the past few weeks. The call was short. Kevin loudly complained about Eric's neglect of the search for his birth mother, though Eric knew from Kevin's voice that it was much more than that. Kevin was jealous. Why couldn't Kevin be more happy for him, now that he'd found someone?

Russ brought two glasses of orange juice. "What's wrong?"

"Kevin's not very happy with me," he replied.

"Why?" Russ sat next to him on the couch.

"Kevin told me that he was upset because I've been neglecting the search for my birth mother, but I think it has more to do with my neglect of him."

"Oh no," Russ said, and put his arm around Eric's shoulders. "I didn't mean to break up a good friendship."

"He'll get used to it," Eric said with a smile.

"Yeah, I guess he'll have to." Russ reached over and kissed him on the lips. "Although maybe he has a point," Russ added. "About the search for your birth mother."

Eric sighed. His letter to the adoption agency had been returned; they didn't have any idea where Marie had gone. "I don't think there's much hope."

"Don't say that," Russ said, lightly kissing his cheek. "You just need to look in the right places."

"Wherever those are," Eric said. He was grateful Russ cared enough to want to help. "I hate to admit this, but sometimes I felt so disconnected from my family. We never seemed to laugh at the same jokes, and my parents were so great at finding their way around, even to new places. I can get lost going to the gym."

Russ gently stroked his arm.

"It was awkward for me to talk about my feelings, especially with my father." Eric began playing with Russ's fingers. "I've often wondered whether I look more like my birth mother or birth father. It's been even more painful over the last few years, since my mom got so wrapped up in genealogy. I don't know anything about my family history, and sometimes it makes me feel like something is missing."

Russ kissed him on the forehead. It felt so good to be comforted without words. Eric had often thought that there wasn't enough touching in his family. Now he had someone who loved to hold him; someone who might always be there. In Russ's arms, he felt safe and comforted. How had he ever survived without him?

After a few minutes of silence, filled with their touching, Russ asked, almost in a whisper, "Would you like to look for a place together?"

Eric leaned back to see the expression on Russ's face. He quickly sensed that Russ felt torn; a part of Russ was still holding back. Yet Russ's eyes held utter longing. "Your eyes are beautiful," he said.

"That doesn't answer my question," Russ replied, smiling.

"I want us to spend as much time together as we can," Eric said, thinking aloud, trying to gauge Russ's reaction at the same time he was trying to understand his own. "I'm already over here most of the time anyway."

"That's true."

Was this the right move? Eric wondered. There was still a great deal that he didn't know about his lover. "What we're really talking about is a commitment."

"Yeah," Russ finally said. "I guess you're right."

"Are we ready for it?" Eric asked for both of them.

Eric was surprised to see tears in Russ's eyes. "Yeah, I think we are."

Eric wasn't sure who made the first move, but they were soon kissing. The feeling of closeness, of skin touching skin and lips touching lips, felt different than it ever had with anyone else. They enjoyed so many of the same things, dancing, the beach, making love; at the same time, Eric realized it was much more than this, more than companionship. There was a feeling of being at one with each other that transcended all else.

The search, Eric realized, might be over. Finding their own place to create a life together would be everything Eric had hoped for. Now, he had to make it come true.

13

Russ's mother ran ahead of him, shouting something he couldn't quite make out. Russ pulled off his T-shirt, threw it on the sand, and went in after her. It was a perfect July day at Pacific Beach. He couldn't recall the last time they'd gone swimming together. By the time he had waded out far enough to dive into the surf, she was already far away, bobbing in the ocean. She'd always been an excellent swimmer, no matter what form she decided to take.

Today, in honor of the sunshine and general vibrancy of his mood, his mother had dropped by the T-shirt stand in the form of a darkly handsome, athletic male, eager for fun. This was one of the most wonderful things about being an elf child. He and his mother had always been able to do most everything together; she could always fit in. He had expressed little interest in organized sports, but had always enjoyed playing basketball with her. They made a good team for pickup games. Actually, she liked sports much better than he did and even joined a men's basketball league for a short time before leagues were developed for women. He would go to the afternoon games at the local YMCA and watch her after school. His father never knew.

When a large wave finally came in, he dived into it and came out the other side. He flipped his hair back, tasting the sea salt on his lips. His body adjusted to the cooler temperature of the water immediately. No need for a wet suit for him, he thought, recalling how he had surprised a bunch of surfers, all wearing wet suits, one winter day.

He swam out to her. "You're amazing."

"Thank you, sweetheart," she replied. "I'm not sure the waves will cooperate with us today."

"The saltwater is enough for me."

"Invigorating, isn't it?" she said. "I haven't seen much of you lately. Why haven't you introduced me to your new boyfriend?"

How she loved to tease him. Russ wasn't sure if he was ready to introduce Eric to his mother. There was no telling exactly what she would do. "I didn't realize that it was important to you."

"Of course," she said, flicking some water at him. "You've reached something of a milestone—what has it been? Several weeks?"

"About that," Russ replied, wiping his eyes.

"You know," she replied, "I can manage to pass for being a little older. I can add some gray streaks. That will age me a little."

"I'm not worried about that," Russ continued, submerging his head for an instant.

"Oh, is there something else you're worried about?"

Russ looked directly at her. "I don't want you to grill him."

"What could you mean?" she said lightly.

"You're going to want to find out everything you can about him in order to protect me." He knew his mother too well.

She gave him a bemused smile. "How do you know that I haven't already met him in some other form? How do you know that I haven't already, as you say, grilled him?"

Although he knew that she was fully capable of doing such a thing, he could tell by the way she held her face that she was toying with him. "I can tell you haven't."

She smiled. "You're right," she pronounced, satisfied. "Russ, who was the person who encouraged you in this little experiment?"

He knew it. Now she was going to take credit for his finding Eric. "You did," he conceded.

"Do you imagine that I would do anything to complicate things for you?" she asked, dipping her head in the water.

He hated it when she used this tone of voice. "No," he replied.

"I'm happy for you," she said, more softly. "I want to meet the person responsible for the happiness of my son, that's all."

He reconsidered. Perhaps he was being paranoid. "I suppose this means so much to me," he began, "that I'm afraid something will happen to ruin it."

"Well, then, don't worry," she said. "Have you met his family?"

"Not yet," he replied. "Though Eric mentioned that we might have dinner with his mother later this week. He tells me that she wants to meet me."

"That's a good sign," she said. "I'd love to host Eric for dinner at my apartment."

"That's very generous."

"What form should I take?" she asked impishly, obviously thrilled.

"How about the one you have right now?" he asked jokingly.

"Do you think that I look old enough to be your mother?" she asked, ignoring his humor.

Why had she come back to this again? "Sure," he responded. "I suppose you do. You could always pass for about forty—old enough to be my mother if I were Eric's age. Besides, I'm not sure he'd be that critical in his appraisal of you."

"Are you telling me that he's gullible?" she asked with a lively gleam in her eye.

He laughed—she was really on a roll. "Perhaps." He hated saying anything so negative about the person he loved, even if it were true.

"I see that you do care for him," she said, softening again.

"We're talking about getting a place together."

Joy swept across her face. "I'm happy for you. You needed someone special in your life, to share your life—at least part of it," she added. "Tell me more about this lover of yours. Is he working?"

"No," Russ said. "He's been talking about getting a part-time job, but so far he hasn't done much about it. I can't blame him. He deserves to have some fun."

"What about his future?"

"He'll be going to grad school at SDSU in the fall," Russ explained. "Maybe he'll pick up a part-time job then."

"No money?" she asked. "Who's going to pay the rent?"

"I think he has money saved for college," Russ said. "He told me his grandparents left him a legacy to help with his education."

"You're going to support him, aren't you?" she asked lightheartedly.

"It looks like it, doesn't it?" Russ grinned. "At least for awhile."

"Have you been faithful to him?"

"That's not something you should be asking," he told her firmly, though he knew it would make no difference.

"You don't need to answer," she teased him. "I can see it in your face—you've been faithful. Probably a record for you."

"Thanks for the validation," he replied grimly.

Suddenly, the crashing of the waves paused, and the surface of the water around them became almost like glass. If he didn't know better, he would have thought his mother had somehow calmed the waters. She dived. He waited apprehensively, even though he knew it was one of her favorite games. What would she turn into? Some kind of sea monster with gills? A dolphin? He felt hands grab both of his ankles and he was pulled under. The water was too cloudy for him to see anything but a large shape moving around. It appeared to be human. They both came up at the same time. He was disappointed. His mother had only changed the color of her hair and eyes, making them lighter.

"Is that all you could manage?" he asked, teasingly.

She dived under again and presented him with not two legs, but one fin. The shiny, darkly green scales sparkled in the sun. She'd become a merman.

He hoped that no one had seen her. "Show-off," he said when she came up for air.

"Never," she replied gleefully. When she dove in again, she had lost the fins and had her feet back. He marveled at her control. For someone so insistent on secrecy, it always surprised him when she decided to show off in public. She really belonged on the stage, consummate actress that she was.

They each tried riding a few waves, but agreed that they didn't pack enough wallop to make it feel like body surfing. They waded back to shore.

"I really do want to meet him," she repeated, once they were on the sand, shaking the water from their hair. "You'll have to tell me what story you've told him, so I won't create any difficulties for you."

A story. Yes, he thought, in the past that's what he would have told a boyfriend—a fabricated saga. "I haven't lied to him," he said, trying not to sound too proud.

"You're joking, aren't you?" she asked.

"No, I'm not," he said, though from the expression on her face he wished he had not been so blunt. "There are just a few things I've left out," he added, hoping to mollify her.

"This could be dangerous," she said very quietly. "You'd be surprised how quickly things can slip out once you start speaking the truth. You have to be very careful. The longer you're with him, the more difficult it will be. What if he asks you how old you are? Or how old I am? Then what would you tell him?"

"Eric is not what you'd call persistent."

Anger spread over her face. "He may not be persistent, but others in his acquaintance might be. Does he have a family who might be persistent? You must conceal certain things about your life and your family."

He hadn't planned on dealing with an angry mother, but here it was. "I'll have to cross that bridge when I come to it."

"You can be exasperating." Her eyes flashed. "Remember what happened to me, Russell Hezekiah Lincoln, before you make a terrible mistake."

"Of course, Mom," he replied, trying to calm her down. Why did the past, especially her past, have to dictate his life?

"Now I'm going to insist on meeting him."

"Not if you are going to act like this," he countered, trying to keep his own anger in check.

She paused, letting the anger dissipate. "You know I'll be perfectly charming," she said. "I'm sorry," she added more gently. "I really am happy that you've found someone. I just don't want you to make a mistake."

He felt like telling her that everything that happens, as she often pointed out to him, happens for a purpose, but thought better of being so impudent. "Don't worry," he said instead. "I won't."

14

Russ and Eric made their way along the winding streets and carefully tended gardens of Mission Hills. Russ had always admired the homes here, which tended to be larger than those in Hillcrest. In old San Diego, this was where the wealthy people had lived, and the neighborhood still retained a genteel quality.

They turned a corner and Eric parked his car in front of a Spanish-style ranch house that appeared to date from the 1930s. "This is where I grew up," he announced.

Russ let out a little gasp. On either side of the house stood a jacaranda tree taller than the red-tiled roof. Both of the trees were awash in purple blossoms. The delicate branches swayed in the light breeze, perfectly framing the entryway to the home. Small flowers, which resembled little hibiscus, had begun to fall, creating a blanket of purple snow that covered the lawn and sidewalk leading to the front door. Russ tried to imagine Eric as a five-year-old, running around the yard, playing with the purple snow. "This yard is incredible," he exclaimed. "These trees are out of this world."

"Beautiful, aren't they? The trees always bloom in early July. Mom has always said that one of the reasons she wanted Dad to buy this place was for the trees." Eric stepped forward onto the carpet of flowers. "Ready?"

"As ready as I'll ever be." On the way to the door, Russ stooped down to pick up a few of the little flowers. Each was a long funnel of purple, as light as the lightest paper. They felt too delicate to hold.

They reached the porch. "Check the bottom of your shoes," Eric told him, lifting a foot to check his shoe. "The flowers can cause stains."

Russ followed suit.

Eric opened the door and they stepped in. "Mom," he called. "We're here."

"I'm in the kitchen, honey."

"Okay," he said to her and added more quietly to Russ, "She usually doesn't like to visit while she's cooking, so don't be surprised if she suggests that we take a drink to the patio."

The house was just as Russ had expected—elegant and neat. It reminded him of open houses he'd seen on occasion, sponsored by real estate agents so intent on creating a good impression that they had removed all indications that the house was actually lived in. Eric was so messy that it made Russ wonder how he had ever survived in such a sterile environment. Then he realized with a pang of guilt that Eric's mother might have done all of this in preparation for his visit. He reminded himself not to be too critical. Eric led him to the kitchen.

Eric's mother, complete with apron, greeted them with a smile. "Hi, honey." She kissed her son on the cheek.

"Mom," Eric said a little too dramatically, "this is Russ."

She extended her hand. "Hello, Russ. I'm glad to meet you."

"Thank you," he replied. "I'm glad to finally meet you too, Mrs. Taylor."

"Please call me Helen."

With her gray hair, she looked almost too old to be Eric's mother, but then, Russ recalled that she had been older than most new mothers when she'd adopted him. They didn't at all resemble each other, at least physically. Helen struck him as dainty—so unlike his own mother. He had the impression that she came from Yankee, New England stock—with a certain tasteful reserve about her that he found appealing. The most striking thing about her, at least on this first meeting, was her graciousness and underlying kindness. He liked her immediately.

"I was just admiring your jacarandas in the front," Russ told her. "They're incredible."

"Thank you," Helen said and smiled warmly. "I like them too. When Eric's father and I moved in, he threatened to cut them down because the blossoms were such a nuisance." She gave him another smile. "I prevailed."

"What didn't he like about them?" Russ asked.

"He was something of a neat freak," she said, moving toward the sink. "The blossoms can stain carpet, even the interiors of cars." She began to wipe one of two blue drinking glasses, which she had apparently just washed. "There are dangers even with the most pleasant and beautiful aspects of our lives."

He couldn't gauge if she meant him to take the comment seriously or as a joke. "You know," Russ continued, "I've seen jacarandas all over town, but yours are the largest I've come across. The way their branches frame your house is amazing."

Eric smiled at him encouragingly and stepped closer to his mother to take the dried glasses. He placed them on the counter.

"Thank you," she replied, pleased. "What amazes me are the numbers of plants from all over the world that do so well here: jacarandas from Brazil, plumeria from Hawaii. The list goes on and on."

Russ felt more at ease. At least Eric's mother and he would have two things in common—her son, and her love of beautiful plants.

"I'm almost finished getting things started here," she continued. "Why don't you men go out on the patio? I've put out some iced tea and soft drinks. I also have some fruit juice here, or would you like something else?"

"Iced tea will be great," Russ replied. "Thank you."

"Thanks, Mom." Eric shot him a glance that said "I told you so" and motioned for him to follow.

"I'll be out shortly," Helen called after them.

Eric led him through a formal living room and a set of partially open French doors to the patio. "She likes you," he whispered.

"I like her too," he whispered back. He felt like he was dreaming. It all seemed too perfect.

"Remember what I said about her cooking," Eric warned him. "It's not one of her strong suits."

As she had promised, drinks were waiting for them on the patio table. Russ absently took one of the iced teas, more interested in the yard and garden, which was just as beautiful as the front yard, though not quite as manicured. The hibiscus were covered in yellow and red blossoms. The focal point of the backyard, though, was the cactus garden. "What beautiful cacti," Russ exclaimed.

"That was my father's thing," Eric explained, with an air of dismissal.

Russ wondered why Eric appeared to resent the garden, or at least his father's interest in it. "It's amazing," he continued, walking across the yard to take a closer look. The garden had such a variety of textures and colors—from light peach to dark green, all beautifully coupled. A few of the cactus plants in the front were in full bloom with luscious pink blossoms. He heard Helen come up behind them. He turned to her. "This garden is incredible."

"Thank you so much," she replied. "Eric's father spent much of his spare time tending to it. I've tried to keep it up the best that I could," she added wistfully.

"Well, I'd say you've done a great job." Russ knelt down to get a closer look at the cactus flowers. "I didn't realize that cactuses bloomed like this."

"They generally only bloom once a year," she explained. "But it can be dramatic."

He cautiously reached down. The flower didn't show any signs of turning toward him, so he knew it would be safe to touch it. "The petals are so soft."

"Quite a contrast," she agreed.

Each cactus flower shot up in a long funnel ending with a cluster of pink petals. Three rows of petals formed a perfectly symmetrical ten-pointed star. Each flower was delicate—especially the inside, a soft well lined with dainty pistils and stamens. Russ's fingers picked up some of the pollen dust.

"Each flower," Helen told him, "only lasts a day—it opens one night and then crumples at sundown the next day."

"I've never seen anything so beautiful," he said. The petals looked iridescent. It was a miracle that something so beautiful and delicate could come out of a plant covered with needles. He touched a flower again—while the tops of the petals were completely smooth, the underside felt a bit sticky. Looking into the depths of the funnel or perhaps catching a whiff of the pollen dust made him giddy, so that when he stood up, he lost his balance—sending his hand into one of the nearby cacti. Two of the needles drew blood from a finger. Russ gasped and grabbed his hand, trying to hide the wound.

"You've cut yourself," Helen said with concern.

"No, it's nothing." Russ smiled, still holding his hand. He didn't have a chance to see if any of the blood had fallen anywhere.

"Let me see," she said.

"Is it bad?" Eric asked.

"No, it will be okay." Russ could already feel the tingling along his hand to the finger—in seconds, it would be perfectly healed. He had to hide it somehow. "Do you have a Band-Aid?"

"Of course," Helen replied. "Come into the bathroom."

Russ followed her, leaving Eric waiting on the patio. When she got the Band-Aid out, it appeared that she wanted to stay and help him with it, something Russ couldn't possibly allow.

"Thank you so much—I'll be fine now," he said, hoping that this would be enough to get rid of her.

"I'll just leave it to you then," she said, slightly bewildered.

He couldn't help it. He felt like a clod. "Thank you," he added and closed the door.

He examined his hand, now completely healed, with no cut or scratch anywhere. The only mark was a faint yellow stain left by the cactus pollen. He tried to wash it off, but with no luck. After drying his hands, he unwrapped the Band-Aid and then realized that in the heat of the moment, he had forgotten which finger had been scraped. "Shit," he muttered. He knew it was either his forefinger or middle finger. He finally decided to wrap both of them.

They were waiting for him on the patio.

"I feel terrible that you've injured yourself on your first visit here," Helen said, glancing at his hand. "Did you cut both fingers?" she asked with surprise.

"Just a little scrape," he replied.

Eric gave him a quizzical look and rolled his eyes.

"Well, dinner will be ready shortly. Why don't we move into the dining room?"

"Thank you," he said, feeling more the fool by the minute. How could he have been so careless? And what if he'd left any of his blood behind?

As Eric and Helen headed into the house, Russ turned back to the garden again, quickly examining the cactus that had scraped him. He couldn't find any signs of dropped blood, which was a relief. Somewhat reassured, he turned back to the house. Eric was standing at the door waiting for him, giving Russ one of his perplexed looks. "Sorry," Russ said. He knew that this wasn't the kind of impression either of them wanted him to make. Eric just shook his head.

Russ sat down with the two of them at the dining room table, which had been set with a full service of china and silverware. It made Russ feel a little awkward—he hadn't expected anything so fancy. "The table looks wonderful."

"Yeah, Mom," Eric agreed, almost as if he were surprised. "It really does."

"I'm so glad you're here," she said. "I've been looking forward to this for a long time."

Russ only hoped that he was making even half the impression on her that she was making on him.

Helen opened a large serving dish. "We're having asopao de pollo," she said. "Caribbean chicken and rice stew."

"It smells great," Eric added, giving him a wink.

"I'll serve Russ first," she suggested, taking Russ's plate. "Eric might have told you that I am not a fine cook by any means, but this recipe looked simple enough. The dish is supposed to be popular in Puerto Rico."

Russ wished that she hadn't put herself down—it smelled terrific.

"What's in it?" Eric asked.

"Chicken, of course," she continued as she served Russ. "It also has sofrito—a mix of tomatoes, onion, garlic, peppers, and fresh herbs."

"Let's see," Russ said, taking his plate. "I think I can detect oregano and coriander."

"You have an excellent sense of smell," she laughed. "Are you a cook?"

"No, just an appreciative eater."

Once she'd served Eric and herself, Russ dug in—it was wonderful, flavorful, and moist. It had been a long time since anyone had bothered to fix a good meal for him. It almost reminded him of how his mother cooked for the family when he was a child. He wondered why she rarely prepared a full meal anymore. "This tastes great."

"Thank you," she said, obviously pleased. "Eric tells me that you're originally from Portland, Oregon?"

"Yes," he said between bites. "I've been down here for several years now."

"Do you like it?"

"You bet." Russ launched into his standard routine of explaining why he and his mother had moved to San Diego, how he'd developed his own business, and how much he enjoyed working on his own. He suspected that Eric had already told her most of it, but he sensed that she wanted to hear it all again from him. She politely listened, now and then asking leading questions, especially about his T-shirt business, but he couldn't tell yet how she was reacting. Unlike Eric, Helen didn't wear her emotions—she was more difficult to read. Perhaps because of this, Russ realized too late that he was going on too long, relaying too much detail. After all, he didn't want it to seem as though he were putting on an act, or trying too hard to please her. He stopped and there was a moment or two of silence that made him cringe.

"I'm just so glad that you found each other," Helen said rather awkwardly. "Eric has never been happier."

Helen's comment surprised him and, by the look on his lover's face, it surprised Eric too. From all accounts, Eric's parents had not been all that likely or willing to share these kinds of feelings. Russ welcomed it as a supreme compliment. "Thank you," he replied for both of them.

"I wonder if I could ask you something," she said. "Eric told me that your middle name is Hezekiah. I haven't come across that name in years. Were you named for a relative?"

"Yes," he replied automatically. "An uncle."

"It's an interesting name," she added, her eyes narrowing. "Was it your father's or mother's brother?"

"I'm sorry—I used the term 'uncle' very loosely." Russ paused, wondering if he should reveal so much. "Hezekiah was actually my mother's uncle."

"Oh, I see," she replied. "Was your mother's family also from Oregon?"

"No," Russ replied, again wondering if he should go on, but he'd promised himself that there would be no lies. "They were from Indiana."

Helen's interest perked up. "Where in Indiana?"

"Valparaiso," he said, feeling more and more vulnerable. The more he revealed, the more he felt something slipping away.

"That's where my great-grandmother Skinner lived."

Now he could appreciate his mother's warning more keenly. Before he'd made a commitment to Eric, whenever anyone had questioned him, he'd usually made up some vague story about his background. The truth could be awkward and he had little experience in conveying it. Who would have thought that his own mother and Eric's mother would share such a connection? "Actually, I've never been there," he added truthfully, hoping to head off any further questions.

"That's a shame, it's a beautiful place. When did your mother live there?"

Russ began wondering if the questions would ever stop. "I'm not sure," he replied—again, with the truth. He felt as though a ton of stones were pressing on him.

"I'll have to talk to your mother about it sometime," she replied.

This, Russ hoped, would never happen.

"I think I told you that my mother is heavy into genealogy," Eric said apologetically. "She's probably going to try figuring out how we're all related."

"I'm afraid my son doesn't approve of my hobby." Helen pushed her plate, still half-filled with chicken and rice, away from her.

"It's not a hobby," Eric continued. "It's more like an addiction."

"There you are," Helen said with finality.

Helen took her time straightening up after the boys left. She thought it was peculiar to be thinking about them this way already—the boys. She carefully rinsed each dish before placing it in the dishwasher. She hesitated to put her nice things in it, but felt too tired to wash and dry everything by hand. It was still odd to think of two men being together. She could accept it intellectually, but she wasn't sure if she had really embraced it emotionally yet. Russ was so frightfully handsome, like a model in a fashion catalogue. It was unreal. Yet he was pleasant to speak with and well-mannered, mature beyond his years. She could see why her son was so crazy about him. She only hoped it would last.

Russ also appeared to be healthy, she noted with relief. So many young men had died, including a few friends of Eric's. Incredibly sad. Eric had told her time and again that he was totally safe and she knew that a monogamous relationship was the best thing for him, yet she was still perplexed why Russ had been so strangely protective of the cut on his finger—she was quite sure that only one finger had actually been bleeding. So odd that he had put on two bandages. She wondered why he was so worried about bleeding. Could it have been that he was afraid of infecting someone with his blood? She couldn't dismiss the thought.

As she finished up the dishes, she absently gazed out the kitchen window to the yard, now blanketed in darkness. Russ had so liked the cactus garden. After she started the dishwasher, she decided to sit on the patio for a few moments to relax. The sodas, she noted with some annoyance, were still on the table. She sat down and opened one of them, smiling to herself. Soon, she wouldn't have to worry so much about things being out of place. She was surprised that this didn't make her at all wistful, only bemused.

The cactus garden looked beautiful even in the darkness. Although most of the color was gone, she could still make out some of the different textures. Taking her soda with her, she went to see if any new cactus flowers had opened.

As she approached the garden, it became obvious that one new flower had opened indeed.

She gasped.

The flower was huge, standing well over two feet above the small cactus from which it had sprung. Even in the darkness, she could see that the flower was a strange red, much darker than any of the others. What was even more fantastic was that the flower glowed faintly, dimly illuminating the cacti around it.

She knelt to get a closer look. All of the pistils and stamens were swaying, even though there was no breeze. She moved back, frightened. No cactus, she realized, ever put out a blossom such as this.

Then she recalled that the flower had sprung up just where Russ had injured himself. She moved closer again. It was definitely blood-red.

Though she didn't plan to touch it, she moved her hand closer to the flower. In response, it turned toward the movement of her hand. She moved her hand back and forward in a little dance with the flower—a delicate ballet unlike anything she'd ever seen. She gazed into it—the farther down into the long funnel her eyes moved, the lighter the pigments became. At the deepest part of the long well, the flower ended in a bright point of light.

15

Dawn came and, as always, Russ woke with the first light. Eric was nestled in his arms, deep in sleep. Russ knew from experience that nothing short of an earthquake could possibly wake Eric. This morning, Russ was thankful for this.

In very little time they'd found an apartment together. In spite of his lack of direction, or perhaps because of it, Eric had a knack for coming across out-of-the-way places—they had just stumbled upon the large second-story apartment, a condominium that had not found a buyer. Eric had taken a wrong turn down an alley on the edge of Hillcrest near the airport and Mission Hills when they found the "For Rent" sign. The apartment took up the entire second floor of a 1920s-era Spanish-style home. It had been completely renovated, with an eye toward preserving as much of the original design as possible.

The apartment was full of windows, light and airy, complete with a large living room, dining area, kitchen, two large bedrooms, and a view of a small canyon filled with king palm trees and giant cacti run wild. The new apartment had more than one exit and plenty of windows large enough for him to crawl through. Then there was the canyon—a perfect escape.

Russ wasn't sure how much longer he'd be able to limit his transformations—he was feeling stuck and sluggish. Although he'd been forced to hide his abilities from his father, he'd always had an outlet with his mother. They'd go on outings together and become whatever their hearts desired. The only troubling thing was that in the more recent past, his transformations had been almost entirely related to picking up tricks. He'd have to invent another reason for becoming someone else. Something, he was certain, had to change. Occasionally, the tingling would start on its own and he'd have to suppress it for fear of taking on a form he'd have a hard time controlling. Although the thought made him feel guilty, Russ looked forward to the time Eric would start classes, but this was at least six weeks away. Until then Russ would have to sneak around more than he liked.

He pulled Eric a little closer to him and Eric barely moved. Russ could see that Eric was dreaming—his eyes were fluttering under closed eyelids. How handsome he was, even after six hours of his face on pillows. Eric's features weren't perfect—the nose was probably too large and the face too long. But taking everything together—the luscious dark of his wavy hair, the pronounced chin and jaw, his youthful exuberance, his boyish charm—Russ couldn't imagine anything more beautiful.

With some care, Russ untangled himself from their embrace, leaving Eric totally unaware of his absence. He quickly slipped on athletic shorts, sweat pants, and one of Eric's ever-present sweatshirts—all the while keeping an eye on Eric, making sure that he remained asleep. When he was absolutely certain that Eric was still dead to the world, Russ quietly stepped into the living room and began a transformation. His body so yearned for it that Russ had a difficult time forming an image in his mind. It was as if his body already had decided what form it would take.

He saw an attractive blond—tall, blue-eyed, and thin, with incredibly long, strong legs—a runner's build. The tingling began and he nearly groaned with relief as everything started to move. Torrents coursed through him, washing out the stagnant energy. The transformation felt instantaneous.

After he was able to open his eyes, he slipped into the hallway and peeked into the bedroom. Eric was still asleep, lying in the same position, completely unaware.

His new body felt wonderful—so strong and ready for action. He slipped out the door, being sure to take his keys. It was still early enough that few people were up and about. His body felt like running, so he ran toward Balboa Park so fast that it felt more like flying. He hoped he wouldn't come across anyone too tempting.

Russ expected to find Eric still asleep. Even so, he found a secluded spot near their apartment to transform back. After he was back to his usual self, he thought the early morning was unusually warm. He hurried home and gingerly opened the door, hoping not to wake him—to no avail. Eric was waiting when Russ walked in.

"I woke up and you weren't here," he said, bewildered.

"I went out for a run," Russ explained.

"I can see that," Eric said as he embraced him. "You feel all sweaty." Russ glanced at the clock—it was already eight. How long had he been running? Where had the time gone?

Kevin walked into the café—without Bird. Eric wanted to talk some things over privately, so he'd asked Kevin to join him at the Deli.

"Hey, Eric," he said, approaching the table. Now that it had been a couple of months since Kevin had started his diet, even Eric could see the weight loss.

The Deli was one of those restaurants that had seen better days—although the food was still great, most patrons had grown tired of the sameness of it. To make matters worse, for a Jewish deli, it wasn't all that Jewish anymore, which removed any chance of appealing to cultural/ethnic chic.

The waiter, a young punk with plenty of facial piercings, took their order right away. Eric went for the pastrami sandwich and Kevin decided on stuffed cabbage rolls. Now that he could get a good look, Eric could see how much weight Kevin had lost. His jowls were nearly gone and Eric could clearly see his bone structure. It reminded him of when Kevin had been younger. The realization sparked memories of neighborhood basketball courts and trying to teach Kevin how to shoot a basket. Kevin's face was again sharp and intense—in fact, he had almost the same expression now as when he'd concentrate on hitting the rim of the hoop. Although Eric appreciated the change, he couldn't help but be a little disappointed for his friend that the weight loss hadn't revealed a more handsome Kevin. "I can really tell that you've lost weight," he offered.

"I hope so," Kevin replied with a chuckle. "I've lost forty-five pounds since you started up with your new boyfriend."

"Isn't that a little fast to lose that much weight?"

"Not really."

"I bet you feel better," Eric said.

"Yeah, I do," he agreed.

"What are you doing for exercise?" he asked. He still couldn't imagine Kevin running or doing much else that was strenuous.

"I dance."

"You mean you're going out!"

"No, I dance in my apartment."

"Oh," Eric replied, disappointed. "Bet your neighbors just love you."

"They got used to it."

Eric could picture various neighbors coming down to complain about a loud stereo and perhaps even louder parrot, only to be faced with a huge man with a manner that could be very intimidating, at least to people who didn't know him well. "You'll have to come out dancing with us."

"Sure," Kevin agreed and was interrupted as the waiter brought the cabbage rolls, along with regrets that they'd run out of pastrami.

"What else can I bring you?" the waiter asked.

"Let me think about it," Eric said.

"It looks like you should have ordered the cabbage rolls too," Kevin said. "Tough luck."

Eric smiled, happy that Kevin's sense of humor had come back—he'd been so depressed after Eric had moved into the new apartment with Russ. "That's okay. I know you'll share."

Kevin shrugged his shoulders and placed two of the rolls on his bread plate for Eric. "How's the new apartment?" Kevin asked.

"We're all settled in," Eric replied, utterly surprised that Kevin had actually given him the food. "It's great having our own place."

"Especially with someone like Russ," Kevin added.

"Yeah," he agreed. Eric thought that he'd give Kevin the more positive things, before he shared his concerns. He didn't want things to appear out of balance. "You know, I always had these fantasies of what it would be like to find someone and become lovers and then find a place together. He's so thoughtful—he really looks out for me." Eric paused. "It's so great to wake up in each other's arms in the morning, have sex, shower together, and then fix breakfast in our own kitchen." He took a bite of the cabbage roll. "That's my favorite time of the day now—morning after we first wake up."

"So, it's the sex."

"No, that's not the only thing."

"What else could you possibly have in common?"

"We both love to dance. We go dancing about three times a week." Eric paused to think. "We both enjoy plants." Another pause. "And we talk."

"Sounds pretty boring to me."

"You don't know what we talk about," Eric said with a smile, not sure that he wanted to share his concerns just yet.

"You're not telling me something," Kevin said, giving Eric a piercing look. "You can't fool me."

Was it that obvious? "Well," Eric began, wondering how he'd tipped Kevin off, but glad he wouldn't appear to be volunteering everything he had to say. "Sometimes I wonder—it seems like Russ is getting edgy. He goes out for runs at the strangest times. One time I woke up in the middle of the night and he was gone. The weird thing was that the doors were bolted from the inside and there was only a window open." Eric took another bite. "Sometimes he's gone when I wake up in the morning."

"And he's been running all these times?" Kevin asked as if he didn't believe it.

"Well," Eric continued a little defensively, "he comes back all sweaty."

"Well," Kevin said and raised his eyebrows. "There are other ways to get sweaty."

"Sweaty as in running, not anything else," Eric insisted. The cabbage rolls were gone, yet he was still hungry.

"Can you really tell?" Kevin had a playful look in his eyes.

"I'm an experienced runner," Eric replied, trying to get some advantage.

Kevin laughed aloud.

"I would know if he was fooling around," Eric insisted. "At least I think that I would." He tried to make joke of it. "No," he continued more seriously, "I have a feeling it's something else." Now that he was talking things over, he felt better. "And there are some other things. Russ is really strange about not letting me use his razors or toothbrush."

"That doesn't sound good," Kevin replied. "Do you think he's positive?"

"I've asked him, and Russ says that he's negative."

"Do you believe him?"

"Yes," Eric replied, although he had his doubts. He was often certain that Russ was hiding something from him—he just wasn't sure what it was. And although Russ was very generous in supporting him emotionally, he seldom shared his own feelings. "I guess it's just learning how to be part of a relationship."

Kevin gave him a look that suggested that was a cop-out, but didn't say a word.

Russ rushed up the stairs and slipped into their apartment, he hoped, unseen. The neighbors might alarm Eric by mentioning seeing a strange man going where he wasn't supposed to be.

He had to admit that there were drawbacks to having a lover. Although he'd found plenty of opportunities to transform, too much of it had to be done behind bushes and in hidden corners of buildings and alleyways. He much preferred transforming at home. In the old days, Russ had made it a point to shun his neighbors so that they never were sure who really belonged in his apartment. Eric, though, had changed that routine—he was too friendly. They were on speaking terms with every neighbor Eric could find.

Often, at night, Russ slipped out one of the windows that faced the canyon, well after he thought everyone was asleep. Lately, this had become problematic since Eric had been sleeping more lightly.

He looked at himself in the mirror—a burly black man with beautiful, large eyes. He had wanted to be something a little different and this black man was ruggedly built, perfect for body surfing, which he'd been doing all morning at Pacific Beach. After Russ had returned to Hillcrest, he'd walked by the Deli and seen Eric and Kevin having lunch together. He figured that he would have at least fifteen minutes alone in the apartment—plenty of time for a relaxed, low-stress, home transformation.

Until he'd started to live with Eric, he hadn't realized how important it was for him to experience frequent transformations. His body now craved the changing—he desperately needed to feel his body shifting, the life force contracting and expanding. The bottled-up energy gave him problems controlling his emotions.

Russ stepped into the shower to wash the ocean from his skin. He felt relieved to be able to shower alone for a change. As the water cascaded around him, he let the transformation happen, slowly, at its own pace. He thought his body might have shifted in stages, since he felt a little confused as he stepped out of the shower stall. He wiped the mirror to look at himself. Russ was back to being his usual self. He smiled at his reflection.

He changed into more comfortable clothes and thought about what he wanted to do. The masquerade was taking a toll on him. Each day he was becoming more nervous and out of sorts, and though he hadn't lost his temper with Eric yet, he had come very close. He felt trapped. If only he could transform at will—but this would mean confiding everything to his lover. Aside from junking the relationship, which he wouldn't do, he could see only one alternative—telling Eric the truth. The only thing stopping him was his mother's warnings, but he didn't think that this would keep him back much longer. He hated living in deceit.

It was a matter of trust. He was almost sure he could trust his lover—almost.

The day started innocently enough, with their usual lovemaking. Eric never felt safer than he did in Russ's arms, and for hours afterward Eric's skin seemed to exult in an afterglow. This in spite of his misgivings—if only Russ would confide in him more. It troubled him profoundly to feel that he didn't really know Russ yet. Of one thing, though, Eric was certain: Russ loved him. Often, this alone was enough to console him.

As he pulled off his T-shirt and undershorts in preparation for his shower, Eric could hear Russ in the kitchen, running the water. Eric hoped it wasn't the hot water, as the shower temperature was impossible to control when hot water was running anywhere else. He turned the water on, but didn't get in. He waited for the steam to begin to fill the room; he enjoyed the vapors from the shower. He waited a little longer, but there was no steam. Perturbed, Eric headed toward the kitchen to see what Russ was doing with the hot water.

Glancing into the living room from the hallway, Eric froze. Russ was crouched in front of Sylvia, their plant gone wild. It seemed as though he were fondling the plant. Eric watched from the hallway, not wanting Russ to see him. As Russ moved his hands over Sylvia, hundreds of the small, waxy leaves subtly turned toward him—wave after wave of swaying, as if in a breeze. Suddenly Russ sat back on the floor and covered his face with his hands. Was he crying? Vines began to creep along the floor, inching closer as if to comfort him.

Eric stepped back, shaken. So his lover could charm plants. No wonder Sylvia had been growing so rapidly. Since they'd moved to the new apartment, the plant had completely taken over a corner of the living room. Eric eased back to the bathroom as quietly as he could, and sat down on the edge of the bathtub.

Eric was careful to mask the turmoil he was feeling until Russ left to work at the T-shirt stand. When Russ embraced him to say good-bye, Eric tried not to flinch. The embrace was just as warm, just as giving as ever. They kissed, and Eric felt the same love.

"Is everything okay?" Russ asked.

"Sure," he said and smiled.

After Russ left, Eric wondered what to do. He couldn't call anyone: he was uncertain whether anyone would believe what had happened.

He could hear Kevin saying "It was probably the wind" and his mother telling him what a good imagination he had. But Eric was quite certain of what he'd seen. He thought back on all the strange things about Russ. The craziness about not sharing razors, toothbrushes, even washcloths. The times he'd awakened to find Russ gone with no explanation. Eric began pacing from one room of the apartment to the next. He paused in front of Sylvia. Her leaves didn't sway to *his* touch. He walked into the bedroom. What was Russ hiding?

There was nothing of Russ's past in any of these rooms, Eric realized. Where was everything? He went back into the hallway and glanced up. There was an old panel in the ceiling that looked like an escape hatch. "This must be a way to get to the attic," he muttered. Eric got a chair from the kitchen. Standing on the chair, he could barely reach to push open the panel. A rush of stale, dusty air blew over him. He felt around the inside of the opening and found a cord attached to a set of folding stairs. After retrieving a flashlight from the kitchen, he quickly unfolded the stairs and climbed up to the attic crawl space.

There were boxes! At least three that he could see. "Russ must have brought these in when I wasn't here," he said aloud. He opened the first box. Old clothes. He moved those aside, and saw photos at the bottom of the box. Several looked like fairly recent photos of Russ with young men Eric didn't recognize. He dug a little further and found photos of Russ with a beautiful young woman with dark hair and flashing eyes. A little further down were older photos, black and white prints with uneven edges, showing a young boy playing alone in a backyard, others showing the same young boy with two adults, probably his parents. Eric looked closer. The young mother looked very much like the young woman standing with Russ in the color photos. He compared the photos. The likeness was unmistakable. Did Russ have a sister?

At the bottom of the box, Eric found old black and white class photos, large 8 × 10 sheets that showed all the members of a grade school class. He looked at the date. 1958. The teacher's name was Mrs. Howard. Sixth grade. Way too early for Russ, Eric decided. But what was Russ doing with this photo? Eric scanned the students' names, and came to one on the third row that stopped him cold. The name was Russell Lincoln. Eric was stunned. Was this an uncle? He compared the class photo with the other photos. It was the same little boy.

Eric continued to paw through the boxes, looking for any explanation. He found report cards, all for Russell Lincoln, all from the 1950s and 1960s. He pulled out a school yearbook for 1965, for a high school in Portland, Oregon, where Russ had said he'd gone to school. He quickly flipped to the index and found the name Russell Hezekiah Lincoln. He turned to the page. There was Russ, looking back at him, a studied, unsmiling image, with straight hair cut in 1960s style. Russ was wearing a thin tie along with a dark blazer, very much in step with the style of that time. Thirty years or more ago.

Eric sat, completely dumbfounded. What was going on? He thought of Russ's embrace, remembered how Russ's green eyes would gaze at him. Was this really the same Russ? What had his lover become?

Something was terribly wrong, Russ could feel it all through his body. A dull, fearful energy coursed through him. What had happened? He thought of his mother. Was she calling for him? The energy wasn't the same. No, it had to be Eric. What had happened to him?

Russ closed down his T-shirt stand, ignoring the odd looks from passersby, intent on returning home as quickly as possible. He didn't worry about how fast he drove. He wasn't even sure he'd stopped at all the lights and stop signs. He rushed into the apartment. "Eric?" he said. "Eric!"

He found Eric in the bedroom, packing. "What are you doing?" Russ asked.

"I didn't think you'd be home," Eric said, not looking at him.

Russ went up to embrace him, but Eric pushed him away. "Don't," he said.

"Why are you packing stuff up?" Russ asked, completely mystified.

"I don't know what's going on," Eric said, finally turning to him, tears in his eyes. "But I'm out of here."

"What happened?" Russ asked. "Tell me, please."

Eric walked over to the bed. "Explain this!" he said, holding up a yearbook.

Russ looked closer. It was one of his high school yearbooks. "What were you doing up in the attic?" he asked.

"This morning, Russ," Eric said. "You were taking care of Sylvia? I saw the plant move."

Russ blanched. It all made sense now. Eric must have gone searching for an explanation. How stupid he had been to care for Sylvia when Eric was home. "I thought you were taking a shower," he stammered.

"That was obvious," Eric replied, continuing to pack. "You still haven't answered my question."

Russ sat down on the bed, crestfallen. What was he going to do now? What kind of explanation could he come up with other than the truth? He was going to lose his love, all for the lies, the deception that had always been his life. He would have to let Eric go. "I'm so sorry."

"I'm sorry, too," Eric stopped and looked at him. "I love you, but I don't know who you are. I can't live with lies. I can't."

"I understand," Russ said frantically. "I understand." The trouble was that he did understand, that he was going to be alone, that he would never wake up with Eric in his arms, never be able to talk with Eric again, and it was too much to ask of himself. He couldn't lose his love. "Please wait," he said. "If I tell you everything, will you promise to give me a chance? Will you stay with me?"

Eric paused, wavering. "You will tell me the truth?"

There it was, the thing his mother most feared, the thing he had always been taught to fear. The truth. But it was either the truth, or choosing to live alone. "Yes, I promise."

"All right, then." Eric sat down on the other side of the bed. "Let's hear it."

Now that the moment was upon him, Russ was uncertain what to do. How could he possibly explain? "I'm not sure where to begin." Russ could see fear creep into Eric's eyes. "I'm very different than most people, and I have special abilities."

"I've already seen what happened with Sylvia."

"Yes, I have a special way with a lot of plants, and sometimes they even move to be closer to me." Russ paused. "And the yearbook?"

Eric nodded.

"I'm quite a bit older than you think I am."

"Yeah," Eric interrupted. "A lot older, but you look just as young as I am. You need to tell me why."

Yes, Russ thought. The truth. "The truth is that I'm an elf child." There it was, he'd finally said it.

"A what?"

"An elf child, a changeling." Russ felt a wave of fear course through him. "I can change my shape at will."

Eric stared and said nothing.

"You don't believe me."

"I don't even know what you're talking about."

"Okay, that's fair," Russ said, trying to come up with another way to explain. "It means I can change my physical form when I want to," he finally added.

"This is too much, Russ," Eric replied, almost annoyed. "Okay, if you're a changeling, let's see it."

"I don't know if I should do transformation right in front of you—it might be too much for you to handle," Russ said.

Eric seemed increasingly agitated. "I think I can handle it."

"Okay," Russ said quietly and moved toward the door. "I'm going to turn the light off—you'll still be able to see this by the light of the window."

As Russ flipped off the light, Eric felt numb at the pit of his stomach—as if everything in his life were about to change for the worse. Although he kept trying, nothing he could imagine could help him connect the Russ he knew and loved with this strange man turning out the light. "You're scaring me," he managed to choke out.

Russ stood close to the open window and slipped out of all his clothing but his undershorts—in spite of the dim light, Eric could still clearly see the details. Russ closed his eyes and stood there for what seemed a long time. Eric resisted the urge to reach out and pull him back to the bed, as if to save him.

"Watch closely," Russ told him softly, with his eyes still closed.

At first, Eric thought that it was his imagination, but he would swear that he could see a slight rippling along the skin of Russ's face. He watched even more closely. More rippling—like waves across Russ's skin. Eric gasped and Russ shifted on his feet in response. The rippling became more pronounced. Eric was terrified—Russ had a look of exhilaration, almost bliss, even while his face began contorting. It was as if some unseen hands were molding him, shoving skin and tissue here and there. Eric wondered why Russ wasn't crying out in pain. It reminded him of seeing a film about experiments done on pilots to test the effects of g-forces. Then the rippling spread down his neck, along his torso and out to his arms and legs. Russ's entire body began to tremble and parts of it grew. At the same time his hair took on a glow.

Eric was so petrified that he couldn't move from the bed. He couldn't take his eyes from his lover's convulsing body. Ripple after ripple, wave after wave washed over him.

Finally, the trembling stopped. Eric gasped again. The contortions had been replaced with a golden light, which seemed to be painted on his form like a watercolor wash.

When Russ, or what used to be Russ, stepped closer to him, Eric drew back. His lover's hair was now blond, his nose had lengthened, his eyes had grown closer together, his arms and chest had expanded, his limbs had grown a couple of inches longer, and Eric could see a sprinkling of freckles on his nose. The man stood before him, sporting an impish smile which Eric knew to be Russ's. It looked so strange to see it on a face he couldn't recognize.

"What do you think?" the stranger asked in a voice that was deeper than Russ's, though with hints of the voice Eric knew so well.

Eric was speechless. This stranger wasn't a stranger but his lover. Eric tried to look deep into the other's eyes in an attempt to find Russ there, but though he could clearly see that the eyes were blue—almost like the sky—it was still too dark to find him.

After he recoverd enough to speak, Eric could only think of one thing to say. "Change back."

16

The window is open. A light breeze and late summer sun dance with the white curtains. The baby watches, waiting for his mother, playing with the rings on the side of his crib. When she walks into the room, he is happy and reaches up to her. She leans over the crib, returning his smile, but doesn't pick him up. He is disappointed. Her long hair swings over him, also playing with the light. He smiles then, happy. As he reaches for the strands of her hair, they gradually begin to change color, almost one by one—a cascade of small and glittering transformations. The baby watches the strands shift from one color to the next, from dark cocoa to light brown, from light brown to auburn, from auburn to strawberry blonde, from strawberry blonde to apple blossom white.

The baby is mesmerized, neither laughing nor crying, very calm. When he finally grabs a handful of her hair, the mother laughs. Her eyes sparkle. Finally, the baby smiles, somehow grasping that this is a first lesson, somehow knowing this is what he will be.

It wasn't at all what Russ had expected. There was such a look of fear and betrayal in Eric's eyes that Russ immediately regretted what he had done. Eric sat transfixed, his hands gripping the edge of the bed. His whole body looked poised to run out of the room. With horror, Russ realized that this was something he could never take back or fix. His eyes misted up.

Russ turned away, facing the open window to revert to his usual self—the self that Eric knew. The sky was a crystal clear dark blue. He knew that there would be no moon tonight. It took him a minute to change back—slower, he thought, than usual, perhaps because of the fear he felt.

After the transformation was complete, Eric drew back when Russ tried to touch him. "You asked me to show you," Russ managed to say, though he thought it sounded ridiculous and accusatory. "Are you all right?" he added more carefully.

"I don't know yet," Eric finally said. He still had the look of betrayal written all over his face. "What are you?"

Eric was shaking. Russ had never seen him so frightened. It was as if Eric remembered nothing that he'd said before the transformation. He'd have to explain everything from the beginning. Russ sat at the far edge of the bed. "I'm a changeling, an elf child," he said in an even voice.

Eric drew even farther back. "What's an elf child?"

Russ took a deep breath. This was going to be much harder than he had ever dreamed. "I can assume nearly any form that I choose, as long as it's living," Russ explained. "You might say that I'm a special kind of human—someone who can do things that not too many other people can do."

"What do you mean 'any living form'?" Eric asked, still shaking.

Eric's reaction was making Russ very nervous. This could be the end of their relationship, and the possibility was chilling. "I can change my appearance to look like any human here on earth—anyone who's young, anyway." He took a breath. "I can also transform my shape into any kind of animal—a bear, a leopard, a moose, an eagle, a fish—whatever."

Eric sat further back on the bed and drew his knees up to his chest. "What about an insect or something even smaller like a microbe?"

"Let's not get carried away," Russ joked.

"No, I'm serious," Eric persisted in a thin voice.

Russ tried to quell the growing fear spreading through him. "That would be pretty hard," he admitted more seriously. "I've never heard of any changeling with the powers to pull that one off. As far as I know, the closer to human form, the easier the transformation."

"Did you say that there are other changelings?" Eric asked.

Russ was relieved to see that Eric's shoulders were loosening up a little. "There aren't too many of us," Russ said.

Eric's brow was furrowed. "How did you become one?"

"It's something that's passed down from one generation to the next."

"Your mother is one," Eric said, as if making an important discovery. "That's why you've been so afraid to introduce me to her."

Certainly, that was a part of it, Russ thought. He edged closer to Eric and was relieved that Eric didn't pull back, though he made no sign of wanting Russ to come any closer. "You may be right," Russ agreed. "If I've been afraid to introduce you, maybe this is why." There it was, he realized. He'd already completely implicated his mother—something unavoidable and certain to pose a major difficulty ahead. Once one secret was revealed, others would tumble down.

"How long have you been able to do this?" Eric asked, finally relaxing his legs, letting his feet rest on the floor.

Russ was relieved that Eric was still asking questions. "Since I was about eight years old. It happens automatically about that age. And then you have to learn how to control it, especially if you plan to keep it secret."

"Is this your true form—what I'm seeing right now?" Eric asked.

Russ recalled the time he'd deceived Eric, the time at the bar when he'd let himself revert to his natural self. Could he ever be entirely sure the man he was that night was his true self? There had been so many changes throughout the years, Russ had long ago lost track of them all. "To be honest, I'm not sure."

Eric raised his eyebrows, incredulous.

"From the time I've been a child, I've been able to make small changes. No one ever noticed. During junior high school, I slowly changed a lot of features I didn't like."

"Such as?"

"Freckles," Russ said.

Eric gently touched Russ's cheek with one of his fingertips. "I recognized you in your high school yearbook."

"Yes," Russ said. "I've kept the same appearance for a long time. It helps keep me stabilized. You've gotten to know me in my usual form, but it's not my true self."

"Could I see your true self?"

Russ was uncertain. If he let himself go again, in an attempt to revert to his natrual self, would Eric recognize him? Would Eric realize that he'd been deceived? Russ didn't want to take the chance. "I couldn't be completely sure of my true self. I may never find it again."

Eric was silent for a moment. "What causes it? Is your body any different from a person's?"

"I am a person," Russ said, a little defensively, and softened the rest of his reply. "I don't know if my body is any different. The process is very natural for me—in fact, I need to change or else I feel stopped up. It starts when I visualize what I want to be, then somehow my body takes over."

"Can you feel when it's happening to you?" Eric interrupted.

"Sure," he replied.

"Doesn't it hurt?"

"It's almost as good as making love," Russ replied.

It didn't appear that Eric believed him.

"I'm serious," Russ insisted. "It feels great."

"It didn't look that way to me," Eric said. "It looked awful." Eric began to shake all over again, but this time, to Russ's relief, Russ was able to move over and embrace him. When Russ patted him on the back, Eric started to softly cry on his shoulder. "It looked so horrible," Eric said. "Your whole face was contorted and you started shaking. There were ripples all over your skin."

Russ pulled him tighter, burying his nose in Eric's soft hair—the familiar scent was comforting. He'd never thought about what it might look like to someone else. It was so natural for him, and the times that he'd been able to keep his eyes open during a transformation while he stood in front of a mirror, the whole thing appeared to be entirely harmless, even beautiful in a way. Russ could feel Eric's tears, wet against his cheek, and wondered if it wasn't his internal joy that colored his reaction to witnessing the transformation himself. When he'd witnessed his mother's transformation, though, there was the same joy. Did it really look so awful? "I'm sorry that it seemed that way to you," Russ tried to reassure him. "I guess it doesn't look like how they do the morphing on TV, does it? Maybe that's what you expected to see."

Only more crying in response.

"I promise that it doesn't hurt."

Finally, Eric returned Russ's embrace. "Is this really you that I'm hugging?"

"Yeah, it's really me." Russ held him tight and rocked with him on the bed. The feeling that he might lose Eric made his head swim—the situation was now beyond his control. He was entirely at Eric's mercy—Eric could leave him tomorrow. He could even tell the world about his secret and someone out there would believe him. No matter what happened, though, there was no turning back. He pulled Eric a little closer—ashamed of how he felt.

"It's too tight," Eric gasped. "You're hurting me."

"I'm sorry." Russ released him.

Eric settled back into his arms. "That's okay, you don't need to completely let go."

The family sits around the dinner table, just finishing up the chicken, rice, and peas. The mother is laughing as she collects the plates. She is beautiful, with her hair of cocoa, eyes the color of old oak, and long, slender limbs. The father watches her, smiling inwardly, crossing his arms, shoving his feet farther under the table. They seldom fight and often make love. Their only child, a young boy of seven, sits with them, very quietly. He feels a tingling up and down his spine that worries him. He wonders if this is what his mother has been warning him about, the hurdle for which she's prepared him.

"Mamma, my back feels funny," he says.

"Your back?" she asks, alarmed.

"Uh-huh," the boy says, now more concerned with her reaction than with the feeling, even though it is becoming more intense.

"Come on," she demands, taking the boy's hand.

"Lizzy," the father says, laughing. "What are you doing getting so upset? This isn't like you at all." The father reaches out to stop them from leaving the dining room.

"No, Herb," she almost shouts. "Let us go."

By this time, the boy's face tingles too and he feels strangely fluid. He can barely stand up.

The mother has to drag him, nearly picking him up, to get him away.

"What's going on?" the father asks as he follows them.

"Nothing."

"Lizzy?" the father gasps.

The mother rushes into the bathroom with the boy, locking the door behind them. When the boy looks in the mirror, a different child stares back at him—someone with high cheekbones, long brown hair, and dark brown eyes.

"Were you playing cowboys and Indians today?" she asks.

"Yes, mother," the boy says. His eyes, filled with wonder, stare back at him from the mirror, so familiar, yet so different. "My eyes."

"What, honey?"

"My eyes look so different, but I still know that they're mine."

"Yes," she says, embracing him. "That's what it's like."

"This is what you've been talking about," he says in a whisper.

"Yes," she whispers back. "Remember, not a word of this to your father."

"I'll remember."

It takes a lot of practice before the boy is able to change back. It's not easy for him to control. His mother patiently explains it to him. "It's a feeling," she keeps on repeating. "Picture the boy you want to be in your mind, very small. Then imagine the little boy growing until he fills up your whole body and pushes out at the skin."

The boy tries it again and again, each time with more success. His body feels so strange, as if he were made of Jell-O or noodles. But it doesn't hurt. It might even be fun, he decides. Finally, it works right. The little boy in the mirror is him again. She makes him do it perfectly at least three times before she lets him out of the bathroom.

When they come out, the father is sitting, waiting for them in the living room, his face ashen.

"Lizzy, is he okay?" he asks, not looking at his son.

"Yes," she answers. "It was a touch of the stomach flu."

He turns to his son with eyes on the verge of turning to fear, then smiles with relief. "There's my boy. For a minute I thought I was going crazy."

It felt so strange to Eric to be in Russ's arms again, knowing that he had become some kind of monster. There was the same feeling of closeness, of Russ's strong arms, of his slightly musky scent, yet Eric knew that he could at any moment become something else, something foreign and unknown.

He had been living with a stranger all these months and didn't know it. Once he had stopped crying, Eric asked, "Why didn't you tell me before this?"

"I've never revealed my secret to anyone," Russ said quietly. "I've wanted to tell you this for a long time, but I didn't have the courage."

"I'm the first person that you've told?" Eric asked.

"That's right."

Eric marveled. No one had ever trusted him with something so important.

"You can't believe how lonely it's been for me."

This was something that Eric could understand. He'd felt the same way—growing up knowing he was terribly different, believing he was the only guy who had a thing for other guys. It had been such a relief when he'd found out that there were others like him. "Did you try to find any other changelings?" Eric asked. "You could've been honest with them."

"There are so few of us. I've only met a few other ones—most of them relatives of my mother's." Russ pulled him closer again. "It's been my mother and me."

Eric tried not to wince—earlier, he had thought that Russ would break his ribs. He had no idea until now just how strong Russ was. "How long have changelings been around?"

"There's a tradition, a legend that's been passed down that the first changeling was born in the Mideast, the son of Mithras, the god of the sun. I think there might have been some mutation. The thing is that a lot of changelings, especially the men, are infertile. The women changelings have a hard time conceiving too, which explains why there are so few of us. I'm my mother's only child."

"What about your father?"

"He wasn't a changeling," Russ said quietly.

"And your father never knew?"

"I don't think he ever did."

Eric couldn't imagine how Russ and his mother could have kept such a secret. Certainly his father must have known. He looked up at Russ's face, trying to picture what it had looked like during the transformation. Russ had said that he could take any form. He wondered if that included the other sex. "Can a changeling alter its sex?" he asked.

"Yes," Russ replied and laughed. "But don't ask me to have your baby. I probably wouldn't be able to conceive and even if I did I wouldn't be able to maintain a female form long enough to bring the pregnancy to term."

The thought hadn't even occurred to him, yet as Russ explained it, he found that he liked the idea of two men having a baby. He glanced at Russ's face again—obviously, he had thought about the possibility. The whole thing was absurd. A man turning into a woman to have a baby. On the other hand, it was strangely sexy. "Are you sure you can't?" he asked.

"Almost positive." Russ nodded.

That meant Russ didn't really know for sure. "Have you tried it?"

"Never mind," Russ said firmly.

The longer they talked, the less fear Eric felt. The longer he heard Russ's smooth voice, the more able he was to push the horrible images from his mind. "How have changelings been able to keep this a secret for so long?" he asked.

"With so few of us, we've never felt powerful."

All of Russ's talk about "we" only emphasized for Eric how different Russ really was. "You are still human, aren't you?" he asked.

"Yes," Russ said, almost glumly. "We are."

How many other things were different about these humans who weren't really human? "How long do changelings live?" he asked.

"I'm forty-eight years old," Russ told him point-blank. "Changelings can live as long as nothing intervenes."

"You don't look like you're forty-eight," he observed.

"I know," Russ said sharply.

"Will you ever age?" Eric asked.

"No, that's one thing I can't do," Russ admitted and looked at him longingly.

It seemed appealing until Eric realized that though Russ wouldn't age, he would. "I'll end up looking old enough to be your father."

"I suppose," Russ agreed. Eric's mind spun with the possibility. He hadn't thought much about growing old until now. He tried to imagine himself as an old man, with a young Russ by his side. Would Russ stay with an old man?

"There are some things I could do to look a little older," Russ offered. "I could learn to move like an older man."

The idea of the odd couple soon gave way to the idea that he might die much sooner than Russ would. "If you're only forty-eight now, I'll be dead a long time before you will." Russ didn't say anything, but Eric could see that his comment had hurt him. Russ had such a look of anguish that it made Eric sick.

He'd grown to take Russ's presence almost for granted; he'd glance over at his lover as they were sitting in the living room and be comforted by the familiar presence. It was as though Russ was literally his other half. Now all that was broken. He wondered if he could ever reclaim that feeling again. Would there be an unbridgable gulf?

"Do you think you can live with this?" Russ suddenly asked.

The question came too quickly for Eric. His immediate thought was "no," though his feelings for Russ prevented him from actually saying it. "I'm not sure," he finally said.

Eric thought he saw a dampness on Russ's cheek and realized that he was silently crying. He looked into his eyes, which were glistening with tears. "Don't leave me," Russ pleaded. "You promised you wouldn't leave me if I told you the truth."

Eric gently touched Russ's cheek, gathering some of the tears. They felt real. "I won't," he said, and regretted his reply. Could he live up to his promise? All he knew was that he wanted Russ to stop crying. "You can stop crying now," he quietly said.

And he stopped.

17

The leaves have all just come out, new and vibrant. It's an early spring, very warm for this time of year. The countryside near Valparaiso, Indiana, is lush, verdant. Sixteen-year-old Lizzy makes her way down the path to her teacher's place. Even though it's Saturday, Lizzy has something she'd like to discuss with Adelaide Mariette Pierce, an important question concerning her uncle and aunt.

The other young people in class call her the teacher's pet, but Lizzy couldn't care less. Most young women her age are doing housework for neighbors, are busy helping their own families on the farm, or are about to get married (or already are). Not Lizzy. Mariette is one of the few people, besides her Uncle Hezekiah, who has encouraged her. Most of the others in this small Indiana town think she's strange. The trouble is, they're right—they just don't know how strange she really is. Sometimes Lizzy wishes she could show them.

Mariette, a widow, lives with her three children fairly close to her uncle's spread. Mariette's husband, William, a railroad man, has been dead for a number of years—killed in a terrible accident. Lizzy remembers the funeral, when she was nine. She can still remember the look on her teacher's face when they led her away from the grave. Pure anguish.

When Lizzy knocks at the door of the small frame house, Mariette calls her in. She's making something at the dining table. "Come in, Lizzy," Mariette says. "You can sample my johnnycake."

"Thank you, Mrs. Pierce," she replies, and steps through the door. The inside of the little house is spartan. Mariette is poor, though she has a rich brother and mother in town. Mariette, Lizzy has heard, is too proud to accept charity from relatives.

Lizzy sits down at the table. She knows she doesn't need permission for this.

"It only has to bake about thirty minutes," Mariette says. "I like mine thin and crisp."

"So do I," Lizzy says. "I've been sampling your bread for some time."

"That's true," Mariette says with a chuckle as she mixes the cake.

"Where are your children?" Lizzy asks.

"Hollis is in the back room reading, I expect," Mariette says. "Kezzie is out back with Minnie. They'll be in after they smell the cake."

At thirty-seven Mariette looks just as old as Lizzy's Aunt Carrie, even though she knows Aunt Carrie is at least ten years her senior. Mariette's face is already lined. Her carriage is proud—from her Vermont upbringing. Even as she fixes the johnnycake, Mariette is dressed up all proper, as if she were going to town. Mariette, Lizzy decides, can't but help look older than she is, considering all she's been through. It takes a strong woman, she knows, to raise children without a husband. Lizzy admires Mariette for supporting her family by working as a teacher. She hopes to emulate her.

"Have you thought about what you might be doing next?" Mariette asks her. "You have learned as much as you can from me. It's time for you to consider opportunities to further your education."

Mariette is no good at small talk—she always cuts right to the point. In this case, Lizzy welcomes the question. Most everyone else assumes that she will be getting married soon, even though she hasn't had a beau yet. "Though I have thought of it, I'm not certain where I should go."

"I know of fine schools in Boston and Pennsylvania," Mariette says wistfully. "My late husband received his education at the college of Hanover in southeast Pennsylvania. A fine finishing school will do you good. If you wish, I will do you the honor of writing a letter of introduction."

"Thank you, Mrs. Pierce, I would appreciate your help."

"You are certainly welcome."

After she pours the johnnycake on the griddle, Mariette turns back to her. "How are your aunt and uncle?" she asks.

Lizzy wonders if her teacher has already heard something about what's going on at her uncle's farm. "Not well," she confides.

"What's the matter?" she asks, sitting down at the table.

"I was hoping to talk with you about this," Lizzy begins, knowing that she can trust Mrs. Pierce. "Aunt Carrie has not been acting like herself lately."

"How's that?" Mariette replies, furrowing her brow.

"She's been awfully quiet lately, especially with my uncle." Lizzy feels a little faint telling this. "She has been sleeping out in the bunk house for nearly two weeks."

Mariette chuckles. "That's been known to happen to a married couple," she adds. "Did they have a spat?"

"No," Lizzy replies. "That's the thing. They didn't argue. When I asked my uncle, he said that he didn't know why either."

Mariette considers this a moment. "That is odd," she finally says, looking off into space. "Have you talked to your aunt?"

"I've tried," Lizzy tells her. "But she doesn't answer me, not a single word."

Mariette taps her finger slowly against the table top. "Lizzy, it is very difficult to know what goes on between two people, especially when those two people are married and have been married for years. Do you want my advice?" she asks, looking directly at her.

"Yes, ma'am," Lizzy replies.

"Let your aunt and uncle take care of their own business. Don't you get involved. They will work things out between them." Mariette stands up to check on her johnnycake. "That's my advice."

Lizzy watches Mariette fiddle with the cake and tries not to feel too disappointed. She had hoped that Mariette would at least offer to talk to her aunt. But on the other hand, she trusts Mariette's judgment. Perhaps, Lizzy thinks, she needs to mind her own business and never mind about her aunt and uncle's. Still there's a gnawing feeling that something's not right. It's in the way her aunt looks at them—something in her eyes that warns Lizzy of danger, but she can't imagine what it is. Then there are all the trips to town that her aunt has taken in the last week, many more than usual. Although Lizzy wants to discuss all of these things with her teacher, by the tone of Mariette's voice, Lizzy knows she won't listen to any more about it. Once Mariette makes up her mind about something, there's no changing it.

When the cake is ready, Mariette goes looking for her children and Lizzy takes a look around the small house. Nearly all of Mariette's scanty possesions have a practical purpose. There are no photographs, no paintings on the rough walls, no mementos. The only thing in abundance is books—books on every conceivable subject, especially geography, history, and literature. Mariette often tells her that she comes from a family of teachers. Anyone, Lizzy thinks, with half a brain would figure that out just by having a look inside Mariette's house.

After a moment, Hollis comes into the room, book in hand, and nods to Lizzy. Hollis, a few years younger than Lizzy, is shy, too shy to speak with a girl, so he promptly sits down and begins reading the book again. Lizzy has always thought he is a fine fellow, someone who will make a good husband one day. She likes his eagle nose and thick dark hair. He is slight, though—from want of proper exercise, she figures. She doesn't attempt to strike up a conversation, already knowing it's hopeless.

Mariette comes back into the house from the front door, after having searched the surrounding yard for her absent daughters. "Kezzie and Minnie have run off again," she says. "I'm afraid they are going to miss some johnnycake."

Lizzy nods. Mariette's youngest children are on the wild side, though to look at them one would think they were both as meek as they come. Sometimes Lizzy feels sorry for them. Mariette never lets them climb in the trees or play any games that would dirty their dresses. They must be little ladies. When Mariette is not around, though, the girls go wild. Lizzy's seen them many a time climbing the trees in their dresses, hanging from the branches like two little Indians.

Mariette cuts each of them a generous helping of johnnycake. Lizzy bites into hers; there's nothing like warm johnnycake. She is surprised how crisp and sweet it is. It smells heavenly. "You're right," she says. "It is better with molasses."

"I told you," Mariette says with a smile. "You take some home to your aunt and uncle."

As she leaves, Lizzy is tempted to bring up the subject of her aunt again, but Hollis is still there. Mariette waves to her from the door.

On the way home, Lizzy holds on tightly to the package of johnnycake, thinking about how many times she's walked down this path since she moved to Valparaiso after her mother died. It has to be at least 500 times, she figures, probably even more. She can barely remember her mother now, only her long blonde hair, always tied back, and her large hands. The day has turned warm, and Lizzy pulls her own hair back. Out of the corner of her eye, she can see Hollis at a distance behind her, pretending he isn't following her. There's hope for him yet, she thinks.

Lizzy falls into deep thought. Her aunt's strange behavior reminds her how uncertain she felt after she first came to her uncle's. Although she knows it's silly, somehow she believes that she may have never belonged here.

Before she knows it, Lizzy is out of the shade of the tall trees and into a clearing near her uncle's house. A good many neighbors complain about how her uncle refuses to clear more of his land for farming. He's often told her how much he likes the trees, and Lizzy has to agree. As she approaches the white farmhouse, she can see her uncle standing on the front porch with Kezzie and Minnie. She has to laugh—while Mariette was searching for them, they were here all the time—and probably set to get the johnnycake after all. He must, she decides, be telling one of his stories. Her uncle has a reputation in town as a crack storyteller, and she's heard him say it's his favorite thing to do. Her Aunt Carrie is nowhere to be seen. All three of them, Uncle Hezekiah, Kezzie, and Minnie, wave at her as she comes up to the porch.

Uncle Hezekiah has just finished a story. They are laughing and her uncle has a flush of success across his face. When he sits down, Kezzie asks him for more, but he says no. Then Lizzy brings out the johnnycake and tears off pieces for all four of them. "You'll never guess where I got this johnnycake," she tells the children.

"Where?" they both ask in unison.

"From a bear!" she tells them.

"A bear?" they both say. Kezzie takes a bite. "My mother made this johnnycake—I know how it tastes!" Kezzie says gruffly, just like her mother.

"Nope," Lizzy continues the game. "A bear gave it to me."

"No, ma'am," little Minnie says.

"I'll bet your mother has been looking for you children," her uncle tells them. "You had better get on home!"

Content with their stories and johnnycake, the two children run off down the path. They look so cute in their matching plaid dresses. Their dark hair flies behind them. Lizzy feels a little sorry for them, confined in long sleeves.

"So, you've been to see the teacher lady," he begins, smiling knowingly. "I hope you gave her our best."

"Yes, Uncle," Lizzy says. "She sent hers too."

"Is she in good spirits?"

"Why, yes," she replies, trying to remember when he had ever asked such a question about Mrs. Pierce—Mariette's temper never seemed to change much. "She's the same as ever."

"I'm glad to hear it." He glances away from her wistfully. "Sometimes I worry about her."

This is a surprise. "Why?"

"She's had a difficult life, as you know. Her late husband, William, was a friend of mine."

Lizzy tries to recall whether her uncle has ever mentioned such a thing. "I didn't know that."

He shakes his head. "You were too young to remember."

"I remember the funeral," she says, recalling the look on Mrs. Pierce's face. Such anguish she has never seen since.

"Is that right?" he asks in surprise. "That was a sad day," he adds slowly, his eyes fixed on some point in the distance behind her.

"What kind of a man was he?" she asks.

Her uncle's face lights up. "To my way of thinking, he was too good for this world." He looks toward her. "He was a dreamer, a gentle soul. Kind and considerate to a fault. He could never see how people would take advantage of him." He wipes the palm of his hand against his knee. "Mrs. Pierce would be beside herself when she learned about how he'd lost out at this job or that. But, Lizzy, he was always true to himself and to his friends and family. You could never ask for a better man."

Lizzy can see that—and see how much her uncle still misses his friend even after all these years. "How did he die?" she asks, not quite remembering that part.

"We were working for the railroad at that time," her uncle continues, a pained expression coming over his face. "Will and I were talking until it looked as though he would miss the train—he was always talking longer than he should. It was already moving, so he waited until he could grab ahold of the caboose. Even that was moving too fast, so he made a run for it." He pauses, as if something is caught in his throat. "He fell in a ditch. He struck his chest up against an exposed beam." He violently smacks the palms of his hands together, making a loud crack. "The doctor we called thought he might have broke a blood vessel."

The story comes back to her now—she sees clusters of folks at church taken with the news, the Sunday before the funeral. No one can talk about anything else. "It must have been terrible for Mrs. Pierce."

"That it was," he agrees. "I wrote his obituary for the newspaper. One of the most difficult things I've ever been called to do. He died in my arms."

Lizzy has seen death before—with her own mother. It comes rushing back though she tries not to remember. Her mother collapses on the bedroom floor, with her hair coming loose and tumbling around her shoulders. Her eyes have taken on the color of honey, she decides. Pure honey.

"Daughter," she whispers. "Always take care. Remember what I've taught you. Be kind. Always know that I love you."

"I love you too."

As her eyes close, her body slowly begins to shake.

The change comes slowly at first. Her body shifts almost imperceptibly, shimmering. Then it comes more rapidly. She groans as her body begins to fold into itself, again and again, in ripples. The ripples quicken into a blur, full of colors, all colors of the rainbow. The whole room seems to blaze with color and a sweet scent fills the air, as if lilacs are in bloom nearby. When the colors begin to fade, the outline of a large bird pushes through the light, slowly taking on a definite form. She has changed into a large bird, very white, very still. The feathers glow with a pure, white light.

"She's a fine lady," Hezekiah says.

At first Lizzy thinks that he's talking about her mother, but realizes after an instant that he's talking about Mrs. Pierce. But Lizzy gets the distinct impression that he's worried about something other than Mrs. Pierce. His face has a haggard aspect, which looks odd on him.

"Would you like to go for a little walk?" her uncle asks. "I have something to tell you."

"Of course, Uncle," she replies.

They head down another path that meanders through some woods. It's one of her uncle's favorites, even though it doesn't lead anywhere in particular.

"You remind me of your mother, Lizzy," Uncle Hezekiah says as they walk. "You're a pretty girl."

"Thank you, Uncle," she says, reaching up to grab a leaf off a maple tree growing along the path. Did he read her mind? she wonders. She can't figure out how he does it.

"Do you remember much about her?"

"No, sir." Lizzy shakes her head.

"I'm sorry to hear that," he says. "Your mother was a wonderful sister. Most all of the young fellas were courting her, or hoping to court her. She had them all running."

Lizzy laughs.

"She was another one who always had a good word to say about someone, or had nothing at all to say. Your mother loved the birds—she was often singing to them." He smiles. "That's how she met your pa. He heard her singing to the birds and started singing back."

"Yes, I remember her telling me that," she says, though she's never grown tired of hearing it. "And then after I was born, he went off to join the Grand Army of the Republic."

"That he did," he agreed. "And never came back."

She still has a photograph of him, the image held by glass. He's in his dark uniform, holding a gun across his chest, anxious to get to fighting. There is a blush on his cheeks, painted on by the photographer; his face is angular and young, not unlike her own face.

"She would've been proud of you," he continues. "She would have wanted you to continue your education, I believe. Have you decided whether you will go off to school somewhere?" he asks, as if he's afraid to hear the answer.

Lizzy is happy that she'll be missed. "Yes, Uncle."

"Well, you know that I will help you," he adds. "It's what your mother would have wanted. There is not much left here for you, I'm afraid."

The woods are glorious, full of maple, oak, and cottonwood. Along the path, thick green grass has already grown a foot high. Flies buzz around them. Her uncle has made her feel so worthy—she knows he is right. She needs to travel and expand her horizons. Marriage, at least for now, is not for her. She looks at him, so grave. She will miss him terribly.

Up ahead, Lizzy sees that there's a clearing, a small meadow with specks of yellow. Could the mustard grass be blooming already? she wonders. Uncle Hezekiah stops. They are at the edge of the clearing. Lizzy walks on a few steps and then turns back to look at her uncle. The sunshine barely catches his face, which is full of joy and expectation. "I want you to see what I really look like, so you can remember me proper," he says, a smile on his face.

In all the years she's lived with him, he's never suggested such a thing. It worries her. "Why do the changing all the way out here?" she asks. "Why not in a room at the house? Wouldn't it be safer there?"

"I don't trust Carrie," he replies. "I think she might have seen me a couple of weeks ago."

"You really think she did?" Lizzy's mind races. This would explain her aunt's odd behavior.

"Not sure," he replies, still smiling.

"Then you shouldn't even do it now," she suggests as forcefully as she can without giving offense. She can't believe her uncle is being so irresponsible—it's so unlike him.

"Don't you worry."

The change comes over him quickly: Lizzy hardly even notices the shuddering of his skin or his moment of vulnerability. There's a slight haze around him as his skin becomes even more smooth, as his chestnut hair becomes even more dark and vibrant, as his limbs lengthen, adding inches to his height. In the final stages of the transformation, he tilts his head back to let the sunlight shine directly on his face. He reaches over his head with outstretched fingers, as if he were capturing the sun's glow. She marvels at his expert control over the process, so different from her own experience.

With the change complete, her uncle drops his hands and looks directly at her, smiling. He's a handsome man, with dark eyes, wavy hair, and broad shoulders, looking as full of life as the green leaves around him. She wonders for a moment if he's only fooling her, trying to impress her with how young he can look. The odd thing is that her uncle's form brings back memories of her mother—her slightly crooked nose, the uneven teeth, the thin legs. No, she decides, this is how Uncle Hezekiah must really look.

The eyes, of course, are the same, she thinks.

"Uncle Hezekiah?"

"Yes, Lizzy?"

"Thank you for letting me see you."

"Always remember me this way."

After Uncle Hezekiah changes back to his old self, they walk toward the house along the path, pausing to admire a huge, ancient maple tree along the way. She can't see the end of the green. Lizzy wonders at her uncle's ability to live with such uncertainty about his wife. She can't imagine living so close to someone, yet being so distant in many ways, so mistrustful.

"Couldn't you just tell Aunt Carrie about us?" she asks.

"Oh no, child," he says, with a laugh. "You must never let on, as hard as it might be." He seems to read the doubt she feels. "No, really, it's much better for them not to know."

"How can that be?" she asks.

"People wouldn't understand, no matter how much they love you," he says, "and what they don't understand, they fear."

Lizzy nods, beginning to understand. It's just like the fear she's seen lately in her aunt's face. "What are you going to do if she saw you?"

"When she's ready, she'll talk to me and I'll reassure her," he says, smiling. "Maybe she was having a spell and didn't know what she was seeing."

They walk on in silence. She can sense that her uncle is hiding something from her—maybe fear, she thinks. "Let me give you another piece of advice," he continues. "Be specially careful of people who follow what the preachers have to say too closely."

"Uncle?"

"That's what worries me about your Aunt Carrie. She's a kind and gentle soul. But her mind is ruled by what she hears in church and nothing else. She's too afraid to follow what her heart tells her. That's why I'd never tell her, because she wouldn't understand it here," he points to his forehead, "even if she understood it here," he points to his heart. "Any kind of ignorance is dangerous, no matter where it comes from."

"I think I understand."

"Lizzy," her uncle says, stopping and facing her, "that's where God is, right here in your heart. Remember that we are all children of God. Do you promise?"

"Yes, Uncle."

"You're a good girl."

On their way back, Lizzy falls behind and her uncle continues without her. She watches him go. She doesn't know what she would have done without him.

Lizzy looks at the trees, counting the patches of moss. She's thinking about what she might want to do if and when she moves away, how soon she might marry. She wonders what her husband will look like, how they will meet, how he'll propose to her. Hollis crosses her mind, but only for an instant. In any case, she hopes that her husband will be as kind and understanding as her uncle. Lizzy tries to reach up into the trees to capture some of their green energy, so vibrant and glowing. She decides that she's glad she's her mother's girl, an elf child.

She holds her hands up, near the lower branches of the tree. Dapples of sunlight dance on them. She lets her fingers grow slightly longer, more slender and delicate. She can almost reach one of the leaves, but decides to let it grow undisturbed.

Mariette, Mrs. Pierce, is right when she says there's a whole world open for her. Lizzy is anxious to try it out. She wants to be free of her life as it is. The possibilities, as she sees it, are endless.

18

Eric held a single red rose in his hands, a gift from Russ. He turned the flower, and two of the petals fell onto the bed. He gently picked them up and was amazed with their softness, like velvet. Although he was deeply frightened, every time he thought about moving back home to his mother's, he remembered his promise. Was there anything he could do to escape its consequences?

He reclined a little further on the bed, their bed. They hadn't had sex since the revelation—Eric couldn't bring himself to share that intimacy, though he finally felt comfortable enough to sleep again, at least for a few hours each night.

Could he abandon his lover? He couldn't shake the image of Russ sitting in front of the plant, hands covering his face, alone. Eric brought the flower closer, wondering at the fine, dark veins threading each petal. The fragrance brought on a smile. In spite of his fear, Eric knew it would be difficult to abandon his love. To stay—Eric's heart raced with both joy and fear. It would be a leap into the unknown, for which he felt inadequate and ill prepared.

Russ had told him it was imperative that he transform, that it was too much a part of him to shut off or ignore. If Russ had to transform, Eric had to learn to live with the changing. He shook his head and smiled again. He would have to witness another transformation, perhaps many of them; this would be the only way for him to finally accept his lover's special ability.

Another problem was the fact that he couldn't tell anyone about Russ's nature. Of course, even if he felt comfortable confiding such a thing to his mother or to Kevin, Eric wasn't sure he would be believed. Keeping quiet would be difficult. Eric hated keeping secrets.

Russ came into their bedroom. He didn't come any nearer than the foot of the bed. "I'm going over to my mother's for a little while. See you soon?"

Eric didn't have the energy to stop him, to tell Russ what his heart had decided. "Yes," he replied and watched his lover quietly leave their room.

Eric remained, lying on the bed, staring out the open window. The solid blue of the sky beyond the confines of the window frame was so inviting.

Russ, against his better judgment, decided to tell his mother about Eric. He knew she would be furious with him, but he had to talk to somebody and his mother was the only one.

It had been a week since he'd revealed himself, but it seemed much longer. Eric had grown more and more quiet, as if he had secrets of his own. Russ didn't have the courage to ask him again whether he planned to move out. Sex between them had been out of the question—every time Russ made any kind of move, Eric withdrew. He feared that if things didn't change, their relationship would crumble; he hoped that by talking with his mother, he'd come up with some idea of how to turn things around.

He stood at her front door, waiting. Nothing had been the same since she sold the house in Portland and moved to San Diego. She had often complained about the lack of space for planting flowers at her new place but had ignored his advice to purchase planters. After all, ceramics were so cheap here in Southern California. He wondered what form would greet him when she opened the door.

There she was—as herself, with cocoa-colored hair and gray eyes, the eyes he remembered so well from his childhood. She was dressed simply in an artist's smock and torn jeans. He could see she'd been painting.

"My son," she said without smiling. She embraced him.

"What's wrong?" he asked as he came in.

"Demons," she sighed, walking over to her canvas, which was set up in the living room. "I'm getting too old for this world."

Her birthday, Russ remembered, was coming up on Tuesday. This would make it even harder for him to ask what he needed to ask of her.

"How do you like it?" She pointed to the unfinished painting.

"A lot," he replied. He saw a meadow, a riot of greens, yellows, and a touch of red, with the sky shocking blue. "Uncle Hezekiah's meadow?"

She didn't have to answer.

"You *have* been struggling with demons," he added.

Her face was expressionless. "There are so many things I can't forget."

It had been a long time since he'd seen his mother as sad as she was today. It was almost as if she knew what he was going to tell her. He sat on the couch to watch her paint. He could feel her scrutiny even though her gaze was completely focused on the painting.

"I have something I'd like to talk to you about," he started.

"You've told him about us, haven't you?" she asked.

Russ wasn't surprised that she already knew. Neither was he surprised by her anger, which he could sense, growing in her, swelling around her. "Yes, I have."

She said nothing, but her paint brush spoke in staccato beats.

"I trust him," Russ said, trying to keep calm.

"I knew it would come to this," she said, with more staccato brush strokes. "What was his reaction?"

Russ was surprised by her control. "It didn't go well."

"What happened?" she asked, not looking at him.

"I tried to tell him, but he wouldn't believe me."

She smiled grimly.

"I had to show him."

She stared at him, furious. "You transformed right in front of him?"

"Yes, I think he went into shock."

"Of course he would," she added with a harsh laugh. "A transformation is not a pretty sight for a human. It must have scared him half to death."

Although Russ was pleased that she would show even a hint of concern for Eric, he could see now that he would get no sympathy. She was concerned about her own safety—and his, of course. "He's withdrawing from me," he admitted.

"I'm not surprised," she replied and began to pound the canvas again with her brush. "I suppose you've told him your life's story," she continued sarcastically.

"Not quite," he replied. "I had to give him some kind of explanation. Otherwise, I'd lose him. I really feel that we can trust him."

"We?" she asked. "Now you have the audacity to speak for *me.* He's a child, Russ, a veritable child. How could you possibly trust his judgment? He's likely to blab things without even realizing their importance."

"You can't say that," Russ said protectively. "You haven't even met him."

"How do you know that I haven't met him?" she asked, glaring at him.

This caught him off guard. "You've already met him," he slowly repeated, growing more angry. "What kind of game did you play with him?"

"A cat and mouse game, of course," she replied sarcastically.

"And you caught the mouse?"

"Of course."

Dozens of scenarios ran through his mind. Did she tag along on one of his jogs in the park? Did she pretend to be his mother? He stared at her, but he knew that it was hopeless to try to intimidate her. "What happened?"

"I took the form of a very attractive man—a big, blond bodybuilder sort that I imagine most young men his age adore."

"Where was this?" he asked.

"At the park," she told him with a smile. "I timed it perfectly."

Now she was playing cat and mouse with him and he hated it. He hoped, at least, that she would tell him the truth. "Get on with it."

"I must admit that he was very loyal," she confessed. "He made it clear that he was not interested in any kind of fling." She continued more softly, "But Russ, he told me—a perfect stranger—about his newfound love, how happy he was, how he had found just the right one and then everything he knew about you."

Russ couldn't help but feel proud. His mother must have seen the look on his face.

"Your friend is a perfectly fine fellow," she said, catching his eyes. "But he's a fool."

Anger flashed through him. "He is no fool." Russ waited for some of the anger to melt away before he continued. "Don't talk about him that way."

She was quiet, except for her brush strokes, which were furious. He could see her changing slightly, even from the back. When she turned to him again, her eyes had become as dark as obsidian. "Trust," she snapped. "What have I told you about trust? What have I told you about human nature?" Her voice cut through him. "People will destroy what is different, Russ, anything that they do not understand." She threw her small paintbrush at him, planting a shock of blue on his shirt above his heart. "People will kill you! I have seen this!"

Even though he could feel her anger all around him, he kept staring in her eyes, trying to make her see into him. He wished she could somehow let go of the fear that had imprisoned her for so long so that she could help him. She finally turned away. He stood and wrapped his arms around her.

"I need you." He could feel her body relax in his arms; he wondered if the anger was also melting away. When she looked at him again, though, her eyes were still obsidian. "Mother?"

"Why don't you introduce your lover to me on my birthday?"

"What?" he asked, perplexed. Although his anger was less, Russ didn't completely trust her. It seemed so improbable that she would want to see Eric, especially on her birthday. It was even more telling that her eyes hadn't changed back yet. "Do you think you could help?"

"I think I might," she replied. "I can be charming. It may be a good idea for me to spend a little time with him," she continued. "Perhaps you're right. Maybe we can trust him."

He couldn't believe what he was hearing. "But on your birthday?"

"Yes," she replied. "I'll meet your lover on my birthday."

The turnaround had come too easily. Yet he couldn't complain, since he had somehow gotten his own way. Would she really help explain things to Eric, to make things easier for him? He wasn't at all sure.

Eric listened closely to the noises from outside, waiting for Russ's return. There was, of course, the dim roar of the city, the conglomeration of street traffic and freeway noise that was a perpetual cushion of sound, usually unnoticed. White noise. Then there were the closer sounds of neighborhood dogs barking, the slamming of car doors, distant radios, and birds chirping. Eric knew that Russ had gone to speak with his mother about them, about how he had revealed his secret.

He didn't move when Russ came into the apartment, nor did he answer Russ when he called from the living room. Eric was almost sure he loved Russ enough to stay with him. Only one small piece of him wanted to run.

"Why didn't you say anything when I called you?" Russ asked him and sat on the edge of the bed.

"I don't know," Eric replied. "Guess I'm still in a daze."

"Are you all right?" he asked.

"Sure," Eric lied. He searched Russ's face, trying to detect any changes. "You talked to your mother about me, about telling me about the changeling stuff?"

"Yes," Russ said and leaned back onto the bed.

"How did it go?" Eric sat up and moved a bit closer. The mix of familiarity and strangeness threw Eric off, as it had for the previous week. There were the same green, glittering eyes, the same thick hair, yet they weren't really the same.

"It could have gone worse," Russ admitted. "She wasn't as angry as I thought she'd be." Russ paused. "She wants to meet you."

This was a shock. He had been waiting for a long time for Russ to say this, but now, under these circumstances, the prospect was frightening. "When are we going to see her?"

"In a couple of days," Russ said. "On her birthday."

Eric brightened. "Her birthday?" Somehow this seemed less threatening. Was she going to accept him then? "Does she like chocolate cake?" he asked.

Russ smiled.

"What did you say to convince her?" Eric asked.

"I said I trusted you."

"That's all you said?"

"Yeah."

Eric studied his lover for a moment, doubtful. "You're not telling me the whole story."

"You need to understand something about my mother." Russ reached out to stroke Eric's hair. "She doesn't trust anyone except me, and now I'm not sure she trusts me completely." He paused. "Don't be surprised at what you see when we go over to visit her. She may not be quite herself."

"Will she at least have the decency to be human?" Eric asked, forcing himself to accept Russ's touch. It felt so odd to be close to him again.

"Who knows?" Russ replied, drawing him closer with an embrace. "She could be just about anything under the sun."

"She won't eat me or anything like that, will she?"

"Probably not," Russ said and playfully growled. His eyes subtly changed to a feline yellow.

"Stop it," Eric snapped and drew away from him.

"It won't be anything like that," Russ answered, holding Eric's gaze with his yellow eyes. "She's not violent."

"Oh, that's great," Eric said. He was sorry he had snapped at Russ. He forced himself to look into Russ's eyes—they shone like a cat's. It was either now or never. Either he would learn to accept this aspect of his lover, or he would have to leave him. "Maybe you should change form again."

"Are you serious?" Russ asked.

"I'm going to have to get used to it, aren't I?" The memory of the first transformation was enough to send chills through Eric. "I might as well start now."

"Okay," Russ replied. "What would you like me to turn into?"

Eric shrugged. Wasn't it enough to agree to witness the transformation? "Something human, male, and good-looking," Eric told him. "Maybe you could keep one thing that looks like you so I can have something to hold onto," he added.

Russ smiled as if he thought the request was cute.

"Change your eyes back to green and keep them that way," Eric said, annoyed that Russ wasn't taking him seriously enough. He braced himself to watch Russ's body contort.

"Okay." Russ stood up. "Where do you want me?"

"Right where you are," Eric said, glad that Russ had stopped smiling. Eric told himself that he had to watch every moment of it. His heart began beating faster. Would it be as horrible as it was before?

The transformation began as it had before, except that Russ didn't strip first. Russ closed his eyes and Eric could see him totally relax.

Eric grabbed the edge of the bed, his whole body tense with anticipation and fear. Everything seemed to happen much more quickly—the color of Russ's hair changed first, from sandy to golden blond. The skin on his face quivered and Eric could see the bones underneath shifting and narrowing. Russ's jaw became more pronounced. Eric's stomach started to turn, but he forced himself not to look away. Wasn't Russ experiencing any pain? The change quickly swept through the rest of Russ's body, with his chest expanding and his arms and legs growing longer. Eric was relieved that this part of the transformation was largely hidden.

This time, it was just a little easier for Eric. He told himself to keep breathing and it would soon be over. When Russ opened his eyes, they were green again. Eric sighed. Russ's eyes were set in a face of utter unfamiliarity. Eric had to admit that it was handsome, but it didn't belong to Russ.

"How do I look?" Russ asked in a voice similar to his old one.

"Handsome," Eric replied, trying not to let his voice quiver. "Especially the eyes."

Russ didn't move toward him, for which Eric was thankful. He wanted some time. The form Russ had taken was beautiful, there was no doubt about it. But it was the eyes that really held him, Russ's eyes. Eric could still see love there for him. He hoped this love would be enough in spite of a hundred different forms.

After a moment, Eric stood and moved toward his lover. At first, he couldn't get his legs to stop shaking. He told himself to keep looking into Russ's eyes—the one constant. He touched his face. The skin was a little smoother than Russ's and slightly more moist to the touch. After a moment, Eric embraced him. Although the body felt different—even Russ's scent had changed slightly, becoming a little stronger—Russ's response was familiar. Eric drew back and looked in his eyes again to get a sense of connection. It was one point of familiarity.

It was too much, this first time touching a stranger who wasn't a stranger, a man who didn't resemble his lover. Eric found that if he kept his eyes closed, he could tolerate the closeness. Even so, it was impossible to relax, even with Russ showering him with kisses. They were kisses from a different mouth. Eric stole a glance at him and saw Russ's face hovering near his own. Were there tears in those green eyes? Eric had to close his own eyes again, though he knew Russ wanted them open. Eric couldn't—he just couldn't find a way to open them without crying.

19

Russ and Eric, cake in hand, walked up to Lizzy's door. Russ knocked. She didn't answer. They looked at each other uneasily. Now what? Russ thought. Eric rang the bell again. Both of them had done nothing but fret all day. This was tempered, at least for Russ, by the promise of intimacy between them. Soon, he thought, they'd be having sex again. It felt so wonderful finally to be able to share everything with another. Now if only his mother would help.

Finally, the door swung open. Russ was relieved—it was not as bad as he thought it might be. His mother stood before them, smiling, a gypsy with long, glossy black hair hanging in ringlets around her shoulders and down her back. She was wearing a skin-tight, long-sleeved rust-colored leotard with a dazzling red wraparound skirt. Her olive skin glistened with perspiration, so Russ knew that she had just gone through the change. Her eyes, still obsidian, glowed.

"You must be Eric," she said, extending her hand.

"I'm happy to meet you." Eric took her hand, trying to balance the cake with the other. "Happy birthday."

"Thank you," she said. "Come in."

Russ glanced at his lover's face, trying to gauge his reaction. Eric, understandably, looked nervous. At least the apartment would seem relatively normal, he thought. There was a TV in the corner, a stereo system along the far wall playing classical music he didn't recognize, a couple of white easy chairs and a sofa—very contemporary and comfortable. The only thing at all out of the ordinary were his mother's paintings. Dozens of them were hanging on the walls, all landscapes and flowers, bright, colorful, and lush.

"What beautiful paintings," Eric remarked.

"Thank you," she said, taking the cake from Eric. "Did Russ tell you I paint?"

"No, he didn't." Eric glanced over at him, as if to say, "Why didn't you tell me?"

Russ shrugged. He hadn't even thought to mention her painting.

"He hasn't said very much about you at all," Eric added for good measure.

"Good," she said, glaring at Russ as she walked over to the dining table, which was already set for three. "Thank you for the cake."

At least she was being cordial, Russ thought. But he could still sense a cool anger around her. And there were those obsidian eyes.

"Would you like something to drink?" she asked.

Neither of them said anything. Perhaps, for Russ's part, it was surprise at her graciousness. He had prepared himself for something very different. Of course, he thought, the night was young.

"I have some wine," she added.

"That would be great," Eric replied. "Thank you."

Russ nodded in agreement.

"Russ, would you pour some for us?" she asked, too politely.

"Yes, Mother," he replied, just as politely. Perhaps, he thought, this would be a long night after all.

"Tell me something about yourself," she asked Eric. "Russ tells me you're involved in computers."

"No, actually, Russ must have been telling you about Kevin, my best friend, who's really into computers. Right now, I'm in a holding pattern until I start grad school."

"Oh, really?" she asked.

This brought to mind his mother's cat and mouse game. Although Russ was exasperated with her, he couldn't say anything. Of course, he hadn't told Eric anything about his mother's covert visit. He hoped his mother wouldn't reveal what she had done—this would only scare Eric even more.

"I'd like to study cartography," Eric added. "I just graduated from college a couple of months ago. I start grad school next month."

Russ could tell that Eric was uptight, though he was surprised at how well he was hiding it. There was only a slight quiver in Eric's voice. He couldn't blame him for being nervous. Even he was nervous.

He just hoped that Lizzy wouldn't go through any transformation in the bathroom and come out as a tiger or some other large animal.

"Well, I'm glad you've found something that you'd like to do," she replied. "You're thinking of the future."

"Thanks." Eric smiled.

Russ could see a hint of relief in Eric's face. He thought his mother was softening a little bit. But then, he couldn't imagine anyone actually taking a dislike to his lover.

"Something smells good," Eric offered.

Russ agreed. "Something does smell good. What is it?"

"Hungarian goulash," his mother said, going into the kitchen to check on it.

"That's what you remind me of," Eric said. "You remind me of a Hungarian princess."

Russ cringed. His mother paused at the oven, her face framed by the steam from the casserole.

"How did you know I was once a princess?" she deadpanned.

She liked him, Russ decided with relief.

When they sat down to dinner, Russ offered a toast. "To my mother—always a princess."

As they ate, Russ was thankful that Eric didn't ask too many prying questions. For her part, Lizzy, loosened by the wine, relaxed enough to ask Eric a few more questions—about his family and their new apartment. All safe, unthreatening. Eric was fairly reserved with his responses, very unlike him. Given what his mother had said to Russ earlier, though, he was pleased that Eric wasn't telling everything and anything. Perhaps Eric would prove her wrong.

It was so odd to see his mother and lover together. He couldn't recall the last time he'd been together with both a friend and his mother—it must have been, he imagined, sometime after high school. Most of his friends had gone off to college or had begun working, as he had done. His father was alive at that time, so the masquerade was still in place. Now it gave him a thrill to have the two most important people in his life, together for once without any charade, and fewer lies. He still didn't trust his mother completely, but her willingness to be civil and even friendly gave him great hope.

Eric insisted that Russ and his mother stay seated at the table while he prepared the cake in the kitchen. While Eric was out of the room, Russ used the opportunity to talk with his mother privately.

"You like him, don't you?" he asked, smiling like a conspirator, or perhaps like a victor.

"Yes," she whispered, looking directly in his eyes. "But that doesn't mean that I feel any differently about your telling him about us."

"Why?" he asked, perplexed. "Don't you think we could trust him?"

"People make mistakes," she insisted. "Even good people. They might mean well, but their mistakes can be deadly. It is not their fault, but that's the way it is. If he makes a mistake, if the wrong people find out about us, you could pay for it. We both may. Now, be quiet."

Eric walked back into the room. The top of the cake was covered with birthday candles.

"Russ, help me out here," he said. "Let's sing."

They sang "Happy Birthday" to Lizzy, and Russ couldn't help but smile. She was obviously glad to have a cake and a song, but yet there was a weariness in her eyes that troubled him.

She blew out the candles on her first try.

"Did you make a wish?" Eric asked.

"Yes," she said, smiling, and turned to Russ. Her eyes were still obsidian. They chilled him. "This is delightful," she said. She pulled the candles out of the cake with abandon and quickly cut a generous piece for each of them.

"My mother used to make me chocolate cake," she said to Eric.

"That's great," Eric replied, obviously pleased with himself. "You know, I wasn't sure how many candles to put on. I hope I didn't have too many."

She laughed, and Russ had to join her. He was relieved that Eric had finally started to joke, even timidly.

"You know we changelings never grow old," she said to Eric.

"That's what Russ said," Eric agreed.

She shrugged as if to say, it doesn't make any difference now. "How old do you think I am?"

"I have absolutely no idea. Russ is forty-eight," he considered aloud. "So maybe you're seventy?"

Russ had to smile—Eric looked so completely mystified.

"No," she said, "I'm more than one hundred years old."

Eric shook his head and began to laugh. "No way," he said, incredulous. "No way!"

She laughed, a deep laugh like Russ remembered from years ago with his father. "Would I deceive you?" she asked, delighted. "Let's celebrate!"

Lizzy pranced over to the stereo and picked out a new CD from the cabinet, which she put in the player.

"What are you going to play?" Russ asked.

"Here," she said, tossing the CD case at him.

"Franz Liszt, *Hungarian Fantasia,* Hungarian Rhapsodies Numbers Two, Five, and Twelve," Russ read aloud. "Johannes Brahms, Four Hungarian Dances. The Berlin Philharmonic Orchestra."

"Let's dance," she said and began to twirl to the music, first slowly and then faster. Her eyes sparkled and she laughed, as if she hadn't danced in a long time. As she moved and swayed, her body slowly changed, becoming even more curvaceous and earthy. A wild Hungarian gypsy princess.

Eric laughed and looked at Russ, joy on his face. He began to dance too.

The energy rushed over Russ as he watched his lover and his mother spin together. He could not believe what he was seeing—the two most important people in his life dancing. His joy was only tempered with the feeling that his mother was acting out a charade, meant either to please him or to cover up something. Her eyes were still as black as night. Still, she was dancing, he thought.

Russ crouched on the floor for a moment to steady himself. Not to be outdone, he brought on a change. His hair grew out longer, turning wavy, glossy, and black as midnight to match his mother's. His eyes turned black too, his nose grew larger, his jaw broadened, his body became more swarthy and strong. If he had decided to become an animal, it would have been a black leopard.

They spun and swayed, Eric, Russ, and his mother, until their breath escaped them.

Eric stepped out of his car, hoping Russ would be at the T-shirt stand. It was imperative that they talk, immediately. He wasn't sure how much more of this he could take. He could still see Russ's mother standing in front of him that morning, her black eyes glittering.

It was windy at Pacific Beach, almost cold, with damp, heavy air blowing against him.

Eric had thought that everything had gone so well at her birthday celebration. He had been so careful not to ask any prying questions. The whole evening he had felt vulnerable—afraid at every moment that she might turn into something disgusting. He hated the way they both watched him, like a bug under glass. After dinner, though, he had thought things had changed. Why did she have to threaten him? he wondered. What could he possibly do to hurt her?

It was hard enough getting used to the idea of his lover being a changeling. And now this, he thought.

At first Eric walked the wrong way down the boardwalk and he went a good hundred yards before he realized his mistake. A gust of wind whipped sand in his eyes. He turned and ran until he got to Russ's T-shirt stand, his heart racing. Luckily, Russ wasn't waiting on anyone. Russ smiled until he saw the look on Eric's face.

"What's wrong?" Russ asked.

"We've got to talk about something right now," Eric told him, out of breath.

"What is it?" Russ asked. "You're shaking."

"It was your mother," he blurted out.

"What about her?"

"She paid a visit to me this morning," Eric said. "She came to the front door but wouldn't come in."

"What did she say?" Russ asked, alarmed.

"At first, I didn't recognize her, because she'd changed from last night." He blinked back tears. "She said she had come over to warn me that I should never say anything about her or you to any of my family or friends. Not anyone." It was becoming difficult for Eric to stand, his legs were shaking so. "She was so angry, you wouldn't believe it. She told me how important you were to her and that if anything ever happened to you, she would come after me."

"Come after you?" Russ asked.

"Something like that," Eric replied. "It was a threat, Russ."

Russ didn't say anything for a moment. Eric could see that he was stunned. "She's just upset. I'll have a talk with her."

Have a talk with her? Eric knew that the threat had been serious. The thought of living with the fear was too much. "Look, I'm not sure I can handle this," he said.

"What do you mean?"

"I'm not sure I can live with you anymore," Eric said. "I'm not strong enough to take it."

Russ jumped over the barrier of the T-shirt stand and embraced him. "My mom wouldn't hurt you—she was scaring you."

"She did a good job of it." Eric stepped away.

"Don't worry," Russ told him. "I'll take care of it."

"I don't know."

"I told you that I would take care of it," Russ said again, this time with a hint of anger.

"You have no right to be angry with me," Eric said. "Not after what you've put me through."

Russ came closer, with tears in his eyes. "Please don't leave me. We can work things out. I know we can."

Eric hesitated. Russ's love held him back; and there was the promise. How many times would he regret uttering those words? He recalled all the times they'd fallen asleep in each other's arms. Eric had felt safe then. Could he ever reclaim the feeling, and would Russ be able to protect what they'd shared? "All right," he said reluctantly. "I'll stay."

20

Lizzy wakes up with a start, hearing loud voices, angry voices. The darkness crowds in around her as she becomes more aware. In her whole life, she's never heard her aunt and uncle argue. She eases out of bed, trying not to make any sound. The voices are too muffled for her to figure out what's being said. Her heart is racing. She quietly steps out of her bedroom and along the upstairs hallway, close to her uncle and aunt's bedroom. There's so little light, even from underneath their door—they must, she realizes, be arguing in the darkness. Her eyes adjust enough to make out the banister and a vague impression of their door. Now she can hear everything.

"What about all the babies?" her aunt asks, as if she were accusing her uncle of something.

"Now, Carrie," her uncle replies in a firm tone.

"All of my babies—stillborn," her aunt sobs. "All the while I thought God was punishing me. But it was you, wasn't it?"

"Carrie!"

"The last baby, the one that didn't have a face?"

"Carrie!" her uncle says more loudly. "It's best not to think of it."

"When haven't I thought of it?" More sobs. "It must be the Devil. You consort with the Devil!" she shouts.

"I do no such thing, Carrie," he replies. "That's the preacher talking."

Lizzy hears some kind of scraping, as if something were being dragged across the floor.

"What curse have I lived with all these years?" she asks, out of breath. "No!" she yells. "Don't you touch me!"

Lizzy hears them come closer to the door and she quickly moves away through the darkness, back down the hallway.

"Don't ask me to live here anymore," her aunt shrieks. "I can't. I just can't."

Lizzy pulls her own door shut and quickly tiptoes to her bed. She's shaking, her aunt's voice echoing. "I can't, I just can't." It's everything Lizzy has feared.

She waits, but hears nothing—no slamming doors, no loud voices. How has he consoled her? Lizzy wonders. She only vaguely recalls the stillbirths, but she does remember her aunt becoming more sullen and withdrawn as she lost baby after baby. The silent darkness is threatening after her aunt's shouts. She opens the curtains to the window just above the bed, but there's no light from the moon. She can't see any stars. Her aunt does know something. Lizzy feels a sense of loss and foreboding. She attempts to make out shapes in the darkness, but there is only black.

In the morning, Lizzy wakes up to find the house strangely quiet, as if it's waiting for something. She slips into her favorite blue dress and quickly opens the bedroom door. In the light, the hallway is almost too familiar, too ordinary. The door to her aunt's bedroom is shut. When she goes downstairs, she finds her uncle sitting at the kitchen table, his hands folded in front of him. His face wears a haggard aspect that she has seldom seen.

"Good morning, Uncle." She sits next to him and glances out the window to see if her aunt is getting firewood.

"Lizzy." He nods at her. "Your Aunt Carrie isn't with us." His hands move, pulling together more tightly. "I expect that she's gone to the preacher."

"Oh, no." She lets out a little sigh.

"Did you hear any of the argument we had last night?" He glances at her, his eyes tired with lack of sleep.

"Enough of it." She crosses her arms. She feels a heaviness all around. "When did she leave?"

"Early this morning," he replies in a tired voice. "I was able to stop her last night, but she slipped away. I didn't think I had slept, but I must have been wrong."

"Do you think she'll be back?"

"I hope so, though that might not make any difference."

Lizzy feels oddly heavy, as if she is about to fall through the floor and slam into the cool earth. She wonders what he means by saying it might not make a difference if she comes back, but she's uncertain whether she really wants to know. "How many stillbirths were there?"

"You don't remember?" he asks.

"I was too young," she explains.

He shakes his head. "There were five." His head tilts back. He's quiet for a long time.

Lizzy waits, uncertain. It's so odd to be here in the kitchen without Aunt Carrie. The kitchen is her favorite place—her domain.

"There's something you should know about our kind," he finally continues. "We are not prolific." He glances at her again. "It's very difficult for changelings to have children. Until I married your aunt, I figured that I couldn't father any, but then with Carrie they just kept on comin'. She must have been specially fertile."

"Why were they all stillborn?" she asks.

Her uncle stands up and goes to the sink to pick up a coffe cup. He walks slowly and hunched over, like an old man. "Most of them were disfigured—the changeling aspect of them didn't develop properly. Their little bodies were all twisted." His voice is shaking now. "I delivered all but the last of them and never let Carrie see them. All but that last one—the little boy without a face."

Lizzy cringes. Is this what she has to look forward to, a family of dead babies?

Her uncle comes up behind her and rests his hands on her shoulders. "It's different for a changeling mother," he tells her in an even voice. "You may not have many children, but chances are that any children you carry will come out all right. It's only the changeling fathers who have trouble; that is, if they are able to father at all." He sits down beside her again. "All of Carrie's praying for a child and look where it led us."

Some of the sharpness comes back to her uncle's eyes. "Lizzy, we may need to move away from here."

As soon as he suggests this, she realizes that running away has been at the back of her mind all along. She pictures them changing form and rushing through the woods, going far enough to catch a train, or transforming into a pair of birds and catching the wind. "If we must, I'll go with you."

"I'm afraid we might not have any choice," he continues. "There's no telling what your Aunt Carrie might decide to tell folks, and the preacher is crazy enough that he might just believe her. I'm scared of what might happen."

"You really think they'll take her seriously?" she asks.

"Some of the so-called leaders in our community don't take kindly to me. They never have." He smiles wryly. "I'm too uncooperative."

Lizzy often has thought this before—though many people adore her uncle, especially some of their closer neighbors. She has heard that a large number of folk consider the family eccentric, and she knows for a fact that many of their comments have been directed at her.

"Even if there's no direct threat to us, folks could make life unbearable. That's what happened to my grandmother. People wouldn't talk to her, wouldn't trade with her, completely shutting her out. She had to move away, along with her children. People can be cruel." He sighs. "Best to start new somewhere."

A new start. It's what she's dreamed about, but it all seems wrong now, contaminated. "When do you think we should leave?"

"Soon." He stands up again. "Within the week. Maybe your aunt will come back home tonight. Then I'll have a better idea."

"If we go, what will we do for money?" she asks.

"There's a considerable sum of money in a bank in Chicago—under our names—family money for emergencies." He pauses, a wave of sadness coming over his face. "It's in the National Bank of Commerce. You'd best remember that." Suddenly his face breaks into a smile. "Would you like to head West, dear girl?"

She immediately thinks of the letters Mrs. Pierce promised her—for schools back East. Perhaps, she thinks, Mrs. Pierce knows of some schools in the West. "That sounds as good as anything," she replies. "Mrs. Pierce might be able to write letters of recommendation for schools out West just as well."

"We won't be able to use any letters of recommendation," he explains with a smile. "We'll need to change our identity."

Of course, he's right. Lizzy feels a bit foolish.

"You start thinking about what you might want to take with you," he says. "Remember, we'll need to travel light."

Later that morning, Lizzy returns to the meadow, half hoping to find Hollis there again. The house is too quiet and she's not sure where her uncle has gone. The meadow will be safe.

As she walks, the image of the baby without a face comes back to her and she's afraid. The sky is finally clearing up; there won't be any rain today. Now that the reality of leaving this place is upon her, Lizzy feels uncertain. She wants to leave, to begin something new, but not under these circumstances. She's never had to run before, or hide.

She thinks about what she could take. There are the photographs of her mother and father, of her uncle and aunt, of herself. Then there's the photo of Mrs. Pierce, given to her only last year. She hopes that she'll have a chance to say good-bye to Mrs. Pierce, though she's not sure how to explain. Then there's Hollis. She knows the Pierces will expect her to write, but she won't be able to. She imagines the pain they will feel as weeks turn into months without a word. Lizzy doesn't want to cause anyone pain, but she fears there won't be any choice.

The West—such a great expanse of wilderness. What will happen to them there? Will they stake a claim to another homestead? Her uncle has talked of Oregon—the land of rain and forests. Then there's always California. She's read about San Francisco, as much of a city as any large city back East. There will be plenty of opportunity to become lost to the world. At least, she thinks more hopefully, they will have each other.

When she begins to head back, she doesn't turn for one final look at the meadow. It's best, she knows, to simply move on.

As she nears the farm, she hears yelling up ahead, a bunch of men yelling. Angry men. She runs off the path into the cover of trees and cautiously advances behind the chicken coop. She can hear the voice of the preacher, like he's reading from the Bible, along with the yelling.

There's a shot.

She moves faster, changing her shape to become smaller, less easy to see, darker to blend in. Men stand over her uncle, next to the coop. He's been shot in the head. She starts to make a noise to divert their attention, but it's too late. "He's being healed," one of the men shouts. "His wound is closing up."

Oh, no, she thinks. Why isn't he fighting back? she wonders with horror. Another shot, point blank in the head. Lizzy spots Aunt Carrie about ten feet away from her uncle. A couple of women are holding Carrie back. She is weeping hysterically.

"This one's healing up too!" the sheriff says.

"It's the Devil," the preacher shouts.

The sheriff fires again, three shots at point blank range. Part of Uncle Hezekiah's head is cracked open and the blood is running out. Lizzy's heart is racing. Is there no way to save him? More yelling. Her uncle tries to get up. His lower half is changing into some kind of animal. A bobcat? A wolf? More shots. Lizzy starts to shake, her whole body tingling with fear. She falls on her side and snaps a fallen branch. Does anyone hear it? Her uncle is almost transformed now, the bleeding has stopped, but two of the men have brought axes from the barn. They start chopping at him. He snarls. Pieces of him fly everywhere.

"Where's that niece of his?" asks one of the women.

Lizzy's body folds into itself, growing smaller and smaller, until she can no longer feel it. Feathers sprout and still she grows smaller and smaller. She doesn't know whether she's a goldfinch, a sparrow, or a lark. It's all instinct. Flight. Her spirit floats around the little body more than it remains in it. She flies up, around the coop, and then into the blue sky.

21

Russ waited until he was relatively calm before going to his mother's, but it was difficult for him to contain his anger. He was also afraid to leave Eric alone that night for fear that Eric would walk out. The whole night Eric slept away from him, balled up on the couch. Whenever Russ reached out, Eric pushed him away.

The morning air was surprisingly fresh and clear. On his way to his mother's, Russ found a darkened nook between two buildings, a perfect place for a transformation. He decided to let everything go—all of the changes, so that he would revert back to his natural self.

The door was already open when he walked up—a foolish thing, he thought. He called her.

"I'm in the bedroom," she called back.

As he approached, his feelings of anger returned. He came to a sudden stop halfway down the hallway. Russ could plainly hear a low buzzing that sounded like a swarm of insects. He hurried into the bedroom.

"Oh, my god," he said in disbelief.

"Hello, son," she said, smiling.

His mother, as herself, without benefit of a transformation, was standing in the middle of a swarm of honeybees. Thousands of them buzzed all around her and in the bedroom. Strands of her long hair were covered with bees; they were even crawling over her face. The noise was deafening.

"What's going on?" he said.

"These are my new friends," she replied and went to her bay window. The bees followed her in a cloud. "A queen bee decided to make her home here and I let her stay. The honeycomb is wonderful to eat."

A large hive had been built around a partially open window. Russ could see the bees coming to and from the hive from outside. Inside, bees were on almost everything—the bed, the vanity, the walls. His mother reached into the hive and pulled out a small chunk of honeycomb. "Would you like some?" she offered.

The bees didn't seem to mind the intrusion at all, although hundreds still swarmed around her. As she got closer to him, the bees started buzzing around him too, but none tried to sting him. "You didn't know your mother was a bee charmer, did you?"

She handed him the honeycomb. He was surprised that it didn't feel more sticky. The comb looked almost like it was dirty, though the little patches of thick golden honey appeared to be relatively clear. Some of the bees landed on his hand and arm, but none stung him.

"You're full of surprises, aren't you?"

"Don't be too glib, or I'll tell my friends here to take care of you," she replied.

"More threats?" he said sarcastically.

"Let's go into the other room," she suggested.

As they walked into the hallway, the bees fell away. "Do you sleep in there?" he asked, eating a corner of the honeycomb.

"They're not active at night," she told him. "As long as I keep the lights off, they don't bother me. In the morning, I don't need an alarm clock."

It was strange, he thought. Neither of them was all that angry, though he was sure she knew why he was there. In the living room, Russ put the honeycomb in a small ornamental bowl and started to lick his fingers clean. "Why did you have to threaten Eric like that?"

"I meant to scare him," she said, her eyes strangely dull, languid. "If he's scared enough, he may not say anything stupid."

Russ had to restrain himself—it seemed to him that she was the one saying stupid things. "Eric almost left me," he said. "You nearly broke us up. Is that what you really want?"

She glanced away. "I'm not sure," she admitted. "I just know that I'm terrified that either you or I will be hurt."

"Can't you leave all that behind you?" he asked.

She turned to him again. "That's easy for you to say. You weren't there."

"I'm sorry," he said. She had a point. "But that doesn't give you the right to threaten Eric. I love him. And he almost left me," Russ repeated. He had to make her understand.

"Well, if he really loves you, what I did won't make any difference."

Russ didn't think that she meant it. "That may be true, but don't you see that you've just driven a wedge between the two of you? How can he possibly enjoy being around you now?" Russ reasoned.

"Perhaps I don't care to be around him."

"Well," Russ replied with rising anger, "Eric is my life partner, so if you want to see me you'll need to see him, too. I want both of you to share what's important in my life and how can that happen now?"

She thought about this for a moment, her face looking tired. "There's not much that can be done to change things now," she finally said.

"You could apologize," he suggested.

"I'll need to think about this," she repeated. "You'll need to give me some time."

He'd seldom seen his mother this way, so resigned to dealing with her demons; the realization made him feel more protective. It was as though she were lost in the sea with no sense of the shore. "Is there anything I can do to help you through this?" he asked hopefully.

"No," she said weakly and smiled. "Just give me some time alone."

As he left, Russ could hear the loud buzzing again when she opened her bedroom door. It didn't seem like a good sign.

Eric waited until Russ was safely asleep to begin gathering a few of his things. He had to be especially quiet, but he had one thing in his favor: Russ was exhausted from his talk with his mother and the stress of trying to keep him there.

Russ had told him that his mother was sorry, that she felt threatened and lashed out. Eric could bring himself to understand why, but he wasn't sure he could forgive. Russ assured him that there was no danger; Eric remained unconvinced. Lizzy's eyes, black as night, kept following him, glaring at him from the corners of rooms and the edges of mirrors. He could feel her watching him, a dark, cold presence on his back.

Once he had collected a few things, he sat down gently on the edge of the bed to say good-bye. He would go to his mother's—perhaps pick up more of his belongings later after things had calmed down.

Russ looked worried, even in his sleep. His brow was furrowed and his eyes were too tightly shut. As Eric sat there, all of the good times came tumbling back—the lazy afternoons at the beach, dancing, eating pizza sitting cross-legged on the floor, moving in together.

It was the sense of closeness Eric would miss the most, the sense of belonging. The trouble was, he still loved Russ in spite of everything. As Eric reached down to give his lover one final kiss, Russ woke up and put his arms around him.

"Hi, handsome," he said, still half asleep.

"Hi there," Eric replied, trying to sound normal. This wasn't the way it was supposed to be.

Russ drew Eric to him in a gentle kiss that lasted much longer than it should have, and Eric soon found himself under the covers. Russ didn't seem to be aware that Eric had his clothes on—at least he didn't let on that he was.

Russ's embrace brought Eric back. How could he consider being without the touch of Russ's hands on the small of his back, without his soft lips against his own? Eric let himself fall into the familiar feeling of being one instead of two. It was impossible to avoid.

When Eric thought Russ might be asleep again, he carefully took off his T-shirt and jeans, tossing them on the floor.

22

The lovers were snuggling in bed in the early morning, sleep yet in their eyes. Russ had one arm draped over Eric's waist while the other cradled his head. Russ searched his lover's face without finding any sign of fear or apprehension. Russ lightly kissed the back of Eric's neck, thankful Eric hadn't acted on his threat to move out. Even though it had been a couple of weeks, Russ couldn't shake the feeling that he might lose his lover. Eric groaned and opened his eyes. Russ wished Eric would go back to his habit of deep sleep, but it had vanished.

"Half of the time, I wonder who I'm going to wake up with," Eric said in a sleepy voice.

Russ smiled. Since he had assured Russ that he would stay, Eric had been growing more comfortable with Russ's transformations. The two of them had begun to have fun with it. Eric moved closer and kissed him on the arm. Russ considered turning himself into some wild man based on a strange-looking model he'd seen advertising Calvin Klein, but decided it was too early in the morning for something so silly. He would tease Eric in another way. "Maybe you should wonder *what* you're going to wake up with."

Eric turned his head. "I suppose you're going to change into something strange?" he asked, almost as a challenge.

"Well," Russ replied. "I could change into some animal—birds or anything in the cat family are my favorites."

Silence. Sometimes Russ wished he could read Eric's mind more easily.

"Don't you believe me?" Russ persisted.

"No, that's the problem. I do." Another pause. "How often do you change into some animal?"

"Only when I'm under lots of stress—you know, bordering on life-and-death situations."

"Oh, I see."

"And then, when I'm incredibly horny," Russ added.

Eric pulled away from him and sat up in their bed. "This is not going to be a normal life, is it?"

"Who ever promised normal?" Russ replied and laughed. "There are benefits, you know," he continued and began to rub Eric's thigh. "Where's your imagination?"

"I don't want to do it with any animals, Russ," Eric deadpanned.

"That's not what I mean, necessarily," Russ said. "Isn't there some guy you've always fantasized about—Tom Cruise, Brad Pitt?"

"Oh, you do vampires too, huh?"

"Tom Selleck? A young Sean Connery . . ."

"We're getting bigger and hairier. . . ."

"Chris O'Donnell . . ."

"A bit closer . . ."

"Batman?"

"You can stop now," Eric said.

"Come on, who did you fantasize about when you were a kid?" Russ sat up on the bed.

"Oh, God!"

"No, come on." Russ began to wonder if Eric had any kind of imagination as a child. "Nothing?" he added, exasperated.

"Let me think a moment," Eric said. "Remember that guy who used to be on the evening news on ABC?"

"What guy?"

"I was really young," Eric explained. "I used to fantasize about the newscaster on ABC. He had a boyish face and kind of blond hair."

"I think I know who you mean."

"He's dead now, though." Eric paused. "Would that make any difference?"

"Not usually," Russ said, trying to remember. Normally he didn't care to change into the form of someone already dead. Strange things could happen. Finally it came to him. "Was his name Frank Reynolds?"

"Yes." Eric smiled broadly. "That might have been the guy."

"You thought he was cute?" Russ asked, incredulous.

"Well, yes," Eric said, a little hurt. "When he was young he was a very handsome man, very newscaster-next-door kind of cute. Don't you remember?"

"Yeah, on second thought, he wasn't too bad," Russ said. Now that Eric was loosening up, Russ didn't want to ruin it. "So, would you like to have sex with a young, very much alive, Frank Reynolds?"

"I don't know yet," Eric told him.

"Why don't we try it? Maybe you can get into it once we start."

"And you change."

"Right."

"Okay," Eric said reluctantly.

Russ could see that Eric wasn't completely relaxed yet, but there was no time like the present.

Russ stood up on the bed, gazing down at Eric, who looked both fearful and expectant. Russ tried to recall exactly what Frank Reynolds looked like all those years ago. He pictured the television, imagined Frank giving the news, and things began to click into place—the fuzziness of the memory sharpened as Russ relaxed and became one with it. Russ laughed to himself—Frank was pretty good-looking after all, in a very clean-cut sort of way. The face would be no problem, but the body, since he had never seen it naked, would be. He decided to use a standard, hunky sort of body with a little hair on the chest and legs, but not massive.

Once the image was set, Russ began to feel the familiar tingling. The tingling became a steady stream of energy, like a waterfall, and Russ lost his sense of place for an instant. He could feel his body shrinking here and there, losing some body hair, finding finer features, and then the snap of recognition, of otherness, the feeling of a complete void coupled the next instant with incredible weight.

The change completed, Russ opened his eyes to see Eric almost smiling, with a look of wonder mixed with uncertainty on his face, his arms outstretched.

"That's not the guy I remembered," he said. "But it will do."

For a long time, there is nothing but blue and green. Her wings flutter ever faster; the air bites in gusts, making it difficult for her to fly. The instant she doubts her ability, she begins to lose altitude. Her wings beat even faster, but to no avail. She doubles back, going to the only other home in which she's ever felt welcome.

She lands in a maple tree near the small house. Though she is frozen with fear, she knows she must begin her transformation soon. There is danger from large animals and she is so small. She hops along the branch until it meets the trunk. Here the tree will be able to carry her full weight when she becomes large again. Another bird—a sparrow—lands near her, its tiny eyes searching. The sparrow calls to her, perhaps to ask where food can be found. She catches herself before she answers—she must not become lost in this smaller world. It might take too long to find her way back to being human.

Her bird ears pick up another song, that of a human, but she doesn't recognize the meaning of its words. She peers into the open window of the house. Is that Mariette? Her difficulty remembering the name tells her she must begin the transformation immediately.

When her heart stops racing, she begins the change, the unraveling that will take her back to being human. It's a relief, an explosion of pent-up energy in the release of a large body kept small for too long. As she gains her limbs again, she loses sight, a momentary vulnerability she's always hated. In the end she has to study her hands to prove that she's human. She counts ten fingers, each with two joints. She realizes, with alarm, that she's completely naked. She hopes Mariette will see her first.

She feels like a rag doll thrown into a tree for safekeeping, except that she is not safe. She will never be safe again.

Before she can climb down, Hollis finds her. She's too weak to attempt to hide. Without a word, he runs into the house. Mariette rushes out. "Lizzy?" she asks. "Please come out of that tree."

Lizzy is not sure she can wave a hand in greeting, let alone crawl down a tree trunk. She can't believe Mariette doesn't comment on her nakedness. Hollis will not look at her.

"They will be searching for you here," Mariette insists. "Hollis, help her down."

So Mariette already knows people are looking for her. Lizzy wonders how long she was flying.

After making his way up the tree, Hollis pulls her to him, holding one of her arms. Pain shoots through her body. He keeps his beet-red face averted as he slowly lets her down into his mother's arms. Mariette is much stronger than Lizzy thought. Her teacher carries her into the house, without a bit of help from Hollis, who awkwardly trails behind them and stays by the door. After Mariette gently places her in a chair, she fetches an old dress and helps Lizzy into it.

"How do you know people will be searching for me?" Lizzy asks, finally finding enough strength to speak.

"They've already been here to look for you," Mariette finishes buttoning the dress. It hangs loosely on Lizzy.

"I'm sorry, I don't understand," Lizzy says, still dizzy from being pulled from the tree.

"Several men were here about an hour ago looking for you," Mariette says, sitting down next to her. "Lizzy, do you know what happened out at your farm?"

The images tumble back. Her uncle's head is cracked open. Blood. "They killed him," Lizzy says, nearly crying. "They hacked him to pieces."

"God have mercy on us," Mariette says. "They said that your uncle was some kind of monster. Lizzy, I've known Hezekiah for years, and his is the gentlest soul I've ever come across, with the exception of my late husband's. My dear girl, you look faint."

Lizzy's eyes flutter. She's not sure whether she feels faint or not.

"Where have you been all this time, Lizzy?" Hollis asks. "Why did you get up in the tree?"

"What happened to your clothes?" Mariette asks.

Lizzy looks from one to the other. Does she dare tell the whole story? How much do they already know? "It was terrible," she says, deciding to tell only a part of what happened. "I heard one of them ask about me, so I got away as quickly as I could. I'm not sure how I came to be here, or how long it took for me to get here." She tries to steady her heart. "My uncle thought there might be trouble. He said that we needed to go away, and not tell anyone about it. He didn't trust Aunt Carrie."

Mariette studies her, and Lizzy cringes. Does Mariette believe her? Will she insist that Lizzy answer all of their questions? She would willingly answer any questions, if she could be sure of their assistance.

"Will you help?" Lizzy asks.

"Young lady," Mariette says, "the ones who killed your uncle will want to kill you, too. Hezekiah was right. You must leave." Mariette stands up. "How can I help you?"

Lizzy is uncertain. She knows she has to run, but where? Mrs. Pierce has offered to write letters of recommendation for schools back East, yet her uncle thought the West would be a better place. She hesitates. Her heart's desire is the East. "I'd like to head East," she says. "Will you write letters of recommendation?" Lizzy asks.

"Of course," Mariette says. "As you will remember, I already offered to write letters for you." Mariette goes over to her secretary, and brings back two envelopes. "Here are the letters. I wrote them yesterday. By providence, I'm sure." Mariette gives her the letters.

"Thank you, Mrs. Pierce," Lizzy says with relief.

"Lizzy," Hollis says, drawing nearer, "How will you pay for the schooling?"

Mariette purses her lips, and stares at Lizzy.

How will she pay for her schooling? Lizzy recalls what her uncle had said. "Uncle told me that the family has an account with a bank in Chicago."

"Will you be able to draw on the account?" Mariette asks.

"I don't know!" Lizzy says, alarmed.

Mariette ponders this a moment, her hands resting on her hips. "My brother is a prominent businessman in Chicago. I believe he will help you. Do you recall the name of the bank?"

"The Bank of Commerce."

"Good!" Mariette says and turns to her son. "Hollis, will you accompany this young lady to Chicago?"

"Yes," Hollis says without hesitation.

Mariette walks to one of the bedrooms. "In the meantime," Mariette says over her shoulder to Lizzy, "you will need some clothes. Hollis, please bring out the horse."

For a few minutes, Lizzy is left alone. She can't believe everything has been settled. She will travel to Chicago, withdraw her family's money, and head East. If only she wouldn't be carrying the memories of the farm and her Uncle Hezekiah. If only he were going with her. How could a life be so completely changed?

Mariette rushes out of the bedroom, carrying a small bag. "Here are spare clothes and some money," Mariette says, handing her the bag. "It's not much, I'm afraid, but it will suffice until you reach Chicago."

"I don't know how to thank you," Lizzy says.

"I've always respected your family. Always. This is my gift to you, and your uncle. Now you must go."

Once Lizzy and Mariette are outside, Hollis helps Lizzy mount the horse behind him. "Come on, Lizzy," he says. "We've got to get."

"I'll never forget you," Lizzy says over her shoulder.

"Hurry!" Mariette says. "I think I hear someone coming. Head out on one of the back trails."

Hollis urges the horse forward. Within a few minutes, the house and Mariette disappear up the trail. Lizzy thinks she can hear horses approaching the house. Only then is she thankful that Mariette hurried them so.

Eric wasn't sure why he woke up—it was only 2:30 or so in the morning. Russ had left a light on in the living room again. Eric got out of bed, careful not to move too quickly and wake up his lover. He glanced at him, sprawled over his side of the bed. There was enough light for Eric to see him clearly—especially his face, part of which was caught in the sliver of light from the door.

Something was wrong, he thought. Eric walked around the bed and approached him for a better look—it was still Russ, but yet it wasn't. The hair was slightly lighter in color and its sheen was gone. The nose was a little longer and slightly crooked, with a few freckles.

Eric gasped and Russ stirred, turning over onto his back, the covers coming off his chest. It was hairier than usual and his muscles weren't as big.

It was Russ, but then it wasn't.

Eric's eyes followed the line of his body in the blankets. His legs didn't seem as long as they ought to. The shape of the face was different, more rounded, not quite as good-looking.

If he hadn't known it was Russ, Eric wasn't sure if he would've recognized him. The body changed again, the face slightly, and Eric lost more of the Russ he knew. He gasped again—this was the same man who had tried to pick him up once right after he'd started dating Russ. It had been at Orion. Eric recalled how much this man had reminded him of Russ and how conflicted he had felt. Eric remembered being surprised that the man seemed happy when Eric told him he was seeing someone.

Here was the same man in his bed. Eric felt light on his feet, as if he could float away at any moment. He shook his head, wondering what other tricks Russ had played on him. He tried to remember guys who had attempted to pick him up. They all became a blur. Eric wondered if there was any way for him to recognize Russ, no matter what form he took. Eric smiled, recalling something Russ said about his eyes, the eyes of an elf child. He would have to learn. Perhaps play his own tricks.

"I need to learn how to recognize you," he whispered.

Russ heard him, at least on some level, because his body started shifting. Russ's eyes fluttered behind his eyelids, a constant movement that spread over his skin. His face changed first, becoming more angular with higher cheekbones; his hair darkened and grew out slightly. The rest of his body shifted, his chest expanded and chest hair retreated into the skin, his limbs lengthened. Eric shook his head.

He opened his eyes, sleepily, and he was Russ again. "What are you doing awake?" Russ asked and stretched. "Why are you standing there looking at me like that?" he added.

"You left the light on again," Eric told him. "I saw you in the light and was remembering the first time we met."

"Oh, really?" Russ asked. He smiled. "Why don't you turn off the light and come back to bed? I'm still sleepy."

"Fine," Eric replied. "I'll turn off the light." Yes, Eric thought. He'd have to learn to be more perceptive, more observant. He slipped back in bed and into another long embrace.

23

Eric somehow convinced Russ to help him with dinner preparations—he especially needed help with the vegetarian lasagna. The chocolate cake was starting to tip over, and he hoped no one would notice. Eric made a last-minute dash around the apartment. For a change, everything was in its place. He only wished that there was more light—they didn't have enough lamps to suit him.

Russ had been the one to suggest a celebratory dinner marking the beginning of Eric's graduate program, but Eric was saddled with making most of the preparations.

Kevin was the first to arrive, with Bird on his shoulder, squawking like crazy. It had been awhile since he'd seen his friend and he was amazed at how much more weight Kevin had lost. For the first time since he'd known him, Kevin looked like he was within a normal weight range for his height.

"You look great!" Eric told him.

"Thanks," he said. "I've lost over a hundred pounds." Kevin put Bird on the back of a chair. "I'm no longer obese," he announced.

Russ joined them and gave Kevin a hug. "You've really made a lot of progress."

"I feel good," he agreed. "I've been dating someone for about a month," he added proudly and a bit awkwardly.

"That's great," Eric told him, genuinely pleased.

"I met him through America Online," Kevin continued. "His name is Jim and he's also a computer programmer. We've been doing things together for about two weeks."

"You should have brought him along," Russ suggested.

"It's too early yet to introduce him to everybody," Kevin replied. "I want to get to know him better myself."

"Is he cute?" Eric couldn't help but ask.

"I think so," Kevin said. "He's about your height, except more slender. He's a blond," he added, looking at Russ.

"How does Bird like him?" Russ asked, smiling.

"Bird tolerates him." Kevin reached down to pet the parrot, only to have her nip at his finger. "She's not fond of change, so she's pissed off at me right now."

"A jealous girl," Russ observed. "How about something to drink? A glass of wine?"

"Sure," Kevin replied and sat on the couch.

As Russ headed for the kitchen, he passed Bird, who hopped off the chair to escape him.

Eric extended his finger to Bird and almost got nipped too. It was like old times. He was relieved that Kevin had found someone. It had been a long time coming. He couldn't help but feel a little sad that he no longer shared things with his old friend. Eric felt as though he'd lost his connection to Kevin, and Kevin's boyfriend only widened the gulf.

"Didn't you say your mom would be here?" Kevin asked.

"Yeah," Eric replied. "She should be here any minute."

Kevin continued in a conspiratorial tone, "Have you heard anything more about your birth mother?"

Eric recoiled from the question. He almost wished that he'd never talked to Kevin about it. "No, I haven't heard anything and don't really want to."

"Why?" Kevin asked him.

"I think it hurts my mom to talk about it," he said bluntly. "Plus, if my birth mother had really wanted to follow through, she would have left some kind of forwarding address at the adoption agency." The feelings of rejection and frustration welled up again. "The whole thing was weird," he continued, his feelings showing. "Here she writes this letter and then within a few months she just vanishes. It's worse than never having heard from her at all."

Russ returned with the wine, giving Eric a quizzical glance. He handed the wine to Kevin.

"I'm sorry that it turned out like it did," Kevin offered.

"That's okay," Eric replied. "You did your best to help out."

Bird let out a piercing squawk.

"She's probably hungry," Kevin said, "and I forgot to bring anything for her to eat."

"We're prepared," Russ told him, starting for the kitchen. "I'll bring something out."

This was a welcome interruption for Eric. Kevin said nothing more about his birth mother. Although Eric was glad Kevin had brought up the subject before his mother arrived, he felt the evening had already been tainted. Soon after they put out some seed for Bird, there was a knock at the door. Eric rushed to answer it.

His mother stood there holding a cactus. "I thought you men might enjoy having another cactus," she explained, hesitating on the doorstep. "This is from the garden at home."

"Thanks, Mom," Eric said and took the plant. There was a small yellow bloom on it. "Look, Russ."

Russ came over and gave Helen a hug. Eric wondered if she would ever hug him back. "Thanks," Russ told her. "It's beautiful."

"I thought that you might like it," she said. "Hello," she greeted Kevin. "You're looking well."

Kevin nodded and smiled at her.

"And you've brought your large friend," she added, reaching down to pet Bird.

"Watch out, Mom," Eric warned her, but it was too late. Her hand was within striking distance.

Only Helen was unsurprised when Bird accepted the pat on the head without even a squawk. Bird peered up at her with one eye. "Don't worry," she added. "Bird and I are friends, you know."

"I'd think twice about doing it again, Mom," Eric said and headed back into the kitchen, his mother following. Eric thought she seemed well. She was wearing a yellow sundress that gave her a youthful appearance. Eric opened the oven to check on the lasagna.

"I never thought I'd see you cooking," she said with a trace of pride.

"Russ has been helping me," Eric explained.

"You're looking a little tired, honey." She ran her hand along his shoulders.

"I'm fine, Mom." The lasagna looked like it was almost ready to take out of the oven. "How does it look?" he asked doubtfully.

"Another ten minutes or so," she said offhandedly. "And things here at home?"

He knew the question was coming—he'd already thought about what he could say. He couldn't lie to her, but he couldn't tell her the whole truth either. He couldn't very well say that he was getting used to having an elf child for a lover, or that the elf child's mother had threatened him. "It's going okay," he said, standing up to face her. "We have our problems, but things are working out."

"Well," she said with uncharacteristic emotion, "if you need to talk to me about anything, you know that I'm here."

He gave her a long hug. He didn't think he could stand to look in her eyes any longer. Thankfully, Russ came into the kitchen. "I need more food for Bird," he said.

Eric's mother helped him with the final touches while Russ opened another bottle of wine and put wine glasses on the table. The lasagna had to cool for about ten minutes, which gave Eric just enough time to steam some broccoli. He wasn't sure it would go all that well with the main course, but he knew that it was supposed to be healthy. Both his mother and Russ said everything smelled delicious. Kevin, on the other hand, didn't say a word. As Eric put out the salad, he told Kevin, "There are a few low-calorie things here."

"Don't worry about me," Kevin replied gruffly.

As they were getting ready to sit down, there was another knock at the door. Thinking it was one of their neighbors, Eric was shocked when he opened the door and found Russ's mother standing there. "Mrs. Lincoln," he said, dumbfounded.

"You can call me Lizzy," she said warmly. "I brought an apology."

Eric couldn't think of anything but the last time she'd spoken to him, threatening him. Now here she was as gracious as she could possibly be.

"You have guests, don't you?" she observed. "I should have called first."

Eric didn't respond immediately. Russ had mentioned that she might come by to apologize, but this was not the right time. Still, she was Russ's mother, and if he slighted her, there might be repercussions. "No," he said, finally getting his breath. "Come on in and join us for dinner."

"Oh, no," she said apologetically. "I shouldn't impose."

"It's not an imposition," he persisted. "There's plenty of food. And my mom wouldn't be too happy with me if she missed an opportunity to meet you," he added with a sinking feeling. He hoped that Russ's mother wouldn't pull any weird stunts.

"Well, if it wouldn't be any trouble," Lizzy said.

Eric glanced behind him and saw that his mother was approaching them—probably having heard him mention her.

"Hello," she said. "Are you Russ's mother?"

"Yes, I am," Lizzy said, faintly smiling. "I'm Lizzy Lincoln."

"I'm Eric's mother, Helen Taylor," Helen said, extending her hand. "I'm so glad to finally meet you. I hope you're going to join us. Eric has been cooking all afternoon."

"I'd love to," Lizzy replied, stepping in.

Eric let Russ handle the rest of the introductions—seeing Russ's mother was enough for him. Here was the woman he'd feared, standing there, being friendly—almost as though she were a different person. Her appearance, he was relieved to see, hadn't changed much. There were streaks of gray in her hair, or what looked like gray. She had put on some weight too, and clothing more suited to an older person.

As he returned to the dinner table, it occurred to him that she must have already known about the dinner—otherwise, why would she have bothered to look older? Certainly not for his benefit. The realization gave Eric a small thrill: he felt proud that he'd figured it out. The only question was if Russ had kept anything else from him. He would have to become more savvy.

Russ had quickly set a place for his mother. Eric and Helen brought the rest of the food out. Once they started to eat, everyone complimented Eric on the meal, even Kevin, who barely touched his. Eric's impression was that everyone was on edge. Bird kept looking from Russ to Lizzy, back and forth, squawking ceaselessly. Kevin finally had to put her in the bedroom and close the door.

One big, strange family. Eric felt like he was visiting someone else's home.

"How long have you known our hosts?" Lizzy asked Kevin.

"I've known Eric for a long time," Kevin said. "I met Russ soon after he and Eric started going out."

Eric tried to gauge each woman's reaction. It always amazed Eric how well his own mother would accept talk about his sexual orientation. It didn't seem to bother Lizzy either. "Kevin met Russ a week or so after I did," Eric added as Bird let out another squawk from the bedroom.

"That bird likes to talk," Lizzy observed.

"She's had a lot of practice," Kevin replied.

"A marvelous creature," Lizzy added with a smile.

Eric hoped she wasn't getting any ideas; he didn't want Kevin to go home without a pet.

"I understand you enjoy painting," Helen said to Lizzy. "Eric told me that the paintings are quite beautiful."

"That's very kind of him," Lizzy said, looking at him.

Eric couldn't tell if Lizzy was pleased or not. Her attention unnerved him and he dropped his fork on the floor. When he bent to pick it up, he noticed that Lizzy's feet, which were cradled in sandals, looked a lot like a man's feet, large and hairy. Suddenly they changed to ladylike, petite feet; the nails were even painted pink. He quickly came back up, hoping he wouldn't appear too shaken. Lizzy didn't even glance at him.

"How long have you been painting?" Helen asked.

Lizzy smiled. "Much longer than I can remember."

"Did you study with anyone?" Helen continued.

"For the most part, I'm self-taught."

Eric interrupted the conversation by passing around the lasagna again, fearing Lizzy would not care for too many questions. The trouble was that he knew his own mother loved to ask them.

"Your son told me that your family originally came from Valparaiso, Indiana," Helen asked once the lasagna, broccoli, and wine had been around the table again.

"He did?" Lizzy asked rhetorically, looking at Russ. "My family lived there for a short time."

"With your uncle?" Helen asked again.

"Why, yes," Lizzy replied, her eyes gleaming.

Eric couldn't figure out why his mother was persisting in asking all these questions. It was obvious, even to him, that Lizzy was getting uncomfortable.

"My family lived in Valparaiso at one time too," Helen added.

"How long ago was that?" Kevin asked.

"They all left before the turn of the century, I believe," she replied.

"In fact, I just received a copy of a letter that was written by my great-grandmother," Helen added, growing more excited. "A distant cousin sent it to me. I brought it along for Eric to read." Helen reached down to pick up her purse, which was under the table.

"That's amazing." Kevin stopped playing with his food.

"You can read it to me later, Mom," Eric said.

"I'm interested in hearing it," Kevin said. "It's not every day that you receive a letter from a long dead great-grandmother."

"That's how I feel about it," Helen agreed.

Eric glanced over at Russ, whose face was ashen.

"What was your great-grandmother's name?" Lizzy asked.

Helen turned to her and smiled. "Adelaide Mariette Pierce."

"Adelaide Mariette Pierce," she repeated in a monotone.

Eric wondered what was going on. It seemed like his mother was going somewhere with this.

"Yes, that's right," Helen said. "Were there any people of that name when your family lived there?" she asked.

"I haven't the slightest idea," Lizzy replied brightly. "I wouldn't mind listening to the letter. It sounds fascinating."

As his mother pulled out the copy of the letter, Eric felt completely at a loss. He couldn't imagine why both Lizzy and Kevin would be interested in such a thing. Russ, he thought, looked nervous.

"The letter was addressed to Celestia, my great-grandmother's sister," Helen began. "The family had the odd tradition of using their middle name. The letter is dated the twenty-third of December, 1908, written from Bemidji, Minnesota. Apparently, Mariette's son had died, though I'm not sure of the cause." Helen glanced down at the letter and started reading it.

> Celestia,
>
> I have found you. Our cousin Katie Skinner provided me with your address. I have terrible news. My son, Hollis, died near Bemidji almost at our very door. He was coming back from teaching school, and no one found him until morning. He seems to have taken a fever, though the Physician was uncertain. By the time we were found and rushed to his side, he was gone.
>
> Had we only known we could have gone to him in less than an hour, and one or the other of our family would have been with him. I do not remember the name of the Physician called to attend him. There is no Special Hospital Physician, we depend upon the City Doctors. Had we only known! So sad! A Stranger among Strangers.
>
> I am thinking of going to California and thought perhaps I would stop over and see you on my way down. Should I see you don't be shocked at my appearance. Old but not as yet feeble sans hair & teeth & wrinkled. Pioneer life for thirty years in the "Wilds of Minnesota" has left its mark. I am seventy-six on Christmas.
>
> I must stop right here or lose the opportunity of this sending to mail. We are three miles from town and only get mail once a week. We'll send this to the ranch as Cousin Katie thought that would find you. None seemed certain where you were.
>
> Your sister,
> Adelaide Mariette Pierce

"Isn't that remarkable?" Helen said as soon as she had finished. "This is the first letter I've ever had of hers—my branch of the family didn't keep old correspondence."

"Who was the son?" Kevin asked.

"My granduncle," Helen told him. "I've already written to the Minnesota Historical Society to see if they have additional information."

"It's a sad story," Lizzy said quietly.

Eric thought Lizzy looked dazed. Russ wouldn't return Eric's look, but only stared at the table.

"The language people used back then was so different," Kevin observed. "Where did you get this letter?"

"From a first cousin, one of Celestia's descendants," Helen explained, putting the letter away. "She had saved it all these years."

"Maybe you could ask her if they have additional information about the son who died," Kevin suggested.

"I'm a bit confused," Lizzy said, reviving a bit and leaning forward. "You asked me about Valparaiso, but this letter was written from Bemidji. That's in Minnesota."

"Yes," Helen explained, carefully watching Lizzy. "Mariette moved to the Detroit Lakes area of Minnesota to homestead. Hollis must have died near Bemidji. I'm surprised those who found him didn't recognize him."

"Mariette must have had a difficult life setting up a homestead," Lizzy reflected. "Are you a granddaughter of Hollis then?"

"No," Helen replied warmly, obviously enjoying talking about her family. "Mariette had three children—Hollis, Keziah, and Minnie. I'm Kezzie's granddaughter."

"I see," Lizzy said. "Did Hollis leave a family?"

"Oh, no," Helen continued. "Hollis was a confirmed bachelor."

"At least Mariette had her daughter's family to take care of her," Lizzy said absently.

"Well, that's true," Helen said. "Mariette lived with my grandmother until her death at the age of eighty-three."

"Eighty-three," Lizzy repeated, her eyes glittering.

Lizzy's behavior was so out of character, Eric thought. There was an awkward silence. Eric had never thought he'd see Russ's mother completely at a loss. His own mother kept staring at her.

"Well, how about some chocolate cake?" Russ suggested and stood up with a flourish. "Eric, can you give me a hand?"

As they left the table, Helen and Kevin continued to talk genealogy. Kevin asked about online genealogy sources. Lizzy didn't say a word.

"What was all that about?" Eric asked him in a whisper as soon as they were safely in the kitchen. "Why are you so upset?"

"We'll have to talk about it later," Russ said. "Why did you have to tell your mother that my family lived in Valparaiso?"

"You did," Eric told him in surprise. "Don't you remember? My mother asked you about all of that stuff."

Russ glared at him. "I told her?" he asked. He dropped his gaze. "I guess I did tell her," he muttered, more to himself than to Eric.

"Come on," Eric whispered and grabbed the cake. It looked even more lopsided than it had earlier. "They're going to wonder what we're doing in here."

During dessert, Eric noticed that Russ seemed to be avoiding his own mother—he wouldn't look at her. Lizzy, for her part, was subdued. Actually, Eric preferred this quiet Lizzy, but Russ's behavior made him nervous. Most of the conversation centered on Eric's new graduate program, which he was to begin in a week, and whether he'd been able to find a part-time job that would work with his class schedule. Eric thought that Lizzy was particularly quiet.

At one point, Lizzy turned to Helen. "I'm afraid I haven't asked Russ anything about your family," she began. "Are there other children?"

"No," Helen said. "Eric is our only one."

"And your husband?" Lizzy asked.

"Eric's father passed away a short time ago," she replied.

"I'm sorry to hear that," Lizzy said softly. "My husband died several years ago. It's a different life without them, isn't it?"

"It surely is," Helen agreed.

24

Moonlight, much brighter than usual, cast shadows along their bedroom floor. If Russ turned his head on the pillow in just the right way, he could hear Eric's heartbeat. He waited patiently, but it took hours before Eric's heartbeat slowed and his breathing became steady and deep. Russ could feel his mother calling him. Every time he heard a slight noise outside, he thought it might be her, beckoning. He didn't know whether she was angry, upset, or both. He only knew he had to get to her.

Now that Eric was sleeping so much more lightly, Russ knew it would take a special effort to escape from their embrace. He grew smaller and more lean. Once he was out of bed, he crouched next to the window, allowing the process to continue. He grew smaller and smaller. Such a drastic transformation was painful, but he felt that he had to get to his mother quickly.

He wanted to fly.

He imagined large eyes and huge wings. His body became more compact and the fabric of him turned in on itself. At last, he sprouted feathers. Then came the blindness. When he came to himself again, he had a brief horror of having a body almost too small for his spirit.

It had been a long time since he'd taken the form of an owl. Few creatures had better night vision. He would have to be careful, though, not to indulge the urge to hunt for prey in the darkness.

He flew into the night. The cool wash of air felt wonderful against his wings. The flapping made very little sound. It almost seemed as though he wasn't flying at all, except for the ground and buildings moving in a mosaic beneath him. He navigated by the light of the moon and could already see her window open for him. He regretted not flying longer.

His spirit was drawn to hers. It made things so easy.

The soft flapping of his wings against the windowsill, he assumed, must have caught her attention. Russ could see her sitting in the darkness of the living room, watching him. He flapped his great wings several times again before the change began to reverse itself. There was the blindness as he lost his feathers, and his body felt a release as it grew larger, though the stretching was painfully slow. He shook uncontrollably. Once he had limbs again, Russ had to rest on the floor to catch his breath; the blindness lasted longer than usual. Still, Lizzy didn't say a word.

"Mother?" he finally was able to ask. His sight was slowly returning. "Mother?"

"I'm getting too old for this world," she finally said in a horribly weary voice.

He had to crawl to where she sat on the floor. He put his arms around her. "I'm so sorry," he said.

"Why didn't I ever return to find them?" she said.

"Fear," he replied simply.

"I could have taken another form," she whispered. "I could have gone back. Poor Hollis."

"You started a new life." Russ felt the strength returning to his limbs and drew her closer to him. "I'm sure he understood that. Besides, you said it was too great a risk."

She hesitated. "You are right," she said. "But I missed Mariette and Hollis. It was a shock to hear of his death tonight. Especially from Helen." She laughed weakly. "She suspects something. She may already know."

"I doubt that."

"You have no idea," his mother persisted. "She is a capable woman, more than you realize."

Russ had thought she would like the fact that Helen was a great-granddaughter of her best friend. "Think of who her great-grandmother was. Why are you so fearful of her?"

"You didn't know Mariette," his mother said and pulled away from him. "She was as tough as nails. If Helen is at all like her, she will be formidable. Don't underestimate her."

"You're being paranoid," Russ said.

"You don't need to psychoanalyze me," Lizzy said. "I've taken care of myself for decades, and taken care of you. I am not paranoid. I'm being sensible, as you should be. It is difficult to predict what may happen. One must be careful and ever watchful." Lizzy paused. "This has been a stressful evening."

For a long while, Russ held his mother in his arms, listening to the muffled sounds of the city at night. He knew that she wouldn't cry. Even so, he could feel sadness all around her. He couldn't imagine what she must be feeling, to finally learn the fate of the people who had saved her, after all these years. Finally, he felt her body relax.

"At least Mariette lived a long life, with family around her," she said quietly. "I wish I could say the same for Hollis. I almost named you after him."

"You never told me that," Russ replied in surprise.

"Well, it's true." Lizzy looked around her. "I'm feeling better now. I should get some sleep, as you should." She stood, took a few steps, and then turned back. "I'm happy that you came to me. You helped." She looked stronger now. "But I know my own mind and I know when there's danger. I sense danger all around you and your lover. You'd best be careful."

Russ didn't bother with another transformation; instead he made do with an old pair of shorts and a tank top that he'd left at his mother's. It wouldn't do to walk home naked, he mused, though he had done it before. It had been a long time since he'd seen his mother so upset and fearful. There was no tellng what she might do. As he made his way home through the dark streets, his mother's warning kept ringing in his ears like a steady bird call.

The next day, the lovers visited Pacific Beach, not far from the most northern point, before the sand gives way to rocks, cliffs, and crashing surf. Russ insisted that they get out of the apartment to enjoy the sunshine. Eric would be starting graduate school soon, and they would have fewer opportunities to lie on the sand on a whim.

The sun felt so hot that they stripped to nothing but their shorts. They lay side by side on a large Mexican blanket Eric had bought in

Tijuana, blue and white like the sky. Russ turned toward Eric, but said nothing.

"Stop looking at me like that," Eric complained. "We're out in public."

"Let the public be damned," Russ replied, laughing. But he rolled onto his back. "What are you thinking?"

"Right now?" Eric asked.

"No, before. While I was watching you."

"I was thinking about your mother, and why she was so upset the other night."

"Haven't we already talked about this?" Russ asked, though he hated being evasive. "Forget it."

"You know we haven't talked about it!" Eric said with an incredulous look. "She really quieted down once my mom started in with her family history. And she seemed to be nervous discussing Valparaiso."

Russ looked out over the surf, watching the few souls playing in the water.

"I knew you didn't want to talk about it," Eric added.

Russ paused, deciding whether he really wanted to reveal anything. If Eric was going to understand Lizzy any better, he needed to explain things, at least to a point. On the other hand, he didn't want to risk his mother's wrath. "Well," Russ began slowly, "our families lived in the same area at the same time."

"I wondered about that," Eric interrupted.

"They knew each other better than you might think," Russ continued. "In fact, they were neighbors."

"You're kidding."

"Your mother's great-grandmother was my mother's schoolteacher," Russ explained. "They were also good friends."

Eric smiled broadly. "It's hard to believe. If I could only tell my mother about this, she would have a field day. Just imagine, my mom would flip out being able to talk to someone who had been close to her great-grandmother."

This was alarming. "You must never let on that I told you any of this. Not to anyone and especially not to my mother."

Eric gave him a you're-not-kidding look. "Do you really think I'm that stupid?"

"Of course not."

"What else do you know about my mom's ancestors?"

"Mariette was one of the few people to encourage my mother." He thought a moment. "I also remember my mother talking about a terrible accident—involving Mariette's husband."

"Yeah, it was a train accident."

"That's right. Mariette was a widow and raised a family by herself. She must have been tough."

"That's what I've heard." Eric paused, considering him. "I just thought of something. We're almost related."

"We are related," Russ reminded him. "We're lovers."

"You know what I mean," Eric said, growing more excited. "Tell me something," he added. "If they were close friends, why was your mother asking questions about Hollis if she already had the answers?"

This was one part Russ wasn't sure he wanted to reveal. "When she was about sixteen, my mother left Valparaiso for the East Coast to attend school. I don't think she kept track of them. The other night, she finally learned what had happened to her friends."

"No wonder she was so quiet after my mother talked about the letter." Eric shook his head. "So that's why you were so upset. You were worried about how your mother was going to react. I thought my mother was giving your mother the second degree."

"I was wondering about that too," Russ said. "Do you think your mother knows anything about us?"

"No," Eric said. "I'm not sure why she was pushing your mother so much. It got me worried too. I was afraid your mother might do something weird." He let eyes rest on the sand caked on his hands. "You've talked to your mother since last night, haven't you?"

Eric, Russ realized, was becoming more perceptive. It delighted him. "Yes," he said, smiling. "How did you know?"

"You were angry with her after the dinner," Eric pointed out. "Now, less than twenty-four hours later, you're trying to help me understand her better."

"Well, do you?"

"Maybe." Eric turned to him. "Is your mother doing okay?"

"Yeah," Russ told him. "Well enough."

They both sat up again, letting the sun drench their faces. Russ let it soak in, feeling more and more relaxed. He considered telling Eric the whole story about his granduncle Hezekiah and his mother's flight. He knew it would appeal to Eric's sympathy for the underdog. He glanced at Eric, so cute lying on the beach towel. Russ felt protective and proud of him at the same time.

"You're looking at me, aren't you?" Eric asked without opening his eyes.

"You look very sexy right now," Russ told him. "Sweat is beading up on your chest."

"Save it for later," Eric replied.

"Yeah. I guess you're right."

Russ was tired of having to hide his affection for Eric in public. He felt a need to be close to Eric at that moment, physically close, that he simply could not satisfy. He continued staring at his lover, watching his chest rise with each breath. Without thinking, Russ leaned over and kissed Eric on the lips. "Love you," he whispered.

Eric sat up. "What are you doing?" Eric loudly whispered, glancing over toward the water.

Russ followed his gaze. Apparently, a couple of guys walking by had seen them. "Oh, who cares?" Russ said.

"I can't believe you just did that!" Eric shook his head and smiled. "You're crazy."

"Crazy to love you?'

"Something like that." Eric laughed. "I'm thirsty. Do you want anything from the taco shop?"

"No, you go ahead."

Eric stood up, brushed some of the sand from his shorts, and started down the beach, toward the winding stairs to the boardwalk.

Russ watched the guys who had seen them. They were laughing, but not maliciously, Russ decided. The guys were young—still in their twenties and fairly burly, as if they worked out regularly. They moved with a bodybuilder's strut. Russ studied their faces—not bad-looking, perhaps on the rough side.

Russ looked away, not wanting to cause any trouble, as if he hadn't already caused enough. He rubbed his face on the blanket. When Eric came back, perhaps he would tell him more about what happened to his mother. If they understood each other a little better, his life would be much easier. The sun felt so heavy on him. When he looked up again, the two guys were already well down the beach, nearly under the pier, well out of the way. He could hardly wait for Eric to come back.

Eric bounded up the wooden steps, rushed past the public rest rooms at the top of the staircase, and then ambled along Diamond Street on his way to the taco shop for a drink. What Russ had revealed about their families amazed him.

The taco shop was not crowded. A short line of people was waiting to place orders. Rock music boomed from speakers hanging at each corner of the ceiling. The cook nodded and smiled at him from behind the counter. It felt good to be recognized. The crowd was young and only partially clothed. Eric felt very much at home here— after all, it was where they'd had their first date.

Eric liked the idea of their families having such a close connection. Russ's mother was sure to like him better now. It was as though fate had brought them all together. He wished he could tell his own mother—she would be in genealogy heaven.

After waiting in line, Eric placed an order for a large Dr. Pepper and an extra large 7UP for Russ, his favorite soft drink. For fun he added six rolled tacos, one of the specials, though he had to wait for them.

On his way back, he sipped the Dr. Pepper, thinking of Russ and what they might do when they got home. Eric was enjoying the few minutes away from his lover; it almost made him feel guilty. He passed a couple of teenagers heading away from the beach, which wasn't as crowded as it should have been. Inland clouds, he figured, had kept people away, in spite of the fact that it was blazing bright on the coast. A perfect time, he thought, immensely satisfied. He stopped at the top of the staircase. He saw Russ lying on the sand, already brown from the sun. He wondered if the tan was natural or if his elf child had been busy again.

Eric decided to hit the rest room and save a trip up the stairs later. He waited inside the door for his eyes to adjust to the dim light. The rest room was filthy—like they all were at the beach, smelling of urine, sweat, and a hint of ocean. He wondered what to do with the drinks and rolled tacos, hating to put them on the dirty floor. He finally placed them in the corner where it was dry and went to the urinal. In a moment he was joined by another guy.

Eric cautiously glanced at the man out of the corner of his eye. His companion was attractive, tall, and well-proportioned. Something about him seemed a little familiar, too, and Eric immediately thought of Russ's mother. Perhaps she was playing a trick. Suddenly, he was very embarrassed and he tried to hurry up.

The guy smiled at him, which Eric tried to ignore.

"Hey," the guy said. "I like the looks of you."

"Sorry," Eric quickly replied. "I'm already spoken for." Now he was almost sure it was Russ's mother. The timing was just too perfect. "I know it's you," he added. "I'm getting sick of your tricks."

The guy gave him a dirty smile that unnerved him.

"I could show you some tricks," the guy said and grabbed him by the arm.

"I said I'm not interested," Eric replied. He tried to pull away, but the guy was incredibly strong. "Look," he said, "this isn't going to do anything to improve our relationship."

"A relationship? You want to be my girlfriend, faggot?" the guy said and grabbed him by the other arm. "Or are you already somebody else's girl?"

"Hey," Eric said. "Let me go!"

"Are you looking for some dick?" He grabbed Eric's crotch. "You wanna suck my big dick?"

"I don't want any trouble," Eric said calmly, in spite of his racing heart. He felt hysteria closing in on him fast. He didn't think Russ's mother would go this far, unless she was serious about her threat. The thought crossed his mind that this could be someone else too, and he wasn't sure what was worse. He searched the guy's eyes for some sign of recognition, but found none. "I just want to leave, okay?"

"You don't want to leave yet, do you?" the guy said. "We haven't had any fun yet."

"Help!" Eric shouted, trying to get away from him. The guy pulled a knife.

"Oh, God," Eric said.

"You yell one more time and I'll kill you, faggot." He forced Eric to one of the toilets. "Let's see how much water a faggot can drink," he said, plunging Eric's head into the water with his free hand.

The smell was horrible—a combination of urine and shit. Eric struggled, in spite of the knife at his neck. He felt it cut into him and he froze, hoping this would be the worst of it. The cut burned like fire. The water felt sickeningly warm.

"Drink it, faggot," he said. "Drink it."

The man was unbelievably strong. He pulled Eric out of the water. "How did you like that, faggot?"

"Please leave me alone," Eric said, the filthy water dripping down his face.

The guy stepped around in front of him, still holding the knife, and kneed him in the groin. Eric doubled over, catching the knife with his face. The pain was unbearable, shooting up and through him, radiating out, throbbing. "Please stop."

Eric felt a blow to the back of his head. Thinking this might be his last chance, he ran blindly for the exit. The guy grabbed his foot to trip him and got on top of him. Eric screamed.

He began to stuff the bag full of tacos into Eric's mouth to gag him. "This will shut you up."

Pinning Eric's arms behind his back, the guy dragged him over to the urinal. The bag jammed in his mouth hurt almost as much as the cuts and Eric fought to keep it out of his throat, afraid he would choke. The pain in his groin was numbing.

"All faggots should die," the man said, pulling Eric's shorts down. "I want to see you piss again." The knife sliced into Eric's penis. Eric screamed a muffled scream and the tacos pushed into his throat, nearly choking him. It was like pissing sheer pain, like pissing rubbing alcohol or acid. His blood spurted into the urinal, turning the dirty white of the porcelain red. Blood everywhere.

Eric passed out and fell down, the pain was so intense. When he gained consciousness, the guy was kicking him over and over. Eric rolled on the dirty floor with the blows. He struggled, but it was no use, he was so weak. He wanted to pass out but he couldn't. Smack. Eric felt a rib break. The pain was everywhere. Smack. Another rib. Smack. Smack. Smack.

Eric felt little pulses behind his eyeballs. The pain was so intense he felt removed from it in an odd way, even though he could hear his bones breaking. There was a roaring in his ears.

Suddenly, he saw his mother looking down at him as he rested at her breast, feeling her warmth, his first mother, the one with green eyes and short, reddish hair, a large building where she left him, his new parents so happy, his first room, his first blue toy truck, Granny and Grandpa, so young, catching dragonflies at the lake, his dark-haired mother making chicken noodle soup, his first dog, the schoolyard, the fight with Steven in third grade, Granny's funeral, everyone in black, crying after being hit with a baseball, his first junior high prom, trying to avoid Cynthia, being taunted in high school, being called "faggot" the first time, his first car, his first boyfriend, Taylor, college and leaving Taylor, the woods near Salem, the trip to Venice and getting drunk on cheap wine, his father's funeral without any tears, college graduation, his mother so proud, snow everywhere, Kevin, computers, Russ, the first time Russ transformed, playing together in bed, Russ holding him, the princess's birthday, the window, the moon.

He was out of his body looking down at it, sprawled next to the urinal. The guy who beat him was no longer there. He was surprised that he couldn't see any blood.

Something yanked him out of the rest room through the roof. He could see Russ lying on the beach, all tanned and gorgeous. For a moment, he was right with him and Russ sat up, looking worried. But he couldn't stay. Something drew him up, away, hurtling into the blue of the sky so fast that it turned white and then very dark, like a tunnel. At the end of the tunnel, he could see a white light, a large chrysanthemum. All he wanted was to reach the white flower, moving ever faster, waiting to touch the softness of its petals.

25

Russ awakened, feeling Eric's presence all around him. He quickly sat up. Eric hadn't yet returned. Something was terribly wrong, he knew it. Worse than anything ever before.

The sun had moved—a good deal of time had passed. He felt dizzy with the heat and what must have been a heavy sleep. He couldn't remember, but he knew that he had been dreaming.

He glanced up at the stairs. He didn't think Eric would lose his way just walking back from the taco shop.

Russ started to run along the sand, and by the time he got to the bottom of the stairs, he heard sirens. The sirens grew louder and louder—he could not will them away. Up above, at the top, he could see a couple of people turning their attention suddenly, and the screaming sirens grew agonizingly loud. By the time he reached the boardwalk, the sirens had stopped and Russ could hear car doors slamming.

Two young men in blue police uniforms were rushing into the men's bathroom. Russ ran in after them. The police failed to stop him. There was Eric on the floor, half naked, covered in blood.

"Eric!" Russ screamed, and rushed to his side. Was he breathing? He had to help him breathe again. The smell was horrible, a mix of blood and piss. The blood looked more black than red on the dirty rest room floor.

The police pulled him back. "Wait a minute," one of them gruffly said.

"This is my friend," Russ said and pleadingly looked at the officer—the officer's face only registered with him for an instant, the short, dark mustache, blue or were they hazel eyes?

The other officer checked Eric's pulse. "I don't feel anything." Another siren—an ambulance?

Russ shook off the officer's hold and dropped to Eric's side. He'd been cut in the groin—blood was everywhere. He took one of Eric's hands but didn't feel any life there. "Oh, god," he sobbed, tears coming down his cheeks. Had he already gone? There was a cut on his face. Russ couldn't see any other damage. There had to be something he could do. He was looking at Eric—it was his body, his face, yet it wasn't Eric. He simply wasn't there any longer.

The siren grew louder and then ceased. Suddenly medics rushed into the rest room.

"Out of the way, please," one of them told him.

He almost pushed them all aside, to take Eric with him, perhaps to the ocean where he could help Eric turn into a fish or, better yet, a bird and take to the sky. But some part of Russ compelled him to stand back. The medics were Eric's only chance.

They began to work, attempting to resuscitate him, thumping on his chest, hooking him up to an IV—it was as if the dirty space had instantly become a hospital room.

"May I talk with you for a moment?" the officer, the one with the mustache, asked him.

Why wouldn't the face register with him? He wasn't really seeing these people—he knew that a moment later, he wouldn't remember them. Russ allowed himself to be led a few steps away, near the entrance.

"You said that you're friends?"

"Yes," Russ replied, completely distracted by what the medics were doing. Why did the officer have to do this now?

"What happened?" the officer asked.

Russ felt himself floating. He could hear himself replying to the officer, but it was as though he were someone else. Did he tell the officer how he and Eric had been down by the water? About the men who saw them kiss? How Eric had gone to get something to drink? Or how he'd rushed up to the rest room when he heard sirens? Then he thought he heard himself ask the officer who had found Eric. Who had called the police? Who could have done this?

"We got the call from a guy who found him," the officer replied. "Someone else is talking to him right now."

Russ forced himself to come back. He wanted to talk with the man who'd found Eric too, yet he couldn't possibly leave Eric's side now. The medics lifted Eric onto a stretcher.

"We're getting a pulse," one of them said to Russ and the officer.

It looked like they were getting ready to take him to the hospital. Russ strained forward to see his face—was he really back? Was Eric really there? "I want to go along," he said.

"Are you family?" came the reply as they began wheeling him out.

"Yes," he said without explanation. He was going along no matter what.

"Let's go," the medic said.

Russ looked at the officer. "Do you need my name?" he asked, afraid the officer would want him to stay.

"You already gave it to me," the officer replied. "You go ahead with your friend. We'll catch up with you later."

Once Eric was wheeled into the ambulance, Russ and two of the medics piled into the back while two others rode up front. There were so many tubes and wires that it was hard to see Eric's face fully—Russ had to lean forward, putting his own face very close to his lover's. Yes, Russ thought, there might be life there. Eric's face was still chalk white, but some pink was returning to his lips, those lips he had kissed so many times. If only he could breathe more life into those lips, that mouth. The medics continued to work, injecting liquid into the tubes, monitoring every sign. "It's looking better," one of them said. "He's starting to fight."

The siren sounded oddly muffled inside the ambulance. Russ didn't get the impression of speed; it seemed more like slow motion. Would Eric ever open his eyes?

"Is there a concussion?" Russ asked.

"Yes," one of the medics told him. "He's also been kicked. Looks like some of his ribs have been broken. There may be internal bleeding."

Russ looked at the young man, the bland face, with—were they blue eyes? He didn't understand why nothing was registering with him. All that he could see was the chalk white of Eric's face.

Suddenly, Russ felt a horrible tingling all up and down his spine. He realized that he was about to transform into something, he wasn't sure what. His stomach was already turning and he could feel his toes retract. This could mean only one thing—he was turning into some animal. He quickly glanced down—luckily his sandals were hiding enough of his feet to mask the change, at least for the present. Russ closed his eyes and tried to get a grip on himself. He concentrated on his current form, the form Eric so loved. He told himself that he had to stay whole so that Eric could recognize him. As difficult as it was, Russ managed to unravel the change. He slowly felt himself relax, the knot in his center loosening. Russ imagined himself whole again, with all ten toes, perfect, ready for Eric to compare with his own, side by side in bed. Gradually, the tingling subsided and he could feel his body relax into its previous form. He opened his eyes. Yes, he was all there again.

"Are you doing okay?" a voice asked him.

"Yeah," he said. "I'm okay."

The ambulance pulled up to the emergency entrance. They scooted the gurney out of the vehicle and into the hospital, with Russ close behind, down a short hallway, to the right, through swinging doors.

"I'm sorry," came a voice. "We need you out here for a moment."

He couldn't follow Eric any longer. He resisted the urge to transform into someone else. Was there a hospital uniform somewhere? He had to be near his lover, but he was uncertain of his abilities. What might happen? What if he began another transformation? What kind of animal might he become?

Another voice, "Could I have you complete some forms?"

Forms? Russ stepped up to the emergency reception desk. He could be filling out a form while his lover was dying. Name, address, insurance. Did Eric have any insurance? Birth date, parents' names—he couldn't even remember the first name of Eric's father. Allergic to any medication? Currently on any medication? Prior illnesses—whole columns of them. Current problem—a sliced penis. Loss of blood. Concussion. Broken ribs. Chalk-white face.

There were so many questions he couldn't answer, so many gaps in what he knew of Eric. Their lives had crossed less than a year ago. Russ realized that he needed help, he had to call for help.

"May I use your phone?" he asked the clerk. What were the telephone numbers? He didn't know them. "Do you also have a telephone directory I could take a look at?" he added. He would call Helen first, then Kevin. As he looked up the numbers, he tried to find the words to explain what had happened, but none came to him, only a horrible feeling.

Suddenly, a hand grabbed his shoulder. He turned. Was this the doctor? The man appeared to be too young to practice medicine. "I need to talk with you immediately," the young doctor said. "Let's sit down."

Helen's hands shook as she gripped the steering wheel of her car. How could this have happened? She had often experienced moments of fear, a silent acknowledgment of the danger that seemed to lurk everywhere. But none of this could compare to the horror of being told that her only son had been attacked and was in the hospital. Russ had not even known the name of the hospital. He had to ask someone. As she waited, holding the phone, the initial shock gave way to momentary hysteria. Perhaps it was just as well that he was away from the phone or she might have blamed him for whatever had happened and accuse him of being some kind of monster who'd endangered her son. As it was, by the time he came back to tell her the name of the hospital where her son might be dying, the feeling had passed, or at least she was able to suppress it.

She was driving much faster than usual—as she went through an intersection, she was greeted with a chorus of car horns and only then realized that she had run a red light. She slowed down enough to see that no one was hurt, she had caused no accidents. She wondered if any of them would sympathize with her if they knew the circumstances. She decided that they probably wouldn't care. They all had their own lives. She was only an old woman, a bad driver, who'd been in their way.

She pulled into the hospital parking lot, trying to imagine what her son's injuries might be. She couldn't shake an image of his face, beaten and bloodied.

Helen rushed into the emergency room. She found Russ slumped forward in a chair. When she sat down next to him, he started up. "Helen," he said, with a wild look in his eyes. "I'm glad you're here."

It seemed to her that he had been crying. "How is he?" she asked. "Have you been able to talk with the doctor?"

"He was called away," Russ replied, nearly sobbing. "I've just been waiting out here. No one has told me anything." His eyes wandered. "I couldn't even fill out the forms."

Helen could see that he was completely beside himself. His forehead was covered with tiny beads of sweat, yet when she touched his arm, it was cool, like marble. "Perhaps if I talk with the receptionist," she suggested. Russ's condition had a strange calming effect on her, as if she could be strong knowing Russ needed her. She left him to walk up to the desk. "You've admitted my son, Eric Taylor. Could you please tell me how he is doing?"

"Just a moment," the clerk replied. "I'll see if the doctor is available. We had another emergency a few minutes ago."

Helen sat down again, not understanding why the clerk didn't tell her anything. Certainly he would know. She debated whether to go through the doors and find Eric—after all, she was his mother. When she reached out to comfort Russ, she noticed that she was shaking again. "What happened?" she asked him.

It took Russ a few seconds to register and understand the question. Helen thought something about him was off, something besides the current dilemma, but she couldn't place it. He seemed like a different person somehow.

"We were at Pacific Beach," he began haltingly. "Eric went to get something to drink. He was gone too long." Russ stopped, as if he had lost his train of thought.

"Yes?" she encouraged him.

"When I heard sirens I ran up the steps." Russ glanced at her. "Eric was attacked in the rest room." He paused again. "It was awful. There was blood everywhere."

Helen cringed and tears began to flow. Her son's blood.

"He'd been cut in the groin," Russ continued in a shaky voice. "The medics thought he had a concussion. They said it looked like he'd been kicked in the ribs."

"Horrible," she said. "Who could have done such a thing?"

"I don't think there were any witnesses," Russ replied.

Helen hesitated, frightened. She couldn't help but feel that the blame rested with Russ. In all the years that Eric had been losing his way, nothing like this had ever happened. A dozen questions flashed through her mind: Who are you? What are you? What have you done with my son? But she controlled herself. Her husband had always admired her self-control. Now there was a bitterness to her memory of this admiration. She almost wished she didn't have any self-control at all. Then she could get all of this out into the open. The main thing now, she reminded herself, was Eric and only Eric.

Finally, the doctor approached them. "Are you Eric's mother?" he asked.

"Yes, I am," she replied and began to stand up. The doctor was so young—it astounded her.

"No, you don't have to get up," he said and crouched in front of them.

"How bad is it?" she asked. The doctor looked very concerned. "I want the truth."

"All right." He took in a short breath. "We've moved your son into intensive care. He has suffered a concussion, massive internal injuries, and a severe cut on his penis. He's lost a great deal of blood and has not regained consciousness." The doctor paused. "I hate to tell you this, but the injuries are so severe that there's a chance he may not make it."

"Oh, no," Russ said.

"What are his chances?" Helen said.

"His condition is serious—it's too early to judge yet," the doctor replied. "But he's young, strong, which will help him."

Before Helen could form her next question, Russ shot out of his chair. "No! Someone is going to pay for this," he said loudly. All eyes in the room were on him.

"Russ!" she said, astounded by the strength of his reaction. "Please sit down. This isn't going to help anything."

"No!" he snapped, his eyes blazing, threatening.

The doctor stood up, as if to protect her. "Please settle down," he said.

Helen was too shocked and upset to be fearful. Suddenly, Russ turned and ran out of the emergency room. Several people in the entryway had to step aside for him.

A weird calm came over the room after he had fled. When she came to herself again, Helen asked, "May I see my son?"

There was no turning back now, no chance to unravel the transformation, no chance to center himself or find the core of his old self. He was transforming into something—likely some kind of animal. There was no point in trying to control it, despite the danger. If he turned into a small animal, he risked being run over by a car. If he turned into a large animal, like a leopard, a tiger, or even a gazelle, he risked drawing too much attention to himself here in the city. The safest thing was to fly. He could only hope that his body would follow a reasonable course.

It had always been this way. Anger was one of the most difficult emotions for him to control and the one most likely to bring about a rapid change. His mother often chided him about this weakness.

In his heart, he sensed that his mother had nothing to do with the attack; moreover, he didn't think it would be possible for her to do such a terrible thing. Yet his anger was taking him places that neither felt right nor made sense. Part of him watched the anger take charge of his actions, felt embarrassed that he had created such a scene at the hospital, despaired when he left his lover. But the anger had become his dictator—he could only watch helplessly.

Russ wasn't aware exactly when the change took place. It seemed as though at one instant he was running faster than he'd ever run before and the next minute he was flying through the air. It occurred to him that the blackout might have blocked his awareness of the transformation or, more likely perhaps, the anger had.

Russ was uncertain what type of bird he had become, but as his anger subsided, he was afraid his transformation might unravel too soon. As he made his descent to his mother's condo, Russ began to feel the unraveling even before he cleared the open window. He didn't realize that he had flown into the bedroom. A swarm of bees immediately surrounded him. Bees were everywhere—covering his wings, buzzing near his bird eyes, burrowing through his feathers to his skin.

He lay paralyzed on the floor as the transformation continued to unfold. At some point, he was blinded, either by the process of the change or by the stings. As the change was taking place, Lizzy must have pulled him from the bedroom. When he regained consciousness, he found himself lying on the couch, her worried face hovering over him. Before he could say anything, the stings— there must have been at least a hundred of them—healed. The dissipating pain felt like the tingling of his limbs after a heavy, motionless sleep.

"What's wrong?" she said, more worried than he'd seen her in a long time.

"Someone attacked Eric," he replied weakly. "In a rest room at Pacific Beach."

"I had a feeling something like this would happen," she said after a moment. "You weren't able to protect him?"

The question stung as painfully as the bees had. "I wasn't there."

Her eyes began to change, growing lighter in color until they were almost amber. "What happened?"

Russ sighed, still weak. "Someone got him with a knife." He hated to repeat everything. He could feel the anger building again. "They must have kicked him too. The doctor said he has massive internal injuries and a concussion. The doctor doesn't know if he will make it."

His mother stared at him, tears filling her eyes. He could sense that her pain was real. Did she really have anything to do with the attack?

"Who's with him now?" she asked.

"His mother," Russ replied, acutely reminded that he hadn't been able to control his emotions enough to stay. He had abandoned them there. Ashamed, Russ started to cry.

"It was too much for you," she said, as if reading his mind. "It was better to leave, instead of transforming right in front of them all."

Her sympathy almost made him more ashamed. His crying stopped.

"You can stay here," she said softly. "Until you can pull yourself together."

Russ didn't tell her the other reason why he felt ashamed. He didn't want to admit that he suspected her. He hoped she wouldn't pick up on his feeling. He tried to dismiss the thought before she sensed his fear.

"Did anything unusual happen before the attack? Were you with Eric anytime before he was attacked?"

He had always wondered at her ability to immediately find the core of a problem. "Yes," he replied. "We were down on the sand. Eric went to get something to drink and then he didn't make it back."

"Was there anything unusual?" she persisted.

The kiss, Russ thought. "I kissed Eric at the beach, before he left for the drink."

"Did anyone see you?" she asked.

"Yes," Russ admitted. "There were two guys who saw us. They were laughing at us." Now he began to feel guilty about his kiss.

"Could they have been the ones who attacked him?" she asked. "Is it possible?"

"Yes," he said, his strength coming back. "I'll need to tell the police about them. They could have been the ones."

"Possibly," she said sadly. "But remember, it could just as easily have been someone else. You can't jump to conclusions."

"No," he said, disturbed by her reasoning. What else did she know?

26

That night at their apartment, Russ dreamed of Eric, as he looked after the attack. There was the dingy rest room, the horrible smell of urine and blood. Eric was lying on the floor in a pool of his own blood. As Russ gazed at his lover, Eric pulled his bloody body up from the rest room floor and faced him. Russ couldn't turn away from the horrible sight. Something held him there. Russ cried out in frustration, but Eric did not move. Eric's body began to change very slowly. The wounds healed, the blood disappeared. Eric smiled at him, a beautiful, joyful smile. Russ tried to speak, but Eric put his fingers to his own lips.

Russ woke up with a start, alone. The moon was shining through the window.

The morning after the attack, Helen diligently watched her son's face, waiting for some sign of awakening. No matter how long she kept her vigil, however, the face remained lifeless. If it hadn't been for the monitors telling her that he was still alive, she might have believed him dead. She wondered if the horrible flourescent lighting was creating an illusion. The doctors said a blow to the head had caused the concussion. A bandage hid the horrible bump above his forehead. The doctors were even more concerned with the internal injuries, which they were certain had been caused by repeated blows to his ribcage, probably from someone kicking him over and over again.

She leaned over to bring her ear near his face, trying to hear his breathing. She could barely detect movement there, perhaps a little stronger than she had felt earlier. This time, she could also feel a suggestion of heat. She pulled back and delicately placed her hand on his forehead. It felt very hot, as though he had a temperature. She glanced around the stark white room as if looking for help. It was cluttered with so many pieces of movable equipment that she felt claustrophobic. A spiderweb of wires and tubes hung around them. The doctor had told her there was nothing she could do, but she refused to go home.

Helen hated the sound of the dialysis machine; she had tried to get used to its rhythm, but she found it impossibly distracting. Eric had been beaten so horribly, one of the specialists said, that his kidneys had failed. The whole idea of her son's blood being pumped out of his body was completely repulsive to her. She had never thought she would be at all squeamish about such things and had even considered being a nurse at one time. Perhaps, she thought, it was different when the patient was your own son.

Earlier she had been forced to send Kevin home. She had delayed as long as she could, but he was too distraught over Eric's condition and she couldn't handle trying to comfort him any longer. He looked so defeated and helpless, like a large, sad puppy. All he could say, over and over again, was how he couldn't believe anyone could do this to Eric. More troubling to her, though, was Russ's disappearance. She thought he should at least have called. She sensed that Eric needed him and, despite her misgivings, part of her wanted him there, threat or no threat. Another part of her, though, was secretly glad that he had remained absent. She couldn't help but think he had something to do with what had happened to her son.

Helen opened her purse. Inside she found the materials she had been poring over for weeks. First, she carefully unfolded Russ's birth certificate. There it was: 1947. Mother's maiden name: Lizzy White. How could he look so young, a middle-aged man? Next she pulled out U.S. Census sheets that she'd found, showing her great-grandmother's neighbors. There was Hezekiah White, wife Carrie, and niece Lizzy. Never had she been more thankful to have an excellent memory. When she'd seen Lizzy's maiden name, and recalled Russ's middle name, everything started falling into place. Although she felt gratified that she'd found these connections, she had yet to fathom their full implications. How could these people possibly be as old as this data suggested? The image of the blood-red, dancing flower kept coming back to her. What could explain this? And now, with Eric so ill, Helen had never been more frightened in her life.

She glanced at the floor. Several magazines lay there, which she had barely looked at. *Ladies' Home Journal* and *Good Housekeeping* seemed trite—articles about gardening, the latest fashions, and recipes did not interest her in the least. She looked back at Eric, wondering if she would ever have need of another recipe to fix something special for him.

Helen slipped the material about Russ back into her purse, fighting back tears. She was sitting by her son's hospital bed, but would it help? There had to be something else she could do. She took Eric's hand. It was clammy. She recalled times she'd held his hand before, especially when he was a young child. He never failed to reach for her hand when they were out in public. He seemed to require that kind of reassurance. She almost always acquiesced. She squeezed his hand. Was he still there? Helen felt Eric's hand stir. His hand was now squeezing hers. She looked at his face. Was there a change? No, his eyes were still closed. But behind his closed lids, Helen could see that his eyes were fluttering. Eric was dreaming! And some color had come back to his face! Helen quickly stood up, dropping her purse on the floor as she reached to press the call button for the nurse. She felt something wonderful was happening.

Helen didn't have to wait long. Even so, she thought Eric was improving by the second, perhaps enough to awaken. The nurse, a young woman in her thirties whom Helen recalled seeing the night before, rushed into the hospital room. "Is something wrong?"

"He squeezed my hand," Helen explained.

"That's wonderful," she said and began taking Eric's pulse. "He looks better, doesn't he?" she added, studying his face.

"His eyelids were moving," Helen told her.

"Looks like he's come out of the coma," the nurse announced. "See this monitor?" she said, pointing to one of the small screens. "This is showing some brain activity."

"What grand news!" Helen felt like clapping her hands. She hoped she didn't look too ridiculous in her excitement. "Eric?" she asked. "Eric!" she said louder.

"He'll come around soon," the nurse told her reassuringly. "I'll put a call in for the doctor. He'll want to see this for himself."

"Isn't there anything else we can do?"

"Keep praying."

After the nurse left, Helen sat back down and took Eric's hand again, but she couldn't feel a response. Even so, she remained hopeful—there was color in his face and it seemed as though he were just asleep. She could detect a slight fluttering behind his eyelids as well. He was mending. She wondered how long it would take for the doctor to arrive. Perhaps the doctor would take him out of intensive care.

"Come on, honey," she said, tenderly smoothing his brow with her fingertips. "Keep fighting. You're going to make it." When she drew near him again, she thought she could detect the scent of urine, which surprised her. She checked to see if Eric had soiled his sheets, but there was no visual sign of urine, only a faint, very faint smell. The thought reminded Helen where Eric had been attacked. She winced.

As she sat back in her chair, she heard someone slip into the room—she assumed it was the nurse, since not enough time had passed for the doctor to arrive. She glanced up. It wasn't the nurse. It was Lizzy.

"You didn't expect to see me here, did you?" she asked.

"No," Helen replied. "I didn't."

It seemed that Lizzy had dropped any pretense of being old enough to have a twenty-year-old child. She was dressed in skintight jeans and a white, short-sleeved blouse that showed off her beautifully lithe figure. Thick brown hair cascaded down her back. What Helen still couldn't believe was how young her face looked—her skin was as smooth as a twenty-year-old's and just as tight. There was no sagging or puffiness anywhere. Her dark eyes glittered. Helen couldn't help but feel shocked and threatened at her sudden appearance.

Lizzy came farther into the room and stopped at the foot of Eric's bed. "How is he doing?"

"Better," Helen answered. "I think he's coming out of the coma, and I'm waiting for the doctor to check on him." Helen felt helpless and uncertain what to do. She glanced at her son. His color was improving, there was no doubt.

"I'm glad to hear it," Lizzy added and smiled at her.

Helen stared, trying to understand. Could she have had anything to do with the attack on Eric? If so, both she and Eric were in terrible danger. Another part of her yearned to know whether this strange woman could help.

"Russ told me how serious the injuries were," Lizzy added, moving closer to her. "Has there been any change?"

"They're concerned with his internal injuries, especially his kidneys. There was also a terrible gash in his groin."

"People can be so cruel," Lizzy added grimly. She reached out to touch him.

Helen involuntarily flinched and Lizzy withdrew.

"I don't blame you for not trusting me," she said.

Helen was surprised by Lizzy's response. She wondered why Lizzy was willing to be open with her. Helen's initial response was guarded—she couldn't shake her fear of this woman, almost numbing in its intensity. But she also realized that there might be something to gain from being honest and open. Even more important, Helen didn't want to lose the opportunity. She reached into her purse and pulled out the copy of Russ's birth certificate, handing it to Lizzy.

Lizzy barely glanced at it. "You are a resourceful woman, like your great-grandmother."

Helen was flabbergasted. Lizzy was admitting she had known Helen's great-grandmother. "What are you?" Helen asked, trying not to sound too harsh.

Lizzy chuckled. "That's a good question. What do you think I am?"

Helen hesitated. She was already regretting falling into this conversation, but there was no turning back now. She could already see, however, that Lizzy was fond of playing games. "Neither you nor your son seem to experience the process of aging," she said carefully. "That's all I know." Helen paused. "You knew my great-grandmother Mariette, yet you look young enough to be my own child."

"You are very much like Mariette—you know how to get to the point." Lizzy smiled again. "How were you able to find me?"

Helen wondered what Lizzy had in mind for them. "The census records for Valparaiso were a part of the puzzle," Helen finally said.

"You've looked at the census?" Lizzy asked with surprise.

"There's a library here that has complete census rolls from 1790 to 1920 on microfilm," Helen explained. "It's the keystone to every genealogist's work. I merely put the pieces together."

Lizzy laughed. "I've been found out by a genealogist." She sighed. "In a library."

Helen didn't take the comment as an insult, though she supposed that she could have. "May I ask you something?"

Lizzy nodded, still smiling.

"*Why* haven't you aged all of these years?"

Lizzy's eyes grew cold and sharp—so much so that Helen was afraid again. Then, just as quickly, Lizzy's manner softened.

"I'm sorry," she said. "I am not accustomed to being asked direct questions about my abilities. Let's just say that I come from a long line of people who do not age. My son inherited this from me. I believe that an ancestor of mine must have had a mutation that took away the body's ability to age. You see, no matter how old I become, I will remain ageless, even to the day of my death."

"How long do your people live?" Helen asked, curiosity overcoming her fear.

"For a very long time," Lizzy replied.

"Eric will age, but Russ will not age." Helen looked at her questioningly.

"That's true," Lizzy replied. "It's a curse not to be able to grow old with the people that you love and, worse yet, to see them die."

Helen looked at her son—she feared he was still in danger. "Did Eric know this about Russ, that Russ was not capable of aging?"

"Yes," Lizzy said, her eyes narrowing. "I didn't agree with Russ's decision to confide in your son, but the decision was not mine to make." She paused. "It's very important to me that this be kept a secret." Her eyes appeared to become darker. "Will you promise, now that you know this of us, to keep it a secret?"

"Of course," Helen answered and then feared she had done so too quickly. But the way Lizzy was staring at her, she would have promised most anything. "It must be terrible to keep such a secret," she offered.

"People have a hard time accepting people for what they are, especially if they are perceived to be different." Lizzy looked at Eric and then back at Helen. "I know you understand this as well as I do."

"Yes," Helen replied. "Unfortunately, I do." Although she knew it was dangerous, she had to ask Lizzy one more question. "I don't mean to be rude," she began, "but was Eric in danger because of what he knew about Russ?"

Lizzy closed her eyes. The expression on her face, a mixture of anger and desperation, frightened Helen to the core, so much that she would have left the room if Eric hadn't been lying there.

Lizzy opened her eyes. They were filled with tears. "Please believe me when I say that I would never harm your son or you. Your great-grandmother was one of the few people who understood and supported me. I would never do anything to harm any of her relations."

"I didn't mean . . . ," Helen began.

"No," Lizzy said firmly. "There is no need to explain. Just know that I'm telling you the truth."

Helen was still. There was no point in arguing with her. Although in her heart Helen believed her, something also told her that she might have been protesting too much, trying to hide something. "I understand," she finally said.

"May I take your son's hand?" Lizzy asked.

Helen froze. She didn't want Lizzy to touch her son but felt that she didn't have a choice. "Of course," she replied, trying not to sound too reluctant.

Lizzy took Eric's hand and closed her eyes. All Helen could do was wait and watch, hoping no further harm would come to him.

27

Lizzy held the hand of her son's lover, allowing her body to connect with his, attempting to get a sense of the extent of the injuries. She could tell immediately that the blow to the head was less severe than they all had thought. Even now, she could feel him swimming up from unconsciousness, ready to break the surface. The other injuries were more troublesome. She sensed terrible harm to his internal organs. The doctors were right, his kidneys had received the worst. She sensed them shutting down, disintegrating.

His vital signs were weak—heart rate, blood pressure. She sensed, however, that he wanted to live. But he would need help, more help than she could give him. Or might be willing to give him.

Lizzy had mixed feelings about the bond her son had forged with these people. She deeply resented having to share her secrets. She still wasn't certain Helen didn't know more than she was letting on. Lizzy found it difficult to read her, just like her great-grandmother Mariette. She had an obstinacy as hard as stone.

However, the more she explored, the more Lizzy sensed Eric's good nature, his boyish exuberance. She could understand why her son loved him. Even in the shadow of his injuries, Lizzy could sense the core of robust, vigorous manhood. His life was full of promise. She sensed his spirit, an innocent heart. Along with all of this, Lizzy felt Eric's love for Russ.

She could feel a slight shift in Eric's body. He was struggling to come back to them. Lizzy liked him in spite of herself. She wished she could say the same of Helen.

Lizzy was fearful, but the fear was now tempered, she realized, with something else. In her wildest dreams, Lizzy never thought she would be able to talk to anyone except Russ about her special abilities. It had given her a sense of peace to be honest, at least to a certain extent, with Helen. The step gave her both a thrill and a feeling of accomplishment. After all these years, in a way it was like coming home again.

Suddenly, Lizzy felt a surge of energy flow through Eric's body, from his head down through his spine, along his limbs, and out through his hands and feet. She opened her eyes. He was coming back to them. She glanced at Helen and smiled. Helen looked so painfully worried—now, at least, she would have some hope. "Come and take my place here," she said. "I think he's waking up."

Helen hurried around the foot of the bed and stood in her place, gracefully taking Eric's hand as Lizzy offered it to her.

His eyes were fluttering. His arms moved, his hand clenched and unclenched. The only thing that troubled Lizzy was the yellowish tinge to his skin. She could see that he had more hurdles to clear.

His eyes opened. "Mom?" he said.

Russ awoke with a start. Had he been dreaming? Was Eric really bloodied, unconscious, and lying in a hospital bed? He looked at the clock. It was late in the day. He'd never slept so long. He'd never imagined it possible.

He rushed to the telephone. Messages were waiting for him and, with a growing sense of panic, he knew they must concern Eric. He replayed them. The first was from Kevin, who wondered if Russ had been to the hospital and asked if he had any news. The second message was from his mother.

"Russ, this is your mother. I've just come from the hospital." A shot of adrenaline surged through his body. "Eric has come out of his coma and is asking for you. Where have you been?" She continued in a more authoritarian tone, "I'm worried about you and don't understand why you haven't been to see him. Please go to the hospital at once. Helen and Eric are expecting you." There was another pause. "And please call me."

The call would have to wait. Russ, charged with the good news, immediately left for the hospital. Joy surged within him. Eric was awake, and Russ wouldn't be alone.

It was so wonderful to see Eric's eyes open, to hear his voice again. Helen attempted to put her arms around him while avoiding the wires and tubes. She kissed him on the forehead, below the bandage. He looked bewildered, but at least he was with her again.

"What happened?" he asked in a raspy voice. "Where's Russ? Where am I?"

"You've been hurt," she replied, blinking back tears. "You're in the hospital." She turned to look at Lizzy, but she had slipped away. How could she have gone so quickly, without a sound? "Russ isn't here right now," she told him, deciding not to let on that Lizzy had visited. "I imagine Russ will be here soon." At least she hoped he would.

"I feel like I've been asleep for a long time."

"Like Rip Van Winkle?" she playfully asked.

"Is it that bad?" he asked and tried to sit up.

"Don't move yet," Helen said, afraid he might dislodge one of the tubes. "You've been in the hospital now for a couple of days."

"Was it an accident?" he asked.

Helen realized that he didn't remember anything about the attack. This worried her. She hoped he hadn't suffered any permanent brain damage. "No," she admitted.

"Then what was it?" he asked, still groggy.

"Honey, someone attacked you at Pacific Beach when you were there with Russ. Do you remember going to the beach?"

Eric was silent and it looked as though he might fall asleep. She wondered why his skin looked so yellow. "No, I don't remember anything like that," he said with his eyes closed. "The last thing I remember was going to bed."

"What month is it?" Helen asked, trying a different tack.

"I'm not sure," he admitted, opening his eyes slightly. "I feel like I want to throw up, but I'm too tired."

"Oh, dear," she said and began to adjust the bedding. She tried to shake off the feeling of despair that came over her—after all, she told herself, he had only been awake for a short time. He was bound to experience some pain and memory loss. As she dabbed his forehead with a wet washcloth, the nurse came into the room.

"How is he doing?" the nurse asked.

"He's talking," Helen replied breathlessly.

The nurse took his wrist to check his pulse. "I'm glad to see you awake. How are you feeling?" she said to him.

"I've been better."

"I bet you have." The nurse turned to Helen. "I should call the doctor again—I know he'll want to see Eric immediately."

"That would be fine," Helen replied.

"I'll be back shortly," the nurse told Eric. She smiled at Helen reassuringly on the way out.

Eric reached out for Helen's hand and she fought the urge to cry. She couldn't help thinking of when she had first taken him home as a baby. He had reached for her hand then too.

After the doctor left them, Eric slipped in and out of consciousness. Now that there had been a change, Helen felt even more anxious, even though it had been for the better. She feared Eric might slip back into the coma and grew impatient for him to improve. Eric looked so yellow, and perspiration had beaded up on his face again. His breathing was shallow.

Just as she was ready to call the nurse again, Helen heard footsteps. It was Russ. In spite of her apprehension, she felt relieved that he was finally here. "Russ, I'm so glad to see you." When she took Russ's hand to lead him to the bed, she was surprised that it was shaking so.

"Hey, Russ," Eric said weakly and smiled.

"Hey, Eric," Russ replied, though he didn't sound pleased.

Helen was taken aback by Russ's behavior. He didn't seem to want to touch Eric. She hoped Eric was still sleepy enough not to notice Russ's reaction. She wondered why Russ seemed so hesitant. She only hoped he wouldn't make another scene.

"Am I going to be okay?" Eric asked. Helen wasn't sure if the question was directed at her or Russ.

"Yes, dear," she replied. Eric looked so vulnerable and lost.

"I'm glad you're here," Eric said, looking at Russ. "I'm really beat." His eyes slowly closed.

Helen moved toward Eric, while Russ remained standing at the foot of the bed, looking completely forlorn. "Why don't you come a little closer?" she suggested.

Russ inched closer. Helen wondered why he was so afraid. "Russ, what's the matter?" she asked.

"I'm sorry, but I'm not feeling well," he replied cautiously. "What have they told you?"

Helen moved closer to him, to whisper, "The doctor was here about two hours ago. It doesn't look very good, I'm afraid. Eric's kidneys are failing, and the doctors are trying dialysis." She was alarmed at the fear she saw in Russ's eyes.

"This is horrible," Russ said. "Wasn't he doing better?"

"Well, he has come out of his coma. That's a good sign."

He looked at her with strange eyes—more yellow than green, like cat eyes. "I can't stand to see him like this," he said, almost pleading with her. "It's too much for me. I keep seeing how he looked when we found him on the floor of the rest room. I can smell the urine now, just like I did then." He nearly choked. "It's a horrible smell."

Helen, who couldn't smell anything, didn't believe her own eyes—she was sure she could see the same yellow hue in Russ's skin as in Eric's. He was nearly beside himself. His breathing was rapid and beads of sweat were forming on his brow.

"What if he doesn't make it?" Russ asked her in the same pleading voice. "I don't want to live without him."

"It will all work out," she said in the most comforting manner she could muster. "We'll make it work," she added, moving toward him, intending to take him in her arms.

"No," he said, backing up. "I'm not well."

Helen stopped. "Let me help you, then," she said.

"I'll be okay," he replied. "I just have to get out of here."

Again? Helen thought. But perhaps it would be best if Russ left. She wasn't sure what would happen if he stayed. "Why don't you come back a little later?"

"Yeah, I'll try," he added sincerely. "Forgive me."

Once he'd left, Helen sat in the chair, taking Eric's hand. Joy had given way too quickly, she mused. Eric glanced at her, perplexed. All she could do was to squeeze his hand. She thought she must be mistaken, but Eric's skin looked even more yellow than it had before Russ had arrived.

After a time, Eric fell asleep. She couldn't detect any movement, not even a fluttering of eyes behind closed lids.

Russ stood outside the hospital's front doors, unable to go any farther. He felt amazingly weak, and he could smell urine on his own breath. He sat down on the sidewalk and doubled over. After a moment, he looked at his hands. His skin had taken on a strange, yellowish hue, like Eric's.

He had been shocked at Eric's appearance, but that wasn't the only thing. The longer Russ stayed, the more unsteady he felt. It was as though he had fallen into step with Eric's body. Russ could feel Eric in a struggle—he saw Eric's blood, thick with poison. It was as if Eric were swimming in a sea of toxins. Eric looked so weak, a shadow of himself.

Helen hardly registered with him at all—though he knew she was trying to protect and include him. He felt at a loss for how to acknowledge her, which made him feel guilty. As he stood in the hospital room, a horrible feeling came upon him in wave upon wave. There lay Eric, and Russ could do nothing.

As he crouched on the sidewalk, Russ tried to shake off the image of Eric, confined to his bed, restrained by tubes and wires, struggling to survive. He had to find a part of himself that wouldn't bend with illness, wouldn't flow in harmony with his lover.

Russ wasn't sure he could sever the connection. His heart was beating too fast. Sweat dripped off his face. He took several deep breaths. He could sense people pausing near him, could almost hear them asking if he needed help. He had to break the connection with Eric. He searched for some small corner of himself, but he found Eric everywhere.

There was only one thing he could find that didn't belong to Eric. It was anger, the anger he felt at whoever attacked his lover. Russ let the anger float around him; its energy was raw and pure. He concentrated on it, letting the anger flow through him.

By the time medics came, Russ could stand. Everything was all right. At least for now. Russ glanced up at the sky. The sunset was upon them, and the sky had taken on a deep red-purple, like crushed grapes.

28

Helen walked down a maze of hallways to the urologist's office. She detested flourescent lights. Nothing appeared as it should . . . the faces she passed, the bulletin boards plastered with notices, the white tiled floor, all glowed with an unearthly quality. It had been a week, and Eric had not improved.

The receptionist asked Helen to step into a consultation room. A few minutes after she took a seat, Dr. Adams, a darkly handsome man she had spoken with only once before, joined her. All the doctors seemed to be too young these days, or perhaps, Helen thought, it was more a matter of her growing older. She began wondering if the doctor was married, or if, perhaps, he was gay. His deep brown eyes and pleasant manner were becoming. Did the doctor know that her son was gay, and would this make any difference in how Eric was treated? She dismissed the thought, passing it off as irrational speculation fueled by lack of sleep. If only she could confide in Dr. Adams, telling him everything she knew about Eric and, especially, about Russ. Perhaps the doctor could cure her heart of skipped beats. "Thank you, doctor, for seeing me," she said.

"We're all concerned for your son," he said.

"What's causing Eric's infection?" Helen asked.

"We can't be certain," the doctor said. "It may be caused by the fistula, the line I inserted in his arm to access the bloodstream for the dialysis. The tissue around the incision is swollen. Unfortunately, antibiotics don't appear to be effective."

Helen nodded in agreement. She could picture Eric, lying in his hospital bed, wracked by fever. She resisted the impulse to start crying. Since the attack, she had felt numb. She hoped she would remember the details of her conversation with Dr. Adams, so she quickly fished pen and paper from her purse. "Eric is so confused," Helen said.

"Yes, if there are complications during dialysis patients can develop low blood pressure, confusion, and even seizures. As you know, the dialysis isn't working as well as we had hoped. Because of this, Eric is also experiencing some of the symptoms of renal failure."

"How dreadful," Helen said. This certainly explained what she'd been observing. Yet, there had to be some solution. "Are there other options?"

"Of course, there's transplantation."

Yes, Helen had already thought of it. "Would you recommend a kidney transplant?"

"In Eric's case, I would," the doctor replied.

"Why?"

"After doing some further tests, we've determined it is likely Eric has polycystic kidney disease," the doctor explained. "It's a hereditary disease in which cysts grow in the kidneys. Eventually, the cysts can almost completely replace the healthy kidney tissue. The attack Eric suffered may have greatly worsened his condition."

A mass of cysts, Helen thought. She imagined them expanding, ever larger. What a horrible legacy from his birth parents. "Why didn't we know about this condition before?" she asked.

"It can take years for symptoms of this disease to manifest," the doctor explained.

"Will the disease spread to a transplanted kidney?" she asked.

"Absolutely not," he said. "In fact, I believe the only chance Eric has to lead a normal life is with kidney transplantation. Dialysis is only a temporary solution, and transplantation is especially needed in this case, given Eric's present condition."

The only chance. The decision was obvious. "What's the next step?" she asked.

"We can use a kidney from a relative or nonrelative, but his chances go up if we use a kidney from a blood relation. People who receive a kidney from a family member generally survive longer and experience fewer complications."

Helen shuddered. A blood relative. "I'm afraid Eric is adopted," she said. "We don't know where his birth parents are."

"Could you find them?" the doctor asked.

Dazzling sunlight momentarily blinded Helen as she stepped out of the medical complex. She had to fumble around in her purse to find her sunglasses, a gift from Eric for her last birthday.

Perhaps now, she thought, Eric wouldn't mind if she were to indulge in her obsession for research. The doctor's challenge continued to echo in every thought. "Now I'm going to find Marie Thompson, no matter what," she said.

The morning came with sunshine streaming through the window, their bedroom window. Russ reached for Eric, even though he knew Eric wouldn't be there. The movement itself was a comfort, a gentle reminder. Only a few days ago, he would have found a warm, familiar touch, soft skin at the curve of the hip, a hairy chest to caress. Eric would have slipped into his arms, with his mouth half open for a kiss. They would have moved together over the bed, pulling back sheets and exposing their bare skin to the new light and to each other.

He opened his eyes to the same light, but the bed was cool to the touch. Why, he wondered, did the sky appear to be a darker shade of blue when framed by their bedroom window? Had Eric put a hex on the space, some signature energy that electrified the sky? Was the deep, deep blue a sign that he might come back?

The anger was still there, helping his body retain its healthy form. Even so, Russ felt that he couldn't go back to the hospital. Seeing the sickness in Eric would be too much for Russ to handle, at least for now. Russ sensed the anger growing stronger. It demanded revenge. "Who did this?" it whispered.

He heard an intense buzzing and a hummingbird flew through the open window. It hovered inches from his head, staring intently at him. He marveled at the creature, so beautiful with its scarlet neck and electric green wings. Russ sensed a movement at the doorway. He immediately thought of Eric. When he turned, though, it was his mother.

The bird flew away. "Making a new friend?" she asked with a smile. When she came closer, her manner became more grave. "What has happened to you?" she asked.

"I may need your help."

She rested her hand on his forehead. "I can detect Eric's illness when I touch you."

He looked up at her in surprise. He could feel Eric through her. "You touched him, didn't you?"

"Yes," she replied quietly.

She had tried to help him. Certainly, this was proof beyond all doubt that his mother had nothing to do with the attack.

"Turn over," she asked, and he complied. Lizzy started working at his shoulders with her fingers. "You shouldn't be around Eric, at least for awhile. You are too vulnerable. You've grown so close that your body is responding to his with complete sympathy." She paused. "I sense a great deal of anger."

"Yes," he said. "It was the only thing that saved me yesterday. Anger helped me break the connection."

She continued to massage his shoulders. "Anger can be a dangerous thing."

Did she already know what he was going to ask of her? "I'd like to find the scum who attacked my lover."

"I thought as much," she replied. "Do you know how many times I've thought of revenge over these many years? I'm not convinced that it would have helped."

Russ felt the energy slip away. Was the sickness returning? "I'd like your help," he repeated.

She removed her hands. "What would you like me to do?"

Russ turned over to face her. His mother's eyes were so soft and warm, brown like chestnuts. "Tap into Eric's memories."

"I'm not sure I should attempt such a thing, Russ." Lizzy looked away. Was there sadness in her eyes?

"I'm sure you can do it. Eric may not remember," Russ continued, "but his body will. This is the only way I'll be able to know for sure."

"That's not it," she said, faintly smiling. "I'm not sure I wish to be a party to revenge, that's all."

A party to revenge. Was that all there was to it? If the attacker went free, how many others would be hurt? Or was he trying to deceive himself? "This may be the anger speaking through me, but I feel as though I must confront whoever attacked Eric. I'm not sure what will happen, Mother, I only know that this is something I must do."

She thought for a moment, her face reflecting a strange combination of despair and anticipation. "I believe that I understand," she finally replied, "and if this is important to you, I will help." She hesitated. Did she want him to change his mind? To stop her? "I'll step into the other room. You shouldn't see this."

After Lizzy left, a heavy silence settled over the bedroom. Soon, he would confront the truth. Russ could feel the anger begin to grow again, and the more it grew, the more convinced Russ was that confronting the attacker would turn back the clock and bring Eric back to wholeness. Some small part of him realized how irrational the thought was, but he couldn't help embracing the idea. In any case, the feeling steeled him for what he now realized would be the confrontation of his life. Soon, everything would again be right with the universe.

When Russ thought his mother would be well into the transformation, he quietly approached the living room door. He knew that she was probably right—seeing Eric's form might be too much for him, but he wanted to witness his lover whole again. Besides, his strength, aided by the anger, was returning. He pushed open the door just enough to peer in without, he hoped, disturbing her. Her back was turned to him. The process of changing looked almost complete. She had slipped out of her clothing so her body would have enough room to expand to Eric's size and form. There was a slight glow as her skin rippled and stretched over growing bones and flesh.

Eric had come back, whole and complete. Seeing the form of his lover again, even from the back, gave Russ a sense of peace and completeness he hadn't felt in days. It was the same back he had soaped up every day in the shower, the same thick, brown hair he had played with, the same muscular body he had loved to hold. Suddenly, Lizzy rested her hand on the wall to maintain her balance. Russ wondered what she was remembering from Eric's body. Then Russ could see bruises develop along the side of Eric's torso.

Russ stepped away from the open door before it was too late. Seeing signs of the injuries brought back the other memories and he could feel some of his newly found strength evaporate. He couldn't let it happen. He wondered why his mother had to experience pain. Couldn't she access the memory without it?

He waited. Soon, he knew that he'd discover the truth, and learn who had attacked his lover. Russ felt more complete, in an odd way, as his anger took over again. Russ seized upon the image of a healthy Eric, imagining them making love in the moonlight from their bedroom window. Soon he'd be able to avenge this loss. Soon, he felt, everything would take its rightful place.

He braced himself. Had she captured the image of one of Eric's attackers? Before he saw her, Russ heard her. "There was only one man who attacked your lover," she said in a deep, disturbingly familiar voice.

A man stood in front of him—a tall, well-built man with short, black hair. Russ gasped. It was Troy.

29

Helen fumbled with her car keys, trying to stop the tears from falling. She wanted to be at the hospital, but she didn't have a choice: she had to do her best to find Eric's birth mother. Helen carefully placed the directions to Kevin's home on the seat next to her.

Eric had frequently told her what an expert Kevin was on the computer. Now she would put him to the test. She shuddered to think of the task ahead—finding her son's birth mother, something she had always dreaded. Helen recalled what her husband often told her: "Darling," he would say, "if you fear something for too long, it may come true." She seldom mentioned her fear of confronting Eric's birth mother, but he seemed to know just the right time to repeat the refrain. With practice, she learned to shut him out, but not the fear. She could never be rid of that.

Though rain had come the night before, the sky was clear, making the glare off the slick streets especially troublesome. Thankfully, Kevin's apartment house was not difficult to find; it did take Helen a moment to navigate the intercom system. It seemed needlessly complicated.

"Come on up," he said excitedly.

She didn't bother waiting for the elevator. Climbing the stairs would do her good. Kevin opened the door with a smile. It looked to Helen as though he'd lost more weight. She was proud of him, knowing what self-control it must have taken to drop those pounds. The apartment was a horrible mess, with clothes and newspapers lying everywhere. Helen tried not to look too shocked or disgusted.

"Sorry about the mess," Kevin apologized.

"That's quite all right," she said with a smile. "Where's your little friend?" She hadn't yet heard a squawk.

"Bird's sleeping, which is a good thing."

"Would you like to get to work then?" she suggested.

Kevin showed her to the back of his apartment, explaining that the computer was in his bedroom. She found it charming when he told her that he hoped she didn't mind. What a gentleman, she thought. She'd seen enough bedrooms in her day, though she did wonder why he didn't set up his office in the living room. She did her best to ignore the mess. They sat down in front of the computer.

"I've been thinking about this," he began. "Let's start with what we know about her."

"Agreed," she said.

"We have her name, bad address, the name of the adoption agency, the address of the adoption agency, and that's about it." Kevin paused. "Some time ago, Eric and I tried a phone number listed for her in Albany, New York, but the number wasn't current. According to the adoption agency, she was moving out to California, but I've never been able to come up with a number for her here."

"That brings us back to the address," Helen said. "Did she leave a forwarding address at the Albany Post Office?"

"No," he replied. "I've already checked that."

"Perhaps there's another angle," she began, thinking. "Let me see the address again." She studied the letter. "She lists an apartment number, which implies, of course, that she was renting."

"That's true," Kevin agreed.

"I wonder if there is a way, using your computer, that we can determine the name and address of the owner of the apartment house where she lived. Then, perhaps, we can ask the owner or the manager if there was a forwarding address." She waited eagerly for his response.

"Yes," he finally responded. "I believe that there might be. There must be an online service for real estate. Let's go online right now and check out one of the search engines."

Helen watched as Kevin handily maneuvered the software for his online service, wincing at the horrible screech of the modem as it hooked up to the service. "What if someone from the hospital tries to call us?" Helen asked, realizing that being online would tie up the phone line.

"Don't worry," he said. "I have two separate lines."

"Oh, I see." She felt completely out of her element.

With a few clicks of the mouse, he was at a search engine. He quickly typed a question relating to real estate online services. A long list of links appeared. "Let's go to one of them," he suggested.

Within a few moments, they had accessed the Web site for a service. From what Helen could read, they would be able to access real estate information from all over the country online, including New York State. This was just what they needed. In reading the information, however, Helen noted that the service would initially cost fifty dollars a month, with additional online charges for each search, charged by the minute.

Before she could say anything about the charges, Kevin began to sign up for the service and to download the software he would need to access it.

"I will reimburse you for this, of course," Helen said.

"That's not important," Kevin insisted. "But thank you for offering."

Helen considered him. Eric had been fortunate in finding such a friend, but she wondered if something more was between them—at least on Kevin's part. It was difficult to tell for sure.

As Kevin downloaded the software, Helen became a little edgy, so she called the hospital. There was no change. Helen left Kevin's number, just in case.

As she waited, Helen noticed a newspaper clipping sitting next to the computer. She began to scan it. It was a profile of a man named Tony Singleton—a common name. The headline read "Tony Singleton. Hard Work Breeds Success." Helen scanned the one-page article. Singleton was an investment banker for a brokerage house back East who'd come home to establish his own consulting firm, the fourth of five boys, growing up in a home "dominated by sports, especially wrestling." He and his wife had three daughters.

"Is this one of your clients?" she asked.

"No," Kevin said with a grunt. "That's someone I met online." "He's a low-life. He two-times on his wife with guys."

"That's terrible," she said. "Why did you clip the article?"

"I thought I'd show it to the guys," he explained. "Once Eric gets better."

Helen took a closer look at the photo. What a darkly handsome, brooding man, she thought. His features were sharp and perfectly symmetrical. She wondered at the secrets his eyes held. How could Kevin know such things about him? She studied Kevin's profile. Did Kevin have any inkling of Lizzy and Russ's special abilities? Lizzy, of course, had implied that Eric had been the only one to know. But Helen recalled that Eric would often confide in Kevin even when he would not confide in her.

"It's up and running," Kevin excitedly told her. "I'm going to log on to the service."

She could hardly believe that the service had taken so little time to set up, and she wondered if it would work. A menu appeared on screen that listed the states available from which to obtain records. Kevin quickly selected New York. Another menu appeared, requesting search by name, address, or parcel number. Kevin chose address.

"What is the address again?" he asked. As soon as Helen read it to him, Kevin rapidly typed in the address and then clicked on an icon that read "begin search."

Almost immediately, the tax information on the property at that address blinked on the screen. It included the name of the owner, Timothy Biddle, and a mailing address and phone number. "Let's call," Kevin said.

Helen dialed the number, trying to keep her heart from pounding so, afraid that the person on the other end might hear it. A man answered, with a voice Helen thought too young to belong to the owner of an apartment building.

"This is Helen Taylor calling for a Timothy Biddle," she began.

"Speaking," he replied. Now her heart really was beating too fast. "Are you the Mr. Biddle who owns an apartment building at Grape Street?"

"Yes, I am," he replied. "What is this about?"

She paused, suddenly uncertain where to begin. "I'm looking for a woman named Marie Thompson who might have rented an apartment from you."

"That rings a bell. What is this about?" he repeated. She could see that this would be more difficult than she had thought. She glanced at Kevin, who was staring at her. It was even more unnerving now that it seemed certain that she'd found the correct Timothy Biddle. What if he chose not to cooperate with them? "Marie wrote my family a letter," she carefully began. "She indicated that she was moving to California, where we live," she paused, groping for the right words. "Marie didn't contact us after that and we would like to find her. We're worried." She decided not to add what they were worried about.

"Are you related?" he asked.

"Yes," she lied. "We are."

"Let me check my records and see if she left a forwarding address." A long silence followed.

"Mrs. Taylor, Marie did leave an address with me, 2537 Ivy Street, Apartment #14, in Los Angeles." There it was. Her hand trembled so as she wrote the address down that she was afraid she might not be able to decipher it later. "Thank you so much," she told him before he hung up the phone. "Should we dial directory assistance?" she suggested.

"No," Kevin said. "I'm not sure it would do any good. I've already checked the latest directories for Marie's number here in California. We'd have a better bet going through the property search again."

Kevin went back to work, connecting to the real estate service. Once again, he typed the address and a name blinked on the screen. It was so terribly simple, almost unnerving. Luckily, this was an investment company, Action Investments. Surely, Helen thought, a phone number would be easily found in this case, though none was listed in the property record. Kevin gave her a thumbs up as Helen dialed information to ask for the number of the investment company. The operator gave her a number. She paused before dialing again, telling herself to calm down. She dialed. A woman answered. Helen decided to get right to the point. She immediately asked the young woman for the name and telephone number of the resident manager of the apartments located on Ivy Street. She had the number within a moment. "Diane Martin?" Helen asked.

A young woman's voice answered, yes. "This is Helen Taylor calling from San Diego," she began. Her heart was fluttering. "I'm looking for a woman by the name of Marie Thompson. We received a letter from her months ago telling us she was moving here to California, but we haven't heard from her." Helen paused, but there was no response, only a sudden intake of air. She glanced at Kevin, who shrugged. "She's related to my son," Helen added.

"I've got some bad news for you," Diane told her in a hushed voice. "I remember Marie. She rented an apartment from me several months ago." Diane paused again. "Marie said that she was going to find a job and told me about coming out here to get acquainted again with family. Later that week, I hadn't seen her in a while and no one else had either. I got worried and went into her apartment." Another pause. "She was dead."

Helen gasped. "What happened?"

"The coroner did an autopsy," Diane replied. "It was a heart attack."

"Oh, my God," Helen said, nearly crying. "It was so important that we contact her. My son needs a kidney transplant and we were hoping that Marie might have been able to help us!" Her heart was beating so hard that she was afraid it would burst.

"Helen," Diane said, "I am so sorry. Are you related? I did talk with Marie's sister after she died. I believe her name was Elizabeth?"

Diane was asking her for confirmation of the sister's name! Helen remained silent, not wanting to offer any lies. Kevin held his finger to his lips, apparently agreeing with her.

"Could she help?" Diane persisted.

Helen told herself to calm down. Marie had a sister. "Yes," she said. "She might be of help. Do you have a number where I could reach her?"

"Yeah, sure," Diane replied. "Just a second."

As Diane went to find the number, Helen took some deep breaths and tried to calm herself. It looked as though Kevin wanted to say something, but he remained silent.

"Helen," Diane told her in a gentle voice. "Her number is 555-1458." She paused. "I'm sorry about this. Let me offer you some advice. No matter what happened between all of you, the important thing is for you to get together again. Family is important."

"Yes," Helen agreed. "Family is important."

When Helen hung up, Kevin reached for the phone to dial the new number, anxious to continue. Helen balked. "I need to use your bathroom, Kevin," she said. "I need a little break from this."

She found that she was unsteady on her feet and felt embarrassed. Helen closed the bathroom door behind her and turned on the water. She cupped her hands to wash her face. The water felt amazingly cold; it was just what she needed.

After all these years, to find out that Eric's birth mother, the person she had always feared, had died, was a shock. For a long time, she had harbored the secret hope that his birth mother would die, so that she would never have to worry about her again. She had daydreamed about this, a daydream that had been a strange comfort. Now that it was reality, she felt incredibly guilty. Eric desperately needed his birth mother and he couldn't possibly have that help now.

Helen searched for a clean towel. Dirty clothes were piled everywhere on the floor. The bathtub and sink were filthy with dirt and rust stains. She wondered how anyone could live this way. She finally found something that looked moderately clean.

The only hope was Marie's sister. Helen had to pull herself together if she was to convince this stranger that she should help them. When she came out of the bathroom, Helen found Kevin waiting anxiously by the computer. "Are you feeling okay?" he asked, with obvious concern in his voice. "I'm sorry if I was too pushy. I get that way sometimes."

"That's quite all right," she said. "This has been a difficult day." Helen sat next to him again and pressed the button for the speaker phone. As she dialed the number, she felt like she was floating. The phone rang several times. A man answered.

"This is Helen Taylor calling," she began. "Is Elizabeth there please?"

"Yeah, sure," came the response. "Lizbeth!" the man yelled.

After a few moments, a quiet female voice came on the line. "Hello?"

Her voiced sounded like a godsend. Now what would she say? Helen glanced at Kevin as she fumbled with the first few words. "You don't know me," she began, "but I'm Helen Taylor." She paused, suddenly choking up. "My son." She paused. "I was trying to reach your sister and discovered what happened to her."

"How did you know my sister?" she asked suspiciously.

Helen placed her hand on Kevin's knee to steady herself. "Marie wrote to me several months ago. She wanted to contact the family who adopted her son twenty-one years ago." There it was—almost all of it out in the open, but Helen didn't feel any sense of relief.

"Oh, no," Elizabeth replied.

"Did you know that Marie gave up a son for adoption?"

"Yes, I did," she replied. "That was so many years ago. Marie didn't tell me that she'd written anyone about this. I never thought she would ever want to find that child, not after what happened."

Helen paused—this sounded ominous. "What do you mean?" Helen asked.

There was a pause on the other end of the line, although Helen could hear breathing. Helen didn't dare say anything else for fear the woman would hang up on her.

"I'm not sure I should tell you this quite yet," she slowly replied.

Under normal circumstances, Helen might push on, but in this case, the most important thing was to find a potential donor, so she decided to let the comment pass. "That's quite all right. I don't mean to pry."

"I don't mean to be rude, but could you explain why you're calling?" Elizabeth asked, with a decided edge to her voice. "You must know that my sister died several months ago. I don't know why you'd want to contact me."

Helen took a deep breath. "My son, Eric, is now twenty-one years old. Just this week, he was horribly beaten, so badly that his kidneys are failing." She looked at Kevin, who moved a little closer to her. "My son has polycystic kidney disease. The doctor suggested a kidney transplant." She paused. "A transplant from a related individual has a better chance of working." Helen couldn't hear any response on the other end of the line. The silence was so deafening that she was afraid that Elizabeth was no longer there. "From a related individual, the success rate goes up to about 80 percent." Helen waited for some response.

Elizabeth finally spoke up. "You want me to give up one of my kidneys?"

This didn't sound promising. "Well, if not you, then perhaps another member of your family. I know it's a great deal to ask, but would you consider having the doctors see if there would be a good match?"

Silence.

"Eric is a wonderful son," she began pleading, afraid that she was sounding hopeless. "He's my pride and joy. I don't want to lose him."

"It's not that," came a halting reply.

Helen thought that Elizabeth might be crying. "What's wrong?"

"It must run in our family—both Marie and I had trouble with our kidneys."

Helen's heart skipped a beat.

"I've been going through dialysis myself. My kidney wouldn't do your son much good."

Kevin pulled away from her and quickly grabbed a pen and piece of paper. He gave a her note which simply read, "Other family?"

Helen smiled at him in thanks. Was it hopeless? To come this far for nothing? "Are there any other family members who could be possible donors?"

"My parents are both dead. They were both only children. I don't have any children, nor did Marie," she hesitated. "Except for the one baby, of course."

Another dead end. Helen thought there had to be something. "What about other family? Anyone from your mother's family? Perhaps you might have second cousins, other relatives who might be able to help."

There was a pause. "I don't know of any." Another pause. "You know, Marie completed a family tree for us a few years back. Let me see if I can find it."

There was another period of silence as they waited. Helen thought it strange that Marie had shared her interest in family history. She heard a rustling in the background and Elizabeth was back on the line.

"It's like I thought," she told her. "As I said, my father, Alan Thompson, was an only child, you see. I wanted to see if I had any second cousins, but the family tree is incomplete."

"What was your mother's maiden name?" Helen asked.

"Skinner," she replied. "Though I didn't know my maternal grandparents. Let me take a look at the family tree."

Skinner. One of Helen's family names. How ironic, she thought.

"My grandfather's name was John Reid Skinner, who married Elizabeth Evans."

Helen was taken aback. Reid was one of her family names, too. "Where was your grandfather born?" she asked.

"Valparaiso, Indiana," Elizabeth replied.

Helen wasn't sure that she heard clearly. "Did you say Valparaiso, Indiana?" she repeated.

"Yes, I did."

This was overwhelming. There were only a couple of Skinner families in the Valparaiso area, and both of them were related. Could it be that she and Eric had come from the same Skinner family? It was incredible. Her hand started to shake. "Can you tell me who was your grandfather's father?"

"Let's see," Elizabeth began. "I really don't see how this will make any difference. This goes back so far." She paused, apparently reading the family tree Marie had prepared. "John Reid Skinner was the only son of Hollis Reid Skinner and Lydia Garrison. Hollis Reid Skinner was the son of John Richard Skinner and Emily Ward Reid, both of Valparaiso, but natives of Vermont. Would you like me to go on?"

Helen couldn't say a thing. Kevin looked at her questioningly.

"Are you there?" Elizabeth persisted.

"Yes, I'm still here," Helen replied. "I'm in shock. Your great-grandfather Hollis was the brother of my great-grandmother Adelaide Mariette Skinner Pierce. We must be third cousins."

"Are you joking?" she said, incredulous.

"Absolutely not," Helen said. "Could you send me a copy of what Marie put together?" She wanted to confirm what Elizabeth had told her.

"I have a computer with e-mail," Elizabeth replied. "Why don't I just e-mail it to you?"

Kevin scribbled down the address for her. "Here it is," Helen told her, spelling it out.

"It will be there as soon as I can scan all of it in," she replied. Hesitantly, she added, "Are you sure this will help?"

"Yes, I believe it will," Helen said. "Thank you."

"Wait, before you hang up," Elizabeth said in a pleading tone. "Please, let's stay in touch."

"Of course," Helen replied. Eric, after all, was Elizabeth's closest blood relative. How strange that Helen was one of her relatives too. "I'll call to let you know how things turn out."

Helen was stunned by the news. She silently watched as, in a matter of minutes, Kevin retrieved the e-mail and printed it out for her. She began reading the family tree information immediately. Marie had done her homework—there was really no doubt that they were third cousins. That would make Eric Helen's third cousin, once removed.

Helen didn't even want to think of the possibility, for fear that it might not work, but she kept asking herself if she was closely related enough to be a good match for Eric. She could give him one of her kidneys, both of which she supposed were good. She could literally give him part of herself. Perhaps she could save him.

"Are you thinking what I'm thinking?" Kevin asked. "You're going to give him one of your kidneys, aren't you?"

"We'll have to see if it's a good match," she replied. She didn't think Kevin believed it either. The world was a much smaller place than she had ever imagined.

On the way to the hospital, Helen, who usually did not give in to spontaneity, decided to stop at her son's apartment to tell Russ the wonderful news.

30

Russ lay on their bed, gazing out the window, waiting for his full strength to return. The blue of the sky was streaked with white wisps of cloud which, he knew, would turn to scarlet at sunset. How many times had they made love there on the bed and fallen asleep to the sound of their hearts beating? He wondered if they would ever be here together again. He brought back the body memory of them lying together, the warm closeness, the softness of Eric's hair brushing against his neck. His strength returned twofold. He decided he was ready.

He stood, naked, in front of the bedroom mirror. This, he knew, would be the most difficult thing he would ever do. He closed his eyes and opened his mind, asking for Eric. He let the thought float. He could see Eric—the bloodied Eric. He tried harder. The injured Eric began to dissolve, the Eric with mangled face and crushed bones. Russ imagined how Eric looked that last time they were together on the beach. Slowly, the image took shape in his mind. Finally, Eric's brown eyes, his wavy dark hair, his smile, his body, began to form. Russ could finally see Eric's face framed in the blue and white, smiling down on him. Once the image was perfectly steady, this smiling image, Russ let it expand, pushing through his skin. There was the feeling of expansion, of fluid motion, throughout his entire body. When he opened his eyes, Eric looked back at him from the mirror. Beautiful Eric.

As Russ leaned toward the mirror, the image of Eric leaned toward him too, until only a film of glass separated them. The lovers kissed.

Eric stood at the end of the earth, where dark ground met foamy sea. Out of the belly of the dark blue ocean, a man floated. Strands of spidery ocean grass clung to his hair, his thin, crusty waist, his scaly legs and webbed feet. Washed ashore, his lips parted, the man awakened. His breath was sweet like cut pears. His teeth were as white as clamshells. His eyes, glittering green, gazed at Eric, puzzled, as if he had been asleep in the dark for too long.

Eric held him fast as the salty water washed over them. An expression of fear settled in the man's face, sculpting the seafoam and brown algae that clung to his skin. A plastic cord had cut into the man's lower leg and webbed foot. Eric reached down to grasp the cord, yet the man didn't flinch. With hands unencumbered by webs, Eric released him.

As the merman swam back out to sea, he beckoned Eric to follow, but Eric held off, uncertain. When they reached the deep, would they . . . would they kiss?

Russ slipped out of their apartment and drove off, trying to recall exactly where Troy's place was, mentally retracing their steps from where they had met. This time, Russ thought, he would not hold anything back.

After a few minutes of indecision, Russ finally settled on a shabby two-story apartment not far from The Pit. There was something about the front door that he recognized—it might have been the papered-over glass window at the top, or the peeling paint. He walked up to the apartment and knocked at the door. There was no answer. He was tempted to simply turn the knob until it collapsed, broken, but he knew this would be foolish. Instead, Russ slipped around the apartment house, easily climbing over a fence and dropping into the backyard. Just as he thought, there were plenty of windows, one of which was slightly open.

Inside, Russ sat on a threadbare couch and waited. He was pleased with himself for maintaining Eric's form without fighting any instability. None of Eric's sickness was returning; in fact, Russ felt as strong or perhaps stronger than ever. It was the cool anger that fed him, the pristine, mercury-silver anger that had been his companion since he'd discovered that Troy attacked his lover. He'd never felt so calm or in control. Russ could wait forever, if necessary, for Troy's return.

The apartment was much as he remembered it, dusty and not lived in. Russ inhaled deeply. There wasn't even a hint of food, only a suggestion of urine and old sex. He quietly crept down the short hallway to the bedroom, Troy's playroom. Here, the scent of sex was much stronger. There was the mat, torn on one corner. Near him lay a bunch of condoms scattered on the floor. Wrestling gear was piled up along one of the bare walls. A full-length mirror hung on the wall next to the door. In it, Russ was startled to see Eric looking back at him. He tried not to gaze at the image too long, for fear the transformation could start to unravel or Eric's sickness would return. Along the mirror's edge, Troy had placed Polaroid photos of various pickups: decked out in wrestling gear, acting tough for the camera, crouched down as if they were about to leap into the fray.

Russ turned away and shed his clothing. Naked, he went over to the pile of wrestling gear and selected a black singlet that fit. He stretched out on the mat. The anger was still there. Russ concentrated on his body, calling on even more strength, crouching in the wrestler's pose, laughing. This would be the match of Troy's life.

When the sun began its descent, the nature of the light subtly changing, Russ heard voices. Russ hoped that the addition of another person wouldn't complicate matters. The door creaked open. He crouched on the mat, waiting for them to enter.

Troy walked into the bedroom with a young, well-built man in his twenties, a baby face of a pickup. Once he saw Russ, Troy stopped in his tracks. His companion also looked surprised.

"I guess I should have told you that I'm not into three-ways," the companion complained. "What's he doing here?"

Troy didn't say a word, though Russ could see recognition in Troy's eyes—and growing fear.

"Hey, what's going on?" the companion asked. After a few moments of silence and no explanation, the young man slipped out of the bedroom with only a furtive glance back.

"What are you doing here?" Troy said. He was amazingly attractive, with a muscular build, severe features, and startlingly brown-black eyes. Compared to Eric, however, he was nothing.

"I want a rematch," Russ told him, rising from his stance and taking a cocky pose. "You had me at a disadvantage the last time."

"You can't be who I think you are," Troy said with narrowed eyes.

"You think I should still be in the hospital?" Russ said and smiled. "Or dead?"

"This is too weird," Troy said, backing out of the room.

"Are you afraid, faggot?" Russ challenged him.

Troy hesitated at the door.

"You pussy," Russ provoked him. Now Russ could see anger overtaking Troy's fear. The anger was something both of them had in common now, Russ thought. Troy stepped forward.

"You are such a prick," Troy said and began to strip. "Do you remember that night at Club Nova? You dumped a pitcher of beer all over this guy I wanted to screw, and everyone thought it was so cute, just like you think you're cute."

So he remembered Club Nova. Had Troy been following them? What else did he know? "Were you stalking me?"

"Shit, no," Troy said with a laugh. "One day, when I was cruising at the beach, I saw you down there on the sand with your boyfriend. He kissed you."

What had possessed him? Jealousy? Of being free enough to show affection in public? "And so you decide to beat the shit out of me?"

"You deserved what you got, and now you're going to get it again." Troy paused and crouched down slightly. "Get ready, asshole."

Troy lunged at him with terrific force, knocking Russ backward. Russ began to laugh as Troy sat on him and pinned his arms down with his own.

"Don't laugh at me!" Troy snarled.

"This will be your only chance, prick," Russ taunted him.

In an instant, Troy snapped his forehead down against Russ's in a savage head butt, three times. Each time, Russ used it to build up his own strength and anger. Troy looked bewildered when his effort seemed to have no effect.

Troy stared down at him with a strange combination of revulsion and longing. Russ gazed upward at the monster who had taken everything away, his face where Eric's should have been.

Russ knew that the time had come. Russ easily freed his arms from Troy's grasp and flipped him over. "Now it's your turn," Russ whispered. Russ didn't bother pinning his arms. He grabbed Troy's head with both hands and gave Troy a few head butts of his own. Troy cried out in pain.

When Russ let go, Troy's forehead already showed a terrible knot and Russ could see that several veins were broken. Troy seemed dazed.

Russ grabbed another singlet and stuffed it in Troy's mouth. When Troy struggled, Russ punched him repeatedly in the ribs until he could feel them break. Russ pulled at the singlet and tied part of it behind Troy's head. "How does it feel to be on the other end of this?" he asked.

There was terror in Troy's eyes. They darted around the room looking for an escape. Anger coursed through Russ's body like quicksilver. Russ repeatedly hammered Troy in the ribs; Troy had to feel everything that he'd inflicted on Eric. At some point, Troy fainted and Russ shook him until he awakened. There was blood trickling from his nose, and a weirdly purple knot on his forehead.

Russ pulled Troy to his feet and grabbed him around the waist from behind. Troy groaned. Russ took him over to the mirror. He wanted Troy to see his own end.

Russ pondered what to do next. He put more pressure on Troy's already broken ribs, but not enough to make him pass out again. Suddenly, Russ thought of the Greek statues he'd studied in art class, how so many of them lack a head. It would be so simple to twist it off.

He gazed at their reflection. It looked almost as though he had Troy in an embrace—as though two lovers were playing a game in front of the mirror, except for the fear in Troy's eyes, and hatred in his own.

But the eyes that carried the anger weren't his own—weren't they Eric's? Russ pushed closer to the mirror. He couldn't see Eric's eyes there anymore—he didn't recognize them at all. He loosened his grip slightly and Troy groaned with either pain or relief. It was Eric's face, but not Eric's eyes. Russ shook his head, trying to make them come back.

Suddenly he was lying in a hospital bed, struggling with wires and tubes. He looked around the white room, but he was alone. He closed and opened his eyes again and he was embracing Troy; both of them were now slumped on the floor in front of the mirror. A wholly different feeling swept through him and he remembered the first time he and Eric had made love. How could a man be so gentle?

Russ let go—the change was unraveling. He couldn't possibly think of finishing what he had started. He looked down at Troy softly groaning from the deepest part of his throat, the blood still trickling from his nose. Russ couldn't believe what he had done.

Russ pulled off the black singlet and struggled with his own clothes—everything was coming apart. Even some of the sickness was coming back. Soon he might be too weak to walk. His eyes closed as his body began to shudder uncontrollably. The blindness came over him and he lay on the mat, not certain where he was, seeing only Eric's eyes, eyes filled with love, watching over him.

At some point, he struggled up. Troy was still lying crumpled by the mirror. Russ slowly pulled himself to it, anxious to see who he had become. It was his own face, his own body, the one with which he had known Eric. He had to look twice to make sure. He stumbled out of the room, leaving Troy where he was. He would have to help himself. Russ had already done enough.

That evening, Russ went to the Coronado Bridge and stopped at the very top. Could he escape what he had done? He flung himself over the railings and rushed through the air, faster and faster, waiting to feel the water slam him to nothingness. But in mid-flight, his body took over, the reptilian, instinctual part of his body, and he felt a change coming. Before he realized it, Russ had become a very large, white bird that flew over the water with expansive wings, on a cushion of air, taking him through a scarlet-streaked sky home.

31

Helen was astonished. There was Eric coming out of his apartment, looking as healthy and vibrant as he had before the attack. She had just called the hospital and they told her there had been no change, yet here he was.

It couldn't possibly be him, but it was. She wondered if she was hallucinating. As he walked closer to her car, she nearly cried out, but something held her back. She eased down in the seat to escape his notice, but she couldn't help but watch.

There was a look in his eyes that she'd never seen in anyone before—a wild, angry sharpness that she found horrible. Piercing anger. He walked as if he were going to battle. He flung open the car door—she knew it was Eric's car—and then slammed it shut again. This wasn't the way Eric walked or acted. The spectacle chilled her.

She decided to follow. He drove with a certainty and purposefulness that would have been impossible for Eric—there was no hesitation at cross streets, no indecision. Helen's mind raced with the possibilities. The person driving the vehicle ahead of her, the person who looked just like Eric, wasn't Eric at all. It was simply impossible.

Helen began to wonder if Eric had been a twin. Elizabeth, Marie's sister, had mentioned only one baby; however, perhaps Elizabeth had never been told about the twin. Had Eric's twin somehow discovered them, or had Eric lost his memory of discovering the twin in the attack? If Eric knew, wouldn't he have told Russ? Perhaps he didn't have a chance. Helen seized on the possibility that the man she was following was Eric's twin brother. It was the only logical explanation, and the thought suddenly made her incredibly happy. There would be a perfect match, a certain cure.

Helen found it difficult to keep up with this mysterious twin—he certainly didn't drive anything like Eric. At one point, she was afraid he might go through a red light and leave her stranded. Soon, however, he began to slow down, as if he were looking for the right place. She tried not to follow too closely.

He came to a stop in front of an apartment house that had seen much better days. She parked down the block and watched as he got out of the car and walked up to the door. He looked so much like her son that it brought tears to her eyes, yet he didn't walk or act like Eric.

When there was no answer, he quickly made his way around the building. She wondered if he was planning to break in. She found this puzzling. Why wasn't he staying at a motel? Was he staying with a friend, and had forgotten the key?

Helen debated whether to go to the door and introduce herself. What would she say? Are you my son's twin? Will you give up one of your kidneys? She couldn't reach a decision. An irrational impulse that she didn't understand held her back. She would have to wait.

After what seemed like a long time, Helen noticed a couple of men walking up the street. One of them looked familiar—as he got closer, she realized that she had seen his face before. She stared at him, without fear of being noticed because he was so intent on his younger friend. They were headed for the same apartment, no question about it. It was then that Helen realized where she had seen the face before—it was the same man whose profile Kevin had clipped from the newspaper, Tony Singleton.

This confounded her. The two of them went into the apartment. After a few moments, Mr. Singleton's young friend came barreling out of the apartment, shaking his head and muttering to himself. Something hadn't gone right, she could plainly see. Once he was safely down the street, Helen got out of the car and retraced the steps Eric's twin had taken in sneaking into the backyard. The gate, however, was locked. She looked around. She saw a large rock that might give her enough height to peer over the gate. With some difficulty, she moved it near. She stepped up on the rock and looked over. A key was not so cleverly hidden in a recess at the top of the gate. She snatched it up, unlocked the gate, and quietly made her way to the back. She glanced in each window but didn't see anyone, only a dreary kitchen and living room. As she made it to the fourth window, the one past the living room, she heard a voice.

She peered in—there was Eric's twin, dressed in a black wrestling uniform, squared off with Mr. Singleton, who was naked. She looked away and crouched out of sight, debating whether she should slip away. She couldn't believe they were going to have sex. They both looked too angry for that. She couldn't imagine what they were doing.

Her heart was racing. Indecision gripped her.

"This will be your only chance, prick."

Suddenly, she heard signs of a struggle, what sounded like several dull pops and then a terrible groan, then more dull pops. One of them cried out. She stood to see what was going on. The man who looked so much like Eric was crouched over the other man, who appeared to be completely subdued. Then Eric's twin grabbed some piece of clothing and began stuffing it into Mr. Singleton's mouth.

Helen crouched down again, unable to watch. This was something Eric would never in her wildest dreams even think of doing.

"How does it feel to be on the other end of this?" someone asked.

On the other end of what? Helen thought about what the doctors had said. Eric had received an injury to his forehead, and something had been shoved into his mouth to gag him. He had been brutally kicked in the ribs. She eased up again to see what was going on. Eric's twin was punching the man in the ribs.

An idea began to form in her mind that she was unable to articulate yet, but she knew she had to be right. There had to be a logical explanation for what was going on. The question was, who was the man who looked so much like Eric that they could be twins? When she looked again, he was holding Mr. Singleton by the mirror, easily, like a man holding a large puppet. He was gazing at them in the mirror—it appeared as though Mr. Singleton had passed out.

Suddenly, Eric's twin let the other man fall to the floor, and fell down himself. Something was wrong.

Eric's twin began to shudder, slightly at first, then building into uncontrollable shaking. He ripped off the wrestling suit and struggled to put some other clothing back on. Helen gasped. His skin was rippling—changing, stretching before her very eyes. His whole shape was changing, transforming into someone or something else. It was a hideous oozing of flesh. The man who was no longer Eric, no longer anyone, closed his eyes and slumped to his knees. He began to take the form of someone else, a form that seemed familiar to her. At a certain point, she was sure who the man was becoming—there was the light-brown hair, the build, the bone structure. When he finally opened his startlingly green eyes, the man was Russ.

The rest of what transpired seemed more like a dream than anything else. She was floating, detached from her senses. She watched as Russ checked in the mirror again; then he stumbled out of the room, leaving the other man on the floor, limp as a puddle of water.

She moved to peer into the living room and saw Russ leave by the front door. She waited until she heard the slam of a car door. His face, the horror of his shifting face, wouldn't leave her.

She wondered what she could do, or even should do, for Mr. Singleton. If she didn't call for help, he might not make it. Her irrational self suggested that leaving him there might just be a good thing. She couldn't imagine why such an idea would enter her thinking—there was absolutely no reason for it. The idea revolted her. Even if Mr. Singleton was the one who had attacked her son.

She made her way to the front of the apartment and slipped inside, pushing the door open farther, making sure not to touch anything with her fingertips. She would have to keep the key to the back gate for now and discard it later. Helen tried to locate the telephone. The apartment did not look like anyone lived there, which she supposed made sense; this, after all, was Mr. Singleton's other life, as Kevin had explained.

By the time she found the telephone in the kitchen, Helen had become more herself again. The feeling of weightlessness had almost gone. She picked up a stray paper towel and used it to grab the receiver. With another bit of paper, she pressed 911. She disguised her voice as best she could, knowing that her call would be recorded. She only gave them the essentials and refused to stay on the line until the medics came.

Helen left the door open to make certain the emergency team would have ready access. She didn't dare check on Mr. Singleton for fear that he might see her and later recognize her face.

32

Eric dreamed of a man again—this one was dark, with an evil face. He didn't want to go back there. He was floating, struggling with the air that pushed him farther and farther from where he wanted to be. There was a terrible sense of being alone. Wisps of cloud blinded him.

He could hear his own heartbeat. Suddenly, he was in a room, a dingy place with a mat, was it a wrestling mat? Dirty walls.

There was the man—Eric recoiled in fear. The man's body vibrated with blows, someone hitting him, punching him over and over again, then the weightlessness, floating. He couldn't yet remember the face, but it was familiar, horribly familiar.

The man was slumped on the floor. Eric could see blood. The man was moving. It was a dream and yet it was not—something in between? It felt good to be moving again, except for the ghastliness of seeing the dark man lying on the floor. Did he hear soft moans?

Suddenly, his body began to shake and the pain became unbearable. He opened his eyes and could see nothing but white. This gradually gave way to strings of pearls draped across him, or were they tubes filled with rubies? Then he realized it was a hospital room. His body was still shaking. He remembered the pain, nurses running toward him. He couldn't die now. He wouldn't.

When he awakened, Eric felt as though his body had been tossed over a waterfall. He opened his eyes to find his mother sitting beside him.

"You had some kind of seizure," she said, looking worried.

Eric let the statement sink in. He wasn't even sure where he was or what had happened to him. He vaguely recalled previous days spent in the hospital, something about being attacked. When he let his mind go for an instant, the image of a stretch of sand came to him, dancing with light. He was still finding it difficult to separate the dreams from the reality. "Am I doing better?"

"Yes," she replied. "Better."

He hoped she would say more without him questioning her. He was so tired. But she remained silent. He didn't remember her hair being so gray. Had she really grown so much older, or had he forgotten? "Tell me what's wrong. I should be getting better, not worse," he finally managed to say.

"Your kidneys have gone bad," she said. "The dialysis isn't working for you for some reason—the doctors don't understand why. You're going to require a kidney transplant. The procedure is going to be done early tomorrow morning. The doctors are trying to get you a little stronger before the operation."

A kidney transplant, what an idea. "Whose kidney?"

"Mine," she said with a smile.

A wave of nausea came over him, but lying in the bed he could do nothing about it. He reached up to touch his forehead but was stopped by a bunch of tubes. He looked at the back of his hand—it was yellow, with what looked like some kind of sores.

"Honey, let me wipe your forehead for you."

The damp cloth felt surprisingly good. Suddenly he saw a field, or was it a garden? Wild and deserted. A narrow path of rough pebbles led to a clearing overgrown with what his mother had always called Queen Anne's lace. Waist-high weeds glistened with foamy film left, he knew, by flying insects of some sort. It was hard to see through all of this to the hospital room. It was as though he were in two places at once. He concentrated on looking at his mother's eyes, hoping this would bring back the hospital room. She had said that she was going to donate one of her kidneys? It didn't make sense to him. "Isn't that dangerous for you?" he asked.

"Not at all."

He knew she was lying. "Why not use another donor?"

"We'll have a better chance using one from me," she explained with that same smile. "The tissue work showed a match of almost seventy percent."

Eric didn't understand fully what she was saying, but it didn't seem possible. "How could it match that closely?" he asked. "We aren't blood relations."

She still smiled—it was almost infuriating. "Yes, we are."

Eric blinked a couple of times—perhaps he hadn't heard her right. "We're related?"

"How am I going to explain this?" she said more to herself than to him. "The doctor said that we'd have a better chance if we could have a kidney from a donor who was related to you." She paused. "Kevin and I were able to trace your birth mother."

Eric felt another wave of sickness come over him. Now there was a blizzard of butterflies in the room, or was it the garden? Huge, heavy blossoms of yellow zinnias poked up through the tall grass, their open faces reaching for the sun. Had they really found her? "Where is she?" he asked.

She ignored his question, wiping his forehead again. Her action had the effect of scattering the image of the garden, but only for a moment. "I was able to speak with your birth mother's sister—your aunt. She told us that both she and your birth mother suffered from kidney disease and that neither of them had any other children or nieces or nephews, except for you."

He sensed that she was leaving something out. A butterfly fluttered by her ear. "How are we related?" he persisted.

"Your birth mother completed a family tree. It turns out that she and I are third cousins, through the Skinner family."

"Third cousins!" he said, not sure what it meant.

"Honey," she said with a smile. "She and I shared the same great-great grandparents."

The room started to spin. The tall grass swayed in a light wind. They were related after all. Leave it to his mother to figure it out. He started to laugh, but it hurt too much. "Have you talked with my birth mother?" he asked.

She glanced at the floor. "No."

Even in his weakened state, Eric could tell that something was wrong. "You aren't telling me something," he added. There was suddenly a red streak across her face, as though she'd been slapped with a scarlet flower that left a trail of pollen.

"No, everything I've told you is true," she replied, frowning.

"It may be true, but you've left something out." He thought it odd that he was able to make such good sense, given how he felt. He seemed to be alternately in his body and floating just above it. "What is it about my birth mother that you don't want to talk about?" he asked slowly.

She studied his face. "I didn't want to tell you this right now, before your surgery."

"Tell me," he insisted.

"When Kevin and I were doing our search, we discovered that your birth mother died of a heart attack soon after she had sent her letter and moved to California." There were tears in her eyes. "I'm so very sorry."

It didn't register with him at first—he suspected that he'd fallen asleep and was dreaming again. After all the wondering and frustration, how could it have ended with her death? The room began to spin a little faster, yet his whole body felt sour and stagnant. He tried to sit up, but he was too weak. The overlay of the garden was still there—it looked as though there might be people in it now. They were dressed in turn-of-the-century clothing, all in white.

His mother wiped his brow again. "I didn't want to tell you," she whispered. Her concern bothered him. He wasn't quite sure why. It might have been because he realized that he didn't care about his birth mother as much as he had once thought. The news had left him dazed, but not sad; frustrated, perhaps, but not angry. His birth mother was dead. He hadn't even known the woman. Yet all the unanswered questions remained: Why had he been given up? Who was his father? What other family did he have? But even thinking of the questions was too much for him right now. He gazed at his mother—she was so worried. Behind her hovered a hummingbird, a small green wisp of a bird with golden wings. Part of him couldn't believe she didn't comment on the loud buzzing it made. Suddenly, Russ appeared behind her as well, somewhere in the garden. Or perhaps he'd just walked into the hospital room.

"Russ?" he asked. The image was gone. "Where did he go?"

Helen looked as though he'd wounded her. "I don't know," she replied, in a way that told him she wasn't pleased.

"What's wrong?" he asked. The room was spinning faster now. He didn't understand why Russ wasn't with him too.

"Nothing," she replied. "I don't understand why your friend hasn't spent more time with you here. Perhaps it's a good thing that he hasn't."

"What makes you say that?" Something, he realized, was very wrong, yet he wasn't sure he had the strength to convince her to tell him.

"He's not been very stable, emotionally, that is," she said guardedly. "I don't think we should talk about this now," she added. "You should get some rest so that you're ready for the operation tomorrow."

He waited, hoping that she would change her mind. Finally, he gave up. Besides, the garden was growing stronger by the minute, on the verge of pushing everything else out. "All right," he agreed.

"You will pull through this," she told him, almost defiantly. "Everything will be fine."

The grass parted to reveal a row of sunflowers and as he began, he hoped, to drift into sleep, the flowers faded and turned black, the wind taking their seeds.

33

Russ didn't sleep that night, anxious with waiting. Eric and his mother were scheduled for surgery at ten o'clock in the morning, which meant that he would have to be at the hospital by at least six o'clock if he was to see them. He was afraid Eric's body was too weak to withstand an operation, but from what he understood from the nurses, there was no choice. Either Eric had the operation, or he died.

The early morning light played tricks with him as Russ drove to the hospital. He kept glancing in the rearview mirror, uncertain whether his eyes were changing color. He took his own car to the hospital, uncertain of driving the other one. Now that the anger was gone, he had no sense of control. When driving Eric's car, Russ found that Eric's lingering scent was enough to prompt his body to begin an unwanted transformation.

Once at the hospital, Russ hurried to Eric's room. He paused just outside, but slipped in when he heard a nurse approach. He didn't want to be booted out.

Eric was sleeping. His skin was a ghastly yellow, now also marred by terrible purplish sores. His body had appeared to shrink since the attack. Russ attempted to quell a growing fear that he would again begin to mirror Eric's sickness, but he simply couldn't stay away any longer. He went to the bed and took Eric's hand. Eric's eyes slowly opened.

"It's my elf child," Eric said in a weak voice. "Am I dreaming you're here? I was wondering if you'd come," he added with no hint of resentment. "Why haven't you visited more?"

The comment stung, though he felt he deserved it. "I'm sorry," he replied. "I couldn't handle it."

"What do you mean?" Eric's eyes had a faraway look that Russ found strange.

"My body was taking on your illness," he explained softly. "I was getting to be as sick as you were each time I came near you. Guess it was a sympathetic reaction."

"You changelings are pretty weird," Eric said, suddenly louder.

Russ placed his fingers on Eric's lips to quiet him. The touch shocked him—Eric's lips were so dry and chapped.

"There's a halo around your head," Eric said with wide eyes. "Are you sure you should be here?"

"I'll be okay for right now," he replied, though he could feel the sickness returning. He wondered if the halo had anything to do with it, or if Eric were simply delirious. "I wanted you to know that I'll be waiting here with Kevin during your surgery."

"That's great," Eric said and sighed.

"You better come through this," Russ whispered to him. "I need you. Do you understand?"

"I'll try my best," Eric whispered back.

"I love you." Russ kissed him on the cheek.

"Me too."

Russ was surprised to find a spectacular view from the seventh-floor waiting room—a canyon filled with eucalyptus trees that swayed in the breeze. He wished he could escape into their limbs and hide among the silvery-green leaves.

Kevin finally arrived, nearly an hour after the operation had begun. Russ was shocked by Kevin's appearance—he'd lost so much weight that he looked almost like another person.

"Hey, Russ," he said in a deep voice and dropped into the chair next to him. "How are they doing?"

"Fine, as far as I know," he replied. "I haven't seen them for hours."

"Were they in good spirits?"

"Eric was totally out of it, he's so sick." Russ didn't want to remember how bad Eric looked. "I'm not sure about Helen," he added. Actually, he thought Helen had been cold with him, but perhaps he deserved it.

"How long do you think it will be?"

"Hours."

"Sorry I wasn't here earlier," Kevin said.

"That's okay." Russ was glad for Kevin's presence. It gave him a sense of connection to his life before the attack. He did wonder, though, at Kevin's buoyant mood. His eyes were dancing with light—or perhaps, Russ thought, it was the movement of the eucalyptus trees he saw reflected there.

"Why are you so happy?" Russ asked.

"Happy?" Kevin asked. "I'm not sure I'd go that far. I'd rather say 'hopeful.'"

"You mean hopeful that Eric will be okay?"

"Yeah." Kevin touched Russ on the arm. "I really think Eric will be okay."

Kevin's touch was surprisingly comforting. "I hope you're right."

"I brought something for you to look at while we're waiting," Kevin announced, pulling out two newspaper clippings. "Do you recognize this guy?" Kevin handed one of them to Russ. "I found this in the business journal a couple months ago."

Russ froze. Troy's photo glared at him. It was the same face that Russ had so recently seen beaten—the same sharp features. He scanned a few bits of the article—married, children, successful broker, well off. The anger began to surge in him, but he remembered Eric's eyes and the flow abruptly stopped.

"Yes, I think I do," Russ said. "Why are you showing this to me?"

"I had a one-night stand with him. Even Eric has met him, once a few months ago, before he started going out with you."

Russ thought of the first time he'd met Eric at the dance club. Eric had met Troy for the first time on that night, too. He looked at Kevin more sharply. How much did Kevin know? "I'm sorry," Russ said, trying not to sound too defensive. "Why show this to me?"

"I thought you might have run into the guy," Kevin explained. "Plus, I have this other clipping. Here."

Kevin pulled out another clipping. "I found this in the newspaper a couple of days ago." He handed Russ the second article. This one was smaller, from the local news section. The headline read "Man Attacked in North Park." "Looks like Troy ran into some rough trade," Kevin observed.

Russ, with his heart beating rapidly, read the article.

> Tony Singleton, a successful independent broker and businessman, was attacked in the North Park area late Tuesday, resulting in severe injuries. Singleton was robbed, stripped naked, and severely beaten. The victim reported that two Hispanic males attacked him as he was walking from his car to visit a client. The men responsible for the attack remain at large. Mr. Singleton was taken to Mercy Hospital, where he is listed in stable condition.

Images and sounds from the dingy little apartment flooded in on him—the bloody face, the sound of Troy's ribs cracking, the way he'd left Troy crumpled on the floor. The guilt came back too—for what happened and what had almost happened.

"Can you believe that he's here in this hospital, right now?"

"No," Russ snapped. He resented Kevin's intrusion. Why did he have to share such an article now? Then, Russ realized he should not react too strongly. He decided to make light of it. "So, you don't think that good ol' Troy was telling the truth about his beating?"

"Hardly." Kevin looked smug. "He just got hooked up with the wrong kind of guy. I guess I should have more sympathy for him, but I can't stand these guys who have to have it both ways."

Even though he was sure Troy wouldn't recognize him, the idea that he had been admitted to the hospital did not sit well with Russ. He wondered if Troy had read a similar article after he'd attacked Eric. Did Troy recall Eric's name? Would he later come after Eric, when he was feeling better again? Russ had never thought of the consequences of letting Troy go without killing him. The realization was unsettling.

"You're worried." Kevin said, breaking his reverie.

"Yeah," he admitted, supposing that he was referring to Eric rather than Troy.

"I have a lot of faith in the doctors," Kevin reassured him. "Eric's mother told me that the tissue match was good."

"That's right." The eucalyptus trees began swaying more strongly.

"Helen is pretty amazing—she really has a knack for research."

"I suppose," Russ replied glumly.

"You're getting along okay with her, aren't you?" he asked.

"I suppose," Russ repeated.

"When she left for your apartment to tell you the good news, I got the impression that she cared about you."

This was something new. "What are you talking about?"

Kevin looked at him, incredulous. "After Helen discovered the family tree information about Eric's birth mother, she was going to drop by your apartment. You must not have been home."

Russ tried not to sound alarmed. "When was this?"

"A couple of days ago—in the afternoon."

"What time?"

"About four o'clock, I guess."

Russ tried to recall. Was that the same time he had gone to Troy's? The whole afternoon was now such a blur that it was hard to recall the exact time. If she had seen him as Eric—no, he thought, she couldn't have. Something would have come of it, if she had. Yet he wondered why she had told him practically nothing about her successful search, especially since she had been excited enough to come to the apartment to tell him in person.

"How did she discover the connection?" Russ asked. "They are cousins?"

"It's a long story," Kevin replied. "But they are really cousins. It makes you wonder how closely we're all connected. The idea that Helen would end up adopting the baby of one of her own cousins without knowing—it's amazing."

Russ was reminded of how Eric had happened to breeze by his T-shirt stand, seemingly by chance. He'd thought he would never see Eric again, but there he was, pawing through his T-shirts and giving Russ the eye. Was this also amazing? Russ gazed out at the limbs of the eucalyptus as they constantly swayed. Each gust of wind brought the branches closer, creating a constant pattern of connection and release. The silvery-green leaves shimmered in the sunlight.

"Eric will be there for you," Kevin said suddenly.

"Thanks." Russ wished he could share Kevin's optimism. Too many things had gone terribly wrong—why should Eric's surgery be any different?

They fell into an uneasy silence, with Kevin quietly reading the magazines he'd brought while Russ gazed out the window. Watching the trees dance with the wind was the only way Russ could remain calm enough to wait. Every moment was torture. After what seemed like an eternity, a rather young-looking doctor, dressed in green operating room scrubs, came out to talk with them.

"Helen is doing fine."

"And Eric?" Russ asked.

"Eric is doing fine, everything considered." The doctor wearily sat in a chair beside them.

"That's great," Kevin said, nearly dropping his magazine. "I knew he'd make it."

"I think he'll pull through," the doctor replied. "Just pray for his body to accept the kidney."

Pray? Russ glanced out the window again. The wind was so inviting. Perhaps he would pray to the wind to take all his problems away. Wouldn't that be simple? he mused.

"Why don't you guys grab some lunch somewhere," the doctor suggested, rubbing his forehead. "They'll both be in recovery for a good hour or so." The doctor stood up and gave them an encouraging, though closed-mouthed, smile as he walked away.

Kevin looked over at him hopefully and Russ nodded. On the way out of the hospital, Russ tried to imagine Eric lying in the recovery room: Did he still look as yellow as he had? Had the sores on his once-smooth skin disappeared? Russ knew that he would again have to wait.

Lizzy stood over the bed, watching Eric sleep. It had been easy enough to slip by the security guards, though she wished she didn't have to dress like one of them, having taken the form of a young guard she'd seen on one of her previous trips. Downstairs, the guards on duty had told her to go home, that she wasn't scheduled for a night shift. When she told them she had to use a rest room, they laughed, teasing her about making such a long trip just for that. Once out of their sight, she found an elevator that would take her to Eric's floor.

What might Eric think, she mused, if he woke up and found a guard standing over him? By the looks of him, though, he'd been given something to ensure a deep sleep. Either that, or his condition was worse than she thought it would be after the operation.

Eric's skin had an awful yellow cast and terrible sores—the final stages, she knew, of kidney failure. His face looked crumpled and twisted, though she suspected he was in no pain. She picked up his hand. It wasn't good. Toxins swamped his body. She could feel the leaden weight of them, crowding him out, pinning him down. She tried to get a sense of how the kidney—his new kidney—was doing. She could feel that it was at the brink of working. There was a good chance that Eric's body might reject it too—even though his body was weak, she sensed it beginning to marshal an attack against the invasion.

Lizzy placed the palm of her right hand on the skin over the incision, as close as she possibly could to the new kidney. Very slowly, she pressed down. Eric groaned. Lizzy relaxed and began to concentrate on the spot, sending short bursts of energy into and around the new organ. She imagined a protective globe of light coming out from her hand and surrounding the whole area. The globe of light gradually took the shape of a diamond—through it, she began to channel different colors, starting with the darkest purple and through the spectrum to a brilliant yellow and then white. She felt an amazing tingling in her hand. She directed the energy into the kidney until it reached a point of saturation. Then, she took control of the form of the kidney cells, urging them to change to more closely match the surrounding tissue. The process didn't take long. The tissue was a good match to begin with; she was merely helping it along.

Gradually, she could feel the kidney come to life and begin working, and, even more gradually, she began to decrease the flow of light to the area. After several minutes, she carefully withdrew her hand. There was still a faint glow around the area; it looked as though she had burned Eric's skin, leaving an imprint of a large male hand. No matter, she thought. The kidney was functioning—that was the important thing.

She thought of Mariette—this was Mariette's great-grandnephew, or some such thing. From now on, Eric would be her family, no matter how many times removed by generation or bloodline.

She couldn't help but smile. She hadn't felt so light and carefree in years and years. Now she only had to worry about Russ.

She slipped out without anyone noticing her. She was going home.

The sky opened up, revealing a tower of clouds in hues of dark purple, lavender, cornflower blue, gentle green, and soft yellow. Eric floated up through the layers of fuzzy color, propelled by a gentle wind. The farther he traveled, the more he felt a sense of release and freedom, like a river of pure water flowing through him. Toward the apex of the tower sat a stone of jasper. The wind brought him closer and closer to it, until he became one with the gem, flying through its interlocking chambers to the other side. The sudden shift in perception momentarily blinded him. When he regained his sight, a bright, blue sky and mountains of white clouds greeted him. Nearby an angel sat in the sun—its eyes like a flame of fire. Eric could hear voices echoing indistinctly.

Eric moved closer, warily. The angel, neither male nor female, was perfectly composed, like a statue except for its blazing eyes. As Eric came closer, however, the angel began to take on another shape. Its transformation was smooth and flowing, with no rippling of the skin, no awkward shifting of bones and flesh. In an instant the angel had become a being with light-brown hair, with familiar features and incredibly green eyes. A hint of a smile graced his lips. There was such joy in those bright emerald eyes—and peace. It was, he realized with excitement, Russ. Eric had come home.

Russ smiled, reaching out to him with elegant, bone-white fingers. Before Eric could respond, though, the angel began to change again. The light-brown hair quickly darkened to black, the eyes glazed over with darkest brown, and the character of his face changed. Eric recoiled. It was the face of the dark-haired man from his dreams—the sharp features, the uncaring, bottomless eyes. This time, though, Eric saw a hint of sadness and loneliness that he couldn't understand. As he looked closer, he wondered why he couldn't see his own reflection in the man's eyes—he almost became lost gazing into them.

Suddenly, all around them, the clouds began to swirl—streaks of red clothed them in blood. When the sky stopped spinning, Eric found himself in a dingy rest room that he recognized. The dark-haired man was still with him, this time with a yearning.

Then it began coming back to him, standing at the urinal, feeling exposed and vulnerable, the first blow, the stench of urine, his face under water, the blood gushing, the horrible pain after being hit again and again. It was all in the man's face, in his bottomless eyes, now filled with pleading.

Suddenly, they both stood in an empty room. This time, the dark-haired man was lying prone on the floor, with blood on his face. At first Eric was confused. Shouldn't he be the one injured, lying on the floor? But he'd been injured in a different time and place. This bare room, after all, wasn't the public rest room at Pacific Beach. They were somewhere else. The man looked up at him with an odd expression. Eric understood two meanings—both a yearning to be close to him and a longing to be forgiven. The horror of the attack was still with Eric, and the fear. Yet seeing the man hurt in a similar way weirdly twisted his perception of the attack. Eric, almost in spite of himself, began to feel compassion for the dark-haired man.

Eric began to struggle to awaken from the dream—he knew it had to be a dream. He tried to move his feet, to feel his feet again; he tried to take deep breaths, tried to turn his head. He had to wake up. The man began to advance on him, still pleading, for what, Eric did not know. Eric struggled harder to awaken, to blink his eyes and force them open, away from the other man's eyes. Finally, when he was sure that he didn't have a chance, that he might suffocate, he clawed his way to the surface.

His eyes opened.

34

Since the operation Helen's joints had ached, particularly her hips, knees, and ankles. It was a strange feeling, as though her joints were filled with fluid. As she stood, Helen could feel them shift, as if they had a life of their own. She had described the sensation to her doctor, wondering if it was arthritis, but he said that she should try to forget about it and the pain would simply go away.

Otherwise, she was recovering quite nicely and didn't feel the absence of her kidney. The operation had left only a small incision, which hadn't completely healed yet.

Though she was overjoyed with Eric's rapid recovery, her elation was tempered by her fear of Russ. She still couldn't imagine what he was.

Helen was afraid she was becoming obsessed with worry. She couldn't think about anything else. For a time, she tried to convince herself that she had been hallucinating that day, though she knew that was not true. The idea of deceiving herself was strangely comforting.

No, she hadn't been hallucinating or even dreaming. What kind of danger did her son face now that he was home again? Helen could barely tolerate being around Russ—a combination of fear and revulsion put her on edge. Increasingly, anger colored her moods too. In an odd way the situation reminded her of the time she suspected her husband was having an affair. She remained quiet through her discovery of scraps of paper with crudely scrawled phone numbers, through mystery callers who would hang up when she answered the phone, and even through his frequent absences. All along, though, the anger had grown, day after day, until she couldn't bear it any longer. He had remained quiet through her tirade, and quiet even after she had become exhausted with berating him. In the days following, without a word of defense or explanation, the calls and absences abruptly ceased.

Helen simply had to talk with Eric about what she had seen before she did something foolish. She was concerned about what Eric might do if his memory of the attack returned. Would he turn in Mr. Singleton? And if he did, what would Singleton have to say about the attack he had suffered? Would he suddenly change his ridiculous story about being attacked by Hispanic men? Even if he did, she thought it was unlikely that Eric would be charged with the attack on Singleton, since at the time Eric was in the hospital, seriously ill. Her real fear stemmed from what Singleton might do to seek revenge. In any case, Helen doubted whether Singleton would be convicted, even if his double life were exposed. Now that Eric was on the mend, she wanted to keep him safe. She supposed she was a coward, but realization didn't seem to matter. Nevertheless, it was a terrible thing, being controlled by fear.

Then there was the other, horrible, revelation from Marie's sister. When Helen called to let Elizabeth know of their success, she again asked about Eric's father. Although she knew this was a sensitive topic, Helen had no idea that Elizabeth's reply would be so disturbing. The news explained much; even so, Helen wished she had never heard it and planned to delay telling Eric for as long as she could. Elizabeth didn't know the identity of Eric's father. No one did. Marie had been raped.

Helen sat down at her computer and gazed at the screen. On it was a chart showing the descendants of John Skinner, the ancestor she and Eric shared. Studying the chart comforted her, even though she knew it by heart. Through the various boxes and lines on the chart, she could follow the direct connection between herself and her son. There was such beauty in the cascade of names all outlined in blue.

It took a good deal of time for her to get ready to make a trek to her son's apartment. Her body was moving more slowly—the operation had sapped a great deal of her strength. She hoped she'd find Eric alone. At the last minute, she remembered to bring the latest news clipping she had found just in case.

Someone had left the door open in anticipation of her visit, and she walked into the apartment without being seen or heard. She paused at the bedroom door, unnoticed. Eric looked radiant, his face glowing. Helen couldn't help but feel joy, too.

The two of them were quietly laughing. Russ was standing over Eric, helping him wash his face with a wet washcloth—she was stunned by how delicately Russ used the rag, by how much love she saw in every movement. When had her own husband ever shown such care with her? She made a noise to stop what she was seeing, uncomfortable with witnessing such intimacy.

"Oh, Helen," Russ turned and smiled at her. "Eric's been waiting for you."

"I'm sorry to interrupt," she said.

"Hi, Mom," Eric piped up. "It's okay."

"Actually," Russ began, "I was just getting ready to go to the beach to sell some T-shirts." He gave Eric a pat on the shoulder. "Have fun."

"Thanks," Eric replied.

Russ smiled at her again as he left. She was thankful he was leaving—she wondered if Eric had asked him to be absent during their visit. She slowly approached his bed. Her joints were aching again.

"Hi, Mom," he greeted her again, more quietly.

"Hello, honey." She gave him an awkward hug. He was looking so much better, more and more like his old self all the time. "I've brought something to show you." Out of her purse she retrieved a printout of the genealogy chart she had put together earlier that morning. She handed it to him.

"What is this?" he said.

"This is a chart that shows how we are related," she explained. Looking at it with him gave her a little thrill. "Here you are." She pointed with her finger. "Here I am. Here are my parents, my grandmother Kezzie."

"Oh, yeah," he said. He studied the chart for a moment. "It's like a sperm chart."

"What do you mean?" she asked, perplexed and on the verge of feeling wounded.

"It shows the progress of all of these little eggs and sperm—sperm through the fathers and eggs through the mothers. It shows how they've all traveled through these people."

She could see the sense of what he said, though she wasn't sure she liked it. After all, her genealogy work helped save his life. She didn't appreciate his making light of it.

"If it were a people chart," he explained, "there would be a big fat line here between you and me to show how strongly we're connected. Like this." He grabbed a pen and drew a thick, clumsy line directly between them. "See?" He smiled.

As he drew the line between them, she felt herself beginning to glow. "You're sweet."

"I know," he glibly replied, putting the chart aside. "I'm glad you had a chance to see Russ before he left."

She took the chart and put it back into her purse. His comment had offered a perfect opportunity to talk about Russ, but she held back. The thought of broaching the subject of her son's strange lover was enough to frighten her. Helen walked to the window to admire a flowering plant that she didn't recognize from the hospital. The plant was tall, topped with broad, loose clusters of magenta and white flowers dappled with dark freckles. "These are beautiful," she said.

"I think it's called a Peruvian lily," he replied. "Russ's mother brought it over for me."

This didn't sit well with her, but she had to admit the flowers were stunning.

"Is there some problem between you and Russ?" he said.

"Why do you ask?" she replied and moved closer to the bed.

"Because you've been very quiet around him," he said. "I can tell something isn't right."

There was no way she could avoid discussing it now."Honey," she said, "I'm not sure even where to begin to tell this to you."

"Is this something about Russ?"

"Yes," she admitted. By his reaction, she could see that he probably already had an idea what she was going to say. "I saw Russ change his form," she explained simply.

He blanched, from fear or embarrassment, she couldn't tell.

"What exactly did you see?" he asked.

"I saw you, or someone who looked like you, change his shape and become Russ."

"Someone like me," he repeated.

"Someone who looked exactly like you."

"You saw the change?" he said, alarmed.

She decided to be as straightforward as she could. "I saw his body change its shape. It was horrible. His skin, muscles, everything moved."

He wouldn't say anything. She was quite sure she had been completely clear. He was, she realized, debating how much he should tell her. "Honey," she said. "Tell me what's going on."

He thought for a moment. "Mom, I'm sorry you had to see that." He searched for the words. "It was a long time before I knew what was going on too," he continued. "Russ is a changeling. He can change his shape into the form of any person he wants to."

The whole thing sounded absolutely absurd, but she knew it was true. "How is it possible?"

"I don't know," he replied. His eyes reflected a combination of fear and exhilaration. "Russ told me that it's genetic, that way back there was some kind of mutation. He's able to change his shape by imagining the form he wants to take. I'm not even sure he knows how it works."

A genetic change, a mutation that created a whole new kind of person, someone with amazing abilities. It was incredible, frightening, and wonderful. She couldn't imagine all the implications. "Russ's mother has these abilities, doesn't she?"

"Yes."

"I had already discovered that they, both Russ and his mother, are much older than they appear to be."

He looked at her, surprised.

"I discovered it through looking at the census records, and ordering a copy of Russ's birth certificate." She smiled—by his reaction, he apparently hadn't realized how resourceful she could be. "I already talked to Lizzy about this."

"You what?" he asked, sitting up in bed.

"Yes," she explained carefully. "I have already talked with her about it." She tried not to sound too proud. "But she didn't admit to being a changeling," she added. "I'm worried about you."

He smiled. "You are pretty amazing," he said. "I've wanted to tell you, but I swore that I wouldn't tell anyone."

"You didn't hear me," she said. "I am worried about you."

He glanced away. "Yeah, I worry sometimes too. It's not easy having a changeling for a lover."

"It's dangerous," she told him. "You could be hurt again."

"It didn't take a changeling to do this to me."

She cringed. "Well, that's true," she admitted, wondering if he had remembered anything.

"I feel safe with Russ," he told her. "And his mother," he added, almost protesting too much, she thought.

Helen immediately thought of Russ's attack on Tony Singleton. "I'm not so sure," she said. There was no point in holding anything back now. "Russ attacked the man who attacked you."

"How do you know?" Eric asked.

"I saw the attack myself."

"You saw the attack?"

She took a deep breath. "I went to your apartment to see Russ and saw you instead—or someone who looked like you—come out of your apartment. I followed this person to another place; then Mr. Singleton went into the same apartment." She knew she was going too fast, but she desperately wanted to get to the point and have this over with. "I sneaked around the back and saw the whole thing through a window. The man who looked like you attacked a man named Tony Singleton. This same man transformed from someone looking like you to someone who looked exactly like Russ."

Eric was stunned. At first, she feared that she had said too much.

"I had a dream," he muttered, still dazed.

"What was that, honey?"

"I had a dream that I was standing in a room, empty except for a wrestling mat. It was a dingy, awful place. There was a man lying on the mat, and there was blood."

He had perfectly described the room—she was dumbfounded. Had it really been him? "You were in the hospital," she said. "It couldn't have been you."

He ignored her comment. "Russ told me that he couldn't visit me because his body would start to become sick, like mine." Eric paused, thinking. "When he took my form, maybe a part of me was there, enough that I could remember what happened."

Helen wondered. It would explain why Russ had been so absent during Eric's illness and might even explain his bizarre behavior. But it didn't in any way justify Russ's attack, which was obviously planned. Why didn't Eric see this? "Look at what he's capable of doing, honey," she said. "He beat a man."

Eric looked troubled. "How do you know the name of the man? Is this Mr. Singleton doing okay?"

"Kevin had an article about him, and said that he'd gone by another name. I believe the name was Troy. Kevin knew him, and apparently you do, too. He was leading a double life. In the article I cut from the newspaper detailing his attack, it was said that he claimed to be attacked by Hispanics. I read another article today about him going home," she said. "He must be doing fine."

"I don't understand how Russ was so sure that this was the guy who attacked me," Eric said, concern on his face. "Are you worried that Singleton might come after me?"

This took her by surprise. Eric was becoming more insightful all the time. She wondered if the attack had brought something out in him; or perhaps it was living with Russ that had done it. "Yes," she admitted. "You are right about that."

"I doubt that he will," he replied. "It sounds like he has too much to hide. I hope you're not going to mention any of this to Russ or anyone else."

His manner caught her off guard. She wasn't accustomed to him taking charge. "Of course, I won't," she replied.

"We need to keep all of this a secret," he told her. "We all have secrets—Russ, you, Lizzy, and me. Even this jerk has secrets that we need to keep."

"I'm not sure I can stand it," she said. Eric's only response was a smile. She could see that Eric was planning to stay with Russ—she couldn't imagine why. "You're going to stay with him, aren't you?"

"I love him," Eric said. "And he needs my help."

She knew it was true—she had seen the love when she walked in. He would stay with Russ no matter what happened, she realized. It had been the same thing with Eric's father. She had loved him enough to endure. She hated the idea of her son going through the same thing. But at least she would be here to help him. She couldn't imagine, though, living with the knowledge of what Russ was while keeping it a secret. She'd want to learn everything about them. In time, she thought, perhaps the secrets would no longer be necessary.

Helen bent to kiss him on the forehead, her beautiful son. Her only son. His eyes looked up at her with such happiness that she almost forgot her pain and fear.

35

Russ thought he was in a dream. He had come so close to killing another human being—he felt that he didn't deserve such happiness, yet the face of his lover hovered over him as they lay together in their bed, finally at home.

He wondered if Eric could see the guilt written all over him; all Russ could see in Eric's face, though, was unblemished joy. Eric beamed down at him.

This was the first time they'd been able to make love since before the attack. Russ reached up to touch Eric's face, afraid that his presence wasn't real, only an illusion. He let his fingertips linger on Eric's smooth cheek and along his jawline, now rough with stubble. Eric's eyes, even in the bright light, were wells of dark, glittering brown—the color of fertile earth. His hair, still wild from their sex, formed a halo of jet-black waves. In spite of Russ's worst fears, Eric had come back to him whole and vibrant.

"This feels fantastic," Eric told him softly. "I missed you."

"Me too," he managed to whisper back.

The image of how Eric looked after the attack edged into his consciousness. How different he looked now, Russ thought. The image of Troy took its place. Both of them were bloody, Eric much more so. Russ had to look away.

"What's wrong?" Eric asked him.

"Oh, I don't know," he said, not willing to be honest quite yet. He wondered how much Eric had seen of the attack on Troy—how much of his dream had blended into the reality of what had happened on that awful day. "I was thinking of your dream," he added. "The one where you saw the empty room and the man lying on the floor by the mat."

Eric gazed at him, a little confused. "I never told you that there was a mat in the room."

This took Russ aback. "You must have."

"No, I didn't." Eric brushed his fingers across Russ's forehead. "Is there something you want to tell me?"

Maybe there was—would telling Eric what he'd done help take the pain away? Or would Eric leave him after discovering what violence he was capable of doing? "I'm not sure."

"My mother talked with me about Tony Singleton."

"She did?" Helen knew, he thought. She must have followed him, as he'd suspected.

"Yes," Eric replied. "She read an article about him being attacked and put in the hospital."

So Eric suspected that he'd attacked Troy, yet Eric wasn't showing any concern or worry. Was it so easy to believe that he was capable of putting someone in the hospital? Russ felt trapped being pinned under Eric's weight, but he made no effort to free himself. "You think that I beat him up?"

"Did you?"

Russ took a deep breath—maybe Eric wouldn't reject him. "I was crazy—all I could think about was making him pay."

"How did you know who did it?" Eric asked.

"My mother took your form and was able to tap into your memories. After she had experienced your attack, or at least after she had remembered your attack, she took the form of the attacker and showed him to me."

"She took my form and was able to remember things that had happened to me?"

"Yeah," he replied reluctantly.

"And then she took his form." Eric looked dazed.

"It's another thing that happens to us—if we take on the form of another person, sometimes the other person sort of seeps through. My mother is particularly good at controlling it."

"That's so weird," Eric said in a quiet voice. "It makes me feel violated."

"It wouldn't hurt you," Russ lamely pointed out.

"So your mother took the form of the guy who attacked me. Did she also tap into his memories to find out who he was?"

"No," Russ replied. "She didn't have to. I recognized him."

"You what?"

"I had met him before."

"That's hard to believe. All of this would be hard to believe if I wasn't already expecting weirdness." Eric stared off into space and Russ was afraid he'd lost him.

"I went to this guy's apartment and beat him up," Russ told him, almost angrily.

Eric turned his head toward Russ again, wearing a pained expression. "I know," he said. "You put him in the hospital."

"I wanted to get back at him for what he'd done to you."

Eric's expression didn't change.

"I don't think I was wrong," Russ added.

"Then why do you feel so guilty?"

"I was ready to twist his head right off." There it was—out in the open. "When I looked in the mirror, I saw you staring back at me. That's when I knew that it wasn't right. You stopped me."

"I stopped you."

"Yeah," he replied, tears filling his eyes. "I'm not sure I can ever forgive myself for what I almost did."

Eric's eyes softened. "I forgive you—is that good enough?"

It was as if Eric had already decided to forgive him—how much did Eric really know? "It's too easy that way."

"You want to be punished?"

"I guess I do," Russ admitted.

"You'll have to do that yourself," Eric said sternly.

"I'm not sure I can."

"I'm not going to force you into anything you're not ready for. You said that you saw me looking back at you—did you take my form when you attacked him?"

Russ wasn't sure he wanted to answer the question. It seemed that Eric was anticipating too much of this, that he'd already had the opportunity to think of what he would say. Though the thought made him uneasy, he decided he had to answer. "Yes, I did."

Without a beat, Eric told him, "Then let me go to Tony and ask for his forgiveness. Maybe he'll ask me for forgiveness too."

Russ suspected that Eric was completely serious, and the thought petrified him. "No," he said. "I don't want you going near him again." Russ gently flipped Eric over and settled on top of him. "Promise?"

"All right," Eric sighed. "If you get off me."

Russ immediately slipped off, realizing that he hadn't been gentle enough. "Did I hurt you?" he asked, alarmed.

"No," Eric told him, a little out of breath. "You just took me by surprise."

As Eric sat up, Russ noticed something across his belly that seemed to be more than just a shadow. "Let me see something," Russ said, moving closer. "Turn a little toward the light." Eric turned and there it was—faint, but still discernible—a handprint. "Look at this."

"Oh," Eric replied offhandedly. "It came back."

"What do you mean?" Russ asked, alarmed.

"I noticed this while I was in the hospital—it was like something had burned an impression in my skin, but it didn't hurt. I didn't think much about it and then the impression went away."

Russ put his hand over the print—his hand fit neatly within it. The print was definitely male. "It's a handprint. See?"

"You're right. It's tingling right now."

"The print is really close to the incision," Russ observed. "I wonder how it got there," he said, though he had some idea.

Eric shrugged his shoulders and smiled. "Maybe it was God, healing me."

Russ couldn't believe how indifferent Eric was. "Yeah," he said. "Maybe it was."

Russ heard a little pecking noise at the window. "Do you hear that?" Russ asked.

"I don't hear anything."

The noise continued.

"Oh, look," Eric said, sitting up. "There's a little bird trying to get in through the window."

Russ turned to look and sure enough, a hummingbird hovered by the window, very near the Peruvian lily that Lizzy had brought over. "Maybe the bird sees the flowers," Russ suggested.

"I guess hummingbirds go by sight, not smell," Eric pointed out, getting out of bed. "Let me open the window."

Russ hated it when Eric got so close to the window, naked. "You'll just scare it away," Russ warned.

"Maybe it's your mother." Eric grinned at him.

"I don't think so," Russ replied, a little offended.

Eric carefully pulled up the window and stepped back. Russ couldn't believe how good he already looked—the light from the window had such a pleasing effect on his skin. Russ could hear an intense buzzing and the little bird flew through the open window and made a beeline for the magenta flowers. Perhaps Eric was right. The little hummingbird was almost entirely dark, electric green—its wings shimmered in the light as it went from one flower to the next, dipping its long beak into the clusters of petals. Eric, who was standing only a few feet away, carefully watched the little bird's progress. With a slight smile on his lips, he seemed utterly content. Then, almost as quickly as the bird had come in, it flew back out again. Some of the flowers were still swaying with the bird's foraging. Eric's smile glittered with the sunlight.

He came back to their bed. "I have a secret to tell you."

This surprised Russ. "I didn't think you could keep one."

"Well, I guess I can't," he added. "Because I'm going to tell this one to you right now."

Russ settled back, though something about the way Eric was watching him was troubling.

"I wasn't sure I'd ever tell you this, but one night, while you were asleep, I saw your body change."

Russ stiffened.

"You'd left the light on and I got out of bed to turn it off. I noticed that you looked different. Then I watched as your body changed more—your hair turned darker, your legs got a little longer, your chest shrank a little, and you even got freckles."

Eric had seen his true form.

"You know, it reminded me of this guy I'd met at a bar, right after we started going out. The guy wanted to pick me up. When I said that I was already seeing someone, he seemed sort of happy about it, which I thought was strange. When I saw you change while you were sleeping, I realized that the man who tried to pick me up that night was really you."

Russ had underestimated him. Eric had figured everything out. Russ couldn't help himself—he started smiling.

"I knew it was you," Eric said, easing up to him and giving him a kiss on the neck.

"Did you think the other guy was cute? I mean, did you think I was cute?" Russ couldn't help but ask.

"Yeah, I did," Eric replied as he nibbled on Russ's ear. "At least from what I remember."

Russ grinned. It was what he had thought all along, but knowing that Eric had found him attractive, for certain, gave him the most amazing feeling of completeness.

"That's how you really look, isn't it?" Eric asked.

Russ felt unwilling to relinquish this last secret. Only one other person knew this about him. "Yeah," he finally admitted. "You're right."

Eric ran his fingers through Russ's hair at the back of his neck. "I knew it." He paused. "Can I see how you really look again?"

"It isn't something I'm fond of doing," he replied, hoping that Eric would give up.

"Come on," Eric persisted. "Can't you do this for me?"

Russ hated the idea. "I'd rather not. Why is it so important for you?"

"Because I'm tired of the secrets," he replied and wrapped his arms around Russ. "I want to see you the way you really are."

Russ turned to look at him. Eric's eyes were determined, but there was something else—incredible love. Was it enough?

"It's important to me." Eric let go of him and stood up next to the bed. He gazed at Russ, a slight smile across his lips. Finally, he reached out his hand. "Come on."

Eric led him over to the full-length mirror they had hung in the bedroom after he'd come home from the hospital. Russ resented being taken by the hand, yet he allowed himself to go along.

"I want to see your reflection too," he added, "so I can see how you see yourself."

Russ had never thought this would happen, sharing so much intimacy. Yed he had waited for this moment to come. Now anything might be possible.

Eric stood behind him, slightly to his right side, and peered into the mirror at the two of them. Russ tried to relax; it had been awhile since he'd seen his true appearance and he had some difficulty imagining how he was supposed to look. He concentrated but nothing came. A mild panic set in. Why couldn't he remember? "I can't remember," he admitted, bewildered and even frightened.

"You can't remember?" Eric asked, incredulous. Eric put his arms around him from the back. "Think back," he suggested. "Think back to the last memory you have of your true form."

Russ thought for a moment, but the only thing that came to mind was how he had looked as a child, before his abilities had taken hold. "The last thing I remember is when I was a kid."

"Why don't you start there?" Eric asked and pulled him tighter.

Russ looked at their reflection in the mirror. It really looked like they belonged together. "Okay," he said. "I'll try."

Eric grinned at the mirror.

"You'd better step away," Russ told him. "I'll never transform with you holding me. I wouldn't want to let go."

"All right," Eric replied and relinquished his embrace.

Russ closed his eyes and imagined the little boy that he had been years ago. The boy came to him almost immediately, shyly smiling. It was so odd—the little boy seemed like an entirely different person. Had he really been that little person? He looked so vulnerable. Slowly, very slowly, he let the boy take over. The tingling started in the base of his spine and traveled up to the base of his neck, and then through his arms and legs. His body felt fluid and he began to shrink. Behind him, he heard Eric gasp.

Russ didn't bother opening his eyes yet; he waited until he knew the blindness would be gone. When he ventured to open his eyes, a little boy was smiling back at him, a boy with freckles and slightly crooked teeth.

Eric, his eyes wide, said, "You were a cute little boy."

Behind him, Eric towered over him. He had forgotten how it felt to be so small among people who were full-grown. He turned to look at Eric and came face to face with a pair of huge thighs. When he looked up at his lover's face, Russ felt dizzy.

"It's time for you to grow," Eric suggested.

Russ turned back to face himself in the mirror again. Ever so slowly, he began to grow, letting the process assume its own rate and course. He was delighted when he discovered that he could watch it happen too—no blindness came over him this time as his body mimicked the aging process. He tingled all over, but without rippling or strain.

Eric watched, completely transfixed.

Russ's body slowly grew, the limbs growing the most at first, along with certain facial features, especially the nose. Seeing his body grow into that of an adolescent brought back many memories too—of the wild times with his mother, hiding their doings from his father, the fights he had at school, the loss of so many friends. He had never experienced an awkward adolescence, but now he understood what people meant. Everything grew at a slightly different rate, at times making his appearance look off-center. All along, though, he had the same freckles and slightly crooked teeth. At what he thought was about the age of sixteen, his nose became slightly crooked. His body hair began to grow out—along with other changes, the broadening of his shoulders, the development of his chest, arms, and leg muscles.

Suddenly, his body grew to be about the same height as Eric's—a growth spurt he had never experienced. After this, he could feel his body settle in. He figured he had to be at least nineteen. Finally, the growing stopped and he was confronted with the man he would have been if not for the changing.

It was slightly different than what he thought—in fact, he was better looking than he had imagined. His freckles had nearly disappeared, but what was left, along with his slightly crooked nose, added an appealing bit of whimsy. He turned to his lover. "This is me. What do you think?"

Without a word, Eric led him back to the bed. Russ automatically sat down, wondering what Eric was thinking. All he could see on

Eric's face was a sort of wild happiness, which gave way to wistfulness, contentment, and longing. Eric, his eyes bright, toppled Russ over, pushing him down on the bed. Eric began to cover his body with wet kisses. Russ had never felt anything like it—his body was awash with delight. The tingling wouldn't stop, a kind of tingling that he'd never experienced before. A wave of joy surged through his entire body.

He was finally home.

Eric eased down over him, his face beaming, hovering over Russ, surrounded by the blue of the sky, framed by the window. Eric's eyes seemed as vast as the sky around him and filled with immeasurable love. "You don't have to hide anymore," he whispered.

Russ's breath quickened. He hoped it would never end.

ABOUT THE AUTHOR

David M. Pierce has taught composition and creative writing at San Diego State University and served as an editor in the trade department for Harcourt Brace. He has worked as a writer and fundraiser for nonprofit organizations for many years and is currently an instructor in the fundraising certification program at the University of California at San Diego. Mr. Pierce holds an MFA from San Diego State University. He resides in San Diego with his long-time partner.